EMBER

ANDREWS & WILSON

EMBER

A TIER ONE THRILLER

BLACK STONE

PUBLISHING

Printed in the United States of America

First edition: 2024
ISBN 978-1-6650-4196-6
Fiction / Thrillers / Military

Version 1

Blackstone Publishing
31 Mistletoe Rd.
Ashland, OR 97520

www.BlackstonePublishing.com

For Tressa & Tenley

AUTHORS' NOTE

Every Tier One novel is a metaphor. This novel, *Ember*, is a reminder about the power and importance of friends and family, of the importance of the "team" component of "Team and Mission before Self." We all feel like Dempsey sometimes, like the weight of the world is on our shoulders, but always remember you're not alone in the fight.

Right now, external forces are focused on creating division and trying to turn brother against brother, sister against sister, American against American. Our enemies dream of America's fall, and they are working tirelessly toward this goal, and division is their weapon of choice. We cannot let this happen. We must remember that, as a nation and a people, our diversity of ideas remains our greatest strength. We do not need to agree with everyone about everything to be one nation, united in purpose, a nation that puts team and mission before self. We must remind ourselves that there are far, far more things in America that unite us than there are that divide us. If we are Americans first, then we can never be truly divided.

We must remain united and strong. Country before party. Team before self.

A&W

PROLOGUE

THE GRAND BAZAAR

TEHRAN, IRAN

TWO AND A HALF YEARS AGO

0935 LOCAL TIME

Elinor Jordan told herself she was in control.

But that was a lie.

The kind of lie that people tell themselves while clinging to the last vestiges of hope.

She pretended to peruse the display of brightly colored silk head-scarves on a table, one of countless such tables here in the main corridor of the Grand Bazaar. With two hundred thousand vendors spread across twenty square kilometers, the Grand Bazaar was the largest market on the planet. The sheer enormity of it, coupled with the hustle and bustle of the crowd, could be disconcerting to the uninitiated. Overhead, intricately painted Persian vaults with pointed arches and intersecting arras lined the ceiling. In the middle of each vault was a round opening, allowing natural light to illuminate the market during the day. For Elinor, however, it felt like a dozen blue irises were looking down on her . . .

Watching her every move.

The air carried a mélange of odors: the sweet tang of brewed tea, the miasma of stale cigarette smoke, the aroma of cooking spices, and the musk of woolen blankets and carpets. Everywhere around her people bartered and bickered, laughed and lolled. She imagined that her American partner, who was keeping close at her side, probably felt like he had been transported back in time. The Grand Bazaar was the opposite of modern internet commerce. Here, shoppers had to rely on their five senses to assess quality and to suss truth from mercantile chicanery. Here, everything was a negotiation, where shrewd perception and posturing ruled the day.

Interestingly, and perhaps fittingly, bartering in the Grand Bazaar was not unlike her own profession. What was espionage if not information commerce, in which buyer and seller come together in a moment of dubious candor and motive to conduct a delicate transaction? Violate either party's trust or truth and the house of cards would collapse . . .

You can do this, she told herself. *You* have *to do this*.

On the outside she projected calm, quiet confidence. But on the inside, Elinor felt her mind unraveling—like the tattered end of a flag whose binding seam had come undone, flapping in the wind. She'd made a pact with herself never to let her feelings compromise her mission—never to let her relationships with her teammates, handlers, or assets infiltrate her heart and corrupt her ability to execute her objectives. Detachment was difficult for any clandestine operative, but it was especially so for double agents like herself. To be an effective double agent, she had to truly understand and embrace both masters. To *survive* as a double agent, she had to develop a duplicitous heart—loving that which she hated one minute and hating that which she loved the next. This schizophrenic existence was on the verge of fracturing her psyche. Contrary to what her psychological evaluations said, hers was a deeply caring and sensitive soul. Like everyone, she needed to love.

And like everyone, she needed to be loved in return.

Last night she'd broken the cardinal rule of her trade and made love to a man she'd intended to betray. The fact that she'd surrendered her body to him was not the problem. Sex was a powerful weapon in her arsenal of influence. No, the problem was that she'd surrendered her heart to him as well.

"We're kindred spirits, you and me," she'd said, her palm pressed to his chest last night before she'd given herself to him. *"Soldiers who've sacrificed everyone and everything we've ever loved to fight for a world where people don't have to live under the shadow of tyranny. I saw it in your eyes the first time we met in Brussels. You've given everything for your country and asked for nothing in return. No one can appreciate John Dempsey better than I can. And the same is true in reverse . . ."*

She hadn't planned to say it. These weren't words she'd carefully crafted to manipulate and seduce him. Quite the opposite: the sentiment had been a confession, a secret liberated from the lockbox she kept in her soul. In that moment, she'd felt so alive and unburdened. Then morning came and, like a bad hangover, those words had come back to torment her.

Now, she could feel Dempsey's eyes on her.

She looked up and met his gaze with a lover's smile. He smiled back, and it made her heart skip a beat. Then, abruptly, he stiffened, and she knew the spell was broken. He'd seen through her, felt her indecision, cued in on her momentary insincerity. She lowered her eyes and drifted away from him to peruse the wares in the next vendor's booth. In her peripheral vision, she watched him follow, his body language now transformed from dutiful companion to stalking hunter.

"Crusader, this is Rome," said the voice of their driver, Farvad, in her microearbud transceiver. "In position."

This was followed by the report from the decoy driver, "Crusader, this is Tripoli. In position."

She acknowledged the reports, pretending all the while to focus on the jewelry laid out before her. An Iranian security guard dressed in a light-green uniform shirt and black pants walked past, eyeing her with suspicion as she gave a coded response in Farsi. This was the third security guard she'd counted in ten minutes, but this was no surprise. Tensions were high after the recent Israeli air strikes, and the city was on high alert.

Dempsey stepped up next to her and took her right hand in his left. She gave his palm a little squeeze and released it.

"Are you sure your *cousin* is coming?" he asked, using their agreed upon code word for Amir Modiri—VEVAK's director of foreign operations, her boss and Dempsey's target. The American operator spoke in English with a passable Irish lilt to correspond with his legend for the op.

"Yes," she said, picking through a pile of woven leather bracelets decorated with beads, silver trimmings, and semiprecious stones.

"How do you know?"

She didn't answer him.

He waited until the shopkeeper struck up a conversation with a nearby shopper to say, "Why here? It's a security nightmare."

"Because it's noisy and crowded. The Grand Bazaar is his preferred venue to meet deep-cover assets face-to-face," she whispered.

"You? You're the asset?" he murmured.

She looked at him with a tight-lipped smile that morphed into an apologetic frown.

I'm sorry, John . . . I never meant for it to come to this, she thought.

But that was a lie, because the duplicitous part of her had.

"Elinor," Dempsey said, slipping his heavily muscled left arm around her waist.

"Yes?" she said, still not meeting his gaze.

"Look at me."

She hesitated, not wanting to comply, but then—tears rimming her eyes—turned to face the man she'd slept with the night before.

"Elinor, whose side are you on?" Dempsey asked, his voice a baritone melody devoid of anger or accusation.

With those words, she felt something crack inside her—like a porcelain doll fracturing, but not shattering, under the tap of a hammer. One ill-placed touch, and she would crumble into a million pieces. She heard a manic laugh erupt from her lips, as if the laugh were coming from someone else.

"I don't know . . . I don't even know who I am anymore."

And that was the hard, uncomfortable truth. She didn't have enough oxygen in her head for two Elinor Jordans. Nor did she have enough room in her heart for conflicting allegiances. This operation would finally do what none had managed to do before: force her to pick a side once and for all.

She blinked her vision clear and held his gaze.

Instead of scolding her or shaking her by the shoulders to snap her out of it, he reached up and wiped a tear from her cheek with his thumb. "Last night you said we were kindred spirits. Do you remember that?"

"Yes," she said, sniffling.

"Do you believe in destiny?"

"I don't know. I never did before, but now . . . maybe."

"Well, I do," he said. "We found each other for a reason. You said it yourself: you needed me last night. To give your father peace before he died. Now I need you to fulfill your end of the bargain. I need you to help me execute this mission for the same reason. Can you do that?"

She hesitated . . .

Last night Dempsey had done something for her that she would always be indebted to him for. In Elinor's father's mind, it was a father's responsibility to protect and provide for his daughter. Only marriage could lift this yoke from his shoulders. In posing as her loving husband, Dempsey had done this and given her cancer-ridden father the ultimate gift.

"I think so," she said at last.

"Are we still a team?"

She nodded.

"Good," he said and pulled her in for a hug.

She pressed into the embrace and clung to him like the trunk of a mighty oak in a storm. She closed her eyes, and the sounds of the Bazaar faded into the background. She felt and heard his heart pounding a steady, fearless rhythm in his chest. And in that moment, she realized there was another option available to her—a choice rather than serving either VEVAK or the Fifth Order.

I choose you, she decided.

That's when the bombs went off.

Chaos erupted in the Bazaar as a series of concussive charges detonated around them. Dempsey shielded her with his body for an instant, then released her. She opened her eyes to people screaming and running in every direction. The operative inside of her retook control, and she scanned the crowd for Modiri. Only when Dempsey took off in pursuit like a heat-seeking missile did she spot the target.

"Rome, Tripoli—Crusader One has eyes on the package. Stand by," she could hear Dempsey say on the comms channel as he barreled into the crowd.

"Copy, One," Farvad's voice said in her ear.

She sprinted after Dempsey. In a footrace, she would have had difficulty keeping up with the American operator, but since he was doing the hard work of lead blocking in the crowd, all she needed to do was follow behind him.

Ahead she could see Modiri, clutching his wife's hand, veering down a narrow passage that bisected the Bazaar's main corridor. She knew from their pre-op mapping that this passage led to an alley used by vendors to deliver goods to merchants at the Bazaar. And it was the same alley where Farvad waited in a delivery van to egress once they'd black-bagged Modiri—once they had "the package."

At least that was the plan . . .

She ran steps behind Dempsey, surrounded by a crush of terrified people fleeing the same direction as they were running, most screaming and shouting as they did. A man with a long gray beard ran two strides ahead of Dempsey, then tripped and fell in front of them. Dempsey hurdled the tumbling man, and she tried to do the same, but her lead foot caught on the bearded man's leg and she went down. She rolled out of the fall onto her left side.

Dempsey looked back over his shoulder.

"Go," she shouted. "I'll catch up."

He turned and kept running.

With a grunt, Elinor got to her feet and followed. To her right, she watched as a uniformed security guard vectored toward Dempsey, blowing a whistle and shouting in Farsi for Dempsey to freeze. After three shrill blasts, the man—who Elinor could tell was not a regular market security guard but a member of an embedded VEVAK security team—pulled his sidearm. To Elinor's shock, the guard fired a round at Dempsey's head. She pulled her pistol, ready to defend her partner, but Dempsey angled left, spun one hundred and eighty degrees, and put a single round in the forehead of the guard in one fluid motion. Without missing a beat, he whirled to face front and was back in the chase like the predator he was.

Reaching the passage where Modiri had turned, Dempsey stopped abruptly and took a knee. Elinor pulled up beside him, clutching her Jericho 941 PSL, and put her hand on his shoulder to let him know she was behind him. He didn't acknowledge her, just popped his head out low for a split second to sight around the corner before pulling it back.

"Clear," he said, then rounded the corner, hugging the wall to the left while she arced right into what she could now see was a dead-end alley.

Scanning for threats, she heard but did not see a metal door slam shut somewhere up ahead. She glanced at Dempsey, and he pointed two fingers at his eyes and then gestured to the second-story windows and rooftops lining the buildings on the right side: *Scan for snipers.*

She nodded and surveyed for protruding muzzles and spotter scopes while Dempsey advanced down the alley lined with storefronts, each with its own door. The crowd noise from behind began to fade, and Elinor was relieved that none of the panicked civilians had followed them down the dead-end passage.

Dempsey checked the first shop's door on the right and found it locked. He glanced over his shoulder to check their six and chopped a hand forward. They advanced to the next door, also on the right, but recessed in an alcove five meters farther down the alley. Unlike the previous door, this one was unlocked and hung slightly ajar. With hand signals, he instructed Elinor to clear right while he cleared left, then counted the breach down in a whisper.

"Three . . . two . . . one . . . go."

He shoved the door open and advanced, sighting over his pistol, while she followed. Instead of opening into a shop as she expected, the door opened to a landing at the top of a descending staircase, which she presumed led to an underground club or basement cellar. A purple-gray plume of smoke billowed up from below, and a red neon sign glowed at the bottom of the otherwise dark and unoccupied stairwell.

"What is this place?" he whispered as he took the lead and descended into the haze.

"A hookah bar," she whispered back as the sickly sweet smell of shisha tobacco flooded her nostrils.

At the bottom of the stairs, they stepped onto a concrete landing and were halted by another metal door, presumably leading into the hookah bar. Dempsey paused and gestured for Elinor to open it so he could lead. For this breach—blind entry into the hookah bar with an unknown number of bystanders and possible hidden shooters in the crowd—Dempsey needed to be unencumbered, with both hands on his weapon.

She acknowledged the signal, got into position, and locked eyes on him.

He exhaled and nodded a countdown cadence:

Three . . . two . . . one . . .

On the zero beat, Elinor pushed the door open, and Dempsey charged into the room, sighting over his pistol. She entered behind him, quickstepping in a low tactical crouch to a position off his right shoulder.

Instead of gunfire, they were met by a room full of wide-eyed stares. She scanned the faces in the crowd over her iron sights.

"Don't shoot us. We don't want any trouble," a middle-aged Persian man sitting on a stool behind a counter said in Farsi.

"Two people, a man and a woman, just entered before us. Where did they go?" Elinor shouted, training her gun on the man who had just spoken.

The man pointed to a doorway with a black curtain on the opposite side of the bar.

"They went through there," Elinor said to Dempsey, nodding at the darkened doorway.

"I'll breach, but you'll have to cover our six. I don't trust any of these guys," he said.

"Roger," she said. She didn't blame him. From the looks of the crowd, she surmised at least a handful of the patrons were involved in organized crime and probably armed.

As Dempsey quickstepped across the center of the smoky lounge, she spun to cover their six and backpedaled as best she could to keep pace. At the edge of her peripheral vision, she saw Dempsey take a knee at the doorway. She scanned right to left in a hundred-and-twenty-degree arc, her back to Dempsey as she covered.

She sensed movement behind her, but before she could turn, three gunshots rang out. She felt a double blow to her back so powerful that it knocked the breath from her lungs and sent her pitching face forward on the floor of the hookah bar. She partially managed to break her fall with her left arm but hit the floor hard. Pain flared in her back, like a red-hot poker had been rammed through her chest. She fought for breath, but all she could do was breathe faster and faster, and with each gasp it felt like no air reached her lungs.

She could hear Dempsey and Maheen Modiri talking nearby, but she couldn't make out their words because her ears were ringing. She realized that her arms and legs were moving—in fact all of her was moving—writhing on the dirty concrete floor in a growing puddle of her own blood. As she struggled for breath, her clouding mind wrestled with a question that wouldn't matter when she was dead but mattered more than anything else while she still lived:

Who shot me in the back?

Amir . . . Maheen . . . Dempsey?

"She's a spy. She works for my husband . . ." Maheen said, the woman's voice tinny and very far away.

It had been Maheen, she realized.

Panic washed over her as she felt all the strength and warmth and will leaking from her body.

Don't leave me, John, she silently begged. *Not here . . . not like this.*

She tried to call out to him, to tell him that she'd made her choice and that she'd chosen him, but instead of words all she managed to do was cough up blood.

Feet appeared in front of her. Not Dempsey's booted feet, but a woman's shoes. Her breath returned, sort of, but instead of hyperventilating, now it felt like she was drowning. She hacked up blood to clear her airway, then gasped deeply, the sound ragged and wrong.

Maheen Modiri kneeled in front of her and addressed her by her Persian name.

"Adina, you have a choice. I can put a bullet through your temple and end your suffering, or you can fight. Which will it be—life or death?"

"Fight . . . life," she said, the sounds uttered more wheeze than words.

The woman gently caressed her forehead and then said, "Okay. I'm calling for a MEDEVAC . . . I know it hurts, but don't give up. I always liked you, Adina. It would be a shame for it to end like this."

Still writhing, Elinor managed to look up and hold the other woman's gaze long enough to wordlessly ask the question burning inside. The question she already knew the answer to.

"Yes, my dear, he left you to die," Maheen said, her own eyes wet with tears as she raised a mobile phone to her ear. "And he's never coming back."

PART I

In fear and trembling, the superior man sets his life in order and examines himself.

—*I Ching, The Book of Changes*

CHAPTER 1

Liu Shazi scanned through powerful digital binoculars, which gave him range and angle data in the left side of his field of view, his eyes settling on the fountain and crowded courtyard outside the temple. From the roof of the Lalit Heritage Home boutique hotel, he had a clear line of sight in all directions north across the Hakha Marg with the safety of distance from ground zero. He could see the crowds filling the market and milling about the historic landmarks of the Taleju Bell and Hari Shankar Temple just beyond. The Patan Museum was out of sight, blocked by the large Bhandarkhal Pokhari with its green wading pool. The Statue of Narsingha sat to his left at the edge of the sunken fountain in Tusha Hiti. He'd chosen this location after an exhaustive search. The geometry had to be perfect for the test bombing to serve its purpose. The kill zone would extend throughout the open square but, he hoped, would not damage the ancient landmarks—other than the fountain—too much. He was still a bit sentimental, he supposed.

He would feel guilty accidentally destroying a World Heritage Site. He looked at his watch.

Where is Umar?

As if manifesting his wish, the Pakistani terrorist Abu Musad Umar—founding member and now leader of al Ghadab—joined Shazi on the roof of the hotel. With his tapered haircut, eyeglasses, and neatly trimmed, short beard, the young terrorist looked more like a college student than a jihadi. When it came to organization and planning, Umar was a genius. His success rate on attacks in the Kashmir-Jammu region was high despite having a limited number of fighters and little money. This was what had caught Shazi's attention and drawn him to seek out the man. As a former counterterrorism operator and expert, Shazi understood how difficult an accomplishment Umar's success must have been. Now that Shazi had augmented al Ghadab with cyber resources, intelligence reports, weapons, and cash, the nascent Islamic terror cell was on the verge of accomplishing great things. If today's test bombing was a success, Shazi would green-light the next operation—the most audacious attack either man could possibly imagine.

"You're late," Shazi said, with a chastising glare.

"Ahmed was waffling. He fears the vest. I needed to talk to him. Give him encouragement," Umar said. He took a seat beside Shazi and opened a notebook computer on his lap. Shazi watched the man and wondered how to best purge doubt and fear from a young warrior tasked with blowing himself up to kill others.

"Can we count on him to go through with it?"

"I believe so . . . but that's why we have two. Just in case."

Umar was a dedicated jihadist. Shazi had learned not to be fooled by the youthful, and somewhat more modern, appearance of the man. While he might not look like the heavily bearded, battle-worn Taliban fighters of the Hindu Kush, he was a blooded warrior. More importantly, he was a true believer. His eyes held the same manic passion and determination of the generation of jihadis he replaced.

Shazi had worked closely with Umar's bombmaker, Zafar Saeed, on improving the directionality and explosive effect of his suicide vest ordnance. He'd taught the man about the Munroe effect—how a blast could be focused or "shaped" using geometry to amplify the damage and penetration of projectiles. In this case, Shazi's goal was to test whether the human torso—when fitted with an array of EFPs, explosively formed penetrators—could deliver compact, high-velocity projectiles directionally and annihilate a specific target through a crowd of interfering bodies.

The two "volunteers" for today's dry run were, like Umar, also true believers. Of course, they didn't know the real mission. They believed the crowd of nonbelievers in the courtyard were the target. He shook his head at the naivety. Jihadists were so easy to manipulate because of their passion, and it astounded him that such blind devotion could exist in a man. Yes, he loved his country and believed in the cause of raising it to a position of power and prestige. But that was a far cry from seeking martyrdom and the supposed forty virgins in heaven who went with it. He felt a small measure of guilt for what they'd planned today. Many innocents would die. The test could have conceivably been done in a controlled environment with simulated targets, but the closer to actual operational conditions, the more valuable the data. And there were other considerations as well. The rank-and-file members of al Ghadab needed a victory like this.

To lead people or influence them, we must first align ourselves with them . . .

He shook off the thought. This was not the time to wax philosophical. He would have time for that after. For now, he needed to be on mission. He put the binoculars back to his eyes.

With tensions in the Middle East ebbing slightly after decades of war with the West, tourists had begun to flock again to the capital city of Nepal, bringing foreign money that the economy desperately needed. After years in the Snow Leopards and then with Guóanbù, it had become almost second nature to Shazi to identify the nationalities of travelers based just on their appearance. Here, through his spotter's scope, he could differentiate the more adventurous tourists from the UK, Europe, America, and the Baltics crowded in the marketplace that Patan Durbar Square became this time of year. Filling the coffers of Nepalese merchants with foreign dollars, these visitors kept Kathmandu afloat.

Being Chinese himself, Shazi felt a guilty pang when he noticed a large group of Chinese tourists moving through the crowd.

Their deaths would not be in vain.

The mission was the mission, and it served a greater good.

He spotted Khaled and Ahmed, their two bombers, moving south through the crowded walk, which narrowed as it passed between the main temple at Patan Durbar and the Hari Shankar Temple. Their sophisticated suicide vests—undoubtedly the most complex ever constructed by the genius bombmaker—were well concealed under their tunics. Then, he noticed that both men were wearing backpacks.

"What are they carrying in those packs?" Shazi said, pulling back from his scope to look at Umar.

"A machine pistol and extra magazines," Umar answered without looking up from his computer.

"Why?"

"So if the vests fail to detonate, they will be able to complete the mission."

Shazi felt his cheeks go red with anger. "If the vests fail to detonate, then the opportunity is lost. Massacring civilians with bullets does nothing to help us prepare for the real mission."

"That's how you and I see the situation, but not Khaled and Ahmed. They have gone to this square to martyr themselves, and one way or another they are going to achieve that end. It is my solemn duty to the martyrs who would make this sacrifice to ensure their mission has purpose." There was a fire in Umar's eyes now. "It impacts my ability to recruit the next martyrs. You must understand this."

The man was a passionate jihadi terrorist, but also extremely bright and pragmatic. And as much as Shazi hated to admit it, Umar had a point.

The two men passed north of the Taleju Bell and entered the open area of the market, which was packed with people. Shazi increased his magnification and wondered if Ahmed might still be having second thoughts. The man's eyes darted back and forth and beads of sweat trailed down his face, despite the dry air and comfortable seventy-five-degree temperature. Shazi began to worry that the kid might bolt—but so long as Khaled's vest detonated, they could still evaluate the design's effectiveness and make any last-minute modifications before the main event.

Shazi watched Khaled pause at the designated mark, five meters from the fountain.

Instead of taking his place next to Khaled, Ahmed suddenly bolted east. But then—to Shazi's surprise—the boy abruptly stopped. Perhaps filled with guilt or a desire to ensure his place in Paradise, he shrugged off his pack and reached inside. The rooftop from where Shazi watched was too far away for him to hear the young jihadi shouting, especially with the din of the large crowd, but he saw that the man yelled the battle cry as he pulled the machine pistol from his bag and hosed down the crowd with 9mm bullets.

Cursing, Shazi shifted his gaze to Khaled, who he could see was holding the detonator in his right hand.

Come on, Khaled, do it. Do it now!

The instant he saw Khaled close his eyes, Shazi dropped completely below the knee wall and pressed his fingers into his ears. He heard the powerful *whump* and felt the building shake as Khaled's vest detonated. A heartbeat later, a second explosion followed as Ahmed detonated his own vest. A moment of eerie quiet followed—save the sounds of brick, rock, and glass falling back to earth—before slow moans from civilians barely alive lifted into the afternoon air.

Shazi rose to look over the knee wall. Umar joined him to survey the damage. The fountain was annihilated, along with a swath of the crowd in a cone-shaped trajectory from where Khaled had been standing. A second arc of slaughter spread out at a different angle from where Ahmed had been. Bodies and body parts scattered in all directions. The left supporting structure of the Taleju Bell had given way and the bell had toppled through the roof of the low building that surrounded it.

The carnage was horrific. Where the happy crowd in the market had once been, now blood, bodies, viscera, destruction, and fire were all Shazi could see. The smells of cooking food had been replaced with that of burning flesh and sulfur.

He dropped down below the wall and returned his binoculars to his satchel.

"So, what do you think?" Umar said, lowering himself to a cross-legged position next to Shazi. "Is it enough to do the job?"

"Oh, yes, it is enough," Shazi said, feeling the overwhelming urge to shake out a cigarette, before remembering he couldn't. He'd quit buying them because otherwise he always smoked in these moments.

Liu Shazi was really trying to make healthier choices, now that he was nearly forty years old.

CHAPTER 2

URBAN COMBAT TRAINING CENTER COMPLEX

CAMP PEARY—ARMY EXPERIMENTAL RESEARCH FACILITY

(SECRET CIA TRAINING FACILITY KNOWN AS "THE FARM")

WILLIAMSBURG, VIRGINIA

0147 LOCAL TIME

John Dempsey led his four-man stick silently through a narrow alleyway, his noise-canceling/sound-enhancing Peltor headset making the fall of his booted feet annoyingly loud. He could hear voices inside the target building, but they were too hushed for him to understand even with augmentation. He held up his left hand in a closed fist, signaling a stop, and took a knee at the corner. Luka Martin and the two nugget members of Ember—Tess Wallace and Andy Fender—tucked in behind him as Dempsey pressed against the dirty brick wall at the end of the alley and peered at the shadows down the street.

"Ember One is Dodge," he whispered on reaching the checkpoint, his barely audible voice loud and clear in his teammates' headsets.

He signaled a split to the three operators behind him and waited as Martin led Wallace—a former SWCC officer—to the opposite wall, giving their four-person squad angles of fire in both directions. Fender, a recently recruited AFSOC PJ, stepped up and squeezed Dempsey's shoulder to signal he was in position. PJs, also called pararescuemen, specialized in combat search-and-rescue ops but were also trained in emergency medical care. Dempsey had worked with many PJs over the years from the Air Force Special Operations Command when he'd been at the Tier One, and he was glad to have one of the Air Force's most elite warriors on the team.

Dude should be a great addition, he thought while battling the overwhelming compulsion to take off his helmet.

The fit felt . . . wrong.

Pre-op he'd confirmed it was his helmet—the same one he'd worn for countless missions—but it didn't *feel* like his helmet. He tightened the chin strap and readjusted his right earmuff. Wearing the helmet and Peltors was driving Dempsey crazy. It seemed like it had been years since he'd worn a headset, much less this streamlined Special Operations battle helmet with NVGs. He'd spent a lifetime in this gear, so why did it feel so foreign to him now? He never imagined it would happen, but he'd come to prefer the freedom of being helmet-free and wearing Ember's microearbud that disappeared in his ear canal. Just like he preferred the form-fitting gel body armor to the heavy, bulky vest he was wearing now. Kitted up like a SEAL, he stuck out like a sore thumb. Equipped with Ember gear, he could operate covertly and blend into any crowd.

Had they let me, I could have executed this mission by myself . . .

And that was the truth. Compared to the assassination operation he'd pulled off at the Bolshoi Theatre in the heart of Moscow, this op was child's play. Dempsey was, well, bored.

"Ember Two is Chevy," said Munn's husky drawl in Dempsey's ear. His longtime friend and teammate was announcing squad two's arrival a block away on the far side of the dark street.

"Ember, Homeplate . . . we have you at Dodge and Chevy," said an unfamiliar female voice from the TOC. "Stand by for overflight data."

Why the hell couldn't Richard Wang be in his ear for this? He didn't need a stranger feeding him information, *especially* information he wasn't sure he could trust. The whole advantage of a team like Ember's Special Activities Division was that they lived, ate, slept, and operated as a unit. They knew every move the other would make, and Wang—who monitored the intelligence stream and fed the team data—knew exactly what Dempsey wanted and when to give it to him.

He decided he didn't care what the stranger told him from some drone pass and would get his information from someone he trusted instead.

"Talk to me, Mother," Dempsey said, querying Grimes, who was set up as overwatch and had her own bird's-eye view.

"Ember One, I hold four armed men standing together and having a smoke break on the east side of the street, five meters from your corner," Elizabeth Grimes, the team's sniper and sometimes mother hen, replied from her rooftop perch. "Two more shooters are standing guard beside the front door of the target house. I see two vehicles, one a Hilux and the other a four-door sedan, parked in front, providing cover for the sentries and a ready egress option if they decided to move the package. One driver in the sedan, no one in the pickup."

"Copy, Mother," Dempsey said. "How are your lines?"

A short pause followed, then she said, "Good lines on the four smokers on the east side of the street. Once the shooting starts, I'll probably lose a line on the two by the door. I can tap the sedan driver though."

He signaled across the alley for Martin to perform a visual scan—pointing to his own eyes and then out into the street. Martin shifted forward, just to the edge of the shadows, and leaned out. Then he shifted back and shook his head, which Dempsey took to mean no angle to engage the four shooters without stepping out into the street.

"Two, sitrep?" Dempsey said, trying his damnedest to stay engaged.

"Two has a line on the shooters on the east side if we move out from cover. Tangos appear to be bullshitting and not paying attention, so could probably drop 'em if they don't scatter too quick. That would let Mother focus on the door sentries and the driver."

This was exactly what Dempsey was hoping Munn would say.

An even better turn, however, would be if the four smokers simply went back indoors. That way Lizzie could take out the sentries with stealth, thereby allowing Ember to breach the target building from the front and back simultaneously and take care of business using preferred tactics. But the clock was ticking, and he knew he wouldn't be so lucky. Based on thermal imagery, the two hostages were being held in the upstairs bedroom of the target house. HUMINT indicated the terrorist leader intended to trade them for cash, but as soon as the raid started, that calculus would change. The bad guys would panic and probably kill the missionary and his wife before Dempsey's team could get up the stairs to rescue them.

"Ember, Homeplate," the female coordinator from the TOC said in his ear. "We have a convoy of three vehicles moving west from the main road toward your position. Thermals show four heat sigs in each vehicle, including drivers . . . ETA is nine minutes."

He felt himself perk up at this news.

Okay, now things are getting a little more interesting.

"One, Two—unless we're made and the inbound convoy is a QRF, then my money says they're planning to relocate the package," Munn said.

Munn was probably right. If Ember had been made, then Homeplate would have indicated the convoy was incoming with speed. Regardless, adding a dozen more shooters to the party dramatically reduced their odds of success. And the minute the two hostages were loaded in the vehicles, the op was over.

"Homeplate, sitrep on the thermals inside the target?" he asked.

"Seven total, including the hostages," the woman reported, her voice strange and robotic. "Two tangos upstairs in the room with the hostages. Two more on the west side front room, which is open to the front entrance. One tango in a small room off the downstairs hallway."

"I thought the single tango was seated in the kitchen, guarding the back door?"

"Um, he was, Ember, but now it appears he's in the bathroom," she said.

"Does he present as standing or sitting?"

"Excuse me?" she said.

"You heard me; is he pissing or taking a crap?"

"Tango presents as sitting, One," she said, her tone clearly put out.

"What about the rear sentry? Is he still pacing at his post?"

"Check," came her clipped reply.

He checked his watch. *They're daring me to try . . .*

A malevolent grin spread out on Dempsey's face. "Homeplate, confirm the drone is armed."

"Drone is armed, Ember One."

"Two, One—change of plans. Reposition to provide cover at the rear of the target house. Hold until my mark."

"Two," Munn said in acknowledgment after a beat, and Dempsey wondered if his old friend could read his mind.

"Mother, hold but be ready to pop melons if the shooters smoking on the street start moving toward the front door."

Another pause, and he could picture Grimes pursing her lips in doubt.

"What's the play, One?" she asked.

He wanted to explain, but if he did, he suspected the adversary would cheat. He didn't trust them.

Instead, he turned to Fender and, with a grin, said, "Do you want to have a little fun?"

"Hell yes," Fender said, a spark now in his eyes.

"FYI, we'll probably die," Dempsey said, clapping a hand on Fender's shoulder.

The PJ shrugged. "I'm game."

He smiled his acknowledgment then shifted his gaze to Martin, who was crouching across the alley with Wallace. Martin shot Dempsey a *WTF* look.

"Reposition to the east by a block, coming around this block to the south," Dempsey said, his voice a whisper, while silently signaling where he and Fender were heading and knowing Martin would put two and two together. "When I call Jackpot, be ready to engage anything moving east."

"Roger that, boss," Martin said with a grin, then chopped a hand and repositioned with Tess Wallace in trail.

"Let's go," Dempsey said to Fender, taking off in a hunched run to navigate the back alleys to the rear of the target house.

"Homeplate, move the primary exfil vehicle into position two blocks east and at the north corner of the block," he said, trying to manage the chess pieces without tipping his hand.

The pause that followed was exceptionally long this time.

"What's the play, Ember One?" Homeplate asked, the woman's voice clipped with irritation.

Dempsey was already moving south, turning east through the dirt parking lot between the two buildings. He hugged the north wall to keep in the shadows.

"The play," he said as he advanced, "is for you to move the primary exfil vehicle two blocks from the X at the north corner. And I need the secondary vehicle two blocks west, ready to pick up Two's stick of four operators."

"Recommend you hold, One," the woman said, followed by an audible sigh. "We can track the vehicles, reposition, and establish a secondary engagement site near the airfield."

Dempsey rolled his eyes at the slip. The female role-player had just revealed that the bad guys would be exfilling at the airfield. In real life, they wouldn't know what the inbound terrorists were planning to do or where they were going.

"Heard you the first time," he said, but with a sharper edge in his voice, "but that ain't how this works. We're the operations team and you're support. So, feed me intel and give me support."

Dempsey took a knee a block east in the long parking lot that ran the length of the building. Feeling the press of time, he glanced at his watch. The number and position of the tangos had already been stacked against Ember, but the twist of the incoming enemy convoy had shifted the odds of a successful extraction to single digits if they tried to perform a conventional breach and exfil according to the pre-op brief. Even if they took the target house and secured the hostages, shooting their way out against the army of incoming fighters was a nonstarter. But if he could capitalize on this window of opportunity while everyone was waiting—this little window that no one would be foolish enough to try to exploit—then maybe they'd have a chance. Which reminded him . . .

"Mother, when I call Jackpot, fall in on Two and his new position for exfil."

"Mother, roger that," Grimes responded, with no judgment or doubt in her voice this time.

"Your plan is to sneak in, grab the hostages, and sneak out the back before the convoy arrives, isn't it?" Fender said over Dempsey's shoulder.

Dempsey turned to see the new guy with a gloved hand clamped over his boom mike to hide the comment from the open channel.

I like this guy already, he thought as he answered the question with a crooked grin.

"Hooah," the PJ said.

They moved as a stealthy two-man unit into position at the rear of the target house where the lone rear sentry was pacing. Dempsey drew his combat knife from the scabbard on the front of his kit and looked at his new teammate. Fender nodded, no words needing to be exchanged for what would happen next. Dempsey made himself small—at least as small as a fully kitted-up operator his size could hope to achieve—and waited until the sentry's back was turned.

At the perfect moment, he surged forward, closed the gap, and clamped a gloved hand over the man's mouth. Instead of plunging the blade deep into the terrified man's brainstem, he smiled and tapped the flat side of the knife on the back of the man's head.

"You're dead," he whispered.

The role-playing guard sighed with annoyance, then laid down obediently on the sidewalk. Dempsey cleared the alley, then signaled Fender to fall in. The former AFSOC operator darted from his covered position in the shadows to Dempsey's side, and together they quick-stepped to the rear entrance of the target house. The two fell in along the brick side wall in a gap between the back door and the kitchen window. Dempsey rose from his low crouch and took a quick peak through the window and found the kitchen still clear. The guy in the bathroom would be finishing up any second.

"The kitchen is clear," he whispered to Fender. "Check the door."

Fender did. Locked, which wasn't a surprise.

Annoyed, Dempsey turned his attention back to the window. After a quick assessment of the design, he inserted his SOG knife into the horizontal gap between the top and bottom panes of the double-hung window. He quietly worked the blade until he dislodged the simple latch with a barely audible click.

Dempsey turned to flash his teammate a toothy, victorious grin.

"Do you crack safes too?" Fender said, with a chuckle.

"I do it all, brother," he said and returned his knife to its sheath.

He raised the bottom half of the window, but it got stuck in the track halfway up. With gritted teeth, he had to put in some muscle to get the window the rest of the way up. It squealed, of course, and the noise made his heart skip a beat.

He held.

"Ready?" he said to Fender when no one came rushing down the hall to the kitchen.

"Ready."

"Ember One is Cadillac," he said softly.

"Wait . . . what?" the woman running Homeplate's comms said, either confused or just pissed off at the audacity of what was happening.

"Metro, Ember One—I will be at your location with the package in under four minutes," he said directly to the exfil driver, who should have repositioned to the new location he'd ordered minutes ago.

"Check," came the driver's reply.

With comms taken care of, he grabbed the window frame, rolled over the sill, and dropped silently in a crouch in the kitchen. A second later, Fender came through the window and landed beside him. Dempsey chopped a hand toward the staircase leading to the second story.

"Ember Three, this is Two," Munn said, taking over comms now that Dempsey had called Cadillac. "Get set in case One is detected and to cover his exfil east. We're repositioning for covering fire on the rear."

Munn gets it . . .

"Three," Martin responded, and Dempsey imagined Martin and Wallace in their crouched stances ready to engage outside.

Dempsey smiled as he reached the back stairs, now out of the sight line from the hallway leading to the front room. He heard a toilet flush and wondered if the dude would notice the open window when he returned to the kitchen. They needed to get upstairs without being detected, or this entire plan would go to shit. With Fender behind him, he ascended the stairs. On the third step, the tread creaked.

Damn it.

"Go; I'll hold here," Fender whispered behind him.

Their Wilson Combat SFX9 rifles were equipped with QUELL ultralight suppressors, so there was a chance that when Fender dropped the kitchen guard, the two guards in the front room would not hear. But not a great chance. They were in the lion's den now, so no turning back.

It was what it was.

Dempsey ascended the rest of the flight, moving fast but trying to be as light on his feet as possible. Another tread creaked near the top, making him cringe, but he kept his attention fully committed forward, trusting Fender to manage his six. He needed to breech before the guys in the front room engaged Fender—or worse, summoned the four guards outside the front entrance.

He heard a single muffled pop behind him as he made the landing at the top of the stairs and knew it was Fender dropping the kitchen guard. Body charged with adrenaline, Dempsey cleared the upstairs hallway with robotic precision. He was in the slipstream of combat and having fun now. He rounded the upstairs banister in a tight button-hook and sprinted toward the closed back bedroom door. He was hoping Homeplate would read the situation and report the position of the shooters in the bedroom without his prompting, but no help came.

He pulled a flash-bang simulator from his kit, breached the door with a swift kick, then pulled back as an explosion of gunfire erupted from inside the room. Spatters of red paint decorated the wall behind him, but he was clear. With hundreds of breaches under his belt, he knew the rhythms of combat better than anyone. He tossed the flash-bang, waited for the chime, then entered the room. In the first millisecond of crossing the threshold, his mind absorbed the tactical picture. An empty twin-sized bed was pushed up against the wall on the right. Huddled on the floor against the far wall were the two hostages—a man and a woman—being covered by a terrorist holding a pistol. To his left stood the second guard, holding a machine pistol. Based on the rules, they had to hold for three seconds to simulate being stunned by the flash-bang.

Grinning on the inside, Dempsey cleared left. He put his Aimpoint sight onto the chest of the first shooter and squeezed twice. Two green splotches blossomed on the man's chest. He swiveled and double tapped the second guard who was standing over the hostages.

"Now, don't die too loudly, fellas," he said, with deadpan delivery. "This is a stealth extraction, and I can't have you messing it up."

The two CIA trainers looked at each other, then collapsed to the floor with loud thuds.

"Bring the rain, Mother," he barked as he quickstepped toward the hostages.

In his Peltors, Dempsey heard a series of *whumps* as Grimes went to work with her sniper rifle, thinning the herd that was the smoking guards outside.

"I'm with the United States Army, and I'm here to rescue you," he said, taking a knee in front of the hostages. "What are your names?"

"We're . . . We're . . ." the woman stammered, playing her part perfectly.

"Don and Bethany Yeigel," the man said.

"Where did your daughter go to preschool?" he asked, pulling a pair of snips from a vest pocket.

"Covenant Day School," the woman playing Bethany Yeigel said as Dempsey cut the black plasticuffs that bound her and her husband's wrists.

Footsteps in the upstairs hallway drew his attention, and he had his rifle up and sighting on the bedroom door in a fraction of a second. An unmarked Fender, who was smiling ear to ear, entered the room.

Dempsey lowered his rifle, relieved but not surprised to see his Ember teammate victorious and uninjured.

"Three KIA downstairs," Fender said. "Mother is engaging the front guard element, but I heard the front door slam open. Plus, that QRF is still inbound."

"One, Mother—two KIA, but two squirted inside the front door. Watch your six," Grimes said.

"Check, Mother," Dempsey said; then, unable to resist, he turned to the two CIA role-playing hostages. "Listen; we've got shooters downstairs, which means we're going to have to jump out the window to exfil."

"What?" the woman said, cutting off his further instructions. "We're on the second floor. Why don't we just take the stairs and go out the back door?" Her voice was no longer that of a scared hostage but an annoyed CIA role-player, now out of character.

"Well, because we can't risk you getting shot," he said with as much earnestness as he could muster. "This way is safer."

The woman turned to her colleague with an *Are you friggin' serious?* expression.

"Listen, it's not a big deal. If you hang from the windowsill, it'll only be eight feet or so from your feet to the ground. Land in a crouch and roll out of the fall. It's easy. If we stay here . . ." he glanced at the other "dead" CIA role-players sprawled on the floor for effect, ". . . we die."

The "husband" ran to the window and flung it open.

"You first, Beth," he said. "I can hold your wrists and lower you another couple of feet."

"Thanks, Don," the woman said, the sarcasm in her voice not masking the real fear she was experiencing.

Dempsey heard footfalls echoing from the stairs into the upstairs hallway, and he shifted his gaze.

"I got this," Fender said and rushed the door, but he stopped short at the unmistakable sound that came next.

Tink . . . thud, gadump, gadump.

The Marine slammed the door closed; shouted, "Grenade;" and scrambled toward Dempsey and the hostages. The simulation grenade exploded in the hall. A real grenade would have torn the door to shreds, of course, but in this case the door was unmarred.

Dempsey turned toward the CIA hostage role-players with an *I told you so smile* and said, "See, if we'd gone that way, we'd all be dead."

Not looking happy at all, the husband lowered Beth as far as he could and dropped her. The woman let out a groan and grabbed at her knee as she hit and fell over but was back on her feet a moment later. Next, Dempsey helped lower the husband while Fender covered the door.

"You next," he said to the Marine and brought his rifle up to sight on the door.

Just as the words left his lips, the bedroom door flew open and two enemy shooters breached the room. Unfortunately for them, Dempsey and Fender were ready with fingers on triggers. They painted the infiltrators' chests green, and Fender gave the stunned-looking role-players a two-finger salute.

"Thank you for your service," Dempsey said with a wink and followed Fender out the window. He performed the same hanging drop the others had and was thankful for the tiny patch of grass in the back courtyard to cushion the landing. He landed in a deep crouch and rolled out of the drop to avoid aggravating the old fracture in his back. He didn't feel anything crack, but he did get a stinger down his left leg as he stood back up into a combat crouch beside Fender, who was sighting and scanning over his rifle.

The backyard was clear to the street, but he heard a burst of controlled fire to the north. Munn's stick finishing their work, he assumed.

"Ember One is Jackpot," he reported. "Intact and moving to the alternate exfil Bravo."

"Mother is closing up the show and en route to Metro Two at Alternate Alpha."

"Two is clear," Munn said on the party line.

"Three is clear," Martin added.

Dempsey turned to Don and Beth, the hostages. "Are you guys for real okay?"

Beth, who was rubbing her knee, glared at him. "What we just did was a safety violation. I should have refused."

"Can you run?" Dempsey said, ignoring the protocol comment.

"We'll see, I guess, won't we?" she said.

"How about you, Don?" he said, turning to the other role-player.

Don was grinning like a kid. "I've always wanted do that. I'm five by. Let's rock and roll and get out of here. If we hump it to Metro One, I think we're gonna win."

"Then let's hump it," Dempsey said with a grin and chopped a hand in the direction they needed to go.

He took the lead, and Fender fell in behind the hostages, creating a diamond formation. With Beth limping, they cut back to the alley then moved north to the corner where Dempsey held them. He cleared the intersecting street, then sprinted a block to the east where the up-armored Sprinter van waited for their exfil.

"Ember One is Lamborghini," he said as he helped the pissed-off Beth and chuckling Don into the van. "The hostages are clear, but we've still got that incoming QRF convoy. Recommend drone strike to finish them off and clear our exit."

There was a short pause and then, "Will take it under advisement, Ember."

Dempsey laughed.

"Ember Two and Mother are Lamborghini," came Munn's satisfied voice in his ear. "Don't be a sore *winner*, Homeplate."

"Ember Three is also Lamborghini," Martin said as he slipped into the Sprinter van with Wallace in tow.

"Well, that was different," Wallace said as she dropped onto the bench seat beside Martin.

"That was badass is what it was," Fender said as he slammed the rear slider door shut.

Dempsey doffed his helmet and annoying Peltor headset and ran his gloved fingers through his hair. As the van pulled away from the curb, he could feel Beth's eyes on him.

"What?" he said, turning to meet her gaze.

"You know they're going to rip you a new one for this. I wouldn't be surprised if they DQ the exercise for a safety violation on the window stunt," she said.

Dempsey pressed his lips into a thin line and stared at her for a moment. A flashbulb memory of him in the bathroom of IK-2 prison in Russia being beaten to within an inch of his life popped into his brain, and here he was getting lectured about the window exfil. The real world was nothing like a training exercise. In the real world of covert operations, there were no paintballs, no pretend grenades . . . no safety stops or do-overs. In the real world, violence was either inflicted or succumbed to.

"You're probably right. But that's okay, because if this was a real hostage rescue, you'd be alive, as opposed to on your knees getting your head sawed off on camera," he said at last. "I'm sorry about your knee."

She didn't say anything else, just looked down at her lap.

"Now I understand," he heard Fender whisper to Martin.

"You understand what?" Dempsey said, shifting his gaze from Beth to his new teammate and then to Martin.

"The Dempsey Factor," Martin said with grin. "I was trying to explain it to our two nuggets, but I couldn't."

"Luka said we'd have to experience it for ourselves to understand," Fender said. "And now, I do."

Dempsey gave Fender a nod and then glanced out the back of the van. *What the hell does he mean by "the Dempsey Factor"?*

Did they mean the Dempsey he had been before Russia—the seasoned and hardened Tier One warrior who had stood up Ember SAD from the beginning? Or did they mean the man he'd become in Russia?

Who did his teammates see when they looked at him now?

Dempsey clenched his jaw. Did it really matter?

He was back.

Ember was back, and he was at the helm.

And we're going to kick some ass.

CHAPTER 3

Kelso Jarvis didn't do guilt.

Guilt was unproductive.

Illogical.

A product of cowardice.

If he screwed something up—which he rarely did—he took owner-ship and remedied the situation. If the mistake could be fixed, he fixed it. If not, he apologized. Either way, whatever the problematic behav-ior, decision, or outcome happened to be, afterward he moved on.

Guilt simply wasn't in his DNA.

At least, it didn't used to be.

But right now, driving to see his dying friend and mentor, Jarvis felt guilty as hell. He'd not visited Levi Harel since the Israeli spymas-ter had revealed he had Stage Four lung cancer. The self-proclaimed "cranky old Jew from Tel Aviv" had dropped that bombshell on Jarvis during the same phone conversation when Jarvis had shared his own diagnosis of Parkinson's disease. Jarvis remembered that particularly miserable day with perfect clarity. It was also the same day he'd accused Petra, once his best intelligence analyst at the Tier One and now his wife, of being a Russian mole.

Not my finest hour.

Echoes of that conversation with Harel played back in his mind.

"What the hell happened to us, Levi?" he'd asked.

"We got old . . . Men like us either go out in a bang before our time or it's death by a thousand cuts. Either way, the Reaper always gets his man, and my number is up."

At the time, the doctors had told Levi he had three months to live. That was eighteen months ago . . .

Jarvis wasn't surprised the spymaster had proven the docs wrong and defied the odds. Harel was a tough old bastard who'd practically written the playbook on cheating death. Still, Jarvis should have made a better effort to come visit before his friend was in hospice care and on his deathbed.

Hence, the guilt.

"Hey, Tony," Jarvis said to get the attention of his Secret Service team leader, and now friend, who sat shotgun in the up-armored Range Rover the Israelis had provided for the convoy.

"Yes, sir?" Tony Perez said, turning in his seat to look over his shoulder at Jarvis.

"Did you remember to procure the special item we talked about?"

Tony grinned and held up a six-pack of Gold Star dark lager.

"Perfect. Did you have any trouble getting it?"

"Took a few calls, but I eventually got 'er done, sir."

"Thanks, Tony. I've got a bet to settle with an old friend," he said with a wan smile, thinking about how he and Levi had been wagering six-packs for nearly thirty years but never seemed to find the time to actually drink one of them together.

Once they arrived at Harel's flat, Jarvis's security detail needed five minutes to secure the area before he could go inside to see his friend. Levi had elected to pass his final days at home under hospice care, not in a hospital connected to tubes and monitors. Jarvis couldn't blame him.

When it's my time to go, I'm going out by HALO.

Tony and a new guy named Rich escorted Jarvis from the Ranger Rover to Levi's front door, which was—strangely—already guarded by an Israeli agent wearing dark sunglasses and a gray suit. The agent nodded at Jarvis, clearly read in on this VIP visit.

Then, it clicked.

"Rouvin?" Jarvis said, sticking out his hand to the Seventh Order operator he'd not recognized at first.

"Good to see you again, sir," Rouvin said.

"How are you holding up, son?"

The Israeli operator shrugged. The man's calm demeanor and easygoing smile very much reminded Jarvis of Shane Smith—Ember's former Operations officer who had died in the attack on the Newport News facility. "I'm managing."

"Difficult times . . ."

"Yes."

"Are you here to augment my detail?"

"No, sir. I'm here to make sure the old man gets to make his peace with you. He made me promise to kill any assassins who might try to take him out before you arrived."

Jarvis laughed at this. "That definitely sounds like Levi."

"Indeed, but I owe him everything, so I'm happy to play along. Besides, I've enjoyed getting to spend these last two days with him. We're all going to miss him very much . . ."

Jarvis couldn't see the eyes behind Rouvin's dark sunglasses, but he knew if he could, those eyes would be red and wet. Struggling to keep his own composure, he gave the Israeli operator's shoulder a squeeze and stepped across the threshold.

"Would you prefer that I wait outside?" Tony said from behind.

When Jarvis turned, Tony was standing next to Rouvin, holding up the six-pack of Gold Star.

He nodded and took the beer from Tony's outstretched hand. "I'd appreciate that; thank you, Tony."

"Yes, sir, Mr. Vice President," Tony said and shut the door behind him.

Jarvis consciously and deliberately tightened his grip on the cardboard handle of the six-pack container to make sure he didn't drop it. He'd been keeping his tremors in check, but the disease loved to rear its ugly head at the most inopportune times. His old nemesis, entropy, was insidious. It had relocated the battlefield to *inside* Jarvis's body because, apparently, it had gotten tired of losing.

"I'm in the study," Harel called, his voice so hoarse and weak Jarvis barely heard him.

The inside of Harel's flat was tidy, organized, and spartan. This was just like Harel—the spymaster would meet his maker with his house in order. All the overhead lights were off, which made the modest foyer and hallway leading into the living room not dark but eerily dim, the only light in the apartment a fading afternoon glow from the setting sun. The air smelled of stale cigarettes and old age. Jarvis made his way through the living room to the study, a second bedroom Harel had converted into an office. The door hung wide open, but he knocked on the doorframe anyway as a show of deference.

"Now you knock, huh?" Harel said from a wheeled hospital bed, where he lay propped up on several pillows. "What happened to barging in like a SEAL without warning or manners everywhere you go?"

Jarvis, who kept a hundred different masks ready for every social situation, put one on now because he didn't want his face to reflect the visceral reaction he felt seeing Harel in the throes of death. Even knowing what to expect did little to lessen the shock of his friend's appearance, which brought meaning to the expression *skin and bones*. Levi had always been of small stature, but the emaciated thing lying in that bed could not have weighed more than a hundred pounds.

"Yeah, well, they tell me as Vice President I'm supposed to act dignified," he said with an easy smile. He lifted the six-pack of Gold Star.

"You waited until I was on my deathbed to make good on our wager," Levi said, with a hint of a smile back. "Typical American."

"If memory serves, *you* lost the last round. This is me picking up your slack and buying the beer that you owe me," Jarvis fired back, scanning for somewhere to sit.

"You can use the chair from my desk," Levi said, raising a spindly finger to point to the left.

Jarvis set the six-pack down on the floor at Levi's bedside while he fetched the chair. The hospital bed took up a third of the study and looked ridiculously out of place with the rest of the decor. He was about to tease Levi about it but stopped himself as he realized why his friend had wanted to spend his final moments in this room. Jarvis quickly and methodically cataloged the room's contents. A candid black-and-white photo of Harel and Prime Minister Shamone laughing together hung on the wall. A piece of scorched Israeli flag sat in a shadow box—a poignant reminder from an incident Harel had never shared with Jarvis. A dozen other mementos and gifts were on display as well, celebrating a life lived both in and out of the shadows during five decades of service to a country he loved. Of course this room would be where Harel wanted to lie in his final moments; these memories and keepsakes were the only "family" the man had.

Jarvis positioned the desk chair beside the bed, took a seat, and pulled two beer bottles from the six-pack resting on the floor. Not having a bottle opener handy, he turned one bottle upside down and used its cap to pry the cap off the other, then handed the open beer to Harel. He opened his own bottle using his wedding band as the catch and his ring finger as the lever.

"Look at you with all the tricks," Harel said, extending his bottle toward Jarvis in a toast.

"Adapt and overcome," Jarvis said, extending his own bottle to gently clink the neck against Levi's.

Both men took a sip and looked at the other. Harel's eyes were rimmed with tears. Jarvis felt his own eyes do the same, and he didn't try to stop it.

"Look at us . . . a couple of real tough guys, huh?" Harel said and chuckled, which made him cough.

"I'm sorry I didn't come sooner," Jarvis said, needing to ease his guilt, perhaps. "That was shitty of me."

"*Pffft*," Harel said. "You're Vice President of the United States. You have better things to do than sit around and listen to the ramblings of an old, dying Jew in Tel Aviv."

"What happened to *cranky?*"

"When you're dying, the cranky is implied."

Jarvis chuckled. "Fair point."

"Anyway, you don't need to apologize. You know that. Men like us understand the rules of the game. We don't hold grudges. The mission comes first."

"I know, but the truth is I'd rather be here with you than dealing with all the bullshit in DC . . ." His voice trailed off. "I never wanted to be Vice President."

Jarvis could feel Death watching them both, like an invisible vulture perched on an invisible tree, waiting patiently but with anticipation. He shook the macabre thought from his mind.

"I'm sorry I missed the wedding," Harel said, seemingly unwilling to engage Jarvis's last comment. "I wish I could have been there. I bet Petra looked magnificent."

"Oh yes," he said, letting himself be transported back to the moment. "She wore this cream-colored pencil skirt that hugged her hips. She was a vision."

"Where did you have the ceremony?"

"The EEOB, in my office."

"Very classy, Kelso," Harel said with a grin.

"It was all Petra's doing. She didn't want a big fancy wedding. I was just along for the ride."

"You know I'm joking. The two of you are the temple; nothing else matters." Harel took another sip of beer and looked at the bottle. "I'm glad you brought Gold Star. It tastes good today."

"Yeah, it does." Jarvis smiled at his friend, who suddenly looked both uncomfortable and exhausted at the same time. In fact, he looked like he was about to drop the bottle. "Do you want me to hold that for you?"

"Thank you," Harel said as Jarvis swept in to grab the tipping bottle. "Do you know what I'd really like, Kelso?"

"What's that?"

"A cigarette."

"Sure. Where do you keep your Noblesse?" Jarvis said, setting the two beers on the floor.

Harel cleared this throat, winced, and in a hoarse voice said, "On my desk."

Jarvis stood and obediently went to fetch the spymaster's smokes.

"You know, this is the part where I'm supposed to chide you for smoking a cigarette while you have Stage Four lung cancer . . ." Jarvis said, his back to Harel as he walked to the desk. He spied a pack of Noblesse and a silver lighter sitting on top of a sealed envelope. He leaned over and picked up the cigarettes and the lighter but left the envelope untouched, ". . . but I'm not going to do that today."

He waited. Levi didn't answer, apparently not taking the bait.

Grinning, Jarvis turned then . . . froze in place.

This moment—the sight of his now dead friend, head lolled to one side and eyes half open, a beam of dusty light across his sallow face— would be seared into his mind forever.

"Oh . . ." Jarvis said as the Noblesse and lighter tumbled from his hand to the floor.

The SEAL inside him spun up into crisis mode, ready to perform CPR and radio for a MEDEVAC, but Jarvis ordered his old instincts to stand down. The final battle was over, and Levi Harel had won. He'd made it to this moment, fighting a year and a half past his predicted expiration date, keeping the Reaper at bay to go out on his own terms.

Lower lip now trembling, Jarvis walked over to the hospital bed and kissed his mentor on the forehead. Then, he closed Harel's eyelids, sat down in the chair, and wept. A thousand memories paraded across the screen of his mind—memories from simpler times. He saw the small but fit man smoking on the beach, one hand in a pocket, as he walked from the surf after a grueling swim while on an exchange tour with Shayetet 13 a lifetime ago. So many things had happened since that day, when a much younger man had introduced himself to Jarvis as Levi Harel. So many times their paths had crossed, and each time the encounter had shaped the man Jarvis had become, all the way to

Harel's sage observations about service when Jarvis had told him how much he did not want to be Vice President.

He let the memories and emotions from the loss wash over him, until eventually he realized the early evening light was now casting long shadows in the room. Finally, he raised his beer to his friend, took a final long pull, then set the bottle on the floor and wiped his tear-streaked cheeks with his sleeve.

When he stood, instead of walking out of the study, he turned back to the desk where the sealed envelope beckoned. He picked up the pack of cigarettes and lighter he'd dropped, putting the smokes back on the desk and the silver lighter into his pocket. Next, he reached out and picked up the envelope. It had a single word on the front, handwritten in compact, neat font.

KELSO

With an unsteady exhale, he placed the envelope into the inside breast pocket of his suit coat.

When I'm ready . . .

He cleared his throat, straightened his jacket, and put on his Vice President's mask.

Then, without a backward glance, he walked out of the flat to call Israeli Prime Minister Shamone with the melancholy news.

CHAPTER 4

Elizabeth Grimes put a thumb on her beer, shook it a tiny bit, then let the foam spray onto the grill, beating back the flames licking the bottom of the thick burgers Munn was tending.

"Hey, stop it," Munn grumbled.

"I'm trying to keep you from burning my dinner, Dan," Grimes said with a chuckle.

"I'm getting a char . . ."

"Yeah, yeah, I've heard that before. You're getting a char to lock in the juices. But right after you say it you always serve me some burned hunk of meat that tastes like charcoal."

"That's bullshit and you know it," Munn said, but he was grinning—and moving the burgers away from where a grease fire was flaring up on the left side of the grill.

"Burning the meat?" Martin asked as he strode over, Richard Wang in tow, and handed Munn another IPA from the stock in the blue cooler by the picnic table.

"Locking in the juices," Grimes said and gave Munn an elbow. He shook his head but laughed good-naturedly. She was glad to be back in Tampa, their training module at the Farm now wrapped up.

"Yeah, right," Wang said, leaning in to check on the meat. "These cookouts are enough to make me a vegetarian."

"You guys are such assholes," Munn said, still laughing. He looked up, and Grimes watched his gaze shift to where Dempsey was standing on one of the large rocks along the water. "God, it's good to have him back."

"Yeah," Grimes said, staring at Dempsey. He was looking out over the darkening water, the last of the sun reflecting pink and orange on the glassy buildings of the Tampa downtown skyline a few miles across the bay. She looked back at Munn, who was shifting burgers away from where yet another grease fire flared. "Maybe you should clean the grill, bro," she said.

"It's a community grill," Munn said, as if that explained everything.

She looked over at Dempsey again, standing alone, staring at the water with a beer bottle dangling from his fingers.

"What did you think of the training op at the Farm?" she asked Munn, trying not to load the question.

Munn glanced at her, and his look suggested he wasn't going there. "Hard to argue with success," he grumbled.

"It would have been way better with me in your ear," Wang said. "I don't know why those CIA buttheads won't let me run comms and signals during the simulations. I would have streamed way more information to Dempsey in the house."

"Yeah, well, they're worried you'll cheat," Martin said.

"How is sharing information cheating?"

"You know what I mean . . . You were in the TOC. You could see all their little tricks and shit. They were afraid you were going to tip things off, but without them catching on until it was too late."

"I would never," Wang said, sounding indignant, but she saw the smile in his eyes.

"Well, you guys know my motto," Munn said. "If you ain't cheatin', you ain't tryin'."

Grimes laughed. She'd heard that old SEAL Team mantra plenty of times. She held her gaze on him until he turned to look at her. "If you'd been leading the op, would you have done what Dempsey did?"

"No, not exactly." Munn laughed as she studied him closely. She couldn't help but wonder if it was a struggle for him to hand the reins back to Dempsey after being the Ember SAD team lead for almost a year. "But I'm not Dempsey. He saw an opportunity and he pounced on it. That's what he does."

"Dempsey's *stealth* breach earned us four or five extra minutes without detection," Martin said, chiming in. "A traditional breach— even one executed perfectly—would have alerted the QRF. I think we still would have gotten to the hostages, but not necessarily without the tangos in the room executing them first. Also, the odds of us exfilling with no blue casualties like we did would have been incredibly low . . . I just don't think it would have happened."

Munn nodded. "You're probably right."

"And if we'd waited for the hostages to be transported off the X and loaded into the convoy, then the chance of success would have plummeted. The stealth entry was the only play to get them out of the target house safely," Wang said. "We needed Dempsey to do, well . . . you know, Dempsey shit."

"And if the pogues running the simulation had authorized the drone strike at the end like Dempsey requested, then we would have bagged the convoy and wiped out the entire cell," Martin said.

"I'm not disagreeing; it just would have been nice to get some more trigger time in the drill for Wallace," Grimes said.

She glanced over at where Wallace stood drinking with Prescott and Lewis. At least Dempsey had taken Fender with him on the entry, but everyone else had been left with precious little to do while Dempsey played Captain America. The newbie caught her eye and raised her beer. Grimes smiled and raised her own bottle back.

I need to get to know both the nuggets—Wallace and *Fender—better,* she silently lamented.

Since Dempsey's return, she'd left the training to Munn, instead choosing to focus on helping JD with his rehab and recovery and spending hours a day on the range and sniper course at the Farm, keeping her own skills sharp.

"The Dempsey Factor is real," Martin said, shaking his head in reverence. "And it's what makes us so badass."

"Exactly," Wang said and nodded toward Dempsey. "I'm glad he's back."

"We're all glad he's back," Grimes said quickly.

"We're finally Ember again," Munn added, then reached for the package of sliced cheese. He started covering the burgers with the thick pieces of cheddar. "Food's up in two minutes."

Grimes nodded, took a pull on her beer, then turned toward the waterfront. "I'll go tell JD before he wanders off . . . walking on water."

That got a laugh from the group.

"And I'll call Buz and tell him that he and Director Casey will be eating scraps if they don't hurry up and get here," Munn added.

Grimes nodded and sauntered over toward Dempsey. He stood on the big rock, motionless except for the slow rise and fall of his massive shoulders as he breathed. The sound of her boots on the rock made him turn.

"You doing all right?" she asked, suddenly feeling awkward. Over the years, with JD she'd gone from skeptic, to awestruck, to crush, to blooded teammate. Hell, they were more than teammates. Dempsey was like a brother, stepping in for the brother she'd lost in Operation Crusader. But since his return from Russia, it felt different.

He felt different . . .

"What do you mean?" he said, and she glimpsed a darkness—like a storm cloud in his eyes—but then it disappeared. "Checking up on me?"

"Not at all. Munn is pulling the burgers off the grill. Figured you were hungry."

"Did he burn 'em again?"

She laughed. "Nah, I supervised carefully this time. I think we're good."

"Well done, sis," he said and shifted his gaze back to the bay again. For a millisecond, she thought she saw him shudder. Then he turned to her and, as if someone had flipped a light switch, was the old Dempsey again. "Man, I'm starving. Even a charred Munn burger will do me good right now."

"Yeah, me too," she said, feeling herself relax. "What do you think about the newbies?"

"They're just about ready, but when it comes to SAD operations, I don't think you know until you know. Once we have an OPORD that gets us downrange, then I can answer that question," he said, but after a pause added, "But Ember nuggets aren't *really* nuggets, are they? The guys we recruit are all veteran operators with years of combat experience . . ."

"But it's hard to pull the team together until we're mucking around in the suck together," she said, finishing where she thought he was going.

"Exactly."

She nodded because there was truth to that. They'd been lucky as hell the last few years. The wildly eclectic team members they'd had—and lost—had always been more than the sum of their parts. Dempsey's superpower was, and always had been, extracting the very best from his teammates.

"And what about you? Are *you* ready to head back into the suck?" she asked, breaching the topic like target compound—fast and direct.

To his credit, Dempsey didn't get defensive and seemed to genuinely consider the question. "I know you're Ember's team mother—both inside and outside the wire . . ." he said. She felt herself bristle at the moniker which she had a love-hate relationship with. She was about to say as much, but he held up a hand and smiled. "It's a compliment, Lizzie. Knowing you're on the long gun covering our six allows us to do what we do. And I'm glad you cover our six back home too. Okay?"

"Okay," she said, "but we weren't talking about me . . ."

He sighed.

"I'm five by, Elizabeth," he said, and his eyes suggested it was the truth. "Russia was hell, but I'm good now. I probably didn't need three months of rehab, but the physical training has made me better. I've put on the muscle I lost, regained strength, and talked to the headshrinkers. I'm good, sis. I'm ready physically, mentally—and yes, even emotionally." He looked at her expectantly. "Hooyah?"

"Hooyah," she said back, conviction in her voice now.

Dempsey embodied the SEAL ethos. Knock him down and he got back up, every time. He was never out of the fight . . .

But how can a person go through what he did in Russia not come out changed?

He held out his beer bottle, which she saw was still nearly full, and she clinked hers against it.

"I'm starving," he said, ending the conversation.

They walked together toward the grill, where the whole team was now gathered. Munn was using a spatula to lift burgers onto buns while long strings of cheddar cheese fell back into the grill, causing it to flare up again. Martin said something Grimes couldn't hear, and everyone laughed.

"Here ya go, teammate," Munn said to Grimes as they approached, handing her a paper plate with an enormous, Munn-sized burger on a bun. "Toppings on the picnic table." Next, the grill master turned to Dempsey. "And for the big guy," Munn said and handed the SEAL two enormous burgers.

Taking a page out of the commanding officer's handbook, Ember's director, Mike Casey, arrived comfortably late along with the unit's Ops O, Buz Wilson. Their tardiness wasn't an ego thing but rather a leadership one. Grimes remembered Jarvis doing the same thing during the early days of Ember. Sometimes, the boss needed to let the kids be kids, to talk freely and bond without supervision. Apparently, the former submarine captain, now leading the world's most lethal and covert direct-action task force, was cut from the same cloth.

"Hey, boss. That's a sharp-looking Hawaiian shirt you got on. Unfortunately, Dan forgot to bring a blender, so we don't have a piña colada for you," Dempsey said, greeting Casey and throwing in some smack talk for good measure.

"No worries. There's probably too many ingredients in a piña colada for you and Dan to remember anyway," Casey said, dishing it back. Then, looking at the twin burgers on Dempsey's plate, he added, "Double fisting as usual, I see."

Dempsey chuckled and took a massive bite of burger.

Moments later the eight SAD members plus Wang, Amanda Allen, Director Casey, and Buz Wilson were all seated at picnic tables and eating. But they were still missing a few.

"Ian and his boys aren't coming?" Prescott asked as he topped his burger with tomato and lettuce, then slathered the bun with mustard.

"No," Buz said. "They're knee-deep in signals."

Everyone, including Grimes, stopped what they were doing and stared at him. The retired CIA spook and Russia expert looked around to make sure no civilians were wandering by within earshot before he continued.

"There was a terror attack in Nepal," he said. "Dozens dead and three times as many injured. All civilians—women and children among them . . ."

"Who did it?" Dempsey said, folding his hands in front of him.

"There's a group claiming responsibility—an ISIS affiliate out of northern Pakistan," Casey said, "but nothing's been confirmed."

"No fucking surprise there," Fender said.

"Are we going to take them out?" Prescott asked.

Casey shook his head. "This isn't an Ember-level event. CIA and JSOC are prosecuting intelligence assets with the help of Navy's Group Ten and Task Force Orange. This is a pretty classic JSOC tasking, actually."

"Except," Buz said, glancing at Casey, "Baldwin isn't convinced that this group—or even ISIS proper—could have pulled off the attack."

"When Baldwin figures it out, he'll tell us," Dempsey said. "And he *will* figure it out. For those of you just coming aboard with us at Ember, Baldwin and his team are geniuses. Pit them against any NSA supercomputer and my money's on Baldwin."

"Maybe we deploy to theater to be ready?" Munn said, speaking up for the first time.

Casey answered for the OPSO. "Not sure where we'd deploy yet, Dan. We'll keep you in the loop, but we have no tasking from Jarvis yet."

"Well, we could suggest it," Dempsey said, backing up Munn.

Casey stared at both of them a moment, his face a mask. "For now this is JSOC, but if Baldwin comes up with something that makes this within our charter, we'll send it up."

Dempsey nodded. Grimes watched his face turn again from granite to soft old Dempsey in a flash. He picked up his burger and took an enormous bite, then used a paper towel to dab juice from his beard.

"In the meantime, I'm going to prep another module for the Farm for next week," Buz said, looking from Dempsey to Munn and back. "I think everyone could benefit from some additional training."

This comment unleashed a chorus of groans from those in earshot of the comment, including Grimes, who couldn't help herself. The last thing she wanted to do was fly back to Virginia for more reindeer games.

"All right," Dempsey said, "but Buz?"

"Yes, John . . ."

"How about you make sure that Wang gets to do his thing in the TOC next time? It's not Ember ops if he's not our ears."

Grimes ticked her gaze to Wang and saw both surprise and gratitude in the kid's eyes.

"I agree," Buz said. "I'll take care of it."

"Oh, and one more thing," Dempsey said, shifting his gaze to Casey. As he did, Grimes saw the storm clouds flare in his eyes again. "Next time you talk to Jarvis, maybe politely remind him that our skills are perishable. The Farm simulations are fine and all, but for Ember to remain effective, we need to be operating."

Casey nodded at the comment, which was clearly directed at him, but said nothing.

"Noted," Buz said after an awkward beat.

When nobody said anything else, Munn cracked a joke and Grimes felt the tension break.

Thank God for Dan, she thought as the team got back to chowing down on their dinner. And soon they were laughing like old times.

CHAPTER 5

"Any questions, ladies?" the SEAL Senior Chief barked at the assembled trainees in the loadout room.

The man's face suggested that the question was not rhetorical, and if anyone had a question then they needed to ask now. Jake Kemper had seen firsthand how seriously the instructors took team safety, especially now that they were advancing in their weapons training and firing live ammunition in a more kinetic environment.

"Okay, good," the SEAL instructor said. "This is a pretty simple course, just to continue to get you comfortable with the fire-and-move techniques we've practiced. We're going to run the course in teams of two like we briefed. For this drill, you're evaluated more on your fire discipline and clear lanes of fire with your partner than accuracy. Tag your partners at any time and you fail. Understood?"

"Yes, Senior Chief," Jake answered for himself and Ketron, along with the six other trainees in the assembly area of the kill house training facility.

"That being said," the Senior Chief said, giving a nod and smile to the other instructors, "you're being trained to be the most lethal fighting force in the world. So: kill the fucking enemy!"

"Yes, Senior Chief," Jake and his teammates said, smiling this time.

"Kemper and Ketron—you lovebirds go first."

"With pleasure, Senior Chief," Randy Ketron, standing beside Jake, said.

In the short time since they'd graduated BUD/S and left the damn grinder behind, Jake had watched Ketron grow not just in skill but in confidence too. BUD/S was where most SEAL candidates failed, so now the students were getting their mojo back. SQT, or SEAL Qualification Training, was graduate school training for the SEALs. The focus was no longer weeding out those who weren't fit for the Teams, and instead shifted toward giving the candidates the skills they would need to operate.

And completion of SQT meant pinning on the coveted Trident and reporting to their first real-world SEAL Team.

"Gear check—you got three minutes."

Jake turned to his teammate. They began checking over their own kits, then the other's, just like they'd drilled the last several days. The classroom training the last couple of weeks had been a welcome break—a time for healing after all the pain and injury of BUD/S—but like the rest of his training class, Jake was ready to get to the good stuff. They'd been lectured on an enormous variety of Special Warfare weaponry, had been tested on disassembling and reassembling those weapons over and over—including blindfolded—and they'd conducted range fire drills. Now, they finally got to shoot and move and feel like actual operators.

"Can't wait for the land warfare block," Ketron said with a grin as his hands flew over Jake's gear.

"For sure," Jake said.

"Do you think, since ours will be at Camp Walker, that we'll have a chance to visit Group Two while we're there?" Ketron asked softly.

Group Two was the home of all the East Coast–based SEAL Teams—Two, Four, Eight, and Ten—based out of Joint Expeditionary Base Little Creek. Camp Walker was located a short distance away in Virginia and was where he and Ketron would be conducting most of their land warfare training.

Jake shrugged. "Not sure, bro," he said, but he understood the reason for Ketron's question.

They just learned that they'd both been assigned to SEAL Team Eight in Group Two—assuming, that is, that they successfully completed the remaining blocks of SQT. Knowing their duty station was a tremendous relief. At first, Randy had been disappointed because he'd hoped to be assigned on the West Coast—to one of the odd-numbered Teams under Group One. Jake, on the other hand, hadn't cared where he ended up geographically. His mom was on the East Coast, but he didn't imagine he would see her much the next few years either way. There had been something appealing about a possible new start on the West Coast. His dad had been an East Coast, Group Two guy, and if Jake had been assigned to Group One, it would have differentiated him from his dad. But then again, the Tier One was on the East Coast, and making it to the JSOC unit was his long-term goal. He wasn't sure if the split of guys selected from Group One and Group Two at the Tier One were the same or not.

He made a mental note to look into that.

What mattered most to him in the short term, however, was being at the same Team as Randy, and so on that front . . . mission complete. As far as advanced schools, Jake wasn't sure which ones they would qualify for, but he would be excited for either sniper school or the Special Operations Combat Medic course. Being an 18 Delta medic seemed exciting and challenging, but he loved the idea of being on the long gun as well. He knew that Randy was most definitely praying for sniper school.

"Let's go, boys," the Senior Chief barked at Jake and Ketron. "Clear left and right as we practiced on the walk-through, then clear the room, meet at the center door, and repeat in the rear room. Hooyah?"

"Hooyah," Ketron responded for both of them.

Jake pressed into the plywood wall beside the fake-looking door and waited for Ketron to squeeze his shoulder from behind, signaling his teammate was ready. Then one of the instructors pulled the rope attached to the empty door handle, opening the door, and they were off.

Jake moved through the door in the low combat crouch, just as they'd drilled for the last week. The master chief had made them go back and forth to chow the first few days in the combat crouch, their finger and thumbs up simulating rifles, and Jake's thighs had burned terribly with lactic acidosis that first night.

Tonight would probably be another rough night too.

He moved left, arcing to clear the corner behind him, knowing Ketron would do the same in mirror image to clear right. Finding no threats, he pivoted clockwise and surged forward. His eyes registered the barren room, devoid of furniture, before he zeroed in on the two targets ahead of him—silhouetted cutouts with cartoon pictures of terrorists on them. Jake put the iron sight of his M4 rifle on the closer target and squeezed twice, then shifted to the other target and double-tapped it as well. As he did, he heard Ketron engaging the same targets almost in cadence, the cracks of their rifles off by only a millisecond. Jake smiled as he surged forward, adding a parting headshot to the second target before stepping left, advancing toward the doorway to the next room.

Instead of surging through the door, he fell in on the left side the doorway, pressed against the wall. Ketron did the same on the opposite, and Jake made eye contact with his teammate. When Jake gave a nod, Ketron pulled the door open and surged through, this time moving left as Jake followed after to clear right.

Jake spun clockwise, clearing his corner, and saw a silhouette with a poster of a terrorist on it, this one crouched beneath the open window. Jake fired twice, smiling as he saw two holes appear center mass, then rotated counterclockwise to clear forward. Two more targets—four more gunshots followed by two to the head of the silhouettes after. Then he turned back to the target by the window and added a headshot there as well.

He surged forward and hollered, "Clear."

"Clear," Ketron echoed.

"All right, secure weapons," a voice said from overhead.

Jake safed his M4 with the flick of his thumb, then held it to his chest, barrel down, and finger outside the trigger guard.

"Safe," he hollered.

"Safe," Ketron added.

Two instructors entered from behind them. They had scowls on their faces, but the instructors *always* had scowls on their faces. Jake couldn't help but grin. He knew they'd nailed the first pass at the drill. He'd watched his rounds hit center mass every time, and now looked at Randy's and saw the same, tight grouping. Ketron grinned back and gave him a nod.

"Well, you're dead, Kemper," one of the instructors said, crossing his arms on his chest.

"How's that, Chief?" Jake asked, surprised and confused. "Did I miss a target?"

"Not inside," the SEAL Chief said. "But you passed right in front of the window like a rookie dumbass. Didn't even clear through it—just sauntered across like you were at the park. So, in the simulation, you got shot from outside the window."

"By who?" Jake asked.

"A sniper, a roving sentry, a twelve-year-old kid with an AK-47 . . ." the Senior Chief chimed in. "It doesn't matter who pulled the trigger. What does matter is that your melon got popped and you never saw it coming."

"Yes, Chief," Jake said, realizing his mistake. "No excuses. Won't happen again, Chief."

But in his mind, a different dialogue was taking place. *I would hardly call it a saunter . . . he knows we're total badasses, which is why he's trying to knock me down a peg.*

"Good," Senior Chief said, piling on with his fellow instructor. "'Cause when you die, you leave your teammate alone and then he's more likely to die. Then the mission fails. And when that happens, your whole damn team dies . . ."

"Roger that, Senior," Jake said.

The Senior Chief gave a nod, but he had a twinkle in his eye.

"Back to the front, and tell Mitchell and Rodriguez to get ready."

"Yes, Senior," Ketron replied for them.

Jake headed through the door with his buddy, feeling the rush slowly ebb. He'd really felt like an operator, and he knew they'd done well. After both scoring in the top three at the static range, they were well on their way.

He heard the soft conversation behind him.

"Accuracy?"

"One hundred percent."

"Shit. On their first run? Time?"

"Thirteen seconds."

Then a laugh.

"Shit, that's probably a record on the first time through. Hell, that's probably better than his old man."

"I don't know about that." Another chuckle. "Jack Kemper was a legend for a reason."

"Dude, we crushed it," Ketron whispered from beside him. "That was fucking awesome."

Jake nodded. He was satisfied, but the ghost of his dead father, the SEAL legend, followed him everywhere here on Coronado. Now, it soured his mood.

"Hey, Kemper."

He turned to see the Senior Chief staring after him, arms folded on his chest.

"Yes, Senior?"

"On the second run, let's split you and Ketron up," the SEAL said. He was smiling, something Jake was pretty sure he'd never seen. Then, to his shock, the man actually winked. "Best to give the rest of the class a fighting chance."

Jake just gave the man a nod, unsure what to say. The SEAL nodded back, then Jake turned and headed to the assembly area where the other candidates waited for their turn at the evolution.

"I can't wait to get to the land warfare block," Ketron said again, his face suggesting he was already there in his mind.

"Me too," Jake said, and he meant it. They were scheduled for the air week next, and he was looking forward to that too. And the combat swimmer block. Hell, he was looking forward to all of it—every damn thing.

If I can just get out from under this ghost's shadow.

As the adrenaline burned off, his mind went back to the grinder of BUD/S. He could almost feel the chill as he prepared to slip into the bathtub full of ice and water for cold-weather conditioning. But that wasn't where his brain was really taking him. For the thousandth time, he replayed the master chief talking softly to him as he shuddered from cold, the man's eyes darkened by the memory of his own haunting by the ghost of Jack Kemper.

"I . . . I thought I saw him once . . ." the man had said.

Then the master chief disappeared from his memory, replaced by the image of the strange, powerfully built officer who had visited him later at the medical clinic. The commander had said he was fulfilling a promise to Jake's father. The ghost of his dad must have haunted that guy too.

Someday, he thought as he exited the kill house, *I'll find out who the hell you really were, and what really happened to you.*

CHAPTER 6

United States President Randall Warner walked along the narrow red carpet beside his Secretary of Defense, through the double doors, and into the opulent reception hall of marble and gold. He wished his wife, Amy, were at his side. The last few weeks he'd become nearly overwhelmed with anticipation of what it would be like to sleep until midmorning, kiss his wife in their own quiet bedroom at the ranch outside of Santa Fe, and then sip coffee at an honest-to-God kitchen table while talking about—*nothing*. At least nothing that mattered.

"They went all out," Secretary of Defense Robert Franks whispered from beside him. "I'll bet the dinner will be amazing."

"If you like Indian food," Warner said with a smile, "this will be the best dinner of your life, Bob."

And Warner did—he loved all spicy foods, but Indian most of all. He'd visited New Delhi once before, almost five years ago now, and still dreamed about the meal he'd had on that visit. But he missed Amy more and more each day as he approached the finish line of his presidency. The end had seemed like an eternity away three years ago, but now it felt like it had arrived in a blink. Eight years as President. So many tragedies and so many triumphs. Now, he just wanted to eat a late breakfast and ride horses before it got hot.

He was sure they'd find purpose in their next season—he and Amy together, side by side—but first he wanted a year of just laying low and enjoying each other. It would feel like being newlyweds again, he thought. At least, that was how Amy was selling it.

Up ahead, the Indian Prime Minister Vihaan Chopra smiled from the podium, which was set up on a dais at the end of the carpet that snaked up the long marble-tiled floor, flanked by opulent pillars inlaid with gold. The pomp and circumstance were decadent, amazing, and flattering—and he wouldn't miss it one bit.

A steak on the grill, a glass of red wine Amy has picked out—and then maybe, dare I dream, a movie on the big-screen TV.

The thought almost made him laugh, so he chased it away. The international press—snapping pictures from every angle as he approached the two steps up to shake hands with a man he truly did respect—would make a mountain speculating about what exactly the American President found so amusing as he approached the leader of India.

Secretary Franks slid away, finding the chair he would occupy in a moment behind the podium, and then joined the applause from the assembled Indian dignitaries. Warner reached out and shook hands with Prime Minister Chopra, the man he was here to meet. They kept their hands clasped, the Indian Prime Minister's firm and dry, and both turned out to the small crowd, posing for the photo op, before Warner leaned in to softly whisper a greeting.

"It's an honor to be here with you, my friend," he said, clasping the man's shoulder with his left hand as he did. "I mean it, Vihaan."

"I'm honored to have you here, Randall," Chopra replied with a genuine smile. "And for the partnership we're forming here. I look forward to chatting about it for a few minutes before dinner—away from the vultures," he added with a chuckle, but then smiled out at the press pool.

"Indeed," Warner said, smiling back. "Me too."

Warner circled the podium and stood behind Prime Minister Chopra as the applause continued for a moment. Then Chopra raised a humble hand, quieting the crowd, and Warner took a seat beside his Defense Secretary.

"It is an honor beyond measure," Prime Minister Chopra said, "to host my friend and a man I admire more than I can say: the President of the United States . . ."

Another burst of applause, and Warner stood briefly again, giving a short wave before taking his seat so Chopra could continue. Warner really wanted to get on with this—the smiling and waving, the photo op, the political nonsense portion of the event—so it could end. He looked forward to talking privately with Vihaan about what they had planned. The partnership they intended to announce was enormous—for both countries. The United States was prepared to invest heavily in India's defense, helping it grow and modernize to defend itself against the rising threats. With a new, modern president in Russia, one tension had cooled, but in its place others grew in what was, it seemed, the circle of geopolitical life. Iran was growing bolder, despite the example that had been made of President Petrov in Russia. China was a threat both economically and potentially militarily as well, as India and the US forged a partnership that threatened China's economic dominance. Pakistan was always a threat to India, of course, and terrorism along the border of the two countries was again increasing.

Another round of applause brought Warner back, and he looked to see Vihaan Chopra smiling and gesturing at him. He raised a hand in confirmation of whatever it was the man had said, accepting some compliment, he assumed. Then the Indian Prime Minister turned and continued his remarks.

As for the United States, the cost of the new partnership in military equipment, trainers, and technology was outweighed, in his mind, by new—and what promised to be explosive—economic gain. American companies, already invested heavily in India, would now increase support for expanding both the technology sectors as well as rare earth metal mining. Truly multinational corporate partnerships meant that, in very short time, America's technology and retail sectors could shift away from their brutal and unsustainable dependence on China.

He smiled, imagining what was going on in the head of Chinese leader Li Yusheng right now. This new and better relationship with Vihaan Chopra and the United States meant that China would no longer have them all by the balls. He didn't care that Pakistan was pissed. They'd been a terrible ally in the decades-long war on terror, and now they would learn that they needed the West far more than the West needed them. This—Warner's last big geopolitical move of his presidency—was one he could be immensely proud of.

He crossed his legs and smiled as Chopra spoke his platitudes about Warner and America, her military, and her companies, but his mind wandered again to Amy and their future. He felt, well, younger than he expected to at the end of this, his second term. He felt like he and Amy had an actual future awaiting them.

The last few months of anticipation for the homestretch had seemed to chase away what had been his almost desperate need to handpick a successor. Did he still wish that Jarvis had agreed to run as the next President? Hell yeah, he did. The man was the perfect choice to finish all that Warner had begun. But maybe now, as he looked forward to his next season with Amy, he understood Jarvis's reasons for declining. Jarvis had served his nation for decades, at great personal cost. Now the former Tier One SEAL wanted—hell, *deserved*—a life of quiet peace with the woman he loved. His country had asked far more than it had a right to of the man. Hell, Warner himself had asked more than he had a right to—running the ODNI, then filling the office of Vice President, all the while running the most lethal and closely guarded covert ops team in the world. Warner imagined—in fact, privately prayed—that the next President, whether his party's nominee or, God forbid, the opposing party's, would see the utility of keeping Task Force Ember alive and in play. No matter your politics, Ember was a powerful and necessary tool.

But it was time for Jarvis to find some peace and happiness. And anyway, Senator Margaret Whalen had stepped up and proven herself to be a passionate and highly motivated candidate for his job as President. Once he reminded himself that he'd played the politics game to get into office himself, he was able to extend her some grace. The truth was, he thought she'd make a great President.

Bob Franks tapped his shoulder and rose, signaling it was Warner's turn to take the podium. Warner stood and gave a humble smile and wave as he joined Chopra at the front for another staged photo-op handshake. Then Chopra took a step back, and Warner took the podium, smiling at the crowd of journalists and the handful of invited guests, Indian dignitaries, and a few White House staffers.

Warner gathered himself, resting his hands on the podium and looking up to scan the teleprompter for the first lines of the remarks his staff had prepared earlier. As he did, his eye caught a motion that seemed out of place. Perhaps his Secret Service detail sensed it too because he saw a blur of motion in his right peripheral vision.

Warner looked down at the line of press photographers kneeling at the front of the flock of journalists. A man with a gray tripod-mounted camera was reaching into a big bag beside him, but instead of a lens or second camera, the man pulled out something else—something small that he held in his left hand, a cord snaking back toward the bag.

The man's eyes burned with hatred as he raised his hand above his head.

Warner grunted as one of the Secret Service agents—Ted Blaise, he figured, judging by the enormous, linebacker-worthy size—crunched into him, dragging him to the floor as the cameraman screamed in rage.

Somehow, impossibly, Warner knew he was dead. Even before he felt the wall of heat and flames engulf him and the searing pain of shrapnel tear through his body, he knew. Time slowed to a crawl, and he had time for just two last thoughts.

First: *I am so sorry I never gave you the next season, baby . . .*

Then: *Find who did this, Kelso, and turn John Dempsey and his team loose to exact vengeance . . .*

Then the heat consumed him, and the blackness swallowed him whole.

CHAPTER 7

Jarvis stared out the dark-tinted rear window of the up-armored Range Rover at the entrance to the Old Cemetery. Harel's funeral was to be a small, private, and expedited affair. For security reasons pertaining to the VIP guests who would be attending, Harel's death had not been publicized, nor had the burial site been announced. Hell, Jarvis and his team had only been told the time and location an hour ago. By Jewish tradition, interment should take place within twenty-four hours of passing. According to scriptural lore, the soul did not depart the body immediately after death. Any mutilation or process that interfered with the natural decay of the body—such as embalming or cremation—was prohibited.

Jarvis had never known his friend to be a particularly spiritual man, but Harel had great and profound respect for tradition. Jarvis had no doubt that Levi's instructions to Rouvin were that the traditions and burial customs of his faith be adhered to however possible.

Today, Harel would be laid to rest alongside some of Israel's most noteworthy and culturally significant figures. Interment in the Old Cemetery was no small feat. The fact that Harel was to be buried here was, as far as Jarvis understood, entirely Shamone's doing. The Israeli PM was giving his friend and fellow soldier the honor the man deserved. The spymaster and the PM went way back, even further back than Harel had with Jarvis.

Shamone and Harel had both joined the IDF and served in Shayetet 13 together. When Harel pivoted into the espionage business, Shamone went into politics, but their orbits never stopped intersecting. It was Shamone who'd appointed Harel to lead the Mossad, and Harel who'd bailed his friend and his country out of countless near-disasters the world had never heard about. Jarvis didn't have the same long history with Randall Warner that Harel and Shamone did, but his relationship with the American President certainly had its parallels.

Except Levi was smart enough to stay out of politics, and I wasn't.

It had been nearly a day since his friend's passing, and Jarvis still had not opened Harel's letter. Last night he'd called Petra to read her in on his final, soul-wrenching visit with the man he'd considered a friend, mentor, and father figure. She'd listened, just listened, without trying to help him sort out his grief. He loved her for that.

Unfortunately, the grieving process wasn't over. Jarvis knew that his friend's final words would give him the closure he needed. But he wasn't ready yet.

I'll know when the time is right.

The most astounding thing was that Harel—by sheer force of will—had stubbornly refused to die until he could say goodbye to Jarvis in person. The expression "living on borrowed time" was more than an idiom in Levi's case. Jarvis smiled, picturing in his mind the Jewish spymaster and Death negotiating the terms of Harel's surrender, only to have the smooth-talking former Mossad chief manipulate the Grim Reaper into getting exactly what he wanted.

Just like he always did with me.

"Sir, Prime Minister Shamone is en route and will be arriving in ten minutes. Security is already in place," Perez said, turning to face

Jarvis from the front passenger seat of their host SUV. "Do you want to stay in the vehicle until he arrives and walk in together, or would you prefer to head into the cemetery?"

"Let's go in now," Jarvis said, feeling antsy and ready to get out of the vehicle. "We'll give the PM the honor of being the last to arrive. His home turf, his moment."

"Roger that."

Perez made a call to check with the external security team and, upon getting the okay, exited the Range Rover. He opened the rear passenger door for Jarvis, who stepped out and immediately squinted in the bright afternoon sun. The Secret Service lead pulled a pair of sunglasses from his jacket pocket and handed them to Jarvis.

"Thanks, Tony," Jarvis said, accepting the shades and putting them on. Most of the time having a close protection detail annoyed Jarvis, but he would miss the little things when his stint as VP ended.

Perez gestured to a gated entry, a cutout in the ten-foot-tall stone perimeter wall that surrounded the cemetery with two iron doors and a bilingual sign announcing the cemetery was currently closed to tourists. Four agents—two from his detail and two presumably from the Israeli PM's detail—waited inside.

Frank Jolly, another trusted agent in his detail, fell in behind Jarvis as he stepped away from the vehicle. Jolly was built like a tank, and Jarvis liked having him in trail. Jarvis followed Perez through the gap between the sawhorse barricades to the gated entry of the cemetery, where the other pair from his detail waited. They formed a box around Jarvis, then followed the stone promenade to the heart of the cemetery, weaving through the rectangular sand-colored pavers. In the middle of the walkway, the stones ran horizontally, creating a ladder effect, but on the right and left sides they were laid lengthwise, which drew the eye into the graveyard.

"And so mounting as it were by steps, let us get to heaven by a Jacob's ladder . . ."

The quote, from an author he couldn't recall, bubbled to the surface from the deep recesses of his mind. At the same time, his synesthesia kicked in and he heard a tone play softly.

Middle F . . . 349.228 Hz

Headstones and obelisks made of blanched concrete and colored marble stood like crooked teeth before him. The ten-acre burial complex was the most crowded cemetery he'd ever seen. And yet it had a strange, disordered efficiency that he recognized instantly.

"This way, Mr. Vice President," Perez said, snapping Jarvis's attention back from the distracted ruminations. "The gravesite is along the northwest wall."

Jarvis nodded, and their five-man formation compressed as they made a left turn onto one of three narrower stone paths, which snaked off toward Harel's plot. Eventually, the stone pavers gave way to a wooden walkway, and up ahead Jarvis spied a small contingent—less than a dozen mourners—already waiting at what he presumed was the gravesite. Just beyond, along the wall forming the perimeter of the cemetery, stood an enormous tree, branches hanging almost to the ground as if in mourning themselves.

He recognized Israeli Defense Minister Levi Danon and the new Mossad chief, Ari Cohen. His gaze caught on a blond woman wearing a black pantsuit, sunglasses, and a hat, not because she was fit and attractive—which she was—but because she was the only person who had not looked up to watch him arrive. Something about her proportions, the shape of her mouth, and the way she held her shoulders . . .

Holy shit, that's Elinor Jordan.

An instant adrenaline dump put him into a state of hyperawareness.

"Is everything okay, sir?" Agent Jolly asked from behind him, astutely cuing off Jarvis's new body language.

"The blond woman wearing a hat," he said. "Who is she?"

"Checking . . ."

Perez and the other agent in front of Jarvis closed ranks, moving shoulder to shoulder, and made themselves into a two-person human shield in front of the VP. Jarvis resisted the compulsion to pull his weapon. Unlike his predecessors, Jarvis always carried a weapon. Perez looked the other way on this protocol violation—first off because he owed Jarvis his life, and second because Jarvis had a pedigree unlike that of any previous Vice President. Jarvis was a lifelong special operator who knew how to handle himself, and Perez knew he was an asset in a tactical situation rather than a liability.

Today, Jarvis carried a Wilson SFX9 pistol, hidden in a pocket-like holster built into his dress shirt. Despite looking like a regular white oxford, the custom-made shirt had snaps under faux buttons for tear-open, easy access. If that woman really was Elinor Jordan—which the machinery of his mind assured him was the case—the odds that he would be drawing his weapon were at least a double-digit number.

The last time he'd heard about Elinor Jordan was after Dempsey had sworn he'd seen her assassinate an informant he'd been interviewing in broad daylight while sitting at a bistro table in Riga. Jarvis had immediately phoned Harel to check the veracity of this claim, and according to Harel, the Seventh Order double agent had spent three days in a hospital in Tehran after being shot in the back by Maheen Modiri and left behind by Dempsey. After that, however, Jordan had disappeared—the presumption being that VEVAK had taken her for interrogation and elimination.

A snippet of that conversation played in Jarvis's head.

"Despite everything, she was like a daughter to me," Harel had said. *"A prodigal daughter, but a daughter nonetheless. I never had one of my own . . ."*

"Are you going to try to find her?" Jarvis had asked.

"Of course I am. I'm a selfish man, Kelso. I want to say goodbye."

He didn't know if Harel had found the answers he was looking for. He didn't know if the spymaster had gotten to say goodbye to his prodigal spy. Was Elinor's appearance here at the funeral her way of paying tribute, of giving Harel the closure the old man had wanted? Or was she here to exact revenge on the former Ember director and boss of the American operator who'd abandoned her?

"Sir, the woman's name is Safra Sivan," Jolly said, whispering in Jarvis's ear. "She's been vetted by the Israeli security service."

The more he studied the woman's face beneath the blond wig, the more certain he became that she was Elinor Jordan. "Israeli passport?"

"No. Belgian."

A smile curled Jarvis's lips on hearing this confirming detail.

Dempsey's first meeting with Jordan had been in Brussels. Was using a Belgian passport her way of sending Jarvis a signal, a subtle confirmation that only he would understand?

"Is that a problem?" Perez asked over his shoulder as they walked.

"Not sure, but I want you to keep a close eye on her."

"Check."

The Israeli cybersecurity apparatus was one of the best in the world. Given her previous top secret security clearance and current disavowed status, Elinor would certainly be flagged as a person of interest. Was it possible that her new NOC was so good that she had cleared every hurdle? Unlikely. Which meant one of two things: either Harel had never reported her as a traitor and threat, or her presence here was sanctioned, possibly even supported, by the Seventh Order.

Was Elinor Jordan back at work with the Israeli equivalent of Task Force Ember? Did Prime Minister Shamone know she was going to be here? Surely he knew of the Iranian double agent discovered within the most covert task force in Israel . . .

On arriving at the gravesite, the small group of guests adjusted their positions to make room for the Vice President and his detail. Jarvis took his spot at the bottom right foot of the casket opposite where Elinor stood, her hands clasping a small bag in front of her. Despite her sunglasses and the effort she made to not look at him, Jarvis could feel Elinor's gaze behind the dark lenses.

As expected, Defense Minister Danon immediately stepped over to greet him. Jarvis shook the man's hand and made small talk, but the tactical part of his brain never shifted focus away from Elinor.

A beat later, Perez leaned in. "The PM has arrived," he said in a low voice.

Jarvis nodded.

The Israeli Defense Minister must have overheard because he paused and glanced over his shoulder toward the cemetery entrance before continuing. While Danon rambled, Jarvis war-gamed out how best to confront Elinor. A part of him wanted to confront her directly, right now, and gauge her reaction. But Shamone would be here in moments, and he wasn't about to brush off Defense Minister Danon, a man Jarvis both wanted and needed to have a good personal relationship with. So, he did the only thing he could do and waited, his mind running countess tactical scenarios.

When Shamone and his detail entered the main gate of the Old Cemetery, all conversation stopped, and the small band of mourners shifted their attention to the Prime Minister's arrival. Jarvis capitalized on the moment to give Perez tasking.

"Go ask Safra Sivan what her favorite restaurant is in Brussels," he whispered.

"Her favorite restaurant in Brussels?" Perez echoed quietly, his voice signaling his confusion.

"That's right; do it now," he said.

"Yes, sir."

Jarvis watched him walk around the grave, up to the woman calling herself Safra Sivan. She didn't appear rattled when the Secret Service agent approached her, nor did she flinch at the question. After hearing her reply, Perez returned and whispered the answer in Jarvis's ear. Jarvis could feel her watching from the other side of Harel's casket.

"My French sucks, but I'm pretty sure she said Les Brassins on Rue Keyenveld," Perez said, confirming Jarvis's instincts. "Then she said to tell you her favorite opera is *Boris Godunov*. Does that mean anything to you?"

It sure as hell does. It means Elinor Jordan is not only alive and well but that she is still very much in the game.

"No, I can't say that it does," Jarvis said, his voice perplexed but his eyes laser-focused on her.

As Shamone and his detail approached, Jarvis had no choice but to shift gears and greet the Prime Minister just like Danon had greeted him moments ago.

"Mr. Prime Minister, it's good to see you again," Jarvis said, extending a hand to Shamone. "Pity it has to be under such melancholy circumstances."

Shamone, a natural and charismatic showman who thrived in social situations, looked nothing like himself. Dark bags hung under the man's eyes and an ashen pallor hung over his face. Clearly, he was taking Harel's death very hard.

"I heard you were there last night when he passed," Shamone said, clasping Jarvis's right hand in both of his own and clutching him tight. "I can't tell you how much peace that brings me. He valued your friendship . . . probably more than you know."

"And the same is true for you," Jarvis said, needing this moment, but a part of his brain still focused on the potential threat Elinor might yet pose. "He had a photo on the wall of his study in a place of prominence. It was a candid photo of the two of you laughing together. Levi spoke often and highly of you."

"Yes, but the latter not nearly with the same frequency as the former, I'm sure," Shamone said and offered a hint of a smile with the quip.

Jarvis gave him a tight smile back. He opened his mouth to make a quip of his own but stopped.

Something was wrong. Shamone felt it too and looked north.

Operating entirely on instinct, Jarvis grabbed Shamone by the shoulder and dropped low, jerking the Prime Minister down with him a mere millisecond before he heard the faint, muffled pop of a suppressed gunshot. Blood spattered his face as the top of the Israeli Prime Minister's left ear evaporated.

As Shamone's nearest bodyguard threw himself on top of the PM, Jarvis pulled his weapon and swiveled to shoot Elinor, who his brain predicted must be holding a .22 LR pistol with a smoking suppressor on the end. But to his surprise, she was unarmed and scrambling for cover. A split second later, his sight lines disappeared as a human shield, comprised of the four bodies of his security detail, enshrouded him.

Chaos and commotion erupted as the rest of the guests realized what was happening.

"Jarvis!" Elinor yelled from where she crouched. "The tree."

He couldn't see where she pointed, but he knew exactly which tree she was talking about—the large, full tree whose bottom branches touched the gravestones. The tree had already registered in his subconscious as problematic because of its proximity to the perimeter wall. The missed kill shot on Shamone would have been straight on for a shooter hiding in the branches or under the low canopy.

Jarvis looked right.

Between Jolly's legs, Jarvis could see Shamone's blood-soaked face. They made eye contact and something inside Jarvis snapped. Flashbulb memories from the failed assassination attempt in Istanbul popped into his brain—where Jarvis, Tony, and Petra had all been shot. They'd both taken bullets for Jarvis, and now he felt suddenly overwhelmed with an illogical desire to mete retribution.

The world didn't have to be this way.

It shouldn't be this way.

Perez clutched his arm and tugged Jarvis toward the exit while calling in the exfil over his radio. "We're leaving—*now.*"

The analytical part of Jarvis's mind knew that retreat to safety was the logical course of action, but the Navy SEAL in him didn't care.

"No," he said, his voice a feral growl as he gave in to the rage.

He jerked his arm free from Perez's grip.

Supercharged by adrenaline and fury, Jarvis hurdled a headstone and zigged onto a narrow path between a row of graves, forcing himself to ignore the urgent call from Agent Perez behind him.

"Stop, Mr. Jarvis!"

The form-fitting, flexible, gel-filled vest he wore under his suit coat, dress shirt, and tactical concealed-carry undershirt was the latest in body armor technology, the same model that Ember had transitioned to for their covert operations. It offered excellent antiballistic protection for his torso but did nothing to safeguard his head. What he was doing was beyond reckless, he knew, but he was in retribution mode. His target was the shooter, whom he fully intended to capture alive if possible.

Apparently, Elinor had the same plan because she was sprinting ahead of him also in hot pursuit. Despite their age difference, he was closing the gap, but just before he caught her, she disappeared under the tree's wide canopy. Jarvis completed a quick one-hundred-and-eighty-degree scan at ground level, searching for a crouching figure or movement before following her under the branches. Once under the canopy, he immediately sighted on her with his SFX9, in case his instincts about her proved wrong.

Elinor, however, was scanning upward with a compact pistol, looking for the shooter in the branches above.

"Clear," she shouted and pointed to the ground. "There's his rifle."

Jarvis followed her gaze to a suppressed Christensen MHR hunter with an optics package that lay abandoned on the top of a grave. Jarvis looked back at Elinor, who eyed a black nylon rope tied to one of the tree branches. It angled down, hung over the top of the perimeter wall, and disappeared from view on the other side.

Jarvis watched as Elinor holstered her weapon and climbed the low branches of the tree, reached across to the high wall, and then hoisted herself onto the top with the ease and agility of an acrobat.

"The shooter must have staged the rope, climbed up this morning, and hid in the foliage," she said, flashing him an *I dare you to follow me* smile from the top. "You stay put, Mr. Vice President. I've got this."

Jarvis cursed under his breath as she disappeared off the other side of the wall. Without a second's hesitation, he holstered his weapon and heaved himself up the tree behind her.

"I can't let you do this, sir," Perez shouted, finally arriving with Jolly at the tree just as Jarvis flung his right leg over the top. "You're not a SEAL anymore. You're the Vice President."

Jarvis grabbed the black rope with both hands and met his lead agent's reproachful glare.

"That's where you're wrong, Tony. Once a SEAL, always a SEAL."

Jarvis wrapped the black rope with his coat and rappelled down the eighteen-foot-tall section of wall faster than he probably should have—partly because he didn't have gloves and partly because there was no way in hell he was letting Elinor kill this assassin. They needed this asshole alive.

He landed on his feet but hit the dirt hard. His whole body felt the jolt, but experience and muscle memory had primed his legs to take the impact like twin shock absorbers. Palms on fire, he straightened up from his crouch to find himself surrounded by . . .

Dogs?

Apparently, he'd landed in an urban dog park—the last thing he'd expected in the dense city of Tel Aviv. The occupants, both canine and human, stared wide-eyed in shock and confusion. A burly dude holding the lead of a muscular boxer pointed at the gate, beyond which Jarvis could see Elinor sprinting away.

"Thanks," Jarvis said and kicked off his own sprint after the former Seventh Order operator.

Ever since Istanbul, Jarvis had given up wearing conventional hard-soled dress shoes. He only wore the new hybrid models that looked like wingtips on top but had a sport sole on the bottom, a decision which was paying off now as he hurdled the park's low gate and churned down the alley, feeling the spry Navy SEAL ultra athlete he'd once been fighting to the surface. After his Parkinson's diagnosis, he'd elevated his level of fitness and training and was in better shape now than when he'd been the Ember director.

What a strange paradox, that he could be stronger and weaker at the same time . . .

Elinor rounded a corner ten meters ahead and disappeared. Jarvis accelerated to his maximum speed, wondering how much of a lead the shooter had on her. Without eyes in the sky, tracking the bastard would require maintaining visual contact. The Old Cemetery was in the heart of Tel Aviv—a warren of tree-lined streets with flats, hotels, office buildings, and restaurants—an easy place to get lost and disappear in.

They couldn't let that happen.

Thighs burning, Jarvis sprinted through the alley, the Wilson SFX9 gripped tightly in his right hand, then burst onto a narrow street lined with parked cars on the left. Ahead, no more than fifty yards, a man dressed in black ran down the middle of the street. He looked back, and the expression on his face told Jarvis everything the operator inside needed to know.

This was the shooter—his friend Prime Minister Shamone's would-be assassin.

Hatred shone in the man's eyes before he looked away and picked up the pace. Elinor was on the right-hand sidewalk, keeping pace with the shooter as Jarvis performed an automatic threat assessment on his adversary.

This guy was the shooter, but based on his build and the way he ran, he was definitely *not* an operator.

A horn blared and tires squealed as the shooter tried to cross through moving traffic. Jarvis watched a motor scooter wipe out and skid to a stop in the middle of the intersection. The fleeing assassin reached down to steal it, but the helmeted driver resisted, not willing to give up his ride without a fight.

Hooyah, random citizen! Jarvis thought. *Gotta love the Israelis . . .*

With a glance over his shoulder, the now panicked shooter abandoned the fight for the scooter and continued fleeing on foot. The would-be killer had given up fifteen meters of lead for his failed effort, and as the man's lead narrowed, Jarvis felt the predator inside push him to close the remaining gap.

Take him down.

Elinor was now side by side with him, her earlier lead now gone, and she reached the intersection just two strides before him and crossed easily through the stopped traffic. Jarvis followed, taking a diagonal vector between two stopped vehicles and the scooter driver.

Jarvis had not studied this area in advance. He'd not committed any of the streets to memory or built a mental map of the neighborhood around the Old Cemetery. As Vice President, he didn't have the need—nor the time—for such tactical preparation. That was the Secret Service's responsibility.

Maybe it was time he revised that policy.

The shooter had continued straight after crossing the intersection and was now running the wrong way down a one-way street. Jarvis followed Elinor onto the sidewalk in pursuit. As an approaching car honked, Jarvis saw the man vector left onto the sidewalk as well.

Gained another meter . . .

Jarvis now ran only two strides behind Elinor and figured he would overtake her by the end of the block. She was fast, but he was faster.

Up ahead, a middle-aged woman walked a small brown dog and shrieked as she jerked the little dog backward, out of the path of the sprinting assassin. The dog barked in a frenzied display of aggression, first at the shooter, then at Elinor, and finally yipping at Jarvis as he ran by. They approached the next intersection, and the shooter turned right instead of risking crossing the heavy traffic.

Thighs burning and lungs heaving, Jarvis passed Elinor and took the lead. Putting his back to her was a tactical risk. He had no reason to trust her. Despite his gut telling him she was an ally, she could be involved in this assassination attempt, functioning as a decoy or even as bait. Hell, she could even be the mastermind behind the whole thing.

But if that were the case, she could have shot him under the tree in the cemetery. Or when he landed in the dog park with his weapon holstered. Neither of those things had happened. She was Harel's self-proclaimed prodigal daughter. Levi had loved her, and so had Dempsey. What did that say about her? And at the end of the day, she'd not handed Dempsey over to VEVAK in Tehran, had she? Dempsey had left her behind, not the other way around. Maybe Dempsey had gotten it wrong. Maybe Elinor had been a double agent working for VEVAK, but her true allegiance had been to the Seventh Order all along.

He jettisoned the distracting thoughts and refocused on the chase as he vectored right onto the next street. But on rounding the corner, he didn't spot the shooter. Unlike the previous two streets, this street was lined with parked cars, walled courtyards, and hedgerows on both sides, creating a literal maze of places to cover and hide. He instantly slowed, leveled his pistol, and scanned for threats. Heart thumping like a piston in his chest, Jarvis forced himself to shift modes from pounding pursuit to systematic search. During the chase, the shooter had been running empty-handed, but that didn't mean he was unarmed.

This feels like an ambush . . .

Elinor caught up to him a beat later and, whether cuing off him or reaching the same conclusion on her own, she instantly mirrored his actions and fell into a combat crouch beside him, pushing out a few meters and angling her search forty-five degrees to his. After clearing their left rear quarter, she turned and their eyes met. In an instant he understood the question in her eyes—were they teammates in this moment or still foes? He gave a slight nod then turned away, clearing his right, before turning back, the question answered. Using hand signals, he instructed her to clear the opposite side of the street while he covered the sidewalk ahead. With a wordless acknowledgment, she drifted left, crossing the street in a rapid cross-step, low in her crouch, like a seasoned operator.

Four slow breaths downregulated Jarvis's heart rate while simultaneously upregulating his situational awareness. He knew that, like a microprocessor, the human mind was capable of operating at different data processing speeds. Race car drivers and fighter pilots were perfect examples of individuals with this ability. As a SEAL operating in a highly kinetic environment, Jarvis had trained his mind to perform similarly, allowing him to scan and react faster than he would under normal circumstances. Being able to harness this capability was one of the things that made men like Dempsey so lethal.

But then, Jarvis was the one who had helped train Dempsey back when he had been Navy SEAL Jack Kemper, and later when he'd become John Dempsey. Jarvis knew what made Dempsey tick.

He knew that Dempsey called this *the slipstream of battle.*

Jarvis called it *jacking his frame rate.*

Mind and senses hyperattuned, Jarvis scanned over the iron sights of his pistol like the weapon was an extension of his own body. Both sides of the street were lined with three- or four-story apartment buildings, each of which had a front courtyard. Most had cantilevered iron balconies on each level. As Jarvis advanced down the sidewalk, he indexed his muzzle over every nook, cranny, and corner where a shooter could be hiding in cover.

Rear car bumper, courtyard entry, gate, hedgerow, rear car bumper, trash can, gate, half wall, hedgerow . . .

To his right, Elinor did the same. But with only two of them, it was impossible to enter and clear every courtyard they passed.

As he approached the third apartment building, the machinery of his mind issued a warning. The shooter had been no more than forty feet ahead of him when Jarvis had rounded the corner, but he'd not seen the man once he'd turned. Which meant that the shooter had taken cover within the first forty feet of the turn.

Jarvis whirled and took a knee.

A gunshot rang out, followed by a second shot a heartbeat later.

At his ten o'clock, a body pitched backward and dropped behind a hedgerow. To his right, at his two o'clock, Elinor stood in a firing stance, smoke rising from the barrel of her pistol.

Jarvis advanced in combat crouch toward where the assassin had fallen, keeping his head below the top of the hedgerow. He popped up and sighted over the hedge, ready to deliver another round, but the crimson hole in the middle of the assassin's forehead obviated the need. He holstered his weapon, then turned to glare at Elinor, who was walking toward him and the fallen shooter.

"Thanks for that," he said.

"You don't look particularly grateful," she said as she reached him.

"It would have been better to take him alive."

"True, but you're the Vice President of the United States. It's also better if you're alive."

"He missed, Elinor."

"His first shot, but would he have missed the second?"

Jarvis pressed his lips into a hard line but decided to let it go. Their eyes met, and in that moment he read more about her than Harel could ever have shared. He saw a brilliant, seasoned operator—but he also saw a loyal teammate willing to risk her own life for his. He wondered if this was what had drawn Dempsey to this woman. "Thanks for having my six."

"Anytime," she said, holstering her weapon.

They stared at each other for a moment, each waiting for the other to make the next move. She broke first.

"Listen, I need to get out of here before law enforcement arrives. But before I do, I have something to say."

"I'm all ears," he said.

"I understand why John did what he did. I would have done the same thing had the situation been reversed. Anyway . . . I was angry for a long time, but not anymore. I forgive him."

"Are you saying this so that I'll understand your motives now, Elinor? Or is this for Dempsey's benefit?"

"Both," she said, glancing down the street in the direction of approaching sirens.

"I'll let him know."

He watched her cast a glance at the body beside the hedge, dark blood still trickling from the wound in his head, eyes unfocused and unseeing.

"You can trust that I will find out who is responsible for this, Mr. Vice President," she said, looking at him again.

Jarvis let out a slow breath and studied her face carefully, but her mask was back up, and they gave up nothing. Harel had trusted her once. Dempsey had as well. But a lot had happened since then—not the least of which was the discovery of her betrayal as a double agent.

"And why would I do that, Elinor? I don't even know who you work for."

"I work for *me*," she said with an ironic little smile. "My days as a blunt instrument of the corrupt state are over."

"I see. So instead of killing people to safeguard freedom, you kill people for money?"

"No. Now I kill people to make the world a better place." She let the sentiment hang for a moment. "Congratulations on your promotion."

Then she was gone. Jarvis watched her for long second, then pulled out his mobile phone to take a picture of the dead assassin. As he did, Perez and Jolly came tearing around the corner onto the street, faces red and weapons drawn.

"Damn, you're fast for an old guy," Perez said as he fell in beside Jarvis. "What the hell, boss?"

The agent was more than a little pissed, and Jarvis knew the anger Perez struggled to contain was well deserved.

"Like I said: once a SEAL, always a SEAL," Jarvis said as he snapped a series of photos of the dead shooter.

"Are you injured?"

"Do I look injured?" Jarvis said.

"That's not an answer. I've seen you look 'not injured' before, when you had a bullet wound to your chest, remember? And you do have blood spatter all over your face. Sir."

Jarvis wiped his cheek, and his finger came away clean. "It's Shamone's blood."

Perez stared at him a long moment, as if trying to decide whether he believed Jarvis or not. Finally, he said, "You know I'm going to get fired for this."

"No, you're not," Jarvis said, clapping a hand on his friend's shoulder. "Because your boss works for me."

"Technically, that's not true," Jolly said.

"Did I say you could talk, Frank?" Jarvis asked, grinning.

"No, sir," Jolly said and looked down, but the man was grinning as well.

The roar of an engine and squeal of rubber on pavement drew their collective gaze to the street corner, where they watched the up-armored Range Rover he'd been borrowing from the Israelis tear around the bend toward them.

"Please don't make us manhandle you into the vehicle, sir," Perez said. "We don't know if this is over. We need to get you secure."

"All right, all right. Exfil me the hell out of here, Tony. We'll let the Israelis deal with the body," Jarvis said, letting Perez and Jolly escort him to the idling Range Rover at the curb.

A few minutes later, once safely inside the vehicle and en route to the airport, Perez insisted on thoroughly checking him over for injuries.

"I told you, Tony, I'm fine," Jarvis said, now jacketless and twisting right and left to prove he'd not been shot. "See, no red on the dress shirt."

Perez's face suggested he was still pretty pissed off, but he finally conceded. "Okay, looks like you dodged a bullet this time, Mr. Vice President—"

"Literally," Jolly piped in from the back seat.

"I know, and I'm sorry, guys. I promise it won't happen again," he said, mustering an earnest expression. But he wasn't sorry, and he *would* probably do it again, because damn, he hadn't felt this pumped up and alive in a very, very long time. "Is the PM okay? I assume they got him out safely?"

"Prime Minister Shamone is safe and secure at an undisclosed location. I also received a text message from one of my counterparts on his detail saying that the PM credits you with saving his life. Apparently the Prime Minister said, and I quote, 'I owe that man my life. I am in his debt,'" Tony said. He raised his eyebrows. "Looks like you've got one helluva favor chit you can cash in whenever you want, sir."

That thought had not occurred to Jarvis because, frankly, SEALs didn't tend to think transactionally when it came to saving lives. But, he realized, politicians certainly did. Tony was right. By saving Shamone's life and running down the man who'd tried to assassinate him, Jarvis had accomplished something that no amount of diplomatic negotiation or horse-trading ever could. The Prime Minister of Israel owed Jarvis his life and would forever be personally indebted to him.

Jarvis nodded and tucked that little gem away for later.

Because if there was one thing Jarvis knew with absolute certainty, it was that someday he would need to call that debt.

CHAPTER 8

RUTH RIMONIM HOTEL SAFED

SAFED, ISRAEL

1540 LOCAL TIME

Liu Shazi sat on the floor at the foot of the queen-sized bed, legs crossed and hands resting on his knees, eyes closed. Slowly, he let the breath flow from his lungs, not pressing it out but letting it find its way as he focused his mind on the middle of a blue sea. In preparation for combat, the Qigong breathing exercise would be radically different and would involve complex but slowly orchestrated movements designed to center and strengthen his Qi, or vital energy, for battle. Such exercise had, he believed in his heart, been central to his surviving situations many of his brother Snow Leopards had not.

But now, he used his mind to push away the disappointment of the failure his puppet terrorist had suffered in Tel Aviv. To do this, he concentrated his breathing in his lower abdomen, belly breathing like a child—a technique the masters of the Qigong called "Original Breath." He felt his muscles slowly unknot, his shoulders sag, his mind clear . . .

I must let go of what I think I know . . .

He felt his pulse slow, falling well below fifty beats per minute.

With it, his mind relaxed in rhythm with his body, opening to all his situation had to teach him.

His mind cleared.

Even when his satellite phone chimed, his pulse stayed slow and steady. Liu rose in one fluid motion from his position on the floor, reaching out with slow, gentle hands for the phone, eyes still closed, but finding his target easily thanks to his new awareness of the room.

"Yes?" Liu asked, phone to his ear, as he slowly opened his eyes.

"It is done?" the familiar voice asked.

"Delhi was a success. Tel Aviv was not," Liu said. He lowered himself back to the floor, resuming his cross-legged sitting position and again closing his eyes.

"You sound disappointed," the voice, raspy from decades of cigarettes, said. "The mission is a success. Delhi was the primary mission objective. The world order is shaken. A partnership being forged is undone. Now assure me that you have not been observed in the company of these jihadists."

"I have been careful," Liu said simply.

"And DNA records from those who participated in the attacks have been uploaded to al Ghadab members in the databases?" the voice asked.

"Of course," Liu confirmed.

"Then everything is as it should be, Liu Shazi," the old man reassured him. "It is time for you to come home."

"Yes, sir," Liu said. The old man was right—the endgame was unchanged by the failure in Tel Aviv.

And yet it was a failure nonetheless . . .

The line went dead, and Liu dropped the phone to the ground, once again focusing his mind on an imaginary lake reflecting the cloudless sky and concentrating on each breath, feeling a calm come over him.

But this time the calm did not completely overtake him, and this was his biggest failure. A lifetime of study in the art of Northern Praying Mantis kung fu, a career in Special Operations at the highest levels, years of study to master the art of Qigong—and still his hubris got the best of him.

"In fear and trembling, the superior man sets his life in order and examines himself."

Until I learn to let go of failure, I can never find peace.

Until I let go of that which I think I know, I can never reach enlightenment.

His breathing finally slowed and his muscles relaxed. He felt control coming to him but then slip away as the image in his mind—the glassy lake reflecting a cloudless sky—quietly morphed into a face.

He stared, in his mind's eye, into the gray eyes of the man who had bested him. He saw, as clearly as if the man had entered his room, the chiseled face of former Navy SEAL Kelso Jarvis. This man was now elevated to the presidency.

That had *not* been Shazi's plan.

Shazi sighed and stood to pack his bag for the next leg of his journey. Despite the hierarchy's satisfaction with the success of his nation's most audacious false flag operation in history, he knew that peace would allude him until he could find a way to complete the mission. His superiors might consider the mission a success, but loose threads meant that the real endgame was still in jeopardy. One more thing must now be done.

As he slipped his sparse belongings and his QSZ-92 pistol into its case, Liu Shazi allowed his mind to indulge a fantasy, a fantasy in which he conducted another operation to finish the mission. There was no peace in his obsession, but he knew himself well enough to find his own path to fulfillment.

He zipped the case shut.

Knowing myself well enough to find my own way to peace. That is perhaps the final, unwritten level of Qigong . . .

CHAPTER 9

"Are you doing okay, sir?" Secret Service Agent Tony Perez asked from the seat opposite Jarvis in the rear of the up-armored Range Rover.

Jarvis looked up, aware he had been ruminating for the last few minutes.

Four minutes and twenty-seven seconds, in fact.

He marveled at how the brief and totally unexpected flashback to the man he had once been—the Navy SEAL Tier One CSO—had sharpened his mind. He felt *alive.* He looked at his left hand, amazed that it appeared rock steady, not even a trace of the usual background tremor he'd learned to accept as his new normal. He saw the blood staining the cuff of his white shirt beneath his suit coat, and as he turned his hand over to inspect how far the bloodstain wrapped around his wrist, he saw no shaking with the movement. He felt strong.

This side effect of his sudden immersion into combat, he decided, was something he needed to talk to some neurological experts about.

"Rock solid, Tony," he replied, setting his jaw.

"Just a few more minutes, Mr. Vice President," Perez said.

"No hurry," Jarvis said and turned to look out the darkly tinted window. There was little to see inside the massive military hangar other than Air Force Two, which was being readied for the flight back to CONUS. The pilots would be completing a flight plan and preflight, and the Secret Service would be readying everything else. The aircraft itself, a C-32A, the military variation of the Boeing 757 airliner, belonged to the 89th Military Airlift Wing. It wasn't as big or plush as Air Force One, but Jarvis didn't care about things like that. Hands clasped behind his back, he watched a small team of black-clad IDF operators patrolling the tarmac outside. An AT variant of the IDF's RAM Mk3 light armored vehicle was positioned in the wide doorway, armed and ready for action.

Jarvis imagined the sour face and scolding lecture he would receive from his boss and friend Rand Warner when he got home for "the stunt he'd just pulled in Tel Aviv." He knew the feeling of youth and strength after the chase would be fleeting, but he still felt energized. Powerful. Like the operator he'd been.

He liked feeling this way.

The smile on his face faded as his thoughts turned back to the reason for his visit to Israel in the first place. A collage of memories of his friendship with Harel flooded his mind. Their professional relationship had spanned decades. The Israeli spymaster had been more than just a friend; he'd been a mentor and lodestar in Jarvis's life—especially the past several years, as Jarvis had been forced to evolve from leading a task force to leading the entire intelligence community.

He shook the thoughts and emotions away and looked at his watch. "Is everyone else aboard?" Jarvis asked.

"Everyone but Mr. Crouch, sir," Tony said, referring to Andrew Crouch, the former intelligence operator who had served in the Texas state legislature before moving to DC to serve in Warner's administration. After the wedding, Jarvis had asked the President's permission to invite Crouch to serve as his chief of staff. Apparently, it was not appropriate for your wife to serve in that job, or so he'd been told. "But he's pulling up now."

Jarvis looked over to see another Range Rover pull up to the steps of the C-32A. Jarvis watched as Crouch hustled out and nearly sprinted up the airstair, an aide in tow with two roller bag suitcases.

Why was the man in such a hurry?

"Understood," Tony said in response to something in his earpiece.

"Are we good?" Jarvis asked.

Tony flashed him a strange look. "They want another minute, sir," the agent said. "I have no idea why or what's going on, but it's strange as hell, right?"

"Indeed," Jarvis said, staring up at the open door to the Boeing.

At the top of the stairs, a flight suit–clad pilot was saying something to the aide with the suitcases. The young man let go of the bag and put his hand over his mouth, and the pilot reached out quickly to grab the black roller before it could tumble down the airstair.

"Come on, Tony," Jarvis said. "Let's go find out what's going on."

Tony nodded, then exited the vehicle and jogged around to open Jarvis's door, but Jarvis was already out by the time he got there. He glanced up the airstair and met the pilot's eyes, but the man looked away and ducked back inside, pulling the roller bag behind him. The younger aide entered next, almost shuffling. Jarvis scanned the empty hangar. The mighty 757 looked suddenly small and forlorn in the wide space. The doors of the chief of staff's Range Rover gaped open, ignored in the hurry to get into the plane. Jarvis felt for a moment as if they, too, signaled open-mouthed surprise and concern.

For a moment, he and Tony were alone in the massive room.

"Stagecoach is coming up," Tony said, his voice picked up by the microphone in his earpiece as the agent moved in tight beside him. Two additional agents scrambled down the airstair, armed with machine pistols, and spread out in the hangar, heads on a swivel.

"What the hell is going on, Tony?" Jarvis asked.

"I swear I don't know, Mr. Vice President," the agent answered.

Jarvis felt a hypervigilance overtake him—SEAL instincts moving into the driver's seat. He watched Tony make eye contact with the other agent at the foot of the airstair. The other man gave him a grim look and just shook his head. The tow vehicle entered the hangar, and two men hooked the Boeing's nose gear to the tow bar. A Secret Service sniper took a knee and stared over his long gun out onto the airfield. The lights on the wing tips of the jet began to flash.

Jarvis bounded up the airstair.

"What the hell is going on, Andy?" he asked as he entered the forward of four compartments of the vice-presidential jet. "Can someone . . ."

He stopped.

Andy Crouch's face was pale, and his eyes were wet, a rare sight for an experienced, blooded, former counterintelligence officer. He held a phone to his ear. A uniformed Air Force senior master sergeant sitting at the main comms console wept openly, her face in her hands.

Behind Jarvis the door was already closed and sealed. Even as the jet was being towed, he heard the pilot spinning up the engine.

"What happened?" Jarvis asked again, but he knew already. "What happened to President Warner?"

"He's . . ." Crouch swallowed hard. "He's dead, sir. There . . . there was an attack. A suicide bomber at the meeting with Prime Minister Chopra. They're all dead. Warner, Chopra, Secretary Franks . . ."

Decades of split-second, life-and-death decisions—dozens of lost teammates and memorials, personal and professional tragedy, even the shock of 9/11—none of it prepared Jarvis for this. He blinked. He told himself he needed to remember to breathe. Not only was his President dead, Warner had also been his friend. Two friends now dead in as many days. The tears that rimmed his eyes were so unfamiliar he didn't even think to wipe them away. Jarvis watched as his handpicked chief of staff looked at his own feet, then rubbed his temples. He remembered that Crouch and Secretary of Defense Franks had served together a long time ago.

So much loss. So much death, again. A lifetime of death and loss.

Then the Navy SEAL, always near the surface, took over. Jarvis began to regulate his breathing, and the tears began to evaporate off his cheeks.

"When?" he demanded.

"It just happened," Crouch said, the tremor in his voice disappearing and his tone turning hard. "There was a suicide bomber who somehow infiltrated the press corps for the event, is what they think. That's from one of our Secret Service agents who was in the hall and survived the blast. There are dozens dead from the American press corps as well. Reggie Buckingham has all hands on deck in New Delhi, of course, and is mobilizing other assets . . ."

"Who?" Jarvis demanded, his voice now cold steel.

"Sir, this literally just happened—almost simultaneously with the attack on the Israeli PM."

"Oh, God," Jarvis said, his voice cracking, the sound as unfamiliar as the tears in his eyes.

What if Shamone hadn't been the target at all? What if someone was trying to take out Warner and me at the same time?

"Passengers of Air Force Two," came the grim voice of the pilot overhead. Clearly, he'd been briefed as well. "Please take your seats and buckle up."

Jarvis dropped into one of the front rows of the ten seats, his mind still reeling as the jet accelerated on the taxiway. Impossibly, the jet was already accelerating on its takeoff roll as Andrew Crouch took the seat beside him and the rest of the security detail and cabin crew strapped in as well.

"Mr. . . ." Crouch seemed to hesitate. "Mr. Vice President. We'll do the ceremony as soon as we are at a safe altitude. The Chief Justice is standing by for a virtual swearing in. There's no civilian press, but the event will be video recorded on both ends, and we have an Air Force photographer aboard, so . . ."

Jarvis turned and held Andy's eyes, the gravity of the situation not lost on either of them. He was about to be sworn in as the President of the United States of America, and America . . . was again at war.

"Do not live stream the swearing," Jarvis said.

Andy looked surprised for a moment but knew to choose his battles. "Understood, sir," he said.

"Once the ceremony is over, I'll need to speak with Petra on a secure line," Jarvis said, his mind furiously prioritizing a myriad of short-fuse tasks. Petra would be his eyes and ears in the White House, but he also needed to get the intelligence community moving on what had happened. And he would need an ally with political savvy as well. "I'll need complete privacy for that call. Then I'll want Reggie Buckingham on a private and secure video chat next, and I'll want to speak to Senator Whalen immediately after."

"Yes, sir," Crouch said, Jarvis's commanding calm refocusing the former spook. "You'll speak to your wife in the stateroom, sir?"

"No," Jarvis said and glanced out the oval window as they climbed. An Israeli F-35 was already tucked in tight on their port wing, and he imagined another would be on the starboard side. Soon, they would be joined by American fighters from the carrier strike group not far away. "All the calls will be from the SCIF."

"Of course, sir," Crouch said. Despite the fact they were still in a steep climb, his chief of staff unbuckled and rose from his seat to get things moving.

Jarvis understood why he offered the stateroom, but his call to Petra—Petra *Jarvis*, now—was anything but a husband-wife call. She was his most trusted adviser, and her mind digested and processed raw intelligence like no one he'd ever met. He would need that mind. And he was about to ask much, much more of her in the coming months, he realized. Her First Lady duties were going to be historical and unprecedented.

And will include something no one will ever, ever know about. No one except me, Mike Casey, and the team at Ember . . .

He would need Margaret Whalen too. He intended to appoint her as Vice President. She would serve beside him for the remaining few months of Warner's—now *his*—term, and he would support her run for the presidency from the Oval Office.

And Reggie—well, Reggie was about to work harder than ever in his life. Thank God the man was both tireless and prescient.

He became suddenly aware of Levi Harel's letter in his jacket pocket, as if Levi himself were calling to him from the grave.

Now is the time for what I have to say, Kelso . . .

He opened the envelope and retrieved the folded, handwritten note inside. He took a deep breath and began to read, and as he did, the chaos aboard Air Force Two began to fade into the background.

Dear Kelso,

When I was a young man, my father told me a parable that changed my life. I share this with you now not because you need teaching, but because sometimes we all need reminding . . .

There once was a wise king who ordered a boulder placed in the middle of the main road leading into and out of his kingdom. The main road was carved into the side of a very steep hill, so this boulder dramatically impacted travel. The king's decision perplexed all, especially his chief adviser, who was forced to listen to the daily complaints from merchants, tradesmen, and most especially the wealthy nobles accustomed to traveling by carriage in and out of the kingdom.

"Why have you done this, sire?" the adviser asked. "It has created hardship and inconvenience where none existed before."

The king nodded and smiled, but he did not explain himself, and so nothing was done.

Days became weeks and weeks became months, but the boulder remained.

Then, one day, a simple vegetable farmer from a neighboring kingdom came upon the boulder while pulling his cart. Unable to maneuver his cart around it, he set about to move it. The boulder was quite heavy, and so he asked other passing merchants for assistance, but they only stood with arms crossed and watched him strain. Finally, using all his might, he rolled the boulder out of the road and down the hill. Underneath where the boulder had been was a shallow hole. Inside the hole sat a bag full of gold coins and a handwritten note from the king:

"Thank you for having the courage and initiative to solve a problem that everyone else was too lazy,

FEARFUL, AND COMPLIANT TO TACKLE. IF IT PLEASES YOU, THE JOB OF HEAD ADVISER AWAITS YOU IN MY COURT."

My DEAR FRIEND, I FEAR A BOULDER LIES AHEAD IN AMERICA'S PATH, AND THE CHOICE TO IGNORE IT OR MOVE IT RESIDES WITH YOU AND YOU ALONE. MAYBE I'm WRONG, AND I HOPE I AM, BUT EITHER WAY KNOW THIS: I BELIEVE IN YOU, AND I LOVE YOU LIKE THE SON I NEVER HAD.

FAITHFULLY AND FOREVER,
LEVI

He stared at the paper for a long moment, then, feeling his chief of staff's eyes on him, he folded it and returned it to his pocket.

"The Chief Justice is ready for you, Mr., umm . . ." Crouch stammered.

"Mr. Vice President," Jarvis said, unbuckling and rising from his seat. "Leave me the comfort of that for the few minutes I have left."

He followed Crouch aft, a hand on the bulkhead to steady himself against the continued steep climb, which had now become a left bank as they turned west. Jarvis passed through the stateroom and then into the conference room further aft, where a handful of people were already gathered, their hands clasped in front of them and faces somber. Chief Justice Benson filled the large screen on the forward wall, his face equally emotional. An Air Force officer whom he didn't know—a lieutenant colonel from her epaulets and a command pilot based on the wings her chest—stood beside the screen, a black leather Bible in her hand. Jarvis gave the woman a nod, noting the tears rimming her eyes.

Jarvis's mind filled with images from his youth—not memories, as he'd been just a baby at the time, but photos that had stirred him during his studies of history: the black-and-white picture of Vice President Lyndon Johnson, one hand on a Bible and his other in the air. The face of the beloved President, eyes blank and unseeing, a sheet pulled up to his shoulders and a chunk of his head missing . . .

Jarvis blinked.

He was no Lyndon Johnson, and Warner had not been killed by a crazed, lone gunman. He was a warrior, not a politician, and Levi was right: for the coming months, that's exactly what America would need.

"Are you ready, Mr. Jarvis?" Chief Justice Benson asked.

"I am," Jarvis said and stepped forward. He nodded to the weeping officer holding the Bible, who gave a grateful nod and sad smile back.

"Sir, please place your left hand on the Bible and raise your right hand," she said.

Jarvis did, clenching his jaw. Yet again, the universe had driven him to a position he never wanted, but one he would execute to the very best of his ability. He supposed Petra was right—that was just who he was.

And it's only for a few months . . .

"Repeat after me . . ."

He listened carefully to the Chief Justice's deep baritone voice. The somber room fell otherwise silent except for the whine of the Pratt & Whitney PW2000 engines. Jarvis pushed from his mind all of the things he would need to do in these months to honor Warner—a man who had given his life for his country.

And to punish those who would dare do such a thing . . .

With his right hand raised and his left on the Bible, his eyes on the flag beside the monitor, Jarvis repeated the oath. As he did, his mind filled with all the times before now when he had, both formally and informally, sworn his allegiance to all that he loved.

His oath at his commissioning as a Naval Officer.

His oath to the office of DNI, then Vice President.

His promise and oath to the Teams, to Warner when he commissioned Task Force Ember, and his unspoken oath to his teammates who still served there.

His recent vows and promise to Petra.

His entire life had been an oath of sorts, a vow to serve that which he believed in defending, with his life, if necessary.

Once again, he would vow to protect and serve all that he loved.

"I, Kelso Jarvis, do solemnly swear that I will faithfully execute the office of President of the United States, and will, to the best of my ability, preserve, protect, and defend the Constitution of the United States . . ."

PART II

The superior man controls his anger and restrains his instincts.

—*I Ching, The Book of Changes*

CHAPTER 10

THE VICE PRESIDENT'S STUDY

US NAVAL OBSERVATORY

WASHINGTON, DC

1144 LOCAL TIME

Petra Jarvis tried to tear her eyes away from the TV, which was on the wall across from where she sat at her husband's impeccably neat and organized desk, but she simply couldn't. The enormous screen was split into four sections streaming the breaking news from CNN, Fox News, BBC, and Al Jazeera—Kelso's favorite mix of viewpoints—but all the feeds were muted as a montage of images filled each newscast between appearances of the talking heads. The front of the palace in Delhi, smoke still rising from open windows and doors and emergency vehicles crowded bumper to bumper in the street; a rear view from what must have been a helicopter, showing an enormous chunk of wall missing and flames still dancing inside; images of the US Navy carrier strike group in the Indian Ocean; video of the White House and the enormous and overt security presence there; the Capitol, the UN building in New York, and even Britain's House of Parliament as the world reacted to the news.

And of course she saw, again and again, pictures from the attack in Tel Aviv, and shaky footage showing what she knew could only be her husband sprinting toward a tree in a low tactical crouch with a pistol in his hand.

Every few moments, the screens would fill with pictures of Randall Warner, the now deceased President of the United States. Then a picture filled the BBC feed of Warner at a state dinner, leaning toward his wife, Amy, sharing some intimate exchange that made them both smile.

They looked happy. She knew how excited Amy had been for his term to end and, in her words, for their lives to begin.

Petra wiped a tear from her cheek, frustrated at the emotion when she should be focused on the most important aspects of this horror show. Her husband was being sworn in as President, she was his trusted adviser, and their nation had been attacked in a way not seen since 9/11. The thought brought a surge of rage through Petra, and for a moment she was again in the mountains of Afghanistan, sitting at a computer in some shitty plywood TOC, doing her best to provide intelligence to help the JSOC SEALs complete their mission and come home to their families.

Almost twenty years had passed since then.

God, it just never ends. Here we are at the beginning, all over again . . .

She waited for a live stream of her husband being sworn in as the next President of the United States but wasn't surprised when it didn't come. Kelso would be unlikely to have the event streamed live. He would prefer to address the nation more intimately when the time was right.

I wish I was there with you, my love.

The biggest surprise in her romance with Kelso had been his easy willingness to admit that he needed her. So many with his background would find that impossible. But then, Kelso operated differently than most people, even the incredible men and women from the JSOC community.

She clicked off the TV, regaining momentary control of the chaotic world she now inhabited. She should be with Amy Warner right now, doing whatever she could to let her friend know she was with her in her unimaginable grief. Well, perhaps not *completely* unimaginable—many times these last two years Petra had imagined losing the man she now so desperately loved. At the thought, her mind filled with Kelso's grimacing face, his white shirt stained crimson after taking a bullet in Turkey. The thought made her reach unconsciously for the scar from her own bullet wound . . .

She glanced at the door. She'd been instructed to be ready for a call from Jarvis any minute and needed to be present for that. Next, she really needed to find her way to Amy. She looked at the remote in her hand, glanced at the large dark screen on the wall, then tossed the remote on the desk like it might bite her. Petra leaned back in the simple black chair.

She'd been a little girl when President Reagan had been shot, but it was one of her most vivid childhood memories. She and her mom had sat in front of their TV as information dribbled in and newscasters speculated. Eventually, her dad had come home early, and they'd all sat there together. She'd watched her mother cry, her dad stoically holding her, and listened to the endless and often conflicting streams of information overlapping with guesses and opinions. Petra sighed. She was now inside of the political machine she'd watched on the TV that fateful day in 1981, which meant she didn't need the gaps filled in by CNN, Fox, BBC, or Al Jazeera. Up-to-date information was a phone call away.

And soon she'd have the most reliable information from the one person she trusted the most.

The door to the study cracked open as if cued by the thought, and her Secret Service detail lead stuck her head in.

"The call will be in the SCIF in a moment, ma'am," Agent Sahran Abib said.

"Thank you," Petra said, a little surprised. "Where is Jackie?" she asked, referring to her own chief of staff, the woman she trusted to run the office of the Second Lady.

Agent Abib hesitated.

"I'm not sure, ma'am," she said. "But Agent Perez made it sound like this call is more . . ." she chewed the inside of her cheek for a second, " . . . off the record."

"I see," she said.

Of course it is. Kelso will have more for me than simply a husband checking in with his wife in a moment of national and personal crisis.

And she suspected she knew what that *more* might be.

When the door closed, Petra walked to the study's corner and placed her left hand on the black glass of a security panel. The magnetic locks of the out-of-place metal door clicked open, and she heard a hiss of pressure as the self-contained room with its own air supply equalized to the office. She pulled open the heavy door to the small personal SCIF that Warner had installed for Jarvis when he took over the vice presidency. They both knew why he needed it after moving over from the ODNI, but she imagined it was never discussed.

Because not discussing it was the point, right?

Whoever took over this office next would likely not need such a room.

She entered and closed the door behind her, hearing the magnetic locks click into place, and took a seat in the comfortable chair facing two computer screens and a bank of other monitors. Just as she did, the small white phone built into the panel chirped softly and she picked it up.

"Yes?" she said.

She could hear nothing besides a slow exhale of breath, but she knew immediately it was him. Her heart filled simultaneously with joy and dread. This was not what Kelso had wanted, she knew, but she believed—especially under the circumstances—it might well be exactly what the nation needed. This was a crisis of incalculable proportions, and she knew of no one else in the world better suited to handle it.

"I love you," Kelso said through the receiver. She closed her eyes. His voice was all business, but she still needed to hear it.

"You too," she said, aware her husband would likely have no similar need in this moment. "How are you?"

They both knew what she meant.

"Angry," he said.

"I understand," she replied, and she did. Kelso was in mission mode. The loss of his friend, the strain of what lay ahead, the implications for the country—these were compartmentalized on the top shelf of his mind for now. "What can I do?"

"How are you?" he asked, and she smiled at the gesture. She imagined this was the last thing on his mind.

"Angry," she said—an agreement, not a mimic. "And ready to help however I can. I know this forces you into a position you never wanted—a position you already turned down."

"It seems the universe had other plans . . ."

"And you'll answer the call. Like you always do." She closed her eyes and pictured the face he would be making.

"No choice this time," he said, and she could practically see his sarcastic smile.

"Is there ever, my love?" she said. "You're headed to Andrews?"

"Yes," he said. "But we're making a stop. We're bringing Rand home with us. I insisted."

"I'm glad," she said, and her voice cracked. "He should come home with you."

Petra suddenly felt the weight of this moment. The President of the United States had just been assassinated on foreign soil. By definition they were at war, and as usual Kelso was at the pointy tip of the spear. Maybe not in the way he would want, but in the way his nation needed. Tears spilled onto her cheeks at the realization of all that lay ahead, for her husband but also for the nation she loved and for those close to her still standing watch over her. She felt overwhelmed and exhausted.

"I will need you more than ever, Petra," Jarvis said, and she heard something in his voice she'd never heard. Uncertainty? That seemed unlikely from the man she knew and loved, but it was something like that.

"I'm here," she said. "I'll support you however I can. I will have your back, and I will be your sounding board."

"I may need more than that," he said, his voice now regaining the cold confidence she was more familiar with.

"Anything," she said, and she meant it.

"Call Mike Casey for me, Petra," he said. "Let him know we need Ember standing by, and make sure he has access to all streams of intel."

There it is. The ask.

"It will be the next call I make."

"I'll see you soon," he said.

"I'll be waiting."

"I love you."

"I love you too."

She placed the secure, encrypted phone in its receiver. Then, suddenly unable to rise from her seat under the new weight she now shared with her husband, she laid her head on her hands on the desk and wept.

She wept for her friend Amy and the loss of President Warner.

She wept for Kelso and the burden he would now carry.

And she wept for the country she loved, and for those keeping watch—who would once again be in harm's way for them all.

CHAPTER 11

Dempsey woke bolt upright in the dark, pistol in hand, disoriented. He clicked on the pistol's light and scanned for threats. As the white beam illuminated the familiar geometry and spartan furnishing of his apartment bedroom, he relaxed. Finding no black-clad intruders, he collapsed back into his pillow.

"I'm home. I'm safe; I'm with my team. Everything is okay," he mumbled.

But why didn't it feel that way?

He clicked the pistol light off, slid the weapon back under his pillow, and stared up into the pitch-black nothing. When he was in the Teams he didn't remember having so many nightmares, but ever since joining Ember bad dreams might as well have been in the job description.

Tonight's dream was a rerun of his subconscious mind's newest fixation. It always started the same, with him going to kill Arkady Zhukov at the Russian spymaster's dacha on the lake. In some versions of the dream, he'd bring a gun but somehow manage to lose it. In others, the magazine would be empty or the trigger wouldn't work. In tonight's version, he forgot to bring a weapon altogether—rendering himself completely exposed and vulnerable.

The dream often had different endings than what happened in real life. Sometimes, Arkady would shoot Dempsey before Grimes's sniper bullet came screaming through the window and split the spymaster's head open in a burst of gore. And in the most twisted permutation, instead of targeting Zhukov, she exploded Dempsey's head instead.

He shuddered at the macabre thought.

Every once in a while, nobody died in the dream. On those nights, he simply had a nice cup of coffee and long talk with the Russian mastermind about life and growing old and about Dempsey's own son, Jake. He liked those nights. In fact, he craved them. It turned out Arkady was very insightful. The old Russian always gave sage advice and understood the hearts and minds of men like Dempsey—men who carried the burdens that others couldn't or wouldn't. In Arkady's case, the man believed he was shouldering the burden of his entire nation, that he and he alone understood how to save Russia from itself. He'd orchestrated regime change and used Dempsey as his blunt instrument.

In tonight's permutation, Arkady had died from Lizzie Grimes's bullet, but the gunshot had robbed Dempsey of hearing what the spymaster had to say about strength in times of adversity. Strength was the yardstick by which all Russians measured themselves. *Strength of body, strength of mind, strength of will*—these were three pillars of survival in a world that tries to break everyone. They were how Dempsey survived six months in Russia's notorious IK-2 prison. They were how he survived now in the aftermath.

"*Zhizn eto sila. Sila eto zhizn,*" he whispered, the Russian coming easily to him, despite having not conversed in months.

Life is strength. Strength is life.

During his first couple of weeks back with Ember, he had slipped up constantly. He'd be in the middle of a sentence, talking in English, and slip into Russian without even realizing it. The polite, worried look on his teammates' faces was always his first clue it had happened again. God, he hated that look—a look reserved for people who were damaged or mentally compromised in some way. Dempsey wasn't damaged or deranged. It just so happened that some ideas were better expressed in Russian. Sometimes, they had better words for certain situations and sentiments.

He missed speaking Russian.

Maybe I should invite Buz over for a beer so we can jawbone in Russian, he thought. He wondered why he hadn't thought of it before.

Russia *had* changed him. He wasn't afraid to admit that anymore. He'd even admitted as much to the brain docs that Casey had made him see. There used to be a time when he was afraid of headshrinkers— afraid that if he opened up and told them the truth he'd be benched and not cleared for duty until they signed off on his mental fitness. Thinking about that now made him laugh.

After Russia, he didn't give a shit what anybody thought about him. Does a wolverine care what a rabbit thinks? No. So why should he? As the expression goes, he'd blasted Doc Abernathy with both barrels. Whatever she asked, he answered. Unfiltered, unabashed. After IK-2, there was nothing anyone could do to humiliate him, intimidate him, or break him down. He had accepted his role in the universe. He was an instrument of retribution, righting the wrongs of the world and bringing things that had tipped askew back into balance. The losses were a necessary cost of this work, work that had to be done in a universe where so few had the tools to do it. Sometimes those losses were friends and teammates, and perhaps sometimes they were pieces of himself. These were things he couldn't explain to someone who'd never paid the price of service and couldn't understand that he'd never had a choice about his true calling in this insane world.

The universe had decided his fate, maybe even before he'd been born.

His mobile phone vibrated on his nightstand.

For some reason, he almost expected the interruption. He grabbed the phone and answered the call.

"Dempsey . . ."

"There's been a major event; we need everyone to come in," Buz said, the Ops O's voice all business.

In his younger years, as Jack Kemper, Dempsey would have pressed for details, his innate curiosity getting the better of him, but not anymore. He hadn't had any bad news for a while now, so he was due; and these days, he'd wait to take his bitter medicine until somebody made him . . .

He kept the radio off during the drive to the secret compound on MacDill that Ember shared with the Tier One JSOC element. Despite working *literally* right next door to his friend and fellow operator LCDR Keith "Chunk" Redman, Dempsey hadn't seen the burly SEAL since he'd gotten back from Russia. This was something he intended to remedy as soon as Gold Squadron got back from wherever they were deployed. He wanted to catch up with Chunk as a friend, but also to find out how Jake was doing in SQT.

He missed his son, and Chunk was Dempsey's lifeline to the boy.

After clearing security and parking in the gravel lot, Dempsey entered the unassuming building that was Ember's headquarters. From the outside, the facility looked like little more than a construction trailer, but the elevator down was a real-life metaphor for Alice's trip down the bunny hole. Hidden below was a secure underground TOC that rivaled the White House Situation Room. He walked through the Ember ops center to the briefing theater—a conference room with a surfboard-shaped, polished wood table surrounded by a dozen chairs— where Director Casey and Buz were waiting. Dempsey wasn't the first of his teammates to arrive, but he wasn't last either.

"John," Director Casey said, greeting him with a grim nod.

"Mike," Dempsey replied.

He took a seat in an open leather office chair at the table. Assembled so far were Baldwin, Chip and Dale, Amanda Allen, Martin, and Wallace. Nobody was talking, and the mood was as tense and nervous as he'd ever seen. He wondered if he was the only one who didn't know what had happened. Munn and Grimes arrived two minutes later—together, Dempsey noted—followed by Wang, Prescott, and Fender, in that order.

Once everyone was seated, Director Casey broke the news.

"At 1458 New Delhi time, a suicide bomber attack took the lives of thirty-seven people, among them President Warner, Secretary of Defense Franks, Indian Prime Minister Vihaan Chopra, several Secret Service agents, staffers, as well as journalists . . ."

Dempsey felt a weight press in on the group as someone gasped, then a silence settled over the room. Casey gave them a moment to absorb the news. Dempsey felt a gaze on him and locked eyes with Grimes, whose face was pale but whose eyes flashed with anger.

He wondered, suddenly, if there was a room far away, just like this one, where a group of people shared the news of another President's death. Had someone like him mourned the death of Petrov, just as he felt his breath taken away by the news of President Warner?

Dempsey shook his head to chase the thought away. It wasn't something that would be useful in this moment.

"Here's what we know . . ." Casey continued.

As Casey spoke, he scrolled through imagery on the room's primary briefing flat-screen, showing the gory devastation of the attack, and Dempsey found himself wondering which of the clumps of recognizable body parts might belong to the American President.

The bizarre thought sickened him.

Dempsey looked down at his lap, and his mind's eye flashed to memories of another suicide attack, an attack that had changed the course of his life forever by robbing him of his SEAL brothers—including Grimes's real-life brother—during Operation Crusader. That other massacre felt like it had happened both yesterday and a lifetime ago. He tried to blink the memory away, but the images lingered stubbornly in the theater of his mind, and the only way he could purge them was to look back up at the carnage on the screen. Warner had never been a teammate, but as POTUS he was an intimate part of the team nonetheless, right? It was Warner who'd authorized Ember's charter, who had put them to work, and who had given them purpose.

So much loss . . .

"Have we positively confirmed that the President is among the dead?" Grimes asked, which was a very Grimes thing to do.

"Yes," Casey said.

"That means that Jarvis . . ." she said, her voice trailing off.

"Is now the President of the United States," Dempsey heard himself say, finishing her sentence, the words strange in his mouth.

Casey nodded. "That's right; he was sworn in aboard Air Force Two—now Air Force One—moments ago. He's in the air and en route to Joint Base Andrews."

"Holy shit," Munn said through a breath. "Does the country know yet?"

"The news just broke," Allen said, looking up from her phone.

The shell-shocked silence that hung over the table as Ember's operators processed the news thickened. After the shock, Dempsey's next most immediate gut reaction was ire—ire directed at Arkady Zhukov. But Zhukov was dead, and Zeta was defunct. Ember's archnemesis for the past three years was no more. Which meant the architect of this attack had to be somebody else.

Somebody new . . .

"Who did it?" Munn asked, his brain having drilled to the next most important question a split second before Dempsey's.

"We're not sure, but Baldwin and his team are working the problem," Casey said. He turned to Buz with a nod, handing the Ember Ops O the reins to lead the rest of the brief.

"There's an ISIS offshoot called al Ghadab Allah—'God's Wrath'—who claimed responsibility immediately after the attacks," Buz said.

"Wait, did you say *attacks*—as in plural?" Munn said.

"That's correct; there was a failed assassination attempt on Prime Minister Shamone of Israel that happened simultaneously in Tel Aviv." Buz paused to use the laptop computer, and a new video filled the screen. "This footage was provided by our Israeli partners. It has not gone public—yet."

Recorded from a distance, the crystal clear video zoomed in on a small intimate gathering inside a cemetery surrounded by a stone wall. A dozen mourners, dressed in dark clothes stood by an open grave . . .

This must be Levi Harel's funeral, Dempsey realized. He knew the Jewish spymaster had been on his deathbed with terminal cancer for some time, but he'd not been told of the old man's passing. A tightness gripped his chest as thoughts of Harel stirred up memories of another Israeli partner—memories best left undisturbed. He chased away the ghost of the female double agent who had burrowed her way into his heart, then blinked the video back into focus.

Three distinct groups stood around the grave. Dempsey quickly identified two of the clusters as close protection details. The third group was the remainder of the mourners. Dempsey's view of Jarvis was blocked by a Secret Service agent, but he could make out the side of PM Shamone's head. A muzzle flash from a large tree along the wall sent everyone into action, and the protection details reacted. But they didn't react as fast as Jarvis, who pulled Shamone to the ground. The small crowd scattered in all directions as agents collapsed to cover the two world leaders.

At the same time, a blond woman separated from the group and took a knee behind a headstone. Dempsey watched her scan in the direction of the shooter, pull a pistol, and take off in pursuit. A split second later, Jarvis launched himself like a missile, separating from his protection detail to follow the woman. Even though Dempsey was only seeing the back of his head, Jarvis's operator movements and gait were unmistakable. But there was also something eerily familiar about how the blond woman moved as well.

"Wait—is that Jarvis?" Munn blurted, catching up with what Dempsey already knew.

"Indeed," Buz said as the blond woman, followed by Jarvis, climbed over the wall and disappeared off-screen to pursuit the shooter.

Martin let out a whistle. "Dude . . ."

"Is there more footage?" Grimes asked, her face all business. "What happened next?"

"As everyone in the room might expect, Jarvis pursued the assailant. By the time his detail caught up with him, he had eliminated the shooter. The assassin—thanks to our new President—has been identified and his body is in Israeli custody."

"Who was the blond woman who pursued the shooter before Jarvis?" Grimes asked.

Elinor Jordan, answered the voice in Dempsey's head. But that was impossible—he'd left Elinor bleeding to death on the floor of a hookah bar in Tehran.

"Probably a Mossad agent. I bet half of the guests were former or active Mossad, since Harel was the previous director," Munn said.

From the corner of his eye, Dempsey saw Munn and Grimes share a look, but he kept his own gaze fixed on Buz. They'd never fully understood his relationship with Elinor, and he didn't want to see the judgment in their eyes.

"We don't know, and the Israelis didn't provide any clarity on the matter," Buz said, "but what they did share was the identity of the shooter—Hameed Abram Asif. He's the son of Abram Asif Kamir, a Pakistani national and an ISIS leader killed by US forces in a raid in western Iraq in 2018. Hameed is a former member of al-Qaeda and a suspected operative for al Ghadab. And with that, I'm going to turn things over to Ian and his team."

"Thank you," Ember's Signals director said. Like all of them, Ian Baldwin was deeply shaken by the events of the last hour. He looked as frazzled as Dempsey had ever seen the man.

The slide on the screen changed to display an intelligence briefing from ODNI on the al Ghadab organization. Prescott and the newbies leaned in to read the summary, but Dempsey knew better. Eventually, Baldwin would ramble his way around the facts, and magically a Rembrandt-worthy picture of the truth would emerge. Dempsey had learned to wait to see the portrait instead of studying the color wheel.

"This is an overview of the membership, financials, and, most importantly, the connections of the al Ghadab organization. You can read the details on the organization for yourself, but what I want to call your attention to is their leader—Abu Musad Umar."

Baldwin clicked the touch pad, and the image changed to show a grayed-out silhouette of a man's head and torso, the kind of placeholder graphic used when a headshot was missing.

"Does *this* man look like he could be the mastermind behind an assassination plot to take out the leaders of three world powers simultaneously? And not just any leaders, leaders of countries that possess three of the most capable, vigilant, and robust intelligence and counterterrorism agencies on the planet?" Baldwin asked.

No one said anything.

"Um . . . looks like the dude's picture is missing there, boss," Martin said with a little chuckle. "Just sayin'."

"That's my point, Luka," Baldwin said, his voice harder than Dempsey had ever heard before. "We don't even know what our enemy looks like."

Dempsey got the sense the cyber genius was more rattled by the prospect that Abu Musad Umar might actually *be* behind the attack than the alternative. Because if Umar was the mastermind, then that would mean that Baldwin and everyone in the room with him—indeed everyone in the entire IC—had missed something completely. They would be starting at square zero.

"During my time at JSOC, I've seen ISIS pull off some wildly brutal and successful operations," Wallace said, speaking up and breaking the tension. "They have the means and the motivation to generate an impressive body count when they put their minds to it. And with Afghanistan now a safe haven for terrorists, and Pakistan an unreliable partner . . . You see where I'm going with this? JSOC underestimated the al Qadar network, and London very nearly paid the price. Maybe this guy, Umar, has taken a page from Qasim Nadar's playbook."

Ember had not been involved in any of the ISR or missions to prosecute al Qadar, but Dempsey had been briefed after returning from Russia on everything that happened. Chunk Redman's team had prosecuted and ultimately neutralized the threat, but it hadn't been easy for them. In proposing a potential parallel here, Wallace demonstrated that she had the insight to become a powerful addition to Ember.

"An excellent observation and comparison," Baldwin said, his voice and demeanor returning to normal. "The al Qadar experience has been a harbinger of an evolving threat. This new generation of terrorists is more dangerous and capable. Also, they think bigger—pursuing stretch objectives with geopolitical implications."

"So, what's *our* next step?" Grimes asked.

"Sit back and wait for a target," Munn grumbled. "Same as always."

"Not this time," Buz said, his gaze sweeping from Grimes to Munn, then settling on Dempsey. "This time Ember is going to conduct our own investigation."

Dempsey perked up at this comment.

"We're headed to New Delhi," Buz Wilson said. "We'll operate under a NOC that's not far from the truth: a counterintelligence task force augmenting CIA assets already on the ground. Director Casey wants us in theater, ready to go at moment's notice for direct action."

"So, this tasking is by order of the President?" Grimes asked.

Casey pursed his lips. "Yes and no. There's a new link in our chain of command. Going forward Petra Jarvis will be our—how shall I put this?—overseer."

"You can't be serious," Munn said. "Our tasking for deep, dark covert ops of the most secret task force in the world now comes through the First Lady of the United States?"

Casey shot Munn a stern look. "Yes, the former chief of staff to the DNI, a woman with two decades' experience in the Special Warfare and Intelligence communities and the person married to the leader of the free world, will be our conduit to POTUS. Is that going to be a problem for you, Commander Munn?"

"No," the lumberjack said sheepishly. Dempsey couldn't help but chuckle at his friend's expense.

Dempsey understood exactly why Jarvis had made this move. As President, Jarvis needed a degree of separation from Ember and the activities that Dempsey and the team carried out in the shadows. Jarvis himself had fulfilled that role for President Warner when he'd been DNI and VP—he had all but said as much to Dempsey during their fateful walk on the beach when Jarvis tasked Dempsey to collaborate with Zhukov to bring down the Petrov regime. As President, Warner could never have authorized such a mission. Now Jarvis found himself in the same unenviable position of his former boss. He could only imagine the conversation during which Jarvis gave up direct control of Ember and passed the reins to Petra.

I bet he couldn't do it, he thought with a shit-eating smirk. *I bet she made him.*

"We head out from the MacDill flight line in two hours," Buz said, tapping his watch for effect. "We're taking the Boeing, but pack for an extended stay. We're on the clock, people; let's roll."

Dempsey glanced around the room, saw no questions, and rose from his chair with purpose. In Russia, he'd been more than a blunt instrument: he'd helped Zhukov plan the most complicated assassination ever attempted and manage the diverse team of Russians with big personalities necessary to pull it off. Now, he was being asked to reverse engineer a double assassination that arguably eclipsed what he'd done in Russia.

That's why Petra was sending Ember to Delhi, right?

Has to be . . .

"All right team, we have our marching orders. Empty your cages and load everything into the trucks," Dempsey said, marshaling his team from the briefing room. "We have no idea what we're headed into, so bring everything. Let's go, people; it's time to get to work."

CHAPTER 12

Jarvis sat at the modest desk inside the Boeing 757 that now served as Air Force One. The plane sat on the tarmac outside the 89th Airlift Wing hangar, as it had now for more than fifteen minutes. He clenched his teeth and tried to focus on the intelligence brief on his computer screen, but it was pointless. He couldn't concentrate. For the first time in his life, he felt both ill-prepared and ill-equipped to complete his mission.

He tried to picture himself sitting in the Oval Office behind the Resolute Desk.

Now that's a frightening thought . . .

Then, as if divinely sent, Levi Harel's words echoed in his mind, the old spy's voice coarse gravel from a million cigarettes: *I believe in you, and I love you like the son I never had . . .*

"Mr. President?" his chief of staff said from the doorway, shaking him from his thoughts.

On hearing his new title, Jarvis realized how much he hated it.

He'd heard it so many times on the flight home from New Delhi, it was akin to fingernails on a chalkboard.

"Yes, Andy?" he said, looking over to his chief of staff.

"The staff feels that you should depart the plane first, sir. We believe that it projects strength and will comfort the American people to see your . . ."

"President Warner will depart the plane first, Andy. I will wait at the top of the stairs and then descend as he is brought around to the red carpet by the honor guard. Have First Lady Warner escorted to the bottom of the airstair to meet me. Together we'll then follow the casket to the hangar for the President's last trip down the red carpet."

"Yes, Mr. President." Crouch had worked with Jarvis long enough to know when it was and wasn't time to debate a decision. "Will you make remarks, Mr. President? We've crafted a—"

"When we enter the hangar, I'll give a brief address."

"Yes, sir. In case you need it," he said and handed Jarvis a sheet of paper with double-spaced remarks in large font.

Jarvis folded the page and slipped it into his coat pocket without looking at it. "Thank you, Andy."

The man nodded.

"This is a difficult time for everyone—for the nation," Jarvis said, noting the dark circles under Crouch's eyes and how pale his face appeared. Crouch was a veteran who'd stared death in the face, but this was a situation for which none of them were prepared. "But we'll get through it. I won't be able to do this without you, so—officially—I hope you'll stay on with me as chief of staff."

Crouch clenched his jaw and nodded. "It would be my honor, Mr. President, but moving forward, if there's someone better for the mission, I'll step aside with no regrets or ill will."

"Thank you for that, Andy," Jarvis said. "But there is not."

"I'll make the arrangements you requested, sir."

"Thanks, Andy. We need to get things moving along. We look indecisive sitting here on the ramp. We exfil in five mikes."

Crouch smiled at the familiar operator slang and seemed to relax.

Jarvis turned back to the oval window and looked out at the sea of cameras and reporters forming a literal wall behind the Air Force senior officers and civilian VIPs. He saw familiar faces—some he knew personally, others not, but he'd met each and every one as part of Warner's inner circle of Cabinet members. The Secretary of State was there, his wife clutching his arm. There was a cluster of senators, and he made out the hunched figure of the head of the CIA.

Spouses held tight to the arms of their significant others.

Tissues dabbed eyes.

"Andy," he called out.

"Yes, sir?"

"Have Petra up in front with Amy. I don't want Amy to feel like she's alone."

From the doorway, Andy Crouch gave him a solemn nod. "Yes, sir."

Jarvis couldn't imagine what Amy must be going through. To lose a husband was horrible under any circumstances, but like this? And just months away from starting the next chapter in their lives . . . a chapter free from politics. Amy and Petra had become friends after Jarvis came on as Vice President, but they'd become especially close over the last few months. Having Petra by Amy's side might help.

Moments later Andy returned and escorted him from the office to the main door of the modified Boeing 757, where his team assembled in formation behind him. He heard stifled sobs from the group before he let out the last of four slow breaths. Then he nodded to the Air Force crew member beside the door, who turned the latch and opened the door.

Jarvis stepped onto the airstair, the cool autumn breeze invigorating him and steeling him against the heavy, somber weight of collective grief all around him.

The timing was impeccable. The flag-draped casket escorted by the Air Force honor guard was making its way from the rear of the aircraft as Jarvis began his descent down the stairs. As he descended, he saw Petra, her hand on the arm of an Air Force colonel in full dress blues. Amy Warner walked beside Petra, escorted by an identically clad officer. The two women and their escorts were walking up the red carpet that extended from the hangar to the foot of the airstair—a long, blood-red trail across a barren swathe of concrete, meant to convey respect but carrying a different meaning today. He caught Petra's eye. Her look, even across the distance, conveyed love and grief, relief and pain, all at once.

The sea of assembled media was unusually quiet. Jarvis knew that scores of cameras were focused on him as he descended. The silence was nearly absolute as the body of the dead President was wheeled toward the red carpet to meet his widow.

The silence, Jarvis thought grimly, *of a divided country now united in grief and anger.*

As a Navy SEAL, he'd been a silent professional. He'd never imagined or desired to be the visible face of such a historic moment. He stepped off the bottom step onto solid ground and returned the salute of the military cadre receiving him.

Then, he turned to the First Ladies.

Amy stared at him with wet red eyes, her lower lip trembling. Jarvis felt his throat tighten. Only a few days ago, they had all dined together at the White House, laughing as Amy shared the couple's plans for next spring. She'd been so exited telling them about all the design changes they had planned for their home in Arizona. Rand had teased her, playing the part of the burdened husband, but the love and anticipation in both of their eyes was clear.

Now, all that sparkle and hope were replaced with dread and loss. Jarvis felt a tear roll onto his cheek.

"I am so, so sorry," he choked in Amy's ear as he wrapped her in an embrace.

She wept on his shoulder, then whispered, "For a man who knew thousands of people, my husband didn't have many close friends. But Rand felt a bond with you. I want you to know that. He loved you like a brother, Kelso."

"I felt the same," he whispered back.

Amy broke the embrace first, and he fell in behind her as she escorted the coffin containing what was left of her husband. Jarvis turned to Petra, who released her Air Force escort and stepped up to take Jarvis's arm. Together, they followed a respectful distance behind the mourning widow.

After twenty feet, the procession stopped, cuing off Amy, who stood hunched and sobbing. She seemed unable to continue, so Petra went to her and put a comforting and supportive arm around Amy's waist. Jarvis gave the two women a moment to console each other before striding forward to join them. Finally finding her strength, Amy took a step while still clinging to Petra, and the procession resumed. They passed through throngs of dignitaries and the press corps along the barricade, dark-suited Secret Service agents along the line at regular intervals—and beyond, kitted-up operators ready to respond at a moment's notice. Jarvis, Petra, and Amy reached the end of the carpet and entered the hangar.

Then the silence ended, as a cacophony of shouted questions from the press began. Jarvis turned and felt anger and irritation rise inside him as the press fished for sound bites, and he inhaled deeply to regain his self-control. Camera flashes began to go off all around him, and the Secret Service moved in to form a tight perimeter. He raised a hand, instantly silencing the din. He remembered how unified the nation had been in the weeks and months after 9/11—and how divided it had become in decades since.

Let this bring us together once again.

For the first time, the burden he now had to carry felt more than he could bear. He let out one long, slow breath but did not feel the usual sharpened focus that tactical breathing reliably gave him. He was a SEAL, a spook, a tactician—and, at times, a killer. None of those things helped him now. Inside him, the SEAL at his core shrugged, at a loss for how to proceed. He felt something unfamiliar bubbling up inside him.

Uncertainty.

Finding nothing else worked, he closed his eyes a moment and said a simple warrior's prayer.

God, please don't let me fuck this up . . .

He opened his eyes.

"I know you have questions," Jarvis said, standing tall and scanning the crowd. "Questions that deserve answers. And when I address the nation later today, I will endeavor to answer all of them. But now, in this moment, I will say this: While the nation mourns the death of a great man—a man dedicated to his god, his family, and his country—you should know we will also be tirelessly pursuing every avenue available to find those responsible for this tragedy. We will find them, we will hunt them down, and we will destroy them." He paused. "That, I promise you."

After a moment, he realized this was a promise he could actually keep. He wasn't a politician, but he was perhaps the world's foremost expert at navigating the tactical uncertainty now ahead of him and his nation. The thought gave him the sense of calm he was looking for.

"Mr. President, is it true that you pursued and killed the terrorist who attacked you and Prime Minister Shamone in Tel Aviv? That you left your Secret Service detail behind and personally took out the assailant? We know you're a former Navy SEAL—"

Bottling his anger at the question, he held the reporter's eyes as he spoke.

"I did what needed to be done," he said softly but firmly, his voice nearly the growl he'd used to lead men in the Teams. "And to those out there who might question my resolve, I say this: now is an ill time to be an enemy of the United States of America."

With that, Jarvis turned his back on the crowd of reporters and VIPs, letting their presence fade into background noise. He focused instead on the coffin containing his friend; on Petra, who was now clutching his arm again; and on Amy Warner, who was barely keeping it together. A receiving area had been set up in the center of the hangar, the presidential seal on display behind it. He placed his hand on Petra's, and they moved aside as Amy walked the last few steps to the area set aside to receive Randall Warner for his last time departing Air Force One alone.

His throat went tight as he watched Amy weep and lean over her husband's casket, while a lone White House videographer recorded the moment for history. Off to the side, the President's Cabinet members and senior White House staff stood in solemn solidarity, most weeping openly. He watched Amy steel herself, straighten up, and smooth her dress. A Navy chaplain moved in beside her, and she took his offered hands, bowing her head as he led her in prayer. Rand and Amy were deeply devout in their faith, and Jarvis knew this Navy chaplain offered something he and Petra could not in that moment.

"Who did it, Kelso?" Petra whispered, her voice tight, low, and full of purpose.

Petra's gaze had shifted from that of a loving, supportive wife to the hard, fiery stare of a blooded Naval Intelligence officer and warrior.

"I don't know." He glanced around and saw no one within earshot. "Did you get the team on task?"

"Yes," she said. "When we get back to the White House and into a SCIF, you can conference with Casey. But we absolutely need a liaison between you and the task force. You're President now, which means you have other responsibilities and priorities . . ."

"This is my number-one priority," he growled, surprised at the emotion in his voice. "*Our* number-one priority."

"I know," she said and squeezed his hand. "But it's not our *only* priority. You're Commander in Chief now. You have a country to lead. Rand made it look easy, but you can't be myopic here . . ."

"I know that," he sighed softly.

But did he really? She was right; Warner made it look easy, but being the President of the United States was the hardest job on the planet.

He did a quick scan to make sure they weren't being eavesdropped on, but all the attention was on the former First Lady, who was kneeling beside the coffin with the chaplain still in support beside her.

"You're the only one adequately read in. The last thing we need is to broaden the number of people with eyes on the group. They're effective only in their anonymity, and now more than ever I need them dark and deadly effective."

She did that head tilt thing she does whenever he said something that missed the mark. "I understand, but how in the hell is the First Lady supposed to accomplish that, Kelso? Hell, it's almost worse than you doing it yourself. There's no plausible deniability with me running this from the shadows."

He shook his head. "I don't give a shit about deniability, Petra, and I don't need it. I gave that to Rand, but I'm no career politician. I make no apologies for what I've done, what I'll do, or how I'll do it. I need security, not deniability. I need to know it's being handled by someone I trust and respect. There is no one else."

Jarvis realized how desperately he needed her to do this. Everything on the horizon felt so foreign and beyond his skill set. He needed to know that Ember was in capable hands. If she could give him this one thing, he might be able to shoulder the rest.

She nodded. "Okay. For now, at least. We can talk about it more once we're back. I'm not afraid of the work, but I want what's best."

He gave her hand a squeeze. "Thank you."

"You're welcome."

"I'm going to appoint Margaret Whalen as VP."

"I thought you might." She smiled tightly, somberly. "It's the right call. We can vet her from inside, because if she's going to serve as your Vice President . . ."

"And the next President," he interjected.

"Okay, and the next President. If she's going to serve as either, we'll need to read her in."

The former First Lady was now rising, helped to her feet by the Navy chaplain.

"We'll cross that bridge when the time is right. Come on," Jarvis said, taking Petra by the arm. "Amy needs us."

"I love you, Kelso," Petra said, and the words were like a warm blanket against a cold, biting wind after a frigid ocean swim.

He looked at his wife. "I love you too, Petra. More than I could ever hope to express with mere words."

She squeezed his arm, and they moved as one to comfort their friend.

CHAPTER 13

EMBER'S EXECUTIVE BOEING 787-9

TAIL NUMBER N103XL

ELEVATION: 35,000 FEET—EN ROUTE TO INDIA

0211 LOCAL TIME

Unable to sleep, Dempsey turned on the cabin lights and swung his legs off the side of the insanely comfortable bed. With an interior cabin size of over 2,400 cubic feet, the Ember Boeing 787 was practically a flying apartment. The luxe long-haul jet had been outfitted with a kitchen, lounge, bunk room, master bedroom suite with private office and bathroom, video conference room, and emergency medical suite in the cargo hold. The team had insisted he take the master suite. With Ember's new additions, every rack in the bunk room was accounted for. He could have pulled rank and forced someone else to take the suite, but as the senior member, that would have been, paradoxically, a show of weakness. Captains of ships did not sleep in the crew's berthing. And so, he supposed, neither should he.

He got dressed, slipped into his camp shoes, and wandered to the lounge. No surprise, he found the usual suspects—Munn, Grimes,

Wang—along with a few of the newbies, sitting on a pair of sofas and happily bullshitting.

"Dude, take my seat," said former Green Beret and Army SF operator Tony Prescott, popping to his feet to give up his spot. "I was just about to turn in."

"You sure?" Dempsey asked, eyeing the vacant spot.

"Yeah, man, I'm fading. Night, y'all."

"Later, dude," Munn said, and the rest of the night owls bid Prescott goodbye.

Dempsey settled onto the cushy leather sofa, which was still warm from the previous occupant's body heat. He let out an old man sigh as he did. No sooner had he settled into the back cushion than he noticed a half-eaten plate of chocolate chip cookies on the coffee table between the two sofas. Each cookie was nearly the size of his balled fist and loaded with chunks of chocolate—legit, gourmet temptations. He leaned in to snag himself one.

"Well, that didn't take long," Munn said.

Dempsey shot his best friend a crooked grin and took a bite. "Dude . . . it's like a hunk of heaven in my hands."

"I know, right?" Martin said. "Tess made them for the underway."

Dempsey turned to look at Wallace and, with a mouth half full of deliciousness, said, "You made these?"

"Yeah," she said, grinning large. "I love to bake. It's kinda my thing."

"I thought driving fast boats and taking bad guys down was your thing?"

"Oh, definitely that too," she said, "but I'm a total foodie. You guys should check out my Instagram. I'm always trying and posting new recipes. If you see something on my feed that you like, just let me know and I'll make it."

"I didn't realize Ember was recruiting bakers," he said with a playful sideways glance at Munn.

"Imagine my surprise," Munn said with a shrug, "but now that we see the benefits of recruiting folks with skill sets outside our tactical requirements, I say we factor that into our decision-making criteria.

I could see us needing someone with barista expertise, a mixologist, maybe a former sushi chef . . ."

"These are seriously delicious cookies," Dempsey said. "Maybe the best I've ever had."

"Thanks," Wallace said, blushing a bit at the compliment.

Grimes, who sat on the cushion next to Wallace, rolled her eyes. He knew Grimes well, and the look on her face told Dempsey everything he needed to know.

You were expecting everyone to haze the hell out of her for baking cookies, but the opposite happened, he thought, trying to suppress a grin.

For as long as there'd been a Task Force Ember, Grimes had been the lone female operator. Over the past few years, she'd completely reinvented herself, and—as with everyone on the team—a big part of her identity was tied to the small, tight-knit group that was Special Activities Division. Being the lone female operator had made her Ember royalty, in a sense. Heck, that's how she'd earned her nickname: Her Highness Lady Grimes. Now, with Wallace in the mix, that dynamic would change for her. She was a pro, so Dempsey didn't expect it to impact her performance. But he could already imagine a bit of a competition firing up between the two women.

A chocolate chip cookie–baking, fast boat–driving, door-kicking shooter versus a beer-drinking, former think tank firebrand, death-dealing sniper, he thought with a chuckle. *Who ever will win?*

Eventually everyone turned in to get some sleep, except for Munn. As she left, Grimes had held eye contact with Munn just long enough that Dempsey noticed. She was leaving the two friends alone—something Dempsey was both grateful for and dreading at the same time. He and Munn had not actually spent any real one-on-one time since Dempsey had come home, and it was long overdue.

Grimes and Munn, his two best friends, had definitely gotten closer in his absence. This neither surprised nor upset Dempsey, though it would have been a lie to say he hadn't occasionally wondered what he and Grimes would be like as something more than teammates. She was smart, strong, confident, and gorgeous . . . but for some reason, that spark simply wasn't there. Dempsey didn't know why. Sometimes he felt guilty because he sensed she was waiting on him—waiting until he was ready—but in his heart he knew that day would never come. For him, dating Grimes would feel like dating his sister.

If I actually had a sister.

Munn and Grimes . . . well, that seemed like a better fit.

Actually, they're probably perfect for each other, he thought. *Too bad they're both too dumb to see it.*

"You want a beer?" Munn asked, getting up from the sofa.

"Sure," Dempsey said, even though he didn't want a beer at all.

The lumberjack returned and tossed Dempsey a can of something he'd never heard of. "Thanks," Dempsey said, cracking the pop-top.

Munn raised his own can in acknowledgment. They took sips and sat in comfortable silence for a long moment.

Then, they both started to talk at the same time.

"You go first, but if you ask me if I'm *okay*," Dempsey said, using finger quotes around the word, "then I'm going back to bed."

Munn chuckled. "I know you're okay, but I am curious about something."

"Fire away," he said.

"What was it like over there, in Russia? You never really talk about it," Munn said.

Dempsey tipped his can and took a long pull on his beer before answering. "Do you mean in IK-2 or Russia in general?"

"Either. Both, I guess."

"Did I ever tell you want they called me over there? What my Russian nickname was?"

Munn shook his head.

"*Rosomakha*. The Wolverine."

"Wolverine like the comic book character or the animal?" Munn said.

"I assumed the animal, but maybe they meant the comic book character. I never asked," Dempsey said with a laugh. "But it doesn't really matter. The point is *Rosomakha* is what I had to become to survive. Every day in IK-2 was a battle—a battle to make it to the next morning alive," he said, his gaze going to the middle distance.

Munn nodded and crossed his legs, signaling he was willing to give a long listen if that's what Dempsey wanted.

So, Dempsey opened the vault.

He told Munn about how the prison used torture interrogation sessions, psychological warfare, and poor living conditions to break him down. He explained the Vory caste system, the activist program, and how he had befriended Alexy Narusov. Finally, he recounted the story of how the "activist" scumbag Churkin had ordered Dempsey to the bathroom for a compulsory dry shave with a bloody razor contaminated with HIV and tuberculosis. That single incident had almost ended him but ultimately had become the defining moment of his IK-2 experience—it had been the moment he fought back, and in doing so won the respect of the Vor Pakhan Makarov.

"Holy shit. What a horror show," Munn said, shaking his head. "I'm sorry you had to go through that."

Dempsey thought about his friend's words. "Why are you sorry? I volunteered for the mission. Besides, what doesn't kill you makes you stronger."

Munn nodded, but they both knew it wasn't that simple. "Tell me about Narusov. What's he like?"

The question made Dempsey smile as a memory popped into his head from his early days at IK-2—sitting with the future Russian President in the cafeteria discussing the two kinds of truth: *istina* and *pravda*, absolute truth and relative truth.

He scratched at his beard. "Alexy is probably the most courageous man I've ever met, because he's not like us."

"What do you mean by that?"

"When we go into battle we're armed and ready to conduct violence of action to achieve victory. We're kitted up with a rifle, pistol, grenades, knife, and so on. Not Narusov. He fights with words. Imagine waging a war against men like us with nothing but your principles."

As he spoke, Dempsey had an epiphany. He understood what his subconscious was trying to tell him in his recurring nightmares. Like a man suddenly looking at his own reflection in a mirror for the first time, Dempsey recognized his greatest fear: being forced to live and operate in a world where he could not fight back the only way he knew how.

"That's pretty deep, bro, especially for a door kicker," Munn said.

Dempsey didn't answer.

"Assuming Narusov wins the runoff," Munn continued, "and becomes the Russian President—which from everything I'm seeing appears to be the case—you'll have one hell of a favor chit you can cash in. That's crazy to think that you'll be personal friends with the President of Russia."

"Yeah," Dempsey said, and his stomach went sour at the thought of being used as a political pawn. If the idea had occurred to Munn, then it most certainly had already occurred to now President Jarvis.

"I can't help but wonder what it must have felt like for you, in the moment right before and right after you pulled the trigger and ended Petrov," Munn said, a look of something near awe and wonder on his face.

"What do you mean?"

"Well, in that moment, you were the most powerful man in the world. You had the will, the authority, and the power to single-handedly topple the Petrov regime. We're talking about friggin' Russia, the world's other superpower, and you took it down from the inside—a feat that mobilizing the entire US military might not have been able to accomplish. It's just crazy to me."

"I guess I never thought about it," he said, but that was a lie.

He'd thought plenty on the matter, both in the months leading up to that fateful moment in the Bolshoi and in the months after. Recently, he had begun to wonder if that mission had been the pinnacle of his career, and if everything he did from now would always be *less* . . . less important, less challenging, less exhilarating.

"You know, it's interesting . . ." Munn said, leaving the sentiment hanging.

"What's interesting?"

"That what you did in Russia has kicked off a series of events that led to Kelso friggin' Jarvis becoming the President of the United States."

Dempsey bristled. "What do you mean by that?"

"Oh, just that it blows my mind that our old CSO—a SEAL for Christ's sake—is now the leader of the free world. The whole Vice President thing was wild enough, but Jarvis as POTUS. I mean, what does that even look like?"

Irritated, Dempsey waved the comment away. "Not that part. The first bit when you said what I did in Russia kicked off a series of events . . ."

Munn screwed up his face. "Isn't it obvious? You eliminating Petrov basically established a precedent that leaders of superpower nations are not untouchable, even in the citadels of their own capital cities. The only assassination attempts in our lifetime were carried out by crazy people—not nation-state players effecting political change. With the death of Petrov, all that changed."

Dempsey felt his cheeks go hot and he sat up straighter. "Are you saying it's *my* fault that Warner and Chopra are dead?"

"What? No, don't be ridiculous. Petrov was a job that needed doing, and that asshole going to hell is the best thing that ever happened to the planet. But what I *am* saying is that we now officially live in a world where regime change via assassination—even for the world's most powerful nations—is officially on the table."

"Why?" Dempsey asked, feeling his face redden. "Because I did my job, you're saying that now the whole world order has changed?"

"Yes. Do you disagree?" Munn said.

Dempsey set his beer down on the coffee table and stood. "I'm going back to bed."

"Come on, man, don't be like that. I'm not pointing fingers, bro. I'm just making an observation."

Dempsey let Munn talk to his back as he headed out of the lounge. Munn's pragmatic approach to life and difficult situations was one of the qualities that Dempsey loved most about his friend. As he stomped away, he knew he was acting childish.

But damn, this particular gut punch hurt.

"JD," Munn hollered loudly, stopping Dempsey before he reached the door to his stateroom.

Dempsey turned slowly back around to face Munn.

"Bro, look, whatever demons you're carrying from your time in Russia, you should know that everyone on this team—but me most particularly—is proud and amazed by what you accomplished. You saved countless lives and likely prevented an escalation in Ukraine that would have led to World War Three. I know that mission came at a cost to you that I can't imagine, but *Jack* . . ." Munn said, using the name of the man Dempsey had once been, the name of the SEAL he'd buried in Arlington to become John Dempsey, the name of Munn's closest friend for decades, "I would have done the same thing given the opportunity. But the truth is, I would have failed. You stepped up when the team, the nation, and shit, dude, when the friggin' *world* needed you. Now you're back and . . . and, well . . ."

Dempsey blinked, felt his pulse slow, and gave Munn the closest thing to a genuine smile he could muster.

"Look, asshole," Munn continued, "I'm just saying that I'm your brother, your best friend, and I'm here for you. If you want to drink a beer or talk about any of this shit in private, I'm always available. What you did in Moscow *was* righteous, and I for one am glad you ended that sadistic Russian bastard. But more than that, I'm glad you're back. I missed you, bro. You've saved my life more than once, JD—in the suck downrange, in a bar in Key West, and now by coming home to lead Ember."

"I missed you too," Dempsey managed, but he needed this conversation to end. Because if it didn't, his best friend might coax another truth out of him, a truth he dreaded contemplating: that Ember might be better off without him. And, even more heartbreaking, that he might be better off without Ember.

Munn gestured back at the lounge. "Come on, let's grab another beer. No more shoptalk. We can just bullshit. I promise."

Dempsey shook his head and reached for the lever to his stateroom door. "Thanks, Dan, but I'm . . . tired."

"Fair enough. Good night, bro," Munn said, his voice sounding apologetic rather than antagonistic.

Dempsey gave a simple wave without looking back. There was no way in hell he'd fall back asleep, but he'd done enough talking for the night.

He needed to be alone.

CHAPTER 14

SQT BARRACKS, ROOM #314

PHIL H. BUCKLEW NAVAL SPECIAL WARFARE TRAINING CENTER

NAVAL AMPHIBIOUS BASE CORONADO

CORONADO, CALIFORNIA

0555 LOCAL TIME

"Come on, dude," Ketron whined from the chair at his desk in their small room. "I'm starving."

"I know," Jake said, grunting as he finished the last four of his fifty push-ups. "Me too." He popped to his feet.

"Why do you do that, bro?" Ketron asked as they grabbed their covers and headed out the door. "I'm all about fitness and being harder than my enemy, but right now I think we get all the PT we need."

Jake laughed—mostly because Randy was right. The last thing he needed was more push-ups, and he wasn't trying to be the class beast or anything. The truth was, he didn't know why he always did a quick fifty before he left the room. He did know it had nothing to do with fitness, though his left shoulder—wonky sometimes after an injury during his competitive swimming days—did feel better when he kept the shoulder muscles tight. But it was more an emotional or even psychological thing. Or maybe just some weird-ass superstition or compulsion.

What he did know was that the tone of classroom instruction was different now, in the wake of President Warner's assassination. He imagined what it would have been like to be in SQT right after 9/11. The nation might now, once again, be on the brink of a war on terror. And if so, the men in SQT right now would be at the tip of the next pointy spear fighting America's next war in the Middle East.

In any case, for now they would spend the morning in the classroom learning more small-unit tactics that they would apply in the afternoon at the range and in the kill house. Classroom instruction was always a great opportunity to have to bang out sets of fifty if you fumbled an instructor's question, so his push-up compulsion did feel more like superstition than necessity.

As he and Ketron crossed the compound toward the chow hall, Jake snapped a salute to one of the rare officers on the compound. The lieutenant commander, dressed in digital cammies with a subdued Trident over his left pocket, gave a relaxed salute back, followed by a nod.

Jake's mind went—again—to the strange SEAL officer who had visited the med clinic during Hell Week. Jake had come to convince himself that so much of that week was fantasy and hallucination. After all, they completed the five-day evolution with a total of about six or seven hours of sleep, spread out in little snippets of thirty or forty minutes. Hell, he'd hallucinated about one of the instructors, Senior Chief Perry, being a great white shark wearing a swimsuit and a whistle, and about his mom calling him to swim out to her in a johnboat with the promise of a warm blanket.

But whoever Lieutenant Commander Keith Redman was, and wherever he'd come from, that man had been real. He'd visited Jake to fulfill some promise to his dead dad . . .

"Was that him?" Ketron asked in a low, conspiratorial whisper.

"What? Who?" Jake asked, confused.

Ketron stole a glance over his shoulder at the officer they'd both saluted, then leaned into Jake.

"Is that the dude who visited you in the med clinic during Hell Week?"

Jake chuckled, mostly to conceal his discomfort. He shared a lot with Randy Ketron—too much, maybe—but he needed someone to confide in. Randy was like a brother after all they'd already endured and would soon become his first lifelong brother in the Teams when they both completed SQT and checked in to SEAL Team Eight. He'd told him about Redman visiting him and how strange it was that he'd never, ever heard of the man—not from his dad, not from the teammates who had visited them after his dad's death, not from his mom. And he'd told Randy about the bizarre conversation with Master Chief White, the instructor who believed he'd seen his dad with some spooky task force in the middle of the ocean somewhere.

"Nah," Jake said, trying his best to sound lighthearted. "That wasn't him. The dude I met was like a fire hydrant. Shit, you're as tall as he was."

Ketron nodded, but his eyes seemed far away.

Jake regretted telling Randy about the encounters with Redman and White. No—he didn't regret telling Randy. He regretted that he'd let that shit creep into his *own* mind, much less infect his best friend. Ketron loved a good conspiracy—whether UFOs, Chinese mind control, or the "inevitable" world takeover by AI and robots. Plus, Jake had been physically, mentally, and emotionally broken during Phase I. Hell, that was the very point of Phase I of BUD/S, and he'd met Master Chief White in Phase II when he was barely recovered. But he was rebuilt now. He'd made peace with the memory of his dad, and he'd given up on pursuing any of the wild-ass conspiracy theories that still floated out there in strange corners of the internet about the most devastating loss in SEAL Team history—the ambush of Operation Crusader in Yemen—and about how his dad might have been connected to it.

Jack Kemper died in Djibouti during Operation Crusader with his teammates and is buried in Arlington. Mom is finally happy. I've found my purpose. It's time to move on . . .

"Jake."

The pull on his sleeve stopped him more than whatever Ketron had been saying.

"Yeah?"

"I said I have something I need to tell you," Ketron said.

On his friend's face, Jake saw the same expression used when he was about to share information about the imminent alien invasion he'd pieced together from the Discovery Channel and the internet. Ketron gestured with his head and stepped off the path to the chow hall and into the quiet copse of trees along the side.

Jake crossed his arms across his chest. "What's up, bro?"

"So, listen," Ketron said, leaning in again. "I know you asked me to let go of the Crusader stuff . . ."

"Randy," Jake protested, but his teammate held up a hand.

"Just hear me out. I know you think all the conspiracy stuff on the internet is bullshit—and honestly, I agree. I love digging into this shit, but it's all in fun, Jake, I swear. I know aliens ain't coming and the robots won't rise against us, and I sure as hell know that the SEALs of Crusader aren't hidden in some mountain bunker or aboard the mother ship."

Jake chuckled at that, despite how uncomfortable Randy's obsession with Crusader had become.

"But there is still some wonky shit, Jake. So, I just want to share two quick things, okay?"

"Okay," Jake said, unable to contain a long sigh. "But be quick, bro. I'm starving."

"Okay, so first off, that dude Redman, the officer that found you at Hell Week?"

"Yeah?"

"So, you were right. He's a JSOC guy. I've got a buddy at Four—not an operator, a support guy who works in cyber. He knows Redman—or knew him, anyway. Your man Redman was at Four before he went to the Tier One. He was the total package: smart as shit, a dude's dude who led from the front. The real deal. My buddy Alex says he wasn't like most cake eaters, and in fact got shit sometimes from the head shed because he always went out, you know? Led the ops personally. But the NCOs—they loved him."

"Okay," Jake said, piecing it together. "Sounds like someone my dad would relate to. So, they must have known each other at the Tier One."

"Except here's the thing," Randy said, and now his face took on a look. "That dude Redman? He's probably at the Tier One now—my buddy is sure of it, like I said—but he was still at Four when Crusader went down. In fact, he didn't leave Four until way after. My buddy thinks that he went to JSOC when they reconstituted the Tier One after the tragedy of Operation Crusader."

Jake nodded. He was curious still about the mysterious Commander Redman, but not impressed.

"Okay," he said. "So my dad knew him when he was in Group Two."

"You said your dad was at Team Eight."

"Yeah," Jake said, but he felt the pull of what Randy was telling him. "So what? Both East Coast. Both Group Two. They could have crossed paths."

"Yeah, but by late 2005 your dad was already at the Tier One. When he left Eight, this Redman dude would have been, like, at best, a brand-new JO—if he was there at all. You see what I'm saying?"

"How did they bond so tight that he followed up on a promise to my dad?"

"Exactly." Ketron folded his arms now with a smug smile.

"Well, here's the problem with that, genius," Jake said, forcing a good-natured smile. "The Tier One was constantly augmented by operators from what my dad would call the 'White Side' teams. Maybe Redman augmented the Tier One, and they did a whole deployment together. Or maybe the Tier One fought beside a platoon from Four back in the day. You've heard the stories, bro. It was the Wild fuckin' West back then in Iraq and Afghanistan. There are a bunch of ways they could have crossed paths, you know?"

"It's just weird," Ketron said. "Will you give me that?"

"Okay." Jake gave a nod to a group of three guys from their SQT class who gave them an odd look as they passed. When they were out of earshot, he said, "I give you it's weird, if you'll give *me* that there are a ton of circumstances that would explain it. There are other ways they knew each other. Or Redman didn't know my dad as well as he claims. So what? What does that prove? Jack Kemper was a legend in the Teams. Everyone wanted to be associated with him. How does that tie to one of your crazy-ass, tinfoil-hat conspiracies?"

Ketron shrugged but looked a little wounded. "It doesn't, Jake. Not alone. It's all the things adding up."

"Okay, what other things? You said you had two things to tell me."

He felt himself getting angry and wasn't sure how to stop it. Ketron was just being Ketron.

"Okay, so look. What do you know about the DNA analysis on the mission?" Ketron asked.

"That they were able to positively identify everyone on the mission—both in Yemen and in Djibouti."

"That's not exactly true," Ketron said, and there was an annoying but infectious gleam in his eye. "According to official reports provided under FOIA requests by lots of different independent investigators"—Ketron's slang for *conspiracy theorists*, Jake knew—"all of the members of the Tier One at both locations were identified by a combination of DNA, personal effects, and 'other means.' Now, we don't have any idea what 'other means' implies," Ketron said, in full-on conspiracy mode now, "but it's weird that it's so vague at all. And here's the big one, Jake." His friend leaned in even closer and took him by the shoulders. "If you inventory all the DNA evidence that was obtained for identification, only two operators are *not* included. One is an operator named Steve Wasserman from the op in Yemen, who was literally at ground zero, and they think he completely evaporated, though they found pieces of his gear that were positively identified as his. You know who the other one was?"

Jake stared at him, not speaking.

"Senior Chief Operator Jack Kemper."

Jake's heart began to race, then he wrestled it under control. "My dad was in that TOC when it exploded. He was evaporated."

The words coming from his mouth made his stomach turn.

"Except the bomber at the TOC in Djibouti didn't deliver a bomb anything like what happened in Yemen, Jake. It was a suicide bomber with a vest or something. Some say he had the explosives shoved up his ass. How does one dude deliver enough explosives to wipe out all

DNA traces of someone? And only one person out of a dozen—including support personnel? You see what I'm saying?"

Jake took his friend by both forearms, removing Ketron's hands from his shoulders.

"Randy," he said, his voice trembling. He took a long, slow breath, closing and then opening his eyes as he did. "Brother, I know you mean well. I do. But losing my dad—first to the Teams and then permanently during Operation Crusader—is a wound I can barely imagine healing from. But I'm close, bro. I am . . . I just . . ." He bowed his head, composing himself. "I can't heal a wound that has the scab picked off again and again and again."

"Dude, I didn't mean to . . ."

"I know you didn't, bro. I know," Jake said, hating the pained look in Randy's eyes. "But I'm asking you to let this shit go. My dad is dead, and I've moved on—me and my mom. I'll always be in the shadow of the legend, I suppose, but I need to find my own path and build my own life. I can only do that by leaving my dad where he is—buried with his teammates in Arlington. Okay?"

"Dude, I am so, so sorry . . ."

Jake shook his head. "You don't need to be. We're good, bro, I promise. Let's grab some chow, sit through class, then hit kill house and show everyone what the best two-man team in SQT looks like."

"Hooyah," Ketron said with a grin.

"Thanks, man."

They rejoined the path, where more candidates were hustling to get fed ahead of class. They fell in with Brent Spivey and Rafael Dominquez, and Jake pushed the intrusive thoughts away, focusing on the mission of the day.

One evolution at a time. Both Mark McGinnis from the SEAL Legacy Foundation and the mysterious Lieutenant Commander Redman had told him this. That had been the key to BUD/S, and he knew it would be the key to success through his whole career.

He sent a quick prayer up for his mom and her happiness, then focused on the small-unit tactics he would need to demonstrate again today.

CHAPTER 15

Jarvis stopped in the doorway to the bedroom and watched the woman he loved stare pensively out the window through the heavy ballistic glass onto the White House grounds, a cup of coffee in her lap. He wanted to just look at her a moment before the reality of the day took over.

It wasn't their first time sleeping together in the White House. They'd stayed there twice before—once before their wedding, after a few drinks had gone late with Rand and Amy, and the other on their wedding night. But last night had held none of the joy of those moments for either of them. They'd arrived in the Lincoln Bedroom late at night, both exhausted. There had been no discussion of where they would sleep, but they'd simply arrived in the Lincoln, hand in hand, without speaking the awkward question out loud. Jarvis couldn't imagine sleeping in the President's suite—in Amy and Rand's bedroom—so soon after the attack.

Apparently, Amy couldn't imagine it either. The former First Lady was at Camp David now, with her daughter and son-in-law and their two kids. Her son would arrive there later today with his family, and if Kelso had anything to do with it, they would stay there as long as they wanted or needed. Kelso had already decided that he would need to take Marine One to Camp David, together with Petra, as soon as possible to spend some time with Amy in person, something he'd not likely get a chance to do today.

Petra either—we have work to do.

"Good morning," he called from the doorway.

Petra looked up, startled.

"Sorry," she said sheepishly. "I didn't hear you."

He walked in, his suit coat over his arm, and took a seat beside her on the couch.

"Tired?" he asked. He knew she'd tossed and turned, but also that she needed strangely little sleep. He had, of course, forced himself to get four hours in preparation for the day. Sleep was a weapon, and he had trained himself to sleep in far more austere situations than the comfortable Lincoln Bedroom of the White House.

"Yes and no," she said and poured him a cup from the silver coffeepot on a tray beside her on the end table. He took a slow sip. "I got a few hours, but I'm still emotionally drained from . . . everything."

He nodded, not sure what to say to that.

"I want this to be our bedroom, Kelso," she said. "Promise me we won't ever move into the President's suite. It's just . . ."

"I know," he said. "I was thinking the same thing. And, anyway, we're just here a few months."

She smiled at that, but he couldn't read her look.

Another time, he thought.

"You'll call on Amy today?" he asked.

"Of course," she said, then looked out the window again. "I just still can't believe it," she said as he took her hand. "It's like a bad dream. It just— I don't know, it just doesn't seem real."

He let the moment draw out and left her to her thoughts. There was really nothing to be said. And she was right. His need to move forward with the business of the nation gave him perspective, but he still found it impossible to believe Rand was gone and Amy was no longer in the White House. Over the years, he'd lost so many teammates and, later, men and women under his command. But not like this.

But for now, there could be nothing else; he needed to focus. The assassination in Delhi and the attempt in Tel Aviv together amounted to a terrorist attack in proportion to 9/11. America was at war; all that remained was to have the IC define the enemy. But Andy Crouch had echoed Petra in correctly pointing out that running the nation was about juggling everything at once, and that included nonmilitary matters. That kind of unfiltered, no-bullshit callout was why Crouch was staying on as chief of staff.

Politics were painful, and he needed a fellow warrior to keep him straight.

Jarvis squeezed Petra's hand, bringing her back. "How is everything?"

"Well, I spoke with Mike Casey briefly on the secure line while you were showering . . ."

He shook his head. That wasn't what he meant. "We'll get to Casey in a moment. How are things for *you*?"

She smiled, tilted her head, and seemed to relax. "It's weird, Kelso. Are you asking me to answer as the First Lady, instead of as the President's Adviser for Counterterrorism?"

"I've asked you to do the impossible—keep a bunch of spinning plates in the air from two demanding jobs at the same time."

She smiled but shook her head. "It's not that. I've been tasked with far more impossible tasks when I worked for you at the Tier One. I can keep the plates in the air. My concern is whether I have the *right* plates up there, you know?"

"I don't," he said, grateful she was now on mission with him. "Tell me what you mean."

"Well . . ." He watched her take a moment, organizing her thoughts, and smiled in awe at her sharp mind crunching numbers on the problem. "In my position as adviser for counterterror, I need for agency leads and task force commanders to trust me to represent their situations accurately and adequately to the President. The CI world has a lot of things going on at once these days—Russia settling into whatever they'll become under their new leadership, the Hermit Kingdom in Korea spinning up their next madness, instability in South America, whatever devious infiltration China tries next . . ." She stopped and smiled. "You know all of this, of course. The point is that I need them to deal with me unfiltered. And, honestly, I don't know if that's possible with the assumed bias they will believe I have. I'm your wife, for God's sake, Kelso. And then, I need to run point as your liaison to Ember . . ."

"Well, that's the real job, Petra. The adviser position gives you access and connections needed to do that." He took his hand off hers. "Petra, with this assassination, we're a nation at war, no matter how or when that becomes official. I respect your advice on the breadth of responsibilities I will have to juggle—something I find overwhelming, if I'm honest . . ."

"You? You're never overwhelmed, Kelso," she said with a soft laugh.

He let out a slow breath.

"That has always been true," he said. A statement of fact, nothing more. "But I'm telling you, as my wife now, that serving as Commander in Chief already feels way, way outside any wheelhouse I've ever operated in."

"Succeeding as Commander in Chief is about surrounding yourself with the right people, Kelso. You've done that with Andy Crouch. You'll find others who you'll be able to lean on as well . . ."

"Exactly," he said. "And that includes you. The points you make about other priorities are more than valid, and the position I've put you in is, indeed, untenable. But I believe . . ." he leaned in closer, ". . . and this I say as both President and your husband, that there is no priority above finding and destroying those responsible for these attacks. Not because I want vengeance—though I certainly do—but because whoever is responsible is still out there, and I promise they are right now planning the next terror attack. This is the most immediate, clear, and present danger to the United States and our allies."

He watched as she digested that, then saw her nod.

"I have Andy to help me balance all of the other commitments, some of which will take time to fully understand," he said. "Hopefully Margaret Whalen will prove an equal ally in that regard. But I need you—someone I trust completely, but who knows Ember and what they can do, and someone who is on their own a genius intelligence analyst—to spearhead the operations of Ember. This isn't me retaining control vicariously through you. This is me, as Commander in Chief, making sure the most valuable tool I have at my disposal is laser-focused on what I believe to be my number-one priority. Right now, that's finding the enemy, out there in the shadows, and putting our direct-action arm to work to stop them. The other position, the adviser position, is a means of access for you. The adviser position . . ."

"Is still an important job, Kelso," she said softly. "It's a job that needs to be done."

He nodded. She was right, of course.

"We only have to keep those plates up there for a few months, Petra," he reminded her. "I know I'm asking a lot. I'm speaking to Margaret Whalen first thing this morning, and I intend to slowly read her in over the coming weeks—or I hope so, depending on what I can glean about her as she steps up. Our priority is to find out who's behind the attacks, have Ember and our other IC agencies cut the head off whatever snake that is, and then have a smooth and peaceful transfer of power in January, hopefully to a duly elected President Whalen. Then, we take a breath and see what's next."

"For us . . . ?"

"For us," he agreed.

"Well, that sounds . . . optimistic," she said with a weary smile. "But first we have to navigate the nation out of the storm and into a safe harbor, and that, my love, is a huge task."

"That's why we're going to do it together," he said, then noticed her downcast eyes. "What's that look for?"

"My concern is that my position as First Lady may make me a liability. The press is already having a field day . . ."

"Screw the press," Jarvis said. "With only a few months in the term, I have the luxury of not having to play their games. I entered the office as a lame duck, so let's try not to care what anyone thinks and just get the work done. Leave the press to me. You are the most talented counterterror intelligence analyst I know, and becoming First Lady doesn't change that. We can't waste that talent because of some outdated expectations for you as my wife. I won't have it."

"All right, Mr. President," she said.

He looked at her, ready to be annoyed that she'd used his title. Then he caught the sparkle in her eye and couldn't help but smile.

"Taking off the wife hat and putting on the Adviser for Counterterror hat, I see," he noted.

"Exactly," she said. "I want to make sure you're all read in before I lose you to the day. Honestly, there's not a ton to tell."

"Well, I have the luxury of waking up beside my top adviser instead of scheduling a meeting," Jarvis said with a grin. "Feed me."

She briefed him on the deployment of Ember's SAD to New Delhi and the Counterterror Joint Task Force NOC they'd created with Reggie Buckingham's help. Then she gave him the rundown on all of Ian Baldwin's suspicions, even sharing the mathematical analyses he used to draw his conclusions, understanding that Jarvis would be one of the few people on the planet to appreciate those details.

"Earlier you said this threat is our number-one priority, and as your senior adviser for counterterror, I completely agree," she concluded. "But we need to let the conventional IC and Ember work to uncover the puppet master. If we simply go nuclear on the al Ghadab cell, we lose that opportunity. We leave an adversary in play who has proven themselves not only capable but appear to have deep, deep intel resources inside the United States . . ."

"Are you suggesting we have a mole?" Jarvis interrupted, his mind going back to the mole they had hunted, and Petra herself had dispatched, while he was still DNI.

She shook her head.

"No," she said. "The new global threat to intelligence is cyber.

Whoever is pulling the strings, I'm guessing that they have very robust cyber capabilities."

"So a nation-state?" Jarvis felt a chill at the thought. If a foreign country had orchestrated the execution of a head of state, they were indeed at war—likely in a world war, in fact. After the covert operation in Moscow, the irony was not lost on him.

"Possibly," Petra said. "But the world is different now, Kelso. Remember the terror cell that the Tier One took down in London? They had the education, expertise, and tech needed to hack into an AI-driven autonomous drone. The truth is, while al Ghadab may not be in that league, we still just don't know."

"Well, we damn sure better find out, and quickly," he growled, a hundred equally horrible scenarios parading through his mind.

As they spoke, he realized how energized he felt. Maybe it was his response to the terrorist attack at the cemetery, or maybe it was the enormity of the task ahead of him. Either way, he couldn't remember feeling so alive and full of energy in a while. Not since he'd become Vice President, at least.

Definitely not since my diagnosis.

He took her hands, and she looked up, surprised by the shift from professionals to spouses, he assumed.

"This may not be where I want to be—or where I imagined we would be as a couple—but it is where we need to serve for now," he said. The fire in her eyes was all the agreement he needed. "In a few months, we'll exfil this damn crazy-ass house, but we'll need to talk about whether either of us is ready to just ride off into the sunset."

The idea of easy days with Petra at his side now felt almost ridiculous. They both had a lot left to give, and he'd not felt more on task in a long time. A fish out of water, perhaps, but on fire. He only wished he could be in the suck with Dempsey and Ember, but those days—those *years*—were behind him. There, he would be a liability now. But here . . .

"So," he said, letting go of her hands and getting back to business. "If Baldwin is right—and I should point out that if he's wrong, it may be the first time—who does he think is the puppet master here?"

Petra nodded but shrugged again.

"He's not committing to any one scenario yet. Not enough data, he says."

"Fair enough," Jarvis said. "Who does the President's Adviser for Counterterrorism think is at the top of the list?" He steepled his fingers. He hated himself for the look, but the energy inside him—the need to *do* something—was getting the better of him.

"I don't have an answer for you, Kelso. We're learning everything we can about al Ghadab in the hope that a deep dive into their connections helps bring some sense to all of this. They've been on our radar for a while, but al Ghadab has always be considered a local cell with regional aspirations. Interestingly, there's evidence they might have exited Pakistan to operate out of India—a move that would buck unconventional wisdom. Planning and carrying out an attack like this on their own seems unlikely based on the profile we've built, but not impossible. But tying together New Delhi with the attack on Shamone and then Nepal . . ." She sighed. "There's a thread there somewhere, I'm sure, but right now, I just don't see it."

He nodded.

A buzzer by the door sounded, and he rose. He leaned in, his eyes on his wife and most trusted adviser.

"Stay on top of Baldwin and his signals team. Maybe they're seeing something the rest of the IC is missing."

She nodded, but her face suggested something else bothered her.

"What?" he asked.

"Kelso, the whole reason for having me run point on Ember is to keep a degree of separation between the office of the presidency and a deep, dark, and unsanctioned task force. If I read you in on every step they take . . ."

Jarvis shook his head.

"I told you I don't care about deniability, Petra. I own my decisions, and deploying Task Force Ember is the best decision we can make here. I stand behind it no matter what."

She placed a hand on his. "I admire you for taking that stand. Hell, we need more of that in politics, but here's the thing, my love: This isn't about you. This isn't about protecting your reputation as the President from fallout if Ember is unmasked. It's about protecting the *office* of the presidency and all that it represents. A scandal of this size—a secret black task force being run by the White House—is more than America, which is already so deeply divided, can stand. Keeping separation between you and Ember is what's best for the United States . . ." she leaned in and gave him a serious look, ". . . Mr. President."

Jarvis let out a long breath. As usual, she was right.

"You're right, and I trust you completely, but as President, I do need to know the tactical, strategic, and political implications of whatever is going on with Ember—along with the rest of the IC. I will trust you to keep me in the loop as needed, using your best judgment, and to check with me about new tasking as you see appropriate. And for those times when you deem separation to be necessary, you can and should rely on Casey to function as my proxy. He has a pragmatic, tactical mind and a strong moral compass. Use him as a sounding board and confidant."

"Okay. I will." She rose, and they hugged.

He walked to the door leading into the east sitting room. When he opened it, he found Andy standing with arms folded, waiting.

"Sorry to disturb you, Mr. President," his chief of staff said, "but we have Margaret Whalen waiting. I took the liberty of having her brought to the Executive Library downstairs, instead of the West Wing."

"Perfect," he said, then turned to his wife, who gave a little wave to Andy. "We'll have more to discuss later, I'm sure," Jarvis said.

"Inevitably," she agreed.

Jarvis closed the door behind him and followed Andy down the Grand Stair, with Tony Perez falling in behind. They continued down to the ground level, where they hung a left to the library. The room was intimate but grand, decorated during the Kennedy administration in the federal style of architecture that Jarvis found stuffy.

He found Senator Margaret Whalen standing alone, somewhat awkwardly, he thought, in the center of the room, hands clasped in front of her. She was dressed in a dark business suit, as usual, and gave him a tight smile.

"Mr. President," she said with a nod. He saw her eyes cut his security detail and his chief of staff.

He turned to Andy and Tony. "Give us the room."

Andy nodded and then he and Perez disappeared, closing the door behind them and no doubt positioning themselves immediately outside.

"Senator Whalen, thank you for coming, especially so early in the morning. I'm so very sorry to not have had this meeting up in the Oval Office . . ."

She seemed to relax and shooed away the comment with her hand. "I can only imagine what you have going on. This is far more comfortable, to be honest."

"Please, have a seat," he said, gesturing to two armchairs separated by a small, round table. "Can I get you anything?" he asked, gesturing to a coffee kiosk in the corner, a rather nice Italian espresso machine. "The coffee down here is better than you might guess."

Whalen laughed but shook her head. "No, thank you, Mr. President. I'm fine. I'm also not ready to have coffee served to me by a sitting President."

Jarvis chuckled and took a seat beside her, folding his hands in his lap.

"What can I do for you, Mr. President?" Whalen asked. "And I mean that sincerely. I view our nation as being at war, even though the enemy is still being defined. You have my full support, and I am eager to serve in any capacity to bring the terrorists who did this to justice."

"I know you are, Senator."

"Please, call me Margaret," she said.

"Margaret. Thank you for that. I wish I could tell you we have identified the threat and are planning our counterattack, but I'm afraid that's not yet the case. But, since you seem willing and ready to serve, I do have something I'd like to ask of you."

"Anything, Mr. President."

He watched her closely to gauge her response to his offer. He'd come to respect her a great deal the last few months, but she was still a professional politician.

"Margaret, I'd like to appoint you as Vice President for what's left of this term of office."

She leaned back, her mouth open in what Jarvis took for genuine surprise.

"Well, I didn't see that coming," she said. "I had assumed you would be asking me to help garner support in the Senate and House for whatever you planned as our response. But this . . ."

"*This* is what the nation needs, Senator," Jarvis said, leaning in.

He could see the gears of her political mind churning. "Why me?" she asked.

"You're a brilliant politician, Margaret," he said, elbows on his knees now. "I, on the other hand, am no politician at all. I would argue I was ill-suited for the job of Vice President for that reason—in fact, I *did* make that argument—but I respected Rand enough to answer the call. For me to serve as Commander in Chief, I need someone serving at my side who knows the ins and outs of the political machine so that I can be effective."

"First off, let me say that I'm flattered and honored you've chosen me, but unfortunately, Mr. President, I can't give you an answer without knowing what your policy priorities will be," she said in confident, measured tones while holding eye contact with him. "You say you need me at your side to govern effectively. I need to understand what the Jarvis administration's agenda is going to be before I can determine if I can add value."

Jarvis smiled. *Brilliant politician* was an understatement. As the party's nominee in the upcoming election, Whalen was leading in the polls by a close but real margin before the attacks. She didn't want to lose that by partnering with someone who might pursue an agenda that deviated from the party and her platform in substantive ways.

"I have a simple answer for your complicated question," he said with an easy smile. "My policy priorities are simple. First, find and punish those behind the attack and assassination of the President of the

United States. Second, don't fuck up everything the Warner administration accomplished over the past seven and a half years. Third, make preparations to hand over the reins to the next administration—an administration that I hope will be led by you."

Now Whalen rose from her chair and paced away from him. Jarvis watched her as she did, trying to read something in her body language.

Finally, she turned to him, arms folded over her chest. "You don't intend to run for President? After all that's happened? That's insane—" She caught herself and now looked somewhat aghast. "I . . . I mean, with all due respect, sir. And I know that phrase usually doesn't imply much respect, but I mean it. Mr. President—"

"Please, Margaret. Call me Kelso."

She laughed.

"I'm sorry, Mr. President, but I'm not ready for that yet."

"Fair enough."

She exhaled and seemed to collect her thoughts. "Quinnipiac University polling released just last night shows you winning the presidency by solid double digits—landslide-level stuff. You're an American hero, Mr. President."

She began to pace, back and forth, just a few steps at a time in front of her chair. Jarvis rose and circled behind his own chair, clasping his hands on the high back of the dark leather. He'd seen her on C-SPAN grilling a tech giant in committee and knew just how formidable her mind was. Thin and fit in her tailored suit, she looked ten years younger than her fifty-four years, even in person.

"The nation needs a different leader now than it did when I threw my hat in the ring," she said with what sounded like resignation. "I believe I would do a damn fine job as President, make no mistake, but everything has changed. The nation has already chosen its next leader, at least informally, Mr. President. The YouTube video of you chasing down and killing the assassin in Tel Aviv has nearly a billion views. With voting only weeks away, there is no candidate on the planet who could beat you in the race. Not one." She sighed, stopped her pacing, and faced him. "You can't possibly be planning to throw all that way."

"I'm not," he said and smiled. "I might not be a politician, but I'm not that naive. I know the importance of political capital. If what you're saying is true, then I will indeed apply that capital for the good of the nation."

"So, you *are* running for President then?"

Jarvis could only imagine the bitterness she must be containing somehow. The attack had been a tragedy, but also an ironic October surprise for someone just weeks away from a likely win. He admired Whalen all the more for the resentment she *wasn't* showing right now.

"Margaret, I intend to leverage all that political capital and throw it behind the candidate I believe best serves the needs of our nation. As Vice President, you'd be perfectly poised to win the election in November and take over the presidency in January."

"Are you serious?"

Jarvis nodded. "I was going to vote for you anyway," he said.

They both laughed.

"I don't know what to say. I'm honored, but I also can't image throwing away the opportunity you have here."

"I'm not," he said, watching her carefully. "I'm doing what I believe to be best for the country."

"Of course," Whalen said.

"I have lost a lot of people close to me over the years, Margaret," he said, still holding her gaze. "I've ordered some into battles they didn't return from and held others in my arms as they gave their last full measure of devotion. I have always tried to live a life worthy of that sacrifice and to honor those lost and the families and teammates they left behind." He took a short step toward her. She was staring at him with what he felt to be misplaced reverence. "Swear to me, Margaret, that you will use this opportunity to become a President worthy of the sacrifice made by President Warner."

She nodded, and he saw her eyes rim with tears. "You can rest assured that I will not only promise, but I will live up to that promise with my dying breath."

"Well then, welcome aboard," he said and reached a hand across the table. He believed her. Whalen shook it, her own hand strong and dry. "We'll make the announcement to the nation together this evening."

CHAPTER 16

While Angad Singh rambled, Dempsey resisted many urges—the urge to grumble, to sigh, to take a nap, to claw his friggin' eyes out . . . to do anything other than sit still and listen to the Indian Counterterrorism deputy director talk. Why did he have to come to this bureaucratic stuffed-shirt goat rope with Buz while everyone else got to stay at the hotel?

Because you're the head of Ember SAD, you dumbass, that's why.

He thought he felt Buz's disapproving gaze on him, but when he glanced at the old-timer, the Ember Ops O was sitting forward in his chair scribbling notes. Dempsey looked down at his own notebook and saw mostly blank pages. The only thing he'd managed to write were the names of the first three Indian task force members who'd introduced themselves before he fell behind and gave up. Indian people spoke excellent English, but damn, they talked fast.

". . . and that concludes the overview of NIA immediate priorities and how we will structure the investigation," said Singh. He was slender, tall, and in his midforties, and he swept his gaze across the group. "Are there any questions from the team or our American joint task force members?"

Yeah, I got a question. When I find the assholes responsible for killing Warner, are you guys going to be mad when I shoot them? Dempsey thought but did not say.

"Okay, if there are no questions, then we—" Singh began to say, but was interrupted by the conference room door abruptly swinging open.

Dempsey shifted his attention to the late arrivals—two Indian men, one older and one younger, both wearing suits. Deputy Director Singh looked displeased at the interruption.

"Excuse me, this is a closed meeting."

The older of the two men cleared his throat and addressed Singh in what Dempsey assumed was Hindi. A tense conversation followed. Dempsey looked at Buz, who raised both eyebrows as if to say, *Don't look at me; I've got no idea what's going on.* The older man must have pulled rank because the newcomers helped themselves to a pair of empty seats at the conference table.

For this engagement, the Ember team was operating under a dual-layered NOC. On the surface, they were members of an international counterterrorism investigation task force operating under NCTC. However, Baldwin and the boys had gone the extra mile and created a second layer of digital bureaucracy that established them as a secret CIA counterterrorism prosecution unit within Clandestine Services. Apparently, this had been Buz's idea, but Dempsey didn't know why the double layer was needed. Dempsey's gut told him he'd find out why eventually. Buz didn't do anything without a good reason.

Singh turned to Buz and Dempsey.

"Mr. Wilson and Mr. Jones, please allow me to introduce two of my colleagues from the Intelligence Bureau—Joint Director Gul Bhatt and Central Intelligence Investigations Officer Dinesh Madhav. They will be participating in the investigation and prosecution of the terror cell behind the attack on our two nations."

Buz nodded. "It's unfortunate our meeting has to be under such dire circumstances. My name is Buz Wilson. I'm the director of the International Counterterrorism Investigation Task Force, a division of NCTC. And my colleague, Larry Jones, is our ground operations team leader. We'd like to thank you and your government for your cooperation and the invitation to participate in this investigation in your country. We know it's difficult when outside teams are operating inside your jurisdiction, which is why our modus operandi is cooperation and transparent intelligence collection . . ."

That last line was a nice touch, Buz, Dempsey thought, chuckling on the inside.

"Do you have anything you'd like to add, Larry?"

It took Dempsey a beat to remember that *he* was Larry.

"Um . . . no, I don't think so," he said, mustering his best play-nice smile. "That pretty much covers it."

Buz shot him a *Thanks for nothing* look.

The middle-aged man in the suit, Joint Director Bhatt, spoke next.

"As Deputy Director Singh mentioned, I am Joint Director Bhatt from the Intelligence Bureau, and I lead the Counterintelligence SIB. My colleague, Dinesh Madhav, is the head of our Counterintelligence Investigations Division. While this investigation will be spearheaded by Deputy Director Singh out of this office, IB will be providing oversight and assistance as required for the duration of the project."

Dempsey noticed the lone female member of the NIA task force, Ria something-or-other, roll her eyes at this comment. There was some kind of tension between the NIA folks and the new IB arrivals, and he made a mental note to ask Buz about it later. Despite hating himself for it, he felt his focus sharpening now that his interest had become piqued by potential interagency tension.

Singh checked his watch, then did something that visibly pissed off the new guys from IB: by announcing with a smug expression that it was time to break for lunch. In the corner of his eye, Dempsey saw Buz's lips curl into a smile underneath his mustache as he closed his writing pad and packed up. Dempsey handed the Ops O his notebook to carry in Buz's briefcase, which earned him an annoyed glare.

"What? I don't carry a briefcase," he said as Buz grudgingly took the tablet and pen.

"I would offer for you gentlemen to join us for lunch," Singh said, addressing the IB newcomers, "but as I was not informed to expect your participation, I've already made the reservation. We will see you back here at 1300 to continue the brief." Singh turned to address the woman, Ria, before Bhatt or Madhav from IB could protest. "Ria, if you could please escort our American guests to the parking garage and our transportation, I will meet you there in short order."

"Yes, of course, Director Singh," she said, then turned to Buz and Dempsey. "If you would come with me, please, gentlemen."

Buz and Dempsey followed the NIA officer, who Dempsey now remembered had introduced herself as a senior counterterrorism analyst. She walked quickly, her heels clicking a quick-paced staccato cadence on the tile floor. On reaching an elevator bank, she ushered them into a waiting car and rapidly pressed the Door Close button before selecting the garage level as their destination.

Talk about an emergency exfil, Dempsey thought with a smirk.

Only when the car began to descend did the woman turn, smile at them, and say, "Deputy Director Singh has selected a very private and trusted dining location where we can speak freely and openly about our cooperation."

"That sounds wonderful," Buz said with a grandfatherly smile.

On reaching the garage level, Ria escorted them to a black SUV with tinted windows parked nose out in an end parking slip. With a key fob she retrieved from her suit jacket, Ria unlocked the door. "You can talk privately inside while we wait for Angad," she said to Buz. "It's not bugged; you have my word."

Dempsey registered two notable developments since their arrival in the parking garage. First, she'd eased up on the formalities, referring to her boss and colleague as Angad rather than Deputy Director Singh. Second, she'd provided an opportunity for him and Buz to caucus in private.

Interesting.

"Thank you, Ria," Buz said simply and climbed into the back seat of the SUV.

Dempsey made a quick scan of the garage for anything out of the ordinary, then checked Ria's face for signs of insincerity or betrayal. Finding none, he climbed in and closed the door behind him.

"What the hell was that all about?" he asked, turning to Buz.

"The IB is the oldest formally established centralized intelligence agency in the world," Buz said, his eyes bright and full, as usual, of wisdom. "It's older than the CIA and quite formidable, with nearly twenty thousand employees. In India, IB is the eight-hundred-pound gorilla when it comes to intelligence collection, counterintelligence, and counterterror operations. But after the 2008 Mumbai attack—a day they refer to as 26/11—the Indian Parliament passed a bill to form the National Investigative Agency, or NIA. In doing so, Parliament publicly named the attack as an intelligence failure, which highlighted IB's incompetence and drew scrutiny on its management, practices, and overall effectiveness. In creating NIA, Parliament stripped counterterrorism investigation and prosecution from IB's charter and gave it to NIA. But, as you can imagine, that's easier said than done. IB still operates in the counterterrorism space. Just like at home, every agency has a counterterror division. If you ask me, IB showing up like they did means they have no intention of letting NIA run this investigation unchecked."

Dempsey nodded, a clearer picture coming together for him. "But that dude Bhatt said he was director of the Counter*intelligence* SIB, not Counter*terrorism*. And what's an SIB, by the way?"

"Subsidiary Intelligence Bureau—functionally a silo of operations inside IB. Each SIB head has the title of joint director. Bhatt is the joint director of Counterintelligence, and him personally coming to this meeting is very telling. It means—and this is just me theorizing—that IB believes there is more to this attack than just an al Ghadab suicide bombing. Also, it's way too high profile to let NIA run the show. IB has already been shamed once by an intelligence failure, and clearly, they did not see this assassination of the Prime Minister coming. If this attack turns out to be something more than al Ghadab getting lucky, then it would be the biggest intelligence failure in the history of the organization. The parliamentary investigations would be brutal and, I imagine, would result in the firing of the agency director and most if not all of the joint directors."

"Are you saying Bhatt is here to cover his ass?"

"Is that really so surprising?"

Dempsey snorted a laugh. "No."

What he heard was everything he hated about the world he worked in. It was why he was grateful to be operating for Ember, outside of the bureaucratic checks and balances. At Ember, he didn't have to give a shit about rice bowl politics. He was given an objective and then the resources and, more importantly, the authority and autonomy to execute.

"Also, before we run out of time, one more thing to keep in mind. As far as partners go, do not make the mistake of confusing IB with MI6 or Mossad. We do not have that kind of trusted, born-from-blood track record with the Indians like we do with the British and Israelis. India is not a member of the Five Eyes. I'm not saying IB is the Russian SVR or Chinese MSS, but we need to proceed with a healthy dose of caution. We need to be prudent and vigilant about preserving our NOC, do you understand?"

Dempsey slow-nodded. The double-layered NOC Buz had constructed made sense now. "Because *we* are going to be part of IB's investigation . . ."

"That's right."

Clever bastard, Dempsey thought with healthy dose of respect for the old-timer. *He's giving IB a veil to pierce on purpose. He knows they're going to try, and when they do, IB will confirm Buz's identity and prior clandestine service with CIA. It's why he's using his real name inside the NOC. But the trail will lead them to Buz's secondary NOC, that we are a direct-action arm of the CIA, rather than a supersecret, deniable, covert task force.*

He looked at Buz—with his cheesy *Magnum, P.I.* '80s mustache—and grinned. The man was truly brilliant and just kept finding new ways to surprise him.

Movement caught Dempsey's attention. He glanced out the side window to see Deputy Director Singh heading toward the vehicle from the elevator bank. Ria Keltker, her surname finally percolating into Dempsey's consciousness, opened the front passenger door and climbed inside. Singh stepped into the driver's seat, which, like in other former British colonies, such as Australia and South Africa, was built for driving on the left side of the road.

"You will have to excuse me if I appear flustered or emotional, but there is tremendous pressure on NIA—on me and Ria in particular—to quickly identify the culprit behind the assassination and mete justice," Singh said, after putting the transmission in Drive and stepping on the accelerator. "We lost our Prime Minister—a man who was popular with the people and respected by Parliament. The question everyone is asking at NIA is 'How could this happen on our watch?'"

"We can empathize with your situation, because we are literally in the same boat," Buz said. "I could not help but notice that you did not take the opportunity to invite your colleagues from IB to join us for lunch . . ."

Dempsey watched Singh glance in the rearview mirror.

"That was intentional, as I fear this will be the last opportunity the four of us will have to talk without IB supervision. Ria and I both were educated in the US. I went to Rice University, and she attended the University of Chicago. We understand Americans—how you work and how you think. You've come here hoping for a collaborative investigation, and that is exactly what we at NIA intend to offer you. The same courtesy does not apply to Joint Director Bhatt and Officer Madhav. With them, your autonomy will be curtailed, and you will be closely monitored for the duration of your stay."

"This lunch will be your opportunity to ask all the questions you want and get unfiltered answers from us," Ria said, turning in her seat. "We will have to be judicious and political after this; otherwise we risk providing IB with a framework they could use to build a case against the NIA for negligence or gross incompetence."

"We appreciate your honesty and the heads-up," Dempsey said, speaking up when Buz left him the window to do so. "We've both been in this business a very long time, and we understand the challenges of 'joint' anything when it comes to counterterrorism operations. It's difficult enough trying to stop bad guys with imperfect information, but having to worry about being undermined by folks who are supposed to be on the same team . . . Well, let's just say we can appreciate the delicacy of your situation."

"Thank you for saying that, Larry," Ria said. "May I call you Larry?"

"Absolutely," Dempsey said, then with a grin added, "I also respond to *knuckle-dragger, door kicker, dude,* and *bro.*"

This earned him a laugh from both Ria and Singh.

Ice officially broken . . .

Dempsey looked out the window as they drove, taking measure of the city. He was well-traveled, but this was his first time in New Delhi. From what he'd seen so far, the world's second-largest city met his expectations: hot, crowded, and chaotic. Motorized rickshaws clogged the streets. The open-cab, three-wheeled taxis—along with mopeds and buses—swerved and honked and spewed exhaust like some wriggling, burping, farting organism consuming every road and alley. The farther they traveled from NIA headquarters, the more densely packed the city became. Roadside merchant stands with fruits and vegetables, clothing, and cheap electronics lined the streets, interspersed with piles of trash. Dempsey did a double take when he saw a cow standing in one of these piles of trash, foraging like a stray dog or raccoon might at home.

"You don't see that every day," he murmured as they drove past.

"You do here," Ria said. "Cows are considered sacred, so they can't be culled, but with over five million of them roaming free, they are becoming more than a nuisance. Spreading disease, causing car accidents . . . it's a mess."

"I would think so," Dempsey said, suddenly craving a nice juicy Munn burger hot off the grill with a hunk of melted cheddar.

They arrived at the restaurant a few minutes later, and Singh turned the SUV over to a valet at the curb. The restaurant host greeted both

Singh and Ria by name and escorted the foursome into a private room. Unlike the malodorous stench of petrol exhaust and trash outside, the restaurant smelled of stewed meat and curry. Dempsey's mouth began to water just at the thought of the coming meal.

Once seated at the table, Singh ordered lunch for the group. The server brought bottled waters, chai, and a plate of appetizers—nuts and fried dough balls covered in sauce.

"That is called *dahi vada*. It is made from lentil flour and topped with yogurt. It is not spicy," Ria said, as Dempsey tentatively reached to spoon a ball onto his plate.

He cut it in half and ate the first bite. "Very good," he said and, before he'd finished chewing, scooped himself another one.

Buz took a sip of his water. "What can you tell us about al Ghadab's activities in Delhi leading up to the attack? Our intelligence did not indicate they had a strong presence in country, and we had zero indicators or trip wires alerting us to an assassination operation."

"As you are undoubtedly aware, al Ghadab is a radical Islamic terror organization that originated in Pakistan. Ria has been tracking and analyzing al Ghadab's operation for the past eighteen months, so I'll turn the discussion over to her," Singh said.

"If you'll humor me for a moment, I think it might be helpful to start with a little history to help put these recent events in perspective," Ria said.

Buz nodded. "By all means."

"As I'm sure you are well aware, the Kashmir region has been a source of conflict and strife between India and Pakistan for decades. Islamabad has supported—both directly and indirectly—a separatist movement in the region, with Pakistani ISI supplying arms and training to mujahideen militants in Jammu and Kashmir. Their goal was to fight a protracted and low-cost proxy war with India using these 'separatists' to consume India's military resources, destabilize the local government, and degrade India's operational readiness in the region. However, one of the unintended consequences of this plan is that along with militance came ideological change, which contributed to radicalization of the fighters. A return to Islamic fundamentalism replaced separatism as the primary driver of operations, and cross-border attacks began to look a lot more like acts of jihad than the fight for independence."

"I'm familiar with the history," Dempsey said, "but when does al Ghadab emerge?"

"Not until recently. The founder of al Ghadab is Abu Musad Umar, a lieutenant from the Islamic State–Khorasan Province who split with ISKP in 2019. He was off the radar for a while, then reemerged in 2020. His first act of terrorism at al Ghadab was an IED attack in the Jammu Poonch district in October of that year. He took credit for several other attacks of similar scope over the next eighteen months. Then, nine months ago, al Ghadab claimed credit for a large attack in Srinagar that killed seventeen. Next came the recent bombing in Nepal, and of course the assassination—which Umar has officially claimed credit for."

"Where is al Ghadab getting its funding?"

"An excellent question," she said. "Originally, we assumed they solicited funding from Pakistani ISI, but we never found proof of this. Drug trafficking is our working assumption, but we've been unsuccessful in validating that. Unlike other groups operating in the Jammu-Kashmir region, al Ghadab has been incredibly effective at concealing its activities and hiding the identity of its members. Because the region is so volatile and active from a terrorism perspective, we maintain a robust ATS presence there. We have a strong informant network and dozens of undercover agents working to penetrate the various cells. ATS had made a lot of arrests in the past twelve months, but none of them have been al Ghadab members."

"What's ATS?" Dempsey asked.

"Sorry, ATS stands for Anti-Terrorism Squad. The American counterpart would be your local SWAT teams that operate at the police level. NIA is an *investigative* agency. We don't conduct field operations and instead rely mostly on ATS when it comes to threat prosecution. Special forces, too, at times."

Dempsey nodded and resisted the urge to smile or look at Buz. The fact that NIA didn't have a direct-action branch and relied on SWAT teams for their field ops made them the perfect partner for Ember. When the time came to take out al Ghadab—assuming the terrorist cell was in fact responsible for the attack—it meant Ember might be able to conduct the hit.

"Tell them your theory on Nepal and al Ghadab, Ria," Singh said. "It's compelling, and I'm interested to hear their opinion on it."

"Okay," she said and turned to look mainly at Dempsey. "Other than an insurrection by Maoist extremists in 2006, Nepal is essentially terrorism-free. While Nepal does have a military, it is very small. Diplomacy and neutrality is Nepal's national defense strategy. Sandwiched between India and China, which both have very large militaries and GDPs, it would be pointless for Nepal to invest in an arms race it has no chance to win. Also, India and Nepal share an eighteen-hundred-kilometer *open* border, allowing free movement of both Indian and Nepalese citizens with cultural, religious, or marital connections on the other side. Combine this with the fact that Nepal relies entirely on its armed police to provide law enforcement, prosecute drug traffickers, and perform counterterrorism activities, I believe Nepal is at dire risk of being exploited by groups like al Ghadab. In my professional opinion, Nepal is one jihadist epiphany away from becoming a global terrorist safe haven."

Dempsey leaned in to meet her gaze. "So you think al Ghadab has already relocated their operations from Jammu-Kashmir to Nepal?"

"Yes."

"That would go a long way to explaining why they fell completely off your radar and how they were able to execute the Kathmandu attack and the assassination bombing here without any chatter in your HUMINT network," Buz said.

"Precisely," Singh said with a look of pride on his face for his young analyst.

A knock on the shut double doors to their private dining room stopped the conversation.

"Come," Singh said. A beat later both doors opened to reveal three servers carrying silver trays loaded with a veritable feast of kebabs, curries, rice dishes, and oven-baked naan.

Dempsey's stomach growled as he anticipated what he knew would be a spicy, delicious meal. He turned to Buz with a grin on his face.

"What are you thinking?" Buz whispered.

"I'm thinking Munn, Grimes, and Wang are going to be jealous as hell they missed this meal. *Suuuuuuckers . . .*"

Buz shook his head. "I'm not talking about the food."

"Oh. In that case, I think it's obvious," Dempsey said, grabbing a piece of hot naan and tearing it in half. "SAD is taking a trip to Nepal."

CHAPTER 17

EXECUTIVE DIRECTOR'S OFFICE

SHANGHAI SECRECY ADMINISTRATION BUREAU (SSAB)

MUNICIPAL BUREAU OF THE MINISTRY OF STATE SECURITY

XUHUI DISTRICT, SHANGHAI, CHINA

1805 LOCAL TIME

Liu Shazi sat with his legs crossed at the knee, staring out the two large windows that formed the corner of the office behind the director's desk. At the moment the desk sat empty, as Shazi waited for the SSAB director to arrive for their meeting. Through the left window, he could see the Lupu Bridge crossing the Huangpu River, connecting the two halves of Shanghai. Through the right, he stared down at the confluence of the Huangpu with the Rihui River, which allowed the compound that formed the SSAB, and the glass skyscraper at its center, to be surrounded on three sides by water. If not for the constantly present haze of smog in China's most populous city, it all might almost be pretty.

Of course, it was only a loosely guarded "secret" that SSAB was actually a front for the Shanghai State Security Bureau, the most active and powerful municipal bureau of China's Ministry of State Security.

From here, the Chinese intelligence machine conducted covert operations around the world—all for the advancement of the people of their great country. While the MSS headquarters was based in Beijing, the SSAB in Shanghai continued to be the most active and effective bureau in conducting overseas operations. Shazi had worked in both the 7th and 18th Bureaus since being recruited to the civilian agency of the MSS from his work as a counterterror expert with the Snow Leopards. In 7th, he had become a master at counterespionage. In 18th, he was given tasking against the single most viable threat to Chinese sovereignty and influence in the world. In other words, 18th was the United States Operations Bureau.

For the son of a wheat farmer from the Fen River Valley, it was an honor to serve at all, and an amazing feat to have risen so high in the 18th, which he considered the most important Bureau of the MSS.

Shazi sighed. He resisted the urge to scratch at his neck—or better, remove his obnoxious necktie entirely. He was not a man designed to wear a suit and fancy shoes. He belonged in the field, doing the hard work that kept China strong and allowed her to grow more powerful by the day—work so many viewed only as a stepping stone to an office such as the one in which he now sat.

"Ah, Shazi," said Director Gua Dongxing as he returned, emerging through a door set in the wall just over Shazi's right shoulder, which Shazi guessed led to a smaller private communications office. "I am so sorry to keep you waiting. It has been that kind of day."

"It is my honor to wait, Director." It was the only acceptable response, even for an operative at Shazi's level. "I am eager to learn of my next tasking in our mission."

"Yes, yes," Gua said, but waved his hand as if the very thought were an annoyance. "First, let us enjoy the moment. You are to be congratulated for your work. Truly excellent. We have canvassed our broad network of assets within the United States, and there is no indication whatsoever that our operation is anywhere on the radar inside the American intelligence community."

"That is good news," Shazi replied, smoothing out the pants leg of his charcoal-gray suit instead of clawing at the collar of his starched shirt. "And al Ghadab has taken credit for the attacks?"

He regretted the follow-up question. It was something he should already know, but truth be told he had done little but sleep since arriving in Shanghai ten hours ago, and he almost never indulged in television. He should have tuned in to the international news ahead of the meeting or checked with 18th Bureau for information beforehand at a minimum.

Gua seemed not to notice.

"Yes, as you predicted. Your time in 7th Bureau has served you well, Shazi, though I suspect your Snow Leopard pedigree has more to do with it. Al Ghadab released a video just a few hours ago, claiming credit for the death of President Warner and the attempt on Shamone. I suspect they felt it gave them more credence to have wounded the head of Israel than to have missed a shot at Vice President Jarvis altogether, eh?"

Gua laughed, his jowled faced jiggling as he did. Shazi smiled politely to conceal his disgust for the man. *To treat the temple that is the body with such irreverence . . .*

"In any case, they claimed credit for Nepal as well, stating that this was the fate of any who shared a bed with the two Great Satans." He laughed again. "Your prediction was correct, Shazi. I was concerned they would fear the attention this would gain from the powerful forces of the American government. Surely, they remember images of bin Laden, of Saddam Hussein swinging from the gallows, of al-Zawahiri's body . . ."

"These are images that energize them, Director," Shazi explained. "They believe they are doing the ordained work of their god and that to be martyred for jihad brings untold power and station in Paradise."

"And the virgins," Gua said with a softer, dismissive chuckle.

"Yes," Shazi conceded, but still this comment indicated that the man didn't fully understand. *How could you, though, having not walked beside the believers of jihad?* "It makes them powerful and fearless allies. I believe it is important that I return to Kathmandu as soon as possible to meet with Abu Musad Umar. A personal congratulations from me . . ."

"To what end, Shazi?"

Gua leaned back now in his oversized, high-backed leather chair. Shazi stared at him for a moment.

"I don't understand, sir," he said.

It was the truth. Surely such a valuable weapon as what they had developed, funded, and connected in the al Ghadab network wasn't something one just left on the battlefield after the first deployment? The potential of this weapon—a weapon *he* had created through blood and sweat—was, at present, limitless. It had taken the Americans an entire decade to decapitate bin Laden from the head of the al-Qaeda snake, and that madman didn't have the resources or support of the covert operators of MSS helping him hide.

"Shazi, this phase of the operation is complete," Gua continued. "We can't risk further connection to Abu Musad Umar now, not with the Americans surely investing every resource into penetrating their organization. Uncovering even a suggestion of a connection to the MSS would be catastrophic to our mission."

"But, Director—" Shazi began.

Gua raised a hand, cutting him off. "The mission is not tactical, Shazi. Our battlefield is not one we create with bullets and bombs. Our battlefield is strategic."

The man rested his forearms on his desk now, leaning forward with faux compassion on his face.

"I know you are a warrior—one of China's best—but our battlefield now is political. It is economic. Our mission is to defeat the Americans on this battlefield from the shadows, and your work now makes this possible. You forced their eyes away from the deal with India and back to their persistent, lurking fears of Islamic terrorism. Our assets inside the United States government suggest that few even knew of the economic-and-defense deal Warner was brokering with Chopra—meaning there is little chance they return to that table with their new leadership. This will allow us to shore up our energy and, if all goes well, our security and defense relationship with India. It will allow us to bring Nepal into our fold and under the umbrella of the security they will want us to provide—security that India has just proven they *cannot* provide. Again, this is thanks to your hard work."

Shazi's mind whirled, and he slowed his breathing, shifting it from his chest to his lower abdomen to allow his Qi to find peace and focus.

My mind is a clear lake reflecting the sky . . .

"Director Gua," Shazi began, his voice now gentle but confident, "all you have said makes sense, and I receive your praise with pride. I do, however, think there is an opportunity here to inflict more damage on the Americans—most especially in India and Nepal as they investigate in the aftermath of the attacks. This will further cripple them—but more on task, it will further undermine their standing and reputation in the region, raising ours in the process."

"Perhaps true, but risky and unnecessary, Shazi."

Shazi nodded. From Gua Dongxing's own point of view, he might even be right.

"The next time we interact with Abu Musad Umar, it should be at his public execution after our Snow Leopards take him from his compound in Nepal and destroy his entire operation," Gua continued. "This is the victory that raises our standing. This is how we convince Nepal, but also India, that we are more effective and reliable defense partners than the United States. And that will lead to economic partnerships with both, which will ensure our economic dominance over the West, removing our only real competitor from the field of play."

Shazi nodded again, showing deference, but was still unconvinced. He had heard this all before and even saw the brilliance of the plan. Despite the grudging respect he had for the terrorist's skill and cunning, he had no issue with betraying and eventually killing Abu Musad Umar. Terrorists like Umar were, in his mind, cockroaches—a plague on the planet, driven by hatred and zeal instead of seeing the greater good. Shazi had been a counterterrorism operator more than long enough to feel no remorse about ending al Ghadab brutally and for good. But only once they had been adequately exploited.

"There is another consideration," Shazi said, folding his hands in his lap, allowing his slow and measured Original Breaths to come from his low abdomen to bring control and peace. His pulse slowed as they did.

Gua raised an eyebrow and gestured with his hand for him to continue. "And what is that?"

"We missed our opportunity in Tel Aviv," he said, the words stinging as he heard them. His hatred of failure was all that kept him from achieving the true peace of his spiritual Qigong. "As a result, we are left with an American President who is far more capable than Warner ever could have been—perhaps more capable than any President in history, at least in terms of the battlefield we have laid out, Director Dongxing. This man is a true warrior. He led the American Tier One SEALs from the highest level. He fought beside the Israeli Special Forces early in his career. Our intelligence on him from 18th Bureau suggests he continued to be active in some capacity with counterterrorism task forces before becoming the director of National Intelligence and then Vice President. His intellect and his connections to the American intelligence and covert operations communities make him a significant threat in his new position."

"I am familiar with the intelligence reports on the new American President," the director said, clearly annoyed at being lectured.

"Of course," Shazi said, feeling the Original Breath technique already effecting the flow of his Qi, calming him. "But I am familiar with the *man*. He will think much differently than any President in history. He cares nothing about self-preservation, only about his mission to his country. He will analyze what he sees from a master warrior's mind and is the only one in this entire equation—the only one on our political and economic battlefield—who might uncover and thwart our plan. We should leave al Ghadab in play until it is time to destroy them, in the hope of an opportunity to kill the new American President. This will increase our chances of success, Director Dongxing."

The director studied him, his eyes darting back and forth across Shazi's face in a way that would have made him uncomfortable had he not already centered his spiritual Qi. Shazi knew better that to underestimate Dongxing. He might never have been the special operator Shazi considered himself, but Dongxing had risen to his position through intellect, cunning, and a reputation for ruthless brutality when he'd once been a field agent for MSS.

"I will take this under advisement, Shazi," Gua said before inevitably offering the reason he would not, in actuality, consider it at all. "You are one of our best operatives, and I trust your instincts. But a movement against the President so soon in the wake of such a bold attack on his predecessor without adequate time to develop a mature series of blinds and real-world covers sounds to me to be terribly dangerous. Our best protection against the West discovering our role in this is to focus our attention on matters that do not require our being linked in any way to al Ghadab. Communication alone is dangerous at this point. Do you understand?"

"Of course, Director," Shazi said with a gentle smile. "It is my job to offer you insight and alternatives, but I trust your guidance entirely."

A lie, but the only possible answer.

"And I respect and appreciate your insight, Liu Shazi," Gua said, his look softening. "You should take some well-deserved time to rest and recover before your next tasking presents itself. The next days and weeks will play out on the political and economic battlefields as I have explained."

"I will," Shazi said, knowing Gua's words were more than just a suggestion.

"The Bureau has several properties in the Maldives which you would find restful and luxurious, I believe. Perhaps I can make them available for you?"

"You are beyond generous, Director," Shazi said with a gracious bow. "But I have close friends I have been meaning to catch up with in Thailand—from my military days—and this would seem a good time to reconnect. I will be available at a moment's notice, of course."

"Of course," the director said, leaning back in his chair and giving Shazi a smile that suggested the meeting was over. "Let us know what you need. If you don't hear from us, perhaps check in in two weeks, yes?"

"Thank you, sir," Shazi said, rising and giving a polite bow, then heading out of the office. He decided he would not let his peace evaporate.

My mind is a still lake reflecting a clear sky . . .

But he would make a call.

After recovering his electronics, which had been secured in one of the small lockers in the lobby of the director's office, he descended in the elevator from the thirtieth floor, his Qi at peace but his mind still calmly running through his options. In the last decade he had learned more about tradecraft than Director Gua Dongxing had perfected in his decades as an assassin operating inside of China's borders. Shazi knew the importance of the chain of command but also that the endgame mattered. He tolerated that chain of command out of respect for the structure it provided. But he worked for the people of China, and for the nation he loved.

Shazi crossed the lobby, passing through the exit of the security checkpoint, and then exited through the double glass doors onto the grounds of the complex and through the traffic circle serving the front of the building. He turned right, then walked across the footbridge spanning the Rihui River, leaving the grounds and heading toward Jiangbin Road to the north.

At the far side of the bridge, he pulled out his personal encrypted satellite phone. From this phone he ran the network of assets he had developed under various NOCs and official covers. He used his fingerprint to open the biometric lock to the phone—any other method would wipe the phone clean instantly—and pressed the number one.

"Yes?" Zhao Feng's voice was soft but even. Shazi could hear street sounds in the background.

"I need you to set up a meeting, Bo," he said, using the nickname he'd given the slightly older man, who was his subordinate but felt like an older brother. They had fought and bled together many times. Feng was no longer officially in the employ of the Chinese government. But the man was still a patriot. Never did his private, profiteering soldiering conflict with the goals of the CCP.

"Of course," Feng said. "I assume I know with who . . ."

"Yes," Shazi said.

He stopped now at the corner of the footbridge. To his right was the Shanghai Marriott Hotel, where he was staying, but only until he could arrange passage to Kathmandu. This he would do using his connections to a myriad of private jet services, many of whom would drop everything to serve him. He had racked up many, many favors over the years.

"I will be there in a day," Shazi continued. "We should meet tomorrow night. Bo, tell no one from the team there."

Feng laughed. "There is no one left from the team here, Shazi," he said. "After the attack, they fled like rats abandoning a ship of fire, brother. I had assumed you had summoned them home."

Shazi pursed his lips and contained his irritation. It was not beyond the authority of Gua Dongxing to recall his team, but it was still discourteous to have done so without involving him.

"Very well, then," he said. "That is for the best. It will be just you and me, brother."

"I will make it so," Feng said. "And look forward to seeing you."

"You as well. We must find time to enjoy some *momos, choila,* and a few cocktails at Maya."

Feng laughed at that—an inside joke from years ago when they had conducted a covert operation in Kathmandu while serving with the Snow Leopards. Truthfully, while he enjoyed the traditional foods, he was loath to put alcohol in his body these days—unlike the soldier he'd been at the time. For Feng, he would make an exception.

"I will have everything in place when you arrive."

The line went dead.

Shazi turned and headed to the Marriott. He would arrange for his flight, leaving time for a workout in the generous gym of the hotel, an hour of meditation, and time to pack his few things.

Chain of command was one thing, but Shazi lived a spiritual life, serving the greater good now that he had grown beyond being the simple weapon of policy he had once been. If he was wrong, then no one would be the wiser. Feng would die before betraying him. If he was right, then it didn't matter what Dongxing felt about his disobedience.

Success for China would erase many, many sins.

CHAPTER 18

SITUATION ROOM

WHITE HOUSE SUBLEVEL

WASHINGTON, DC

1155 LOCAL TIME

President Jarvis glanced at his watch as he thanked the small contingent from his defense team for the briefing. He had an important call to make—important to him, at least—and it was getting late where the man he would call was located. This meeting had been necessary, but not entirely informative. As a veteran of Special Operations, a JSOC SMU commander, and former DNI, he could piece together on his own what sort of military posture was needed to address the threats to the country that were still out there—both the threat from those responsible for the attack and the inevitable threat from the opportunists who would seek to capitalize on the destabilization in the aftermath. Still, he had to remind himself that, as President, the most important weapons he had at his disposal were the minds of the bright and talented men and women serving around him.

"I agree with the positioning plan," Jarvis said, glancing at his watch again. He had a lunchtime briefing from his Secretary of State in a few minutes. "Extending the deployment of the *Ike* seems warranted, and I completely agree with the plan to position the carrier strike group in the Arabian Sea. This is the show of force we need while we determine just where the threat is. Expedite a replacement for the *Eisenhower* in the Med while you're at it."

There were tense nods all around, and Jarvis rose.

"We can reconvene this afternoon or as events warrant," he said before he left the room, Andy in tow.

"Anything you need ahead of the lunch with Secretary of State Baker?" his chief of staff asked.

"One quick thing," Jarvis said, turning to the former spook. "I need to make a call on an encrypted line from down here before I head up. Just me in the room. Private. I have the number and will connect myself."

Andy nodded but didn't look happy at being kept in the dark.

"Use number two," he said, indicating one of the small breakout rooms to their right. The entire Situation Room was a giant SCIF, of course, from the large TOC-style conference room traditionally portrayed as the Situation Room in films and television shows to the myriad of smaller conference rooms surrounding it in the sprawling complex underneath the White House. "I'll clear the line."

Jarvis patted the man's shoulder.

"I'll meet you upstairs in the Oval ahead of meeting Baker. I'll only be a few minutes, but apologize for my being late."

At that Andy smiled for real.

"I'm sure Secretary Baker will understand, sir," he said.

"Apologize anyway," he said. He valued promptness above a lot of things. He came from a world where five seconds late could mean life or death.

"Will do, Mr. President," Andy said and headed for the door out of the SCIF.

Jarvis entered the small conference room and closed the door behind him, hearing the magnetic lock engage. He sat at the head of the table beside the silver phone, which had a red light on it. He picked it up, but there was no dial tone—or any sound at all. He replaced the receiver and was about to go find someone to help him when the red light turned green. Apparently, Andy had arranged for the phone line.

He picked up the receiver again and dialed the number he had memorized. There was no ringing in the receiver, but a familiar voice came on after only a moment.

"Yes?" Dempsey said in his ear, clearly unsure who was calling him on his secure phone.

"John, it's me. Kelso Jarvis."

There was a short pause, but when Dempsey spoke there was no surprise in his voice. Jarvis imagined that very little surprised Dempsey these days.

"I didn't expect a call from the President, sir. I'm flattered, but I wonder if this is a good idea—under the circumstances."

Jarvis felt more glad than ever that he'd decided to make the call.

"Leave that to me, John," Jarvis said. The silence suggested Dempsey would do just that. "I regret that this is the first time we've spoken since you came home," he began, and just saying it filled him with that very regret.

"First time since our walk on the beach in St. Pete, sir," Dempsey said. "But I never expected a call. You gave me a choice of how to continue serving my country, and I chose. I'm glad it worked out. No regrets, sir."

Jarvis realized that Dempsey was giving him the reflexive *sir* from their time together when they served at the Tier One. Jarvis knew that Dempsey would reserve higher respect for the Tier One CSO and former head of Ember than he likely would for whichever politician sat in the Oval Office.

"Still, we owe you a great debt, John. *I* owe you. And, maybe more to the point," he said, realizing Dempsey would feel no such debt, "I'm proud of what you did and what Ember is doing now."

"We're glad to be out here, sir. This is what we do . . ."

There was something in his voice, though.

"But?" he prodded.

"No *but*, sir," Dempsey said. "But maybe I'm a little surprised to be here in the capacity we're operating in. We're direct-action operators, Mr. President. It feels weird to be sitting in on board meetings with the Indian intelligence community and assisting in investigations. It seems like we should be black-bagging shitheads, finding the head of the snake, then cutting it off."

Jarvis couldn't help but smile. As usual, Dempsey seemed to underestimate everything he brought to the table.

"Well, John," he said, "perhaps we thought that you might be the one man on earth capable of bringing a unique insight into the tactical complexities involved in assassinating a head of state. Not the direct-action piece—any high-level operator can do that—but the chess pieces that would have to be moving behind the scenes. What we need is someone who can help us identify those responsible—the bastards at the top of the pyramid—so that I can unleash Ember to do what it does best."

"And that is?"

"Eliminate the threat, John."

The silence stretched out long enough that, for a moment, Jarvis thought the call might have dropped.

"We can do that, sir," Dempsey said finally. "I trust you will be able to remove any . . . barriers that might present themselves."

"I'm sure I can, John. Any problems with tasking or support, just let Buz and Mike know."

"They are both exceptional, sir. The perfect men for the job," Dempsey said.

"I agree," Jarvis replied.

"Is that why you called? Were you worried I needed a pep talk?"

"Nah," he said.

"So there *is* something else . . ." Dempsey said.

"Only one thing," Jarvis said. "I wouldn't be the teammate I wanted to be if I didn't make the time to thank you personally, John."

"Thank me?" the operator said, clearly confused. "For what? I'm just doing my job, sir."

"Maybe," Jarvis said. "Maybe it's for me, then. But I needed to thank you. For Russia, for this, for heading up Ember's SAD . . . For all of it, John. I know what you sacrificed to be here."

Jarvis thought of Jake, once a boy and now a man in the SEAL training pipeline—an apple that had fallen very close to the tree.

"It's all I know, sir," Dempsey said softly. "Maybe it's what I was made for, I don't know. But I do know that my sacrifice is nothing compared to the teammates we've lost, the men of Crusader, those we lost at Ember, including Shane Smith—and now President Warner. I'll fight with my last breath to make sure their sacrifices are honored, sir."

"I know, John," Jarvis said. "Me too. I promise, son."

"I never doubted, sir."

"Good luck, John," Jarvis said, feeling a sudden and unfamiliar wave of emotion. "And good hunting."

"Thank you, sir," Dempsey said.

Jarvis broke the connection by setting the silver phone back in its receiver. He stared at it for a long moment. He realized that, through his relationship with Dempsey, he maybe understood better how Harel had felt about him. Harel had shaped the leader Jarvis had become, softly and quietly, one conversation at a time over decades. Kelso owed much of who he was to that process. And now, with Dempsey, Jarvis felt the obligation to pay Harel's style of mentorship forward.

So many sacrifices from so many people. And Dempsey's story was just one long lifetime of personal sacrifice, wasn't it? But that was the job they'd both signed up for, and Dempsey had confirmed his ongoing commitment to that mission on the beach in St. Pete when he'd agreed to go to Russia.

I believe in you, John . . .

If anyone could find the way to mete vengeance on those responsible, it was John Dempsey and the SAD from Ember. And that would make the nation safer.

As President, he owed it to those who had gone before to make sure Ember got that job done.

CHAPTER 19

THE IMPERIAL HOTEL

DELHI, INDIA

2228 LOCAL TIME

Elinor Jordan could not recall the last time she'd been this nervous. Not before an op. Not before outing herself to Jarvis in Tel Aviv. Hell, not even before she thought VEVAK was going to execute her in Tehran. She balled her hands into fists to stop them from shaking as she paced her luxury suite . . .

This nervousness—it was what John Dempsey did to her, and she wasn't sure why.

That's a lie, her inner voice reminded her. *You know exactly why. You broke the rules. You opened your heart and let him in. And now you're about to do it again.*

She considered aborting.

The timing was terrible, and reuniting with Dempsey would only be a distraction from her mission. She'd promised Vice President Jarvis—now President Jarvis—that she would help find the mastermind behind the assassination attempt in Tel Aviv. Her investigation had taken her to Delhi and, no surprise, the same had happened with

Task Force Ember. Now Dempsey was here staying at the same hotel as she was. How could she *not* capitalize on the opportunity to do the thing her heart demanded, no matter how illogical?

It wasn't fear of capture or consequence that had her so worked up; it was fear of rejection—a pathetic, juvenile fear rooted in insecurity but also in the hope that the half truths they'd told each other had been more than mutual manipulation. Hope that the intimate night they'd spent together in Tehran had meant something to him too. Hope that her decision in the Grand Bazaar to put Dempsey above her mission had not been the product of a mental breakdown or post-coital confusion.

"Get a grip, Elinor," she said to herself in Hebrew. "You're doing this for *you*, not for him."

She blew air through pursed lips and marched out of her hotel room without checking her makeup or outfit in the mirror. The walk from her suite in the hotel's northeast wing to his in the northwest wing took less than five minutes, which was fortunate because five minutes wasn't enough time to lose her nerve. She'd thought about contacting him covertly and arranging a private meeting somewhere off the grid, but why go through all the extra trouble? Showing up out of the blue and knocking on his hotel room door seemed as good a plan as any.

He's either going to let me in, slam the door in my face, or shoot me. I'm okay with any of those outcomes, she thought with a macabre smile.

She paused outside his door to listen. The spotter she'd placed across the street, watching the room with a thermal imaging scope, had assured her that Dempsey was alone. For her to go through with this, he needed to be alone. That was her only prerequisite.

Not hearing any voices, she knocked on the door three times, took a step back, and stood in line with the security peephole.

She smiled.

No, don't smile.

She relaxed her mouth and resisted the overpowering compulsion to slip into one of the many characters she could become that would make the pending confrontation easier.

Don't do it. No masks tonight.

She did, however, raise both hands, palms forward, so he could see she wasn't armed.

She heard footsteps inside the room, then nothing, except for her own pulse pounding in her ears. She waited for what felt like hours. Finally, the lock clicked, the handle turned, and the door swung open, but only partway. He looked different than she remembered him—harder, more chiseled, and for the briefest of moments, haunted.

"Is it really you?" Dempsey asked, staring at her. But his face didn't register the shock she'd expected. Had Jarvis told Dempsey about their encounter in Tel Aviv? Or perhaps he just knew she was still alive. Dempsey, it seemed to her, always *knew*.

"Yes, it's really me."

They stood in silence for a long moment, the uncertainty a suffocating fog between them. She felt her bottom lip begin to quiver. Dempsey stared at her, shielded behind the partially opened door, his stance seemingly poised for action. His left hand rested on the doorframe and his thick left leg blocked the opening. She noted how his booted right foot was set as a doorstop to keep her from rushing and pushing it open. And she had no doubt that his right hand gripped a weapon behind the door, his finger probably inside the trigger guard.

Then he said something she did not expect, his gaze steady, his face a mask, and his voice a low growl.

"Are you here to kill me, Elinor?"

"What?" she said, gobsmacked. "Of course not. How could you think such a thing?"

He pursed his lips and studied her. His eyes, those eyes that had stared into her soul, that had been an infinity pool she'd lost herself in at her father's apartment in Tehran, were now deep, dark holes devoid of emotion or information.

This was Dempsey on mission.

"How could I not? When I left you, you were a double agent—an instrument of VEVAK," he said, then something flashed in his eyes, something emotional rather than tactical. "What are you now?"

"A reasonable question," she said. She continued showing him the palms of both hands. She turned slowly around so he could see there was no weapon on her back. "But if my mission was to kill the elusive John Dempsey after tracking him to his hotel room in Delhi, where he was staying under a well-secured NOC, then why would I bother knocking on the door? If I were still an instrument of VEVAK, don't you think you'd be dead already?"

He considered that a moment, then gave a curt nod.

"Step back from the door," he said, and she immediately complied.

He opened the door wide, raising the pistol in his right hand as he did—a custom subcompact she'd not seen before, though the *WC* engraved on the slide suggested it was a Wilson Combat build. She moved all the way to the far wall across from his door and allowed him to expertly sweep the hall in both directions. Then he stepped back into his room and gave her a nod.

"You can come in now," he said softly and gave her a wide berth as she entered, staying out of easy reach, his pistol still in his hand, trigger finger outside the guard but ready.

She walked past him slowly, hands still up at chest level, then she turned to face him as he kicked the door closed behind her, spinning the dead bolt and securing the secondary latch above the handle. His eyes never leaving her, he used a booted foot to slide a wooden doorstop into place and kicked it in tight.

"What are you doing here, Elinor?" he asked.

She shrugged while chasing away a million lies that entered, unwelcomed, into her well-trained covert operative brain. She settled on the truth.

"I wanted to see you. I wanted—I don't know—closure, I suppose. Isn't that what normal people call it?"

His mask cracked and he smiled. "We're not *normal* people."

"No, we're not," she said, her eyes falling to the pistol in his hand.

Dempsey snorted a laugh and then took a step toward her. She tensed, but the gun in his hand still had a finger outside the trigger guard. Dempsey was the most skilled—and lethal—operator in the world. If he meant to end her, she would be unable to stop him. She knew that when she came to his room.

He paused in front of her, mere inches away. He opened his mouth to say something but shocked her by pulling her in for a hug instead.

"I'm sorry I left you behind," he said softly in her ear as his thick, powerful arms wrapped around her. "So very, very sorry . . ."

Tears came unbidden, streaming down her cheeks as she pressed herself into his broad chest. She could feel and hear his heart pounding a steady drumbeat. She threw her arms around his torso and hugged him back. They stayed like that, bonded in apology, until finally he released her.

She felt him slip his pistol into his rear waistband. "This feels like a dream," he said. "When I left you, you were dying . . . How did you survive?"

"It was touch and go there for a while, but I fought. I wanted to live," she said, her accent thicker than usual, something that happened when she was emotional.

"Maheen Modiri put two bullets in your back. Why would she turn around and save you?" he said.

"I don't know. Pity, maybe, but after you left, she gave me a choice between life and death. I chose life."

"And what about VEVAK . . . ?"

"I got out," she said, smiling and wiping the tears from her cheeks.

"How?"

"It's a long story."

"I've got time," he said, folding his arms across his chest.

"I'll tell you when I'm ready," she said, and after a pause, "I'm not ready, John."

He seemed to soften a bit at her earnestness. "Okay."

"Do you know about Levi?" she said, changing from one uncomfortable topic to another. Just saying his name caused a sudden hollowness in her chest. Since the funeral, she'd thrown herself into this mission to avoid having to process her grief and guilt over her mentor's death. She would have to deal with both, but . . .

Later.

"Yes, I know about Harel. And I watched a CCTV recording of the funeral and the assassination attempt."

"Jarvis told you I was there?"

"He didn't have to," he said with a crooked smile. "And you look better as a brunette than a blond, by the way."

"I'll take that as a compliment," she said, feeling some of the warmth returning to her chest.

She stared at him for a long moment, recommitting every detail of his rugged, handsome visage to memory.

As if reading her thoughts, he said, "It's been so long, Elinor. I was beginning to have trouble picturing your face." The words sounded heavy, as if weighed down by regret. And maybe something else. Longing?

"I hope you're not disappointed."

"No," he said with a hesitant chuckle. "Far from it."

She surveyed the room, looking for a place to sit. He had the thick curtains drawn, no surprise, but other than that the room looked virtually undisturbed. The design was the mirror image of her own suite, and the only difference between her room and his was that his duffel bag sat open atop a bench that he'd dragged beside the bed. She nodded at a love seat positioned against the wall opposite the room's en suite sitting area.

"May I?" she asked.

"Be my guest. Can I get you something to drink? I have bottled water and soda in the mini fridge, or we can order room service . . ."

"Water is fine."

He fetched two bottles of cold water and returned to sit on a chair he pulled over from the desk by the window, leaving plenty of space between their legs. He alternatingly unscrewed and screwed the cap of his own water bottle while she tried to think of what to say next. When she'd imagined this reunion—which she'd done half a thousand times—it had never happened like this. This was going far better and far stranger than any of her fantasies.

"It feels too easy. I didn't expect it to be this way," she heard herself say, mortified that she'd actually put the thought to words.

"I know," he said, looking at the water bottle in his hands instead of her. "I always assumed, if you somehow did manage to survive, that you'd want to put a bullet in my back and leave me on the floor to bleed to death just like I did with you."

"You didn't pull the trigger, John. Maheen did."

"Does it matter?"

"Fuck yes, it matters."

He met her gaze. "So . . . you don't hate me."

"I'm not going to lie . . . for a long time, I was very angry with you. I blamed you for my suffering. For my pain. For my mistakes. But I've moved on from that place. It wasn't your fault; it was mine. My fate was of my own making, not yours. You have a SEAL's heart and a warrior's mind—you put the mission first, as you should have. As I would have done had I been in your shoes."

He looked at the ceiling, as if asking heaven for help. "That's the rub, isn't it? A SEAL never leaves a teammate behind. But I left you."

"I forgive you." When he didn't respond, she pushed. "Look at me, John . . . look at me."

Grudgingly, he dropped his head to meet her gaze. In his eyes, she saw the angst and regret of a man who'd punished himself for two and a half years for leaving her to die on the floor of that hookah bar. She'd wondered for that same two and a half years if it had bothered him. She'd asked herself a million times if he'd ever cared about her or if she'd simply been a means to end. Now, as she watched his eyes briefly rim with tears, she finally had her answer.

"I forgive you," she said again.

"Thank you," he said, his voice barely a whisper before he stiffened and checked his emotions.

Like gravity from a dark star, she felt a powerful aura from him. She closed the distance and pressed her lips to his, but he didn't kiss her back, which made her feel instantly foolish.

"I'm sorry; I shouldn't have done that."

"I . . . I want to, but I don't understand what *this* is. I can't trust myself, and I'm not sure I should trust you."

He stood abruptly, almost reflexively, to put physical distance between them. She watched the cords of muscle ripple in his forearms as he clenched his fists.

"You're a master manipulator—one of the most talented spies in the world, Elinor. You deceived the great Levi Harel. You deceived the Seventh Order, Task Force Ember, and your handlers in Iran."

She felt her chest tighten in reaction as she watched him pace, his gaze fixed on her. She thought of a caged tiger, moving back and forth in front of the thick glass at a zoo, watching the prey it wants but can't have.

"But most importantly, you deceived *me*," he continued. "Where have you been, Elinor? What have you been doing all this time? Who are you working for, and why are you in New Delhi?"

A flash of indignant anger, fueled by embarrassment and disappointment, almost made her lash out at him. But she stopped herself. She'd sprung a lot on him and not given him any time to prepare. What kind of operator would he be to accept her on her word, at face value? Dempsey knew better. He'd thought she was dead, and it wasn't fair for her to expect him to cycle through the gauntlet of confusing emotions and thoughts that she herself had two and a half years to reconcile.

"You're right," she said in a controlled and measured voice. "This a lot spring on you out of the blue. Those are all fair questions, so I'm going to do my best to answer them."

He dropped his hands from his hips, looking both surprised and relieved by her calm candor. Maybe coming here hadn't been a mistake.

"It's probably easiest if I start at the beginning and tell you everything that happened," she said, tapping the empty seat cushion beside her.

With a throaty grumble, he looked at the space she offered on the love seat, then took the seat across from her instead.

For the next thirty minutes, Elinor told him everything: how Cyrus had executed Maheen Modiri after Dempsey fled. How the hookah bar owner had called an ambulance and the paramedics had arrived moments before she blacked out from blood loss. How VEVAK had authorized her surgery and post-op care at the best hospital in Tehran, only to brutally interrogate her after she was discharged. And how instead of being executed as a traitor, a legendary retired female spy from the ranks of VEVAK had helped Elinor orchestrate her escape from Iran and start a new life. Though she kept the woman's name to herself, Elinor explained how the two of them became friends, a pseudo mother-daughter relationship that both women desperately needed.

"What about your father? What happened to Ciamek?" he asked during a pause.

Even though she'd been expecting the question, it still hit her like a gut punch.

"He passed away from his cancer, about three months after you left."

"I'm sorry," he said. "I didn't know him well, but he seemed like a good man, and I know you loved him."

"It was a very dark time for me, but at least my dad died at peace."

"So, he died believing that we were . . . married?"

"Yes," she said with a wan smile. "He liked you very much."

"In that case, it must have been hard keeping the ruse going," Dempsey said.

"Oh yes, because I very much hated you at the time."

After an awkward beat, they both burst into gentle laughter. It felt good. The entire conversation had been more cathartic for her than she'd expected. They'd both spoken their truths and unburdened themselves, and she finally felt her body relaxing. She looked at him and noticed that the tightness in his jaw and neck were gone now. Equally telling, his eyes no longer seemed to be scanning her face and body language for signs of insincerity, as they had been since her arrival.

"So, you don't work for VEVAK, and you didn't go back to the Seventh Order. Who do you work for, Elinor?"

She sat up a little straighter and shot him a proud smile. "I work for me, John. Only for me . . ."

"You're freelance?"

She nodded but did not get the reaction she expected.

He screwed up his face and blew a little disdainful puff of air through pursed lips, as if she'd just announced she was a contract killer—which sometimes she was. Then, just as quickly, his face changed again, and he sat back in his chair, his eyes going wide with epiphany, as some puzzle piece clicked into place.

"It was you in Riga, wasn't it?" he said, wagging his right index finger accusingly at her. "You killed Michael the Broker."

"Yes, that was me," she said, aware that the confession could either further the trust and understanding they'd built tonight or tear it all down.

"I knew it," he said, shaking his head. "I told them it was you, but no one believed me. Hell, they thought I was crazy or suffering from PTSD or whatever."

She fixed him with a coy smile. "Sorry I killed your scumbag."

"He wasn't *my* scumbag, but I needed information from him, and you robbed me of that opportunity." His eyes went to the middle distance, and she could see him reconstructing the event in his mind. "You had to be working for someone, Elinor. And that someone was working against us that day."

His face did not look pleased, and his voice had gone cold.

"Not exactly," she said, trying to placate him with another smile. "I'm not at liberty to disclose my client or why it was better for the world that Michael the Broker died that day—other than the obvious—but I could have killed him in his hotel room or en route to the pub. I didn't. I let you have your meeting. I gave you plenty of time. If you couldn't seal the deal, that's on you."

The scowl on his face dissolved and morphed into something resembling grudging acceptance. "Nice work with the whole *Thomas Crown Affair*, shell-game escape you pulled off after. I thought I had you for sure."

"Thanks. I'm pretty proud of that one. It's not easy to outfox Ember."

"You've done it twice now, if you count tonight," he said. "We must be slipping."

"Or maybe my team is just that good."

"Your team?"

"Of course; you didn't think I work solo? That would be a death sentence in our line of work."

"True," he said, then narrowed his gaze. "So, what, you're a merce-nary now who sells her services to the highest bidder?"

"No." She had worked very hard to reconcile this matter in her own mind but hearing the words from him still stung. "I'm not a mercenary, John, though I get why you would think so. I'm a contract problem solver who only takes jobs I believe in. It's not about the money for me. It's about making the world a better place, though I don't expect you to believe that right away after all that's happened. Maheen Modiri was right when she said, 'The time has come for the vendettas of a few angry men to no longer determine the fate of millions.' Maybe it was because I was dying when she said it, or maybe it was because it was wisdom I needed to hear; I don't know. But either way, that sage comment was burned forever into my brain. I no longer work for corrupt governments. I no longer serve those thirsty for power. I don't work for nihilistic old men with personal agendas or vendettas they disguise as patriotism. I decide what is just and what is not."

"Mm-hmm, I've heard that before," he said. She thought he was going to say something more, but he didn't.

"You, of all people, should understand this better than anyone. What you did in Russia—paving a path for regime change from Petrov to Narusov—served the greater good. That's what I do now, John. I work in service of the greater good. In this way, we're the same."

His face darkened, and she instantly regretted revealing that she knew about his operation.

"How do you know about Russia, Elinor?"

"After it happened, I did some investigating. I was curious who had the balls and the mettle to take down Petrov. Imagine my surprise when I figured out that it was you. Of course it was you. Who else could have pulled off this most impossible of missions?"

His face remained stoic, but he held her eyes. When he didn't say anything, she felt the conversation had reached a fork in the road, and he was leaving it to her to choose where it went next. But whether he would accompany her down the path she selected was another matter altogether. Butterflies took flight in her stomach as she made her decision.

"Join me, John," she said, leaning forward and looking at him with all the courage and earnestness she could muster.

"Join you how? I don't understand."

"Leave Ember. Come work with me. Can you imagine what we could accomplish together? Can you imagine all the good we could do? All the wrongs we could right when we don't have to serve the whims and machinations of bureaucrats? You don't have to be a slave to the machine anymore. I've found another path for us. Let's walk it together."

He stared at her in silence for a very long moment. When he spoke again, his words hit her like a punch to the gut.

"I'm glad you came to Delhi. I'm glad we talked . . . but you need to understand there is no *us*. A part of me admires your decision to cut ties with the political machine—if that's really true—but I'm with Ember. And I have a job to do."

She felt her cheeks go hot with . . . embarrassment? Anger? Repudiation? All three? She couldn't tell how or what she was feeling in the face of this swift and decisive rejection. She swallowed and forced herself to quickly regroup.

That was foolish, chastised the voice in her head. *You acted on a whim. What did you expect him to say?*

If she had truly planned this moment in advance, she would have known that his rejection was a given. Of course he would say no. If he didn't, she would have had reason to doubt his sincerity. Asking Dempsey to leave Ember was like asking him to cut off his right arm. This was not something he would do spontaneously.

No, to win him over would take time, patience, and persistence. To win him over, she would have to play the long game. But that was okay; she was good at the long game. If she'd learned anything from her long road to recovery, it was how to be patient and persistent.

"You're right. I'm sorry, I overstepped," she said, smiling and sitting back against the sofa cushion. "You're on mission. You have a job to do . . ."

He crossed his arms and glared at her.

"Look, John, I'm sorry. I take it back. Forget I said it," she said and forced herself to say nothing else until he responded.

When he did finally speak, what he said was typical John Dempsey.
"Okay."

"I know you are going to say no, but I'm going to offer anyway. If you want my help with prosecuting al Ghadab, I have resources I can contribute."

"No," he said and abruptly stood. She watched his face cloud with something, maybe indecision or maybe something else. "We're not hiring, Elinor, and if we were, we don't hire mercenaries. It's good to see you, and I'm glad you're okay—that you've found a new season or purpose or whatever. But our President was just assassinated, and I need to find those responsible and end them. And all of this," he said, gesturing broadly to her and the rest of the world at large, "is a distraction I simply cannot afford to indulge."

She fixed him with a closed-lip smile and took a page from his playbook. "Okay."

Give him time. He's not ready.

"Okay, what?" he said, clearly expecting an argument.

"Okay, I understand," she said and got to her feet. She pulled a business card from her pocket and handed it to him. "This is how you can reach me, when or if you change your mind."

He took the card. "Is this for business or personal contact?"

"For you, John, there is no distinction," she said with a hint of a smile.

He slipped the card into his pocket.

They stood in silence, facing each other. Only half a meter separated them. She felt a compulsion to cross the chasm and press her hand to his chest, over his heart, as she had done on the night they'd stripped their souls and bodies bare two and a half years ago. But she didn't dare touch him. No, she would leverage the silence, harness the separation as tools to lure him back to her. She would make him remember this moment—when she stood within his reach, was willing and ready for the taking—and he let her walk away. Whether it took months or years, she would wait for him because he was her kindred.

He was her soulmate.

"Well, then, I guess this is goodbye," she said, taking a step toward the door.

He nodded and walked past her. "Let me get the door for you," he said and opened it.

"Thank you," she said. She paused, giving him an opportunity to hug her, which he did not take.

"I'm glad you're okay, Elinor, and I'm glad you came to see me."

"It was good to see you too. Good night, John."

"Good night."

She stepped out into the hall, and he shut the door behind her.

Feeling his invisible gaze on her back, she held her head high and walked away. Instead of feeling dejected, she felt buoyed. She'd taken the first step, and despite his best efforts to hide it, she'd seen a crack in his armor.

A hopeful smile spread across her face.

CHAPTER 20

Ian Baldwin woke one minute before his alarm went off, which was the norm for him.

He felt rested but not refreshed—also the norm.

He swung his legs off the side of the mattress. The moment his size-fourteen feet touched the floor, the motion sensor under his bed detected the movement, triggering the smart home program to illuminate his bedroom gradually, with luminosity increasing at a rate of 5 percent per second, stopping at a dim, but not too dim, 30 percent. The window shades, which were electrically powered, would open automatically at sunrise in forty-eight minutes.

He wiggled his feet into his house slippers, then picked up and donned his eyeglasses, which he kept on the nightstand. With the world in proper focus, he padded to the bathroom and took care of satisfying the routine, but necessary, bodily functions associated with waking up.

Next, he dressed without showering.

Contrary to popular opinion, showering every day was biologically suboptimal, as it stripped away natural oils and impacted the epidermal microflora, thereby increasing susceptibility to both dry skin and infection. As someone who did not perform manual labor or engage in strenuous daily physical exercise, the only time he perspired was when he was outside in the heat, something which he minimized to the maximum extent possible since moving to Florida, which was both too humid and too hot for his liking. He did, however, like living near the ocean.

Also of note, as someone who was not genetically predisposed to body odor, showering every third day was perfectly reasonable from an olfactory perspective.

He walked out of his bedroom and headed straight to the gourmet kitchen, where his electric tea kettle was already heating up. Like the bedroom lights, the kitchen lights automatically brightened upon detecting his presence, but they increased luminosity at a faster rate and stopped at 75 percent brightness. While he waited for the kettle to come to a rolling boil, he scooped himself a bowl of overnight oats—topped with a dollop of crème fraiche and a quarter cup of antioxidant-rich blueberries. He ate standing at the dining island, which he'd had modified to bar-counter height. At six foot four, standard counters were too short and made him stoop. The dining island was topped with an extra-thick slab of beautifully grained sequoia-brown quartzite quarried in Brazil. This particular slab was beautiful in both pattern and color, and he sometimes found himself staring at it for minutes at a time.

The three-story luxury home—located just off Tampa's swanky Bayshore Boulevard—had been designed by Roth & Hardy architects for the previous owner, but it perfectly fit Ian's modern design aesthetic and sensibilities. He'd paid 3.1 million dollars, cash, for the house fully furnished when Ember HQ had relocated from Virginia to Florida. His wealth would probably come as shock to most of his colleagues, but there was no reason it should. The stock market was nothing more than the world's most complicated, dynamic data set. The same disciplined, predictive algorithmic approach that he used during his day job to break enemy encryption schemes and find terrorists could also, quite easily, be applied to buy and sell equities and stock options. But if asked about the source of his wealth, his default answer was to say that he came from family money. As general rule, Ian preferred integrity to dishonesty in most situations, but he simply could not tolerate the pressure or responsibility of managing his colleagues' money. He'd made that mistake once before.

Never again.

I am not a hedge fund.

The electric tea kettle, which he could hear boiling, beeped three times and turned off.

He fetched it and poured the steaming hot water into the mug on the counter he'd prepared last night, with a bag of English breakfast at the bottom. While his tea steeped, he ate his overnight oats and thought about the assassination of President Warner.

I will identify the men responsible and bring them to justice. Every last one of them.

The sound of footsteps on the main staircase leading up from the lower level drew his attention.

"Morning," Chip said on reaching the top.

"Good morning, Chip," Baldwin said to his junior analyst, who was presently crashing on Ian's gaming room sofa.

For reasons which eluded Ian, the young man preferred to sleep on the sofa instead of in either of the two unoccupied guest rooms. Ian wasn't really sure how long Chip had been staying with him this time. Sometimes the visit was only a few days; sometimes it would last weeks. Ian had no idea where Chip actually lived because Chip never talked about his place. When not at work, Chip spent all his free time gaming online.

Ian paused his mug midraise to his lips.

Maybe that's why he sleeps on the sofa?

Dale, whose spinal cord injury sustained during the Zeta attack on the old headquarters in Virginia left him disabled, lived on base. Dale was also a gamer, and together Dale and Chip dominated just about every online game there was.

At least, so they said. Ian had no reason to doubt the veracity of the claim.

"May I?" Chip asked, gesturing to the container of overnight oats and snapping Ian out of his rumination.

"By all means," he said and resumed taking a sip of his tea. Whatever Ian ate or drank at home, Chip followed suit. Not, Ian presumed, because Chip appreciated or deferred to Ian's culinary preferences, but rather because when it came to health and hygiene, Chip always defaulted to the path of least resistance.

"Would you like me to drive this morning?" Chip asked after wolfing down his breakfast.

"Why yes, I would, Chip, thank you."

As someone with an unblemished driving record, Ian was perfectly capable of driving himself to work, but he preferred not to. Driving was stressful. He preferred to be driven. And Chip seemed to enjoy driving the Land Rover, but most especially the Aston Martin.

After Ian finished his breakfast and tea, Chip loaded the dishes into the dishwasher and the two men left for work in the Land Rover. As the crow flew, Ian's house was a mere four miles from MacDill, so even with the worst of traffic, the commute never took longer than fifteen minutes. Proximity to the base was his primary criteria for residence selection in his line of work. When crises happened, he needed to be able to get on base quickly. Certain commands like the Tier One and Ember were cleared to use a "nonpublicized" secure entrance that avoided the long lines and traffic of the main entrance in the event of emergencies.

Today's drive, from garage to gate, took ten minutes.

After clearing the armed checkpoint, Chip navigated the back roads to arrive at the Ember facility, collocated on the Tier One compound. From the outside, the compound looked unassuming, like a series of construction trailers set up by contractors doing work on MacDill. A wooden picnic deck separated the Ember trailer from the JSOC trailer where LCDR Redman, Senior Chief Riker, and the impressive young analyst Whitney Watts worked. Inside the trailers there were real offices, but both trailers had been built around an elevator shaft that led to a hurricane-proof underground operations complex. Even if the entire south Tampa peninsula went underwater, the watertight Ember–Tier One complex would survive and continue to operate unscathed.

The nature of their work required both organizations to be unaffected by things as banal as weather.

One of the changes under Mike Casey's leadership was the reorganization of Ember's operations center into something akin to the conn of a submarine—where all the different specialists gathered in one dynamic information-processing node to optimize communication, collaboration, and backup. The former submarine captain had definitely taken the "submerging" metaphor to heart when it came to the underground complex, a thought that always made Ian chuckle. At first, Ian had been skeptical of the idea. He liked the old setup, where he and his boys worked independently in their little cyber-skunkworks and came out to brief the team when they had something worthy of briefing. But Casey had put the kibosh on that on day one. He told Ian that on the Los Angeles class submarines, the sonar team was located in a separate "sonar shack" and reported findings over the speaker system to the officer of the deck. But on the Virginia class attack sub, the Navy had made a change and brought sonar into the control room. Like Ember cyber, the sonar techs had resisted the change at first, but the benefits of an integrated operations center, where all watch standers could see and hear the same information in real time and back each other up, had paid big dividends to war fighting capability, reactivity, and safety.

The same, he said, would be true with Ember.

After two weeks of working the new way, Ian agreed. Buz, Amanda, Mike, and even SAD members like Grimes and Munn when not deployed, contributed regularly with ideas to help improve the cyber prosecution of adversaries. They didn't understand the technical machinations of what his division did, but they brought an out-of-the-box perspective he valued. He assumed that this mission—the hunt to find the al Ghadab mastermind behind Warner's assassination—would be no different.

"Hey, dudes," Dale said, spinning his wheelchair to greet Ian and Chip with a smile as they entered the Ember ops center.

After a prolonged and difficult period of depression, anger, and physical therapy, Dale now showed signs of accepting his injury and embracing life and his work again. The young man had proven himself to be quite resilient and had bonded, strangely enough, with Doctor Munn. Ian had always liked Munn, but seeing the way he took a personal interest in overseeing Dale's treatment plan and recovery had given him even more respect for the surgeon-turned-shooter. Dale, from the waist up, had put on a significant amount of muscle and last month had traded his electric wheelchair for a carbon fiber, manually powered rig that he could take on what he called "fun runs with Munn."

"Good morning, Dale," Ian said, surveying the dual monitors at Dale's workstation. "I see you've been busy this morning."

Dale spun in place to face the monitors. "I started pulling entries on all known members of the al Ghadab terror network from the various databases we have sharing privileges with so we can identify persons of interest, build master files on each of them, determine hierarchy, and start tracking their comms."

Building master case files was going to have been Baldwin's instruction first thing this morning, but with increasing frequency his junior analysts were taking the initiative to work ahead. This development delighted him, and while he would have liked to take credit for it himself, it was probably more a product of Director Casey's ethos of self-determination and resourcefulness.

"Excellent idea," Ian said, settling into a Capisco chair and rolling into a spot beside Dale. "Show me what you have so far."

"Sure," Dale said and proceeded to walk Ian through the fourteen different terrorist profiles, plus the data he'd pulled from NSA, NCTC, Interpol, and the Five Eyes databases.

As the young man talked and indexed through the pages, Ian noticed a pattern, and he silently logged each occurrence into his working memory, which was quite formidable. He waited to speak until Dale was done with the tour of all fourteen files.

"I noticed something interesting," he said, then pointed to Dale's trackball. "May I?"

"Sure," Dale said and handed it to him.

With the efficiency of a machine, Ian indexed through the pages, looking at the update history on the NCTC files for each of the terrorists Dale had identified.

"Interesting . . ."

"What do you see?" Dale asked.

"All of these NCTC files were updated in two batches from the same source—the SSEUR database," he said, referring to the SIGINT Seniors Europe shared intelligence network, a.k.a. the Fourteen Eyes.

"That's not unusual," Chip said. He was standing behind Dale, looking over both men's shoulders. "I've seen this guy's name, A. Creed, for at least two years. He manually initiates updates on all files on a weekly basis, pulling new data from partner databases. It's quite impressive because not all the databases are configured for automatic push updates. SSEUR is one of them."

"Mm-hmm," Ian said, but he was already logging into the SSEUR database to look at the source files. "Chip, please dictate the entries aloud. Dale, record them as I go."

"Roger that," Dale said, fingers poised on the keyboard.

"File for Raheem al Gazi updated August 8 by T. Molina, CNI, at 0212 GMT . . . File for Ahmed Matri, updated August 14 by T. Molina, CNI, at 0127 GMT . . ." he said and continued for the seven remaining updated files before finally stopping. "What do you see?"

"All records were updated by the same dude, T. Molina at the Centro Nacional de Inteligencia in Madrid," Chip said.

Ian nodded. "Yes, and?"

"All the records were updated during roughly a two-hour period independent of date," Dale added.

"Do either of you find that time window odd?"

"Yeah, it's the middle of the night," Chip said.

"The middle of the night in *Madrid*," Baldwin said, "but it's the beginning of the workday in Beijing."

"Hold on. Are you saying the Chinese hacked these records?" Dale asked, his eyes going as wide as saucers.

"I'm merely exploring a hypothesis," Ian said, clicking back into the NCTC record for Ahmed Matri. "Let's look at the Matri file preupdate. As you know, NCTC saves the file history so that no data is lost or overwritten because of an update. Ah, yes, precisely what I feared."

"Matri's record is basically blank before the update," Chip said.

Ian clicked over to al Gazi's file and looked at the preupdate file as well. This data on al Gazi was similarly sparse preupdate. He turned to look at his two protégés. "It seems as though someone decided to do our homework for us before the assignment was announced. It is possible that T. Molina was tasked by CNI to investigate and build files on al Ghadab, but I suspect that is not the case. Dale, I want you to find out if T. Molina is a real person employed by CNI working in the Madrid office. Chip, I want you to reach out to our contacts in Mossad and Jordanian GID and see what they're willing to share on al Ghadab personnel. I'm particularly interested in the files on the updated members."

"On it," Chip said.

"Ditto," Dale added.

Ian stood and gave Dale's shoulder a brief squeeze, something he never used to do but seemed to be a leadership trait practiced by Dempsey and Munn. "Strong work."

"Thank you," Dale said, then with a chuckle added, "but you're the one who saw the pattern."

"Ember is a team," Ian said as he walked over to brief Mike Casey, who'd just arrived from the elevator. "We did it together."

CHAPTER 21

Dempsey took a final pull on the beer he had grabbed from the mini fridge an hour ago, still staring at the blank wall as his mind churned through his conversation with Elinor Jordan. He needed to read someone in on the situation—professionally—but he also desperately needed to talk to someone personally about the emotions the encounter had dredged up in him. He set the empty bottle on the hotel writing desk and paced the room while shaking his head.

A part of him wanted to walk straight to Munn's room and spill the tea about what had happened, but then he imagined Munn's reaction:

"Dude, we need to black-bag her and hand her over to the Seventh Order. I'm grabbing a pillowcase," Munn would say.

"We're not black-bagging Elinor," he'd fire back.

"Give me one good reason why not."

"Because I'm into double agents who speak five languages, have the occasional mental breakdown on mission, and come back from the dead.

Also, she looks really great naked and is the only person I've slept with in three years . . ."

"*That's messed up. We're definitely sending her to Israeli prison.*"

Dempsey sighed.

Then there was Grimes, but that scenario played out even worse in his mind. He could imagine Lizzie listening patiently to the entire saga without interruption. When he finished, she would stand up wordlessly, grab a pistol, and march toward the door:

"*Where are you going?*" *he'd call after her.*

"*To do what you should have done in Tehran.*"

Nope. He couldn't talk to Grimes either.

Which left Wang:

"*Dude, did you* really *tap that? Elinor is fire. Talk about a real-life Bond girl. I say we recruit her into Ember . . ."*

Sighing again, he picked up the encrypted satellite phone and pressed 7 on the speed dial to call the last person he wanted to discuss this matter with but the one person with whom he had a professional obligation to do so.

"Casey," the former submarine commander answered after half a ring, forcing Dempsey to wonder if the man ever slept. "Everything all right, John? Where are you?"

"My hotel, sir," he said, the *sir* almost reflexive muscle memory from his past. "And I'm fine. Sir, confirm you're secure on your end."

"We're secure, John. What's up?"

Dempsey let out a long sigh then dove in, retelling *most* of the details of his encounter with Elinor.

When he was done, there was a long pause.

"Do you believe her, John?" Casey finally asked. "Were you able to get a sterile read on her tells and body language? You know this woman; you've worked with her. Did this feel like a honeytrap encounter to you?"

He hesitated a beat, then, hedging, said, "I got a good read on her. I don't think that was what this encounter was about."

"And you're confident that she is not working for an enemy

player—VEVAK, for example—and that, most importantly, she is not a threat to our current operation?"

Dempsey considered the question. What did he really believe about Elinor? She had ultimately picked him over VEVAK in the Grand Bazaar, hadn't she? She could have shot him the back, but she'd chosen to cover his six in that hookah bar. So why did VEVAK let her survive? Simply to interrogate her after nursing her back to health, as she'd claimed? Could he believe her wild tale about escaping and starting a new life? She seemed so proud when she told him how she had liberated herself from the establishment to become master of her own destiny. Her words echoed in his head:

I work in service of the greater good.

"My gut tells me she is not a threat," he said at last. "Not at the moment anyway."

"All right, John," Casey said. "Who else have you told?"

"No one," he said, a bit taken aback by the question. "Not yet, anyway. I called you first . . ."

"Very well," the submarine skipper said. "Keep it that way for now, okay?"

"Okay," he said, drawing the word out. "May I ask why?"

"Do you remember the video of the attempted assassination in Tel Aviv?"

"Yes," he said, already knowing what was coming next.

"We have since confirmed the blond agent who pursued the assassin was Elinor Jordan. Jarvis confirmed this. It was my intention to read you in, but with all that's going on I thought the distraction would be unwarranted."

"I understand, sir," he said, deciding there was no reason to mention he'd suspected as much at the time and not said anything.

"By the way, that surveillance video cut off at the wall, but we now know what happened after: Jordan assisted POTUS in taking down the shooter. She also offered her assistance in tracking down the cell responsible for the attack. She had plenty of opportunities to turn her weapon on Jarvis, so he believes that her presence at Harel's funeral was legitimate, as was her offer of help. For now, Jarvis wants to leave her in play. That said, if she contacts you again, let me know immediately. In the meantime, I'll inform Baldwin, and we'll tag her and her team for signals collection."

Dempsey nodded but said nothing, not sure what there was to say.

"Get some sleep, John; you've got bigger concerns than Elinor Jordan to worry about. The investigation and prosecution of the group behind the assassination is where I want you focused."

"Absolutely, sir."

"Good luck in Nepal."

"Thank you, sir."

The line went dead. He set the sat phone on his nightstand, then stretched out on the bed. A good night's sleep—that's what his body and mind really craved. Ember was leaving for Kathmandu at dawn to commence a joint operation with Indian Intelligence to locate and capture Abu Musad Umar.

I need my head in the game, not in the clouds.

"I've got my friends, I've got my job—the last thing I need is Elinor and all her emotional baggage mucking everything up," he grumbled as he climbed into bed after turning off the lights.

But if that was true, then why couldn't he get her out of his head? Why did her offer to leave Ember and start a new life with her not sound so crazy the more he thought about it? Why was he thinking about it at all?

Maybe the man who came home from Russia is not the man who left.

That, at least, was what Doc Abernathy had proposed in one of their sessions. In fact, it seemed a recurring theme for the headshrinker—how traumatic events change us and moving forward requires embracing who you have become. He'd discounted the comment at the time as headshrinker mumbo jumbo bullshit—after all, what she viewed as significant trauma was a day at the office for someone with twenty years in cover operations like him—but what if she was onto something?

"I don't have time for this shit," he murmured and let out a long, exasperated sigh. "I just need to go to sleep. Everything will feel normal and clear in the morning."

He tried relaxing the muscles of his face and slowing his breathing, but even with these tricks it took an eternity before sleep finally granted his petition for voluntary unconsciousness.

Once asleep, his dreams took him back to Tehran to relive the events of the Grand Bazaar, but as was often the case with dreams, his brain switched things up. Instead of confronting Amir and Maheen Modiri in the basement hookah bar, he and Elinor found their opponents to be Arkady Zhukov and Grimes—with Dempsey shooting the Russian spymaster and Grimes double tapping Elinor in the back. Rather than leaving Elinor behind, this time Dempsey hoisted her into a fireman's carry and took her with him. He made it to the white panel van waiting in the alley for them to exfil, but instead of finding Farvad in the driver's seat, Ivan Makarov was behind the wheel, grinning at Dempsey with his gold teeth.

"You want to go fast, da?" the Russian mafioso said and mashed the accelerator. "I take you to hospital."

"Hurry, Ivan. She's fading fast," he said, cradling Elinor's limp, cold body in his arms.

But Makarov didn't take them to the hospital, at least not a real hospital. Instead, Dempsey found himself standing in the infirmary of IK-2 with the sadistic Doctor Orlova presiding over the abandoned ward.

"There is nothing I can do," the Russian woman said with indifference while staring down at Elinor, whose naked gray corpse was lying supine on a stainless steel autopsy table instead of a hospital bed. "She's already dead."

"No!" he shouted and grabbed the Russian prison doctor by the shoulders and shook her. "Do something. Save her!"

"Why do you care what happens to this woman?"

"Because—because I need her."

His watch alarm woke him. He sat bolt upright, clutching his Wilson SFX9 pistol, confused. It took him a full second to remember where he was. He removed his finger from the trigger and collapsed back into his pillow. The final words he'd spoken in his dream came back to him as an echo.

Because I need her.

If that was true, it was something he simply did not have time to wrestle with right now. He was on mission.

After showering and packing up, Dempsey met the rest of his team in the lobby and headed to the black SUVs waiting to drive them to the airport. Instead of riding with Munn and Grimes like he would normally do, he loaded up in the vehicle with the newbies and Wang. Dan and Lizzie would see right through him, and he needed time to get his headspace square and his armor on. The commute took longer than he anticipated because Delhi traffic was terrible.

When their driver finally pulled onto the tarmac to park by the Boeing, Dempsey noticed theirs was not the only black SUV dropping off passengers. Fifteen meters away, Buz was shaking hands with Ria Keltker from NIA while three male Indian Intelligence officers were grabbing luggage from the back of their vehicle.

"Looks like we've got riders," Fender said, leaning up against Dempsey to peer out the window.

"Lucky us." Dempsey jerked the lever to open the door.

After grabbing his own bag, he moved toward Buz to greet Ria. He wanted to just climb the airstair and find somewhere to be alone, but he knew he had to fulfill his role as team leader and tactical liaison.

"Morning," Buz said with a nod, his eyes hidden behind a pair of Ray-Ban aviators.

"Morning," Dempsey said and flicked his gaze to Ria. "Good morning, Ria. How are you today?"

"I'm well, Larry," she said, using his NOC. "How are you?"

"I'm good," he said. He noticed she was dressed for fieldwork rather than in a black pantsuit like yesterday, a sign that hopefully this wasn't her first rodeo. "Did you and Deputy Director Singh get everything sorted with IB yesterday afternoon after we left?"

A curious smile curled her lips. "I think that would be an opportunistic appraisal of the situation. What's the American expression? We've decided to 'agree to disagree' on the best path forward with the investigation."

In the corner of his eye, Dempsey caught Buz chuckling silently at this comment.

"Ah, so they don't know about this, huh?" Dempsey said.

She touched her nose and pointed at him.

Damn, I like this girl already.

"Well, in that case, we better get moving before they do," Dempsey said with a chuckle of his own. He theatrically chopped a hand at the plane and was starting for it when Buz stopped him.

"Ria, we'll catch up to you," Buz said. "I just need to have a word with Larry real quick."

"Certainly," she said with a nod and strode off toward the airstair.

"What's up?" Dempsey asked.

"CIA arrived in Delhi this morning with a contingent of heavy hitters."

Dempsey shrugged. "So?"

"We need to stay one step ahead of them or we risk getting side-lined for political reasons. I asked Director Casey to push hard for boundaries with DNI Buckingham and encouraged him to direct the CIA team to interface with IB. We'll let the two eight-hundred-pound gorillas beat their chests and dance in circles, and hopefully they'll be distracted long enough for us to do our thing. But . . . that means we can't set this joint op with NIA on fire if things aren't working on the timetable we want. Do you know what I'm sayin'?"

Dempsey could have been offended by the comment, but the truth was that was something he'd be liable to do. Sitting still and twiddling his thumbs was not in his DNA. "Yeah, sure, all right."

He slung his pack over his shoulder and turned toward the plane.

"Oh, and John . . ." Buz said, calling after him.

He turned and met the Op O's gaze.

"Khorosho, chto ty vernulsya," Buz said in Russian.

A grin spread across his face. "Thanks. It's good to be back."

Once on board, he again passed on sitting with Munn and Grimes in the lounge to take a seat opposite Ria in the conference room.

"This is a very nice plane," she said with a wide-eyed expression. "I've never been on one so nice."

"Yeah, it's a pretty sweet ride," he said and reached across the table to flip a little black plastic dust cover and reveal a 120V outlet in the tabletop. "There's power if you need it for your computer."

"Thank you," she said, unzipping her computer bag. "Looks like I'll need an adapter. That plug is the American standard."

"Well, I can't help you there," he said with a smile.

Martin, Prescott, Fender, and Wallace entered the conference room carrying duffel bags over their shoulders, jawboning as they did. Martin was wearing a short-sleeve polo that showed off his biceps. The bulge of Prescott's SOB holster was visible beneath the tight Nine Line T-shirt he wore. Dempsey glanced at Ria and saw her eyes tick to his teammates, studying them.

"Don't mind us," Martin said as they cut through the room. "Just moving gear before takeoff. Be outta your hair in a second."

Dempsey took the opportunity to make a quick round of introductions between the foursome and Ria. When they'd cleared out, he turned his attention back to Ria and the business at hand.

"I was thinking about our conversation over lunch yesterday . . ."

"Yes, go on."

"You said that Umar was a lieutenant in the Islamic State–Khorasan Province but split with ISKP in 2019."

"That's correct," she said, opening the lid to her computer and powering it on.

"What about before? What do we know about his life and activities before joining ISKP?" he asked, wanting to build a more complete picture of their adversary.

"An excellent question, but unfortunately one that I do not have a satisfactory answer to. We don't have any pictures of Umar. We don't even know if Abu Musad Umar is his real name or one he adopted during the radicalization process. The limited profile I've been able to build of Umar is based on information extracted during the interrogation of a pair of midlevel al Ghadab members who were captured during a raid a year and a half ago."

"If that's all you got, that's all you got," Dempsey said, leaning in to prop his elbows on the table. "I'd still like to hear it."

"Certainly; I just wanted to temper expectations," she said. "What I know is this: Umar was born in Pakistan, most likely in poverty. We believe both his parents are deceased and that he has no siblings. We don't think he had any formal education. We don't know his exact age, but we think he was twelve or thirteen when he joined ISKP circa 2014–2015. He may have bumped around other groups, which is common, or maybe he stayed with ISKP the whole time. What we know for sure is that he received his training there before joining or founding al Ghadab in 2020."

"But you're not sure?"

"No. One guy says Umar founded al Ghadab; another claims he was already a member when Umar joined. But what is undisputed, however, is that Umar is running the show now."

"What is he like as a leader? What are his aspirations?" Dempsey asked.

"He's smart, ambitious, and computer savvy. Oh, and he pays well. That's very important. He takes care of his fighters and their families."

Dempsey rubbed at his scruff. "Its impressive that he's managed to maintain his anonymity. You'd think somebody, somewhere would have snapped a picture of this guy by now."

"Yes, it's frustrating," she said and pursed her lips.

"Let's talk about the assassination bombing," he said, shifting in his seat. "The postblast imagery I saw piqued my interest . . ."

"How so?"

"Well, both the yield and directionality were impressive. This wasn't your typical S-vest. To get that device through security and deploy it with that level of directional accuracy and lethality required a high level of engineering and explosives knowledge. Since we're lacking information on Umar, maybe the bombmaker is our starting point."

"I like the way you think," she said with smile. "I'll put out queries to my network of asset handlers."

"Do you have a well-established HUMINT network in Nepal?"

"It's a work in progress. I've been working with the Nepalese for the past six months, and the progress has been slow. But after the attack in Kathmandu, they are highly motivated to prosecute threats in country."

He nodded. "Have you secured a base of operations for us?"

"Yes. We have a dedicated safe house for ISR activities," she said.

"Excellent. But what about intervention activities, in the event we identify a cell or HVT?"

She hesitated. "I would have to get authorization and coordinate with the Nepalese for any sort of direct action."

He met her gaze and saw the unspoken question in her eyes.

During their indoc meeting yesterday, Buz had lied. They'd presented themselves under an NOC as a counterterror investigation unit from NCTC. But Ria was smart. This wasn't her first rodeo—or whatever expression they used in India. She'd said she'd coordinated capture/kill missions and worked with operators from India's regional Anti-Terrorism Squads multiple times while prosecuting terror cells in Jammu and Kashmir. She knew what operators looked like, how they talked and carried themselves. He'd seen her taking a measure of his teammates when they'd cut through the conference room. Surely she was connecting the dots.

He smiled, breaking the tension. "I suppose we'll cross that bridge when we come to it."

On the inside, he felt a little pang of guilt for his new colleague and international partner. Because when, not *if,* they found an al Ghadab den of shitheads in Kathmandu, Ember was going to take it down. That much was certain.

If there was one thing he'd learned over the years as an operator, it was that asking for forgiveness was a helluva lot more expedient than asking for permission. These days, Dempsey was done with asking for permission.

CHAPTER 22

During his tenure as Vice President, Jarvis had attended many Cabinet meetings.

This was the first one he was expected to lead.

The massive, oval, mahogany table dominating the Cabinet Room had been a gift from Richard Nixon and used by every administration after. As there was no "head of the table" position for an ellipse, Jarvis's chair was situated on the middle of the table's east side. Per tradition, his chair was two inches higher than the rest and had an engraved brass plaque on the back that simply read "THE PRESIDENT." Every other chair was fitted with a similar brass plate listing the occupant's title.

The Cabinet consisted of twenty-five members—fifteen executive department heads and ten Cabinet-level officials—plus the VP. Of the twenty-six highest-ranking officials in the executive branch of the United States, Jarvis had picked only one of them himself—Margaret Whalen, who he had appointed as Vice President. Everyone else in the room was a Warner appointee, nearly half of whom had two-term tenure. And the only person at this table with less experience than Jarvis was Margaret, so it wasn't like he could count on her for backup.

Jarvis had always admired how smooth and effectively Warner had run Cabinet meetings.

If he had to give a name to Warner's approach, he'd call it the hub-and-spoke method—with Warner at the hub and all the principals on spokes. Warner had never explicitly made a procedural rule that he directed all the conversational traffic, but the protocol was obvious to Jarvis within the first ten minutes of his first Cabinet meeting. Warner would open each meeting with a quick overview, prioritizing the agenda items. Then with each topic, he would lead the discussion like an orchestra conductor, calling on the relevant Cabinet members to speak, using hierarchy and topical relevance to guide the discussion. If someone got too long-winded or decided to use their opportunity to preach from the pulpit, Warner would cut them off midspeech with a by-name thankyou—a smackdown that was known at the White House as the "Warner whack." By managing the conversations in this way, Warner's Cabinet meetings tended to flow in an orderly, timely manner.

Prior to this morning's Cabinet meeting, Jarvis had caucused with Andy—his chief of staff—about protocol and procedure. In that conversation, he'd learned Warner's predecessor had been famous among the White House staffers for his "free for all" approach to Cabinet meetings, which often resulted in heated and protracted debates with multiple speakers talking at the same time. Clearly that method wasn't going to fly, so Jarvis decided he'd use Warner's method.

Besides, everyone in the room has already been trained in it.

When he'd entered the room, he had, for a moment, felt the enormous weight of his new position, made heavier still by his visceral belief that this might be the one position he was ill-suited for. But the moment he took a seat, all those emotions faded away. He was in mission mode. As a SEAL officer, he'd always felt an incredible, paradoxical calm descend on him just as he entered battle. The more shots fired at him, the slower his pulse rate as he analyzed, reacted, led, and fought.

The same was true today. He was on mission now and would give this his all, lead from his gut, trust his advisers, and get shit done. As a SEAL and later as head of Ember, he'd embodied the ethos that a leader might sometimes be mistaken but never in doubt. That ethos might be more important today, and for the next few months, than ever before in his life. The team around this table were individually the best of the best—but they needed a leader.

Right or wrong, today that was him.

He felt his pulse slow.

He glanced at his watch, then looped his gaze around the oval table to assess the emotional temperature of the room, surveying the faces and expressions of his Cabinet. If he had to summarize the mood in a single word, that word would be *tension*. To break that tension and ease the collective anxiety, he decided that simple, heartfelt opening remarks were needed.

"First, let me begin by expressing my sincere gratitude and admiration for everyone in this room," Jarvis said, kicking things off with humility. "Obviously, none of us foresaw being in this situation, and I'm so incredibly grateful to have this amazing and experienced team of leaders to help guide me, and the country, through a very difficult time and transition. President Warner was not only a stalwart leader and patriot, but he was a lodestar for this nation. He was an inspiration and friend to everyone in this room, and he will be deeply missed . . ."

He paused and let the words settle in, watching the faces around the table. About a quarter of the Cabinet members were visibly fighting back tears, which was a testament to how admired and respected Warner had been by the people in the room.

"Unfortunately, for the rest of us, the void he leaves behind is a big one, and it will require all of us working together to weather the storm and keep the country on track," he continued. "Now, I know that many of you have questions about the terror group responsible for the bombing in Delhi and the attempted assassination of Prime Minister Shamone in Tel Aviv. I know you also have questions—and probably concerns as well—about the priorities of my administration and how those priorities will impact the work in each of your respective departments. I want you to know that your questions and concerns are important to me, and they will be addressed in due time. But for the moment, I think the simplest and most expedient way to address them en masse is to tell you that I've made the decision to forge ahead with the plans and policies that were developed and approved by President Warner. Let me say it again: the Warner agenda will carry on through the end of the term . . ."

He could practically hear the room sigh with collective relief. Just like that, the tension was broken. *This* had been the invisible elephant in the Cabinet Room, just as he predicted it would be. No one liked change, especially major change at the eleventh hour. Even if he had been interested in overhauling Warner's policies—which he wasn't—doing so now would be both practically and strategically imprudent. His focus needed to be on maintaining stability and predictability for the nation's domestic affairs amid all the turmoil created by Warner's assassination.

He glanced at Andy, and his chief of staff gave him a nod of affirmation.

So far so good . . .

". . . The only caveat to that pledge, however, pertains to defense and counterterrorism activities. We're going to go after the bastards responsible for these attacks with the laser-guided focus and extreme prejudice of a JDAM, that much I promise you," he said, summoning his command voice and posture for this statement. Though Jarvis knew that leading the President's Cabinet was very different from leading a room full of seasoned Special Operators in the Teams, he also knew that leadership principles crossed that wide chasm of personality types. Teams yearn to be led, and this was how he led—with confidence and passion, and always from the front.

After seeing numerous nods of tight-lipped approval, he softened a little, reserving some of the hard-ass SEAL bravado for another setting. "Given this is our first Cabinet meeting, I think that it is appropriate and important to give each and every one of you an opportunity to voice your thoughts and feelings on the situation we find ourselves in. That said, time is a precious commodity for everyone in this room, so I ask that you limit your remarks to two minutes or less."

"May I speak first?" asked a well-dressed and confident woman across from him, who he recognized as Kristin Mendelson—Warner's, and now his, press secretary.

"Of course," he said, waving his hand to indicate she had the floor.

"Well, I hoped it might set the tone to know how public perception—and of course the press—are framing the transition."

Jarvis clenched his teeth and tried not to let his disdain for this subject reflect on his face. The truth was that it *did* matter if he wanted to get things done—both in his own mission of finding and eliminating the current threat and honoring Warner's policy legacy through the election.

Andy cast a nervous glance at him—either reading his look or just knowing him well. "I don't think—"

But Jarvis cut him off with a raised hand.

"No, she's right, Andy," he said. "It matters if we want to have the support to follow through on President Warner's priorities. Go ahead, Ms. Mendelson."

"Thank you, Mr. President," the press secretary said. He found that the title she addressed him with was already starting to feel less jolting as he settled into mission mode. "Sir, very reminiscent of 9/11, the country has galvanized around you in a very powerful way. Actually, in a way never seen before—owed, perhaps, to media reports of you running down and killing the terrorist responsible for the assassination attempt of Prime Minister Shamone."

Jarvis felt the eyes on him and was suddenly uncomfortable. In his world, these were actions you didn't talk about or even acknowledge, much less concern yourself with public opinion over after the dust settled. He was a SEAL. The country knew it, and everyone in this room knew it. He was aware that already the media had been unable to resist dubbing him a wartime President whose bearing and pedigree "rival that of Eisenhower and Roosevelt." The latter comparison, he knew, would become even more prophetic when they eventually learned of his Parkinson's diagnosis.

"Let's move on, please, Kristin." The media reports dubbing him "Rambo" for running down and killing the terrorist in the Tel Aviv attack were, in some ways, more problematic than the degenerative disease he was hiding, but both were optics problems for another day.

"Of course, sir, but my point is that it matters. We're a day into this, and your poll numbers reflect a nearly unanimous favorable rating. I bring it up, sir, because we have the support we need to finish this term very strong and push through almost anything we want. It would be political suicide for members of Congress to oppose you on anything but the most radical of agenda. And should we pursue serving another term . . ."

She let it hang there, and now the entire room stared at him.

"We will not be discussing the next administration now, or anytime soon," he said, shutting that down hard and fast. "In a few weeks, the American people will decide who will lead them next, but we have far too much on our plate to waste time on that here today. There is an enemy out there, still poorly defined, who have made it clear they wish to do harm to our nation. We will focus on that and on President Warner's agenda. Are we clear on that?"

He felt his temperature rising and struggled to get it in check. The threat out there, the powerful force in the shadows, waiting to attack again—that, he knew, was the boulder in the road that Harel had prophesied for America. With only a few months as President, he had no intention of walking around it. He would not move it either.

I will destroy it with every weapon at my disposal . . .

"Of course, Mr. President," Mendelson said, unshaken. No wonder Rand had chosen her as press secretary. "I meant only to let the room know that, for now at least, we have relatively unconditional support of the American people. We should capitalize on it while we can. These things can be quite fleeting."

"Understood. And thank you, Kristin, for speaking your mind. Your point is important and noted."

She gave a curt nod and jotted something in her leather notebook.

"Who's next?"

To Jarvis's relief, most of the Cabinet members spoke with measured brevity, expressing their grief at Warner's death and pledging their support to the new administration. A few of the wild-card personalities in the room took the opportunity to tag on a grievance or an "expression of concern" related to policy areas germane to their department, but Jarvis handled them with a simple assurance that he would schedule time to discuss their concerns in dedicated meetings in the near future. The final twenty minutes of the meeting he used to let DNI Reggie Buckingham and Secretary of State Baker field questions about current counterterror intelligence activities and the foreign relations impact of the attacks.

He adjourned the meeting, and as he did, he felt an unexpected wave of exhaustion wash over him.

Funny. I feel more wiped out after a Cabinet meeting than I did running down that jihadi assassin in Tel Aviv.

He made sure not to show it, however. He had a gift for reading people and giving them exactly what they needed when they needed it. He had a knack for empowering people to perform, and he put those gifts to work now. He put aside his disdain for politics and worked the room as if it weren't his first time, shaking hands to personally engage with the Cabinet members who he'd not gotten to know particularly well during his short tenure as VP.

One of those individuals, April Jennings, made sure she didn't miss her opportunity to get time with him before he retired from the Cabinet Room to the Oval.

"Mr. President," Jennings said, intercepting him and blocking his path to the exit with her tiny five-foot-two frame. "April Jennings, director of the Office of Science and Technology Policy."

"I know who you are, April," he said with a smile as he shook her hand. "What can I do for you?"

In his peripheral vision, he saw Andy repositioning to off his right shoulder, ready to intervene and shut the sidebar down at a moment's notice if necessary.

That's my right-hand man, Jarvis thought, grateful for the young man's instincts. *He's already shaping up to be my political version of Dempsey, locked and loaded with words instead of ammo.*

"Sir, I heard and appreciated what you said about forging ahead with the plans and policies under the previous administration—"

"Let me stop you right there, April," he said. "I don't consider the Warner administration as the *previous* administration. With the election around the corner, I consider myself as his duly appointed steward to take his legacy to the finish line."

"I apologize," the woman said, though with little apology in her eyes. "And, I completely agree, and I think you misunderstood my meaning. It was just semantics . . ."

As much as he was tempted to jump on this second misstep, he held his tongue. Squabbling with a junior Cabinet member after his first Cabinet meeting as POTUS didn't achieve the optics he was looking for.

". . . Anyway, as I was saying, I heard what you said about not wanting to change policies and plans, but I was hoping you might consider reevaluating one particular recent decision that the President made that will have profound consequences from foreign relations, research and development, and future East Asian policy perspectives."

"And what decision might that be?"

"The decision not to renew the US-China Science and Technology Agreement. In case you're not familiar with the STA, it's an agreement that has been in place for over forty years that promotes lab-to-lab, university-to-university, and scientist-to-scientist cooperation between China and the United States. Under the agreement, leading scientists and academics collaborate in fields such as physics, chemistry, biomedicine, material science, quantum computing, artificial intelligence, and others."

"I'm familiar with the STA," he said, meeting her eyes with an unblinking stare.

"Yes, of course you are," she said, with an embarrassed chuckle. "Um, but are you familiar with all the negative consequences of *not* renewing the agreement? The OSTP's recommendation to President Warner was to renew the agreement, not to let it lapse. I personally support renewing the agreement and lobbied vociferously that we continue the tradition of collaboration, open and free dialogue, and the sharing of best practices and data sets with China."

"Lobbied vociferously, huh? Like you are right now?"

"Uh . . . yes. Sir." She blushed but stood her ground, holding his gaze.

"As someone who has spent his career fighting for ideals I believe in, I respect your passion and tenacity on this matter. Tell you what, April, you have two minutes to make your case why I should deviate from Warner's decision and renew the agreement."

She hesitated a beat, apparently taken aback by his reaction. "Well, first off, Mr. President, the agreement carries a tremendous amount of symbolism. It signals to the world that the United States and China are partners when it comes to furthering the technologies and breakthroughs necessary to tackle the greatest challenges on the horizon—such as climate change, future pandemics, curing cancer, space travel, and renewable energy sources. Second, as of 2020, China overtook the US as the world leader of published research. China surpassed the US and the EU in terms of total research output, and while their output is growing, ours is shrinking. If we let the agreement lapse, we'll lose access to all their research, data sets, and advancements. And lastly, the moment the agreement lapses, China will recall all of their top minds who are presently working and contributing at our leading institutions—places such as Stanford, Johns Hopkins, and MIT, to name a few. Moreover, Beijing will order all American researchers working in China to return home. This will create an instant brain drain, and all current projects will come grinding to a halt."

"If I'm to read between the lines, you're saying that we get more out of the agreement than China does?"

"Yes, and at China's current pace of rapid development, we, not China, stand to be the losers going forward, missing out on all of their advancements in fields such as quantum physics and computer science, where we are currently falling behind."

He pursed his lips, forcing himself to dial down his own vitriol on the subject, and responded, with a little more condescension than he'd intended, "I have a different perspective on the matter, it would seem."

When she didn't respond, he continued.

"When we entered into this agreement in the late 1970s, China was an R & D backwater. We gained nothing from the agreement then, and they gained everything. And as we educated and shared our knowledge with them, the Chinese government created a robust espionage program to infiltrate our universities, think tanks, corporations, and national laboratories with trained spies and civilian informants. This network of in-country assets, working in combination with Chinese hackers and clueless American patsies throughout academia, orchestrated the greatest theft and transfer of intellectual property in the history of the world. You say that, going forward, we'll be the ones missing out by canceling this agreement. Well, you may be right, April. Maybe the damage is already done and beyond recovery. But I, for one, am willing to take that chance. The days of educating our enemy are over. If China is so good at innovating, I say let them prove it."

"Whoa, okay," she said with real surprise on her face. "I guess I'll take that as a hard no."

That comment made him smile. "Like I said, we'll be forging ahead with the plans and policies the administration already has in the works."

"Understood, Mr. President," she said, chastened. "I'll let Secretary Baker know. Thank you for your time."

He nodded at her and turned to Andy. "Let's head to Oval. I have a feeling it's going to be a very long day. I hope you didn't have any plans for the evening."

Andy shook his head and chuckled. "The moment you put your hand on that Bible and Air Force Two became Air Force One, I cleared my calendar until next January."

He clapped his chief of staff on the back. As they moved to leave, Jarvis paused, turning to look back on the empty room. He'd never expected, not in a million years, that rooms like this might one day be his new battlefield. But it was the hand fate had dealt him, and as with every battlefield he'd ever stepped foot on, he intended to understand it, prepare for it, and conquer it. To do that, he would need the people he'd assemble here, including Andy. But, more than anything, he would need Petra. Already, he felt eager to find her, share with her the details of his first Cabinet meeting, and get her insights on how to make the next one go even better.

Like every battlefield he'd fought on, he would win on this one with his SEAL ethos.

Team and mission before self . . .

CHAPTER 23

POTALA PALACE GARDEN

LHASA (CAPITAL CITY)

TIBET AUTONOMOUS REGION, CHINA

ELEVATION: 12,100 FEET

1311 LOCAL TIME

Lungs burning from the exertion of the climb and head light from the altitude, Shazi eyed a nearby park bench, but his ego prevented him from expressing his desire to sit and catch his breath. Ever vigilant, observant, and attuned to the condition of those around him, Shazi's mentor, Zhao Feng, spared him.

"If you don't mind, my friend," his mentor said, "I would like to sit a moment and enjoy the view."

"Who am I . . . to deprive you . . . of such a moment?" Shazi said in between breaths.

They both grinned and took a seat, letting their gaze settle on the northern façade of Potala Palace. Despite being in excellent physical condition, the combination of climbing stairs and the thin altitude had left Shazi panting. Located on the Tibetan Plateau—the highest and largest plateau in the world—the city of Lhasa was nearly three times higher than Kathmandu and two and a half times the altitude of the famous "Mile-High City" of Denver, Colorado, in America. Shazi's blood was not acclimated like that of his mentor, who had settled here in retirement.

"It is quite an impressive palace," Shazi said of the former fortress, built in the Dzong architectural style of monasteries throughout Tibet and Bhutan. The steep, inward-sloping brick walls, flared roofline, and two-tone white-and-red-ocher color scheme made the Tibetan seat of government both iconic and easily recognizable.

"Did you know that Potala Palace was the residence of the line of Dalai Lamas for over three hundred years?"

"Yes, I did, Bo," he said, using his mentor's nickname.

"Did you also know that I have Tibetan blood flowing in my veins? That is why altitude does not affect me like it does you, my lowland brother," Bo said.

"It has nothing to do with lineage. It's the amount of hemoglobin you're carrying. You've adapted to the altitude, whereas I have not."

"Not true. Tibetans have a genetic advantage—a mutation to the EPAS1 gene governing hypoxia. They call it the *super athlete* gene. My hemoglobin levels are the same as yours. But my lung capacity is higher, and my blood vessels and chemistry are modified for better dilation and oxygen-carrying capacity."

Shazi shook his head. "You snake. All this time you told me that it was your training and meditation that kept you one step ahead of me, old man. When, in reality, it's this high-altitude mutation."

Bo smiled. "Yes, I know, but it made you work much harder, didn't it?"

They both laughed at this and, when the moment was over, sat in comfortable silence until Bo took the lead.

"Tell me, Shazi, why have you come here? What troubles you?"

Shazi inhaled deeply through his nose, then let the breath out slowly. "After recent events, I am questioning my . . . my purpose."

"Are you sure it is your purpose you are questioning, or is it perhaps your methods?" Bo said, his voice a gentle wind.

"Maybe both."

"Unburden your mind. Give shape to your darkest, most disturbing thoughts first."

Shazi looked at his hands in his lap. For a fleeting instant, he saw blood dripping from his fingertips. He flinched and turned to Bo.

"You saw something," his mentor said. "You manifested your darkest thoughts. What did you see?"

"Blood on my hands—the blood of the innocents."

Bo nodded. "A dark and disturbing thought indeed. Tell me: Are you responsible for the bombing in Delhi?"

"I did not press the button, but I facilitated and planned the operation."

"And now you feel guilt for what you have done," Bo said. It wasn't a question, nor an accusation, just a statement.

"When I was a Snow Leopard, my job was to stop terrorists. To find and put down men like Abu Musad Umar. For the past year, I have been living with jihadis. To influence them, I had to be accepted by them. To be accepted by them, I had to be respected. And to be respected, I had to embrace their ideology. Now, I fear their madness has infected me. It is not until this moment—when I have distance, both physical and emotional, from Umar—that I see this."

Bo did not respond for several long seconds. When he finally did, his words took Shazi by surprise.

"In 1937 Japan invaded China. The Japanese did not limit their aggression to soldiers. They murdered millions and millions of our people, raped hundreds of thousands of our women, and used biological warfare to spread disease and pestilence. Before the Japanese, the British seized control of Hong Kong, colonized Burma, wrestled Nepal from Chinese control, and dominated our seas. The Russians annexed territory in the northeast. The French colonized Vietnam and took control of Indochina. The list goes on."

"I know our history," Shazi said. "A century of humiliation, subjugation, and atrocity."

"Yes, but *why* did this happen? *How* could it happen? For a millennia China was the world's only superpower—the world's most advanced culture, with innovations in agriculture, engineering, medicine, and chemistry unknown in the rest of the world. How could the world's mightiest nation, with a massive population and land mass, be subjugated by two tiny island nations like Britain and Japan?"

"Because we were not prepared to defend ourselves. We did not have a modern navy capable of rebuffing the British or Japanese war machines."

Bo nodded. "Over the centuries, the ruling class became arrogant, self-indulgent, and complacent. The emperors did not monitor foreign innovation, nor did they study the methods and tactics of enemies across the sea. The price we paid for their hubris was measured in the blood of millions of innocent Chinese. The Party understands this. The Party has learned from the mistakes of the past and vowed to never let China be dominated, subjugated, or cede a centimeter of sovereign land to a foreign adversary. The MSS is the instrument that makes keeping this vow possible."

Shazi knew all of this, of course, but sometimes it was good to be reminded of such things. Maybe this was why he'd come to visit his teacher.

"Do you believe that war is noble?" Bo asked, sitting up a little straighter as he did.

Shazi didn't answer immediately.

"Why do you hesitate?" his mentor asked. "It is a simple question."

"You taught me that the difference between a warrior and a mercenary is purpose. That a warrior fights for a noble cause while a mercenary fights for personal gain. My purpose is and always has been to serve China. Is that not noble?"

"It is noble, but that was not my question," Bo said with a patient smile. "I asked you if war was noble."

"If the purpose of the war is noble, then committing war must also be noble."

Bo nodded, and so Shazi continued.

"I understand this, but some acts of war—like the pillaging and raping of our people by the Japanese soldiers—are clearly not noble."

"Every warrior must decide where the line between noble and

ignoble resides," Bo said, measuring his words like the teacher he was. "This is something you must decide for yourself. The false flag operation you conducted in Delhi killed two emperors—one American, one Indian—who together were forming an alliance imagined with one purpose and one purpose only: to diminish China's economic and military dominance in the region. The tactics and methods of war must evolve or China will suffer the same fate tomorrow that it suffered in the last century." Bo bowed his head toward Shazi. "You have learned all that I can teach you. You are a true and noble warrior."

Shazi bowed his head in deference, but his mentor's statement was untrue.

I will never be as wise as you.

"Gua has instructed me to take time off," Shazi continued, frustrated. "After, he plans to give me new tasking. He is satisfied with the outcome."

"And you? Are you satisfied?"

"No," Shazi confessed. "The operation in Israel failed."

"Jarvis was the intended target?" Bo asked, making the leap in logic that few others could.

Shazi nodded. "And I fear that in this failure I have made things worse. Yes, we rid ourselves of an emperor, but in his place, we now have a general."

"I see. This is a problem, both for you personally and for China. If you follow Gua's orders, the nation could suffer. If you disobey, then you are a mercenary. What are you going to do?"

"I don't know. I was hoping you could help me find the true path."

The old warrior patted Shazi's knee, then stood. "To see what is right, and not to do it, is want of courage and principle."

"That's not helpful."

"When I see him in the next life, I will tell Confucius that you said that," Bo said with a chuckle and began to walk away.

"Where are you going?"

"To climb some more steps. I made a reservation to tour the palace.

Come on, let's go . . . Unless, of course, in the face of adversity your plan is to give up."

I suppose I deserve that, Shazi thought as he leapt to his feet and strode into the lead.

"High-altitude mutation be damned; I'm beating you to the top, old man."

CHAPTER 24

NIA SAFE HOUSE

JUST OFF GOLFUTAR ROAD

NORTHERN EDGE OF KATHMANDU AT

    SHIVAPURI NAGARJUN NATIONAL PARK

KATHMANDU, NEPAL

1115 LOCAL TIME

Coffee in hand, Dempsey walked from the kitchen, past the bunk rooms, to a staircase leading down to the spacious furnished base-ment that had become their ops center. Ria had told him that the exterior doors to the safe house were hardened, the windows made from ballistic glass, and all the comms had UPS battery backups and utilized cleverly concealed antenna arrays on the roof. Obviously, NIA had not slapped this safe house together just for this operation. The Golfutar Road house was a mature, evergreen site they'd used before—or someone had.

At the bottom of the staircase, Dempsey stepped into a wide room, with banks of flat screens on the wall, a communications station, and a large conference table where Grimes and Munn were leaning over Ria's shoulder and peering at the screen of her open laptop. Wallace was seated to Ria's right. Buz paced behind them, apparently deep in thought, and to Dempsey's shock, Richard Wang was at the far end of the table, working intensely on his own laptop. Two of Ria's other three NIA agents sat across from the group at Ria's computer, leaned together and talking in hushed whispers.

"Did I miss something?" Dempsey asked, taking a pull from the coffee in his hand.

"Glad you're here, Larry," Buz said. "We've had a development."

Dempsey cocked an eyebrow.

"I took your suggestion from yesterday to leverage our local asset pool to investigate potential bombmakers with the skill to create the type of device that killed our Prime Minister and your President," Ria said. "We have a hit."

"Excellent. Let me get the rest of the team," Dempsey said and hollered up the stairs for Prescott.

A moment later, a chorus of booted feet came pounding down the stairs. Prescott arrived with Fender and Lewis in tow. Together they took their seats at the far head of the table.

"Here, I can put it on the big screen," Ria said.

Dempsey took a seat beside two NIA agents on Ria's team, one of whom was named Ravi something and seemed like Ria's second-in-command. The other man's name he couldn't pronounce—and neither could anyone else, for that matter—so they'd taken to calling him Dak, which the younger agent didn't seem to mind. The third and final NIA agent on the crew, Amir Yadav, was not with them at the safe house. Dempsey remembered Yadav's surname easily, maybe because it had a Russian ring to it.

An image of a man dressed in a traditional *shalwar kameez*—what Munn still insisted on calling a *man dress*—and a Pashtun cap and sunglasses filled the screen. The man's weathered face wore a grim and serious expression, with pinched lips mostly hidden under a bushy beard.

"This man is Zafar Saeed," Ria began and tapped her computer to show a higher-resolution image of what Dempsey immediately saw to be the same person. This time, however, it was a full-body shot of the man, his beard now closely trimmed, wearing slacks, a gray sports coat, and a black shirt. "This is also Zafar Saeed, taken this morning in front of an electronics store in Patan, a suburb just south of Kathmandu proper," she continued. "Here in Nepal, he is using the alias of Kiran Bir Khatri—a registered name with credentials, including a birth certificate. As Zafar Saeed in Pakistan, he was a well-known bomb-maker and midlevel leader in Lashkar-e-Taiba—translated as 'Army of Righteousness'—a powerful terror organization in Pakistan with the stated goal of merging the entire Kashmir region of India with Pakistan under the flag of a global caliphate."

"We're familiar with Lashkar," Prescott said. "We looked at them for something inside Pakistan not long ago, but they seemed to have faded into the shadows a bit."

Dempsey nodded, but he wasn't sure he was familiar with the organization other than from a few high side briefs he'd scanned. Whatever Tony was talking about must have been while he was still inside Russia, hunting Petrov.

"Indeed," Ria said. "They are still a threat, but much of their senior and midlevel leadership has defected to other, more aggressive and kinetic organizations, such as ISIS, AQAP, and, it would appear, al Ghadab."

Two new pictures filled the screen: a better picture of the electronics store Ria had referenced and then, on the other half of the screen, a very poor image of a dark room with workbenches set up in a U shape.

"Our asset has confirmed that from this electronics store in Patan, Saeed is running a bombmaking cell as part of al Ghadab. It is believed that he is far more than just a bombmaker, however, and that he is perhaps a high-level leader in the organization, at least locally. While he does not appear to have leadership in global operations, Amir's asset believes he may be the number-two guy for the operation in Kathmandu. We believe this cell runs all operations in India as well."

"Can you share all raw signals intelligence you've collected on Saeed with us?" Grimes asked.

Ria gave her a sheepish smile but shook her head. "Regrettably, I cannot. I routed a request through my chain of command to share our source data, but it was denied."

"By Singh?" Buz asked, his annoyance obvious.

"No," Ria said. "The director understands the importance of sharing resources as a team. But he was overruled."

"By IB?" Dempsey pressed.

"Not directly, as we do not fall under their chain of command. But they do have considerable influence at higher levels of government."

"Well, ain't that some bullshit?" Munn said, snorting and shaking his head. "Some joint task force we are."

"I am sorry," Ria said, and Dempsey knew she was. "If there was anything I could do . . ."

"It doesn't matter," Dempsey said, but knew it did. Hopefully, Baldwin and the boys back home could find another way to get it. In the meantime, he'd order Wang to start collecting in parallel. "We have a location and a target. That's all we need to conduct a raid. Time to start planning. We hit the electronics store tonight."

"Impossible," the agent he knew as Dak said. "We're not authorized for any such operation—"

"And we're not staffed for it," Ria said, cutting her agent off. "I can probably get authorization for a direct-action mission, but we will need to wait to get a strike team from the Garud Commando Force or Navy MARCOS."

"It needs to be 22 SG," Dak said, referring to the Indian Black Ops team Dempsey was very familiar with. They were some of the most elite operators in the world, by reputation at least. "Any operation must be deniable if we're going to conduct it inside of Nepal on a short timeline."

"Not necessary," Dempsey said, looking at Buz, who didn't give him the nod but didn't shut him down either. "You have us. These types of operations are our *specialty*."

"What? No," Ravi said. "You are investigators like us. This is a direct-action mission on a terrorist cell."

Dempsey saw Ria's jaw muscles tighten. "It appears our American partners have omitted some details about their capabilities, and perhaps even their charter."

"What are you saying, Ria?" Ravi said, still not getting it.

"I am saying that they are a direct-action team for the CIA." She folded her arms, her expression going smug as she pierced the first layer of Ember's NOC—just as Buz had predicted. "Nevertheless, I can't authorize a capture/kill operation targeting the bombmaker, Saeed."

"With all due respect, Ms. Keltker," Buz said, speaking for the first time, "we don't need your authorization because we don't fall under your chain of command."

Out of the corner of his eye, Dempsey saw Richard Wang offer Munn a fist to bump, but Munn, to his credit, shook his head with a *Not the time* look on his face.

"Even if you could get permission from your leadership—" she said.

"I already have permission," Buz countered, his voice even and calm. "ODNI has given me autonomous authority over this operation, Ms. Keltker. Mr. Dempsey here will put together a mission with his team to take Saeed and any intelligence we can acquire off the X."

"We should conduct the hit dressed as Nepal special police," Munn said to Dempsey. "The uniforms might keep Umar from bolting too quickly once he hears we took his bombmaker. It could give us a day or more of extra time to find him."

"I like that," Grimes said.

"Me too," Dempsey agreed.

"I thought your name was Larry Jones," Ria said, lifting a very unsurprised eyebrow.

"Looks like you got me," Dempsey said with his best Team-guy grin. "I'm John."

She shook her head.

"This is why the CIA has the reputation that it does," Dak said.

"Look," Buz said, ending the bickering before it could begin. "Our team is making this hit on the people responsible for the death of our

President and your Prime Minister. This is our best lead so far. We'll bring anyone we can take off the X back here, along with whatever else we can uncover from the site. We'll share all the information we have . . ."

"Unlike some people," Wallace said with a snort.

"Yeah," Wang added.

"That's enough, Richard," Dempsey said. He looked at Wallace and gave a curt shake of his head. "Ria is operating inside her own ROE, and we'll do the same. We'll share anything we find for sure."

"I know you will," Ria said, fire in her eyes, "because I'm going with you."

"What?" Ravi protested. "Ria, you can't. We must wait for 22 . . ."

"Have you not been listening, Ravi? They're going tonight, with or without our consent," she said. "We can't wait for 22 SG. And we're not *all* going, just me. You, Dakshasha, and Amir will stay here. I will be the lone representative from NIA."

Dempsey studied her determined face and looked at Buz, who shrugged and nodded.

"Okay, Ria," Dempsey said. "We'll place you on the op."

"Oh my God, Ria, you're going to die," Dak said.

"No, she won't," Dempsey said, giving Dak a hard look that wilted him on the spot. "I'll keep her safe. That is also what I do." He turned back to Ria. "You'll be fine."

"I know." She met his gaze, and in her eyes, he saw both fire and courage.

"Finish your brief, Ria," he said to her. "And after, we'll get some satellite coverage lined up for the op to augment whatever SIGINT collectors and surveillance you have in place."

Ria stared at him a moment and grudgingly accepted the power shift. As of this moment, everyone in the room now understood who was running the show.

"Okay," she said. "The electronic store is located on a road called Fulbari Marg Purba between Thecho Chapagaun Road and the F102 highway here . . ."

Ria clicked the mouse and a map filled the TV screen.

Dempsey glanced at Grimes, who gave him a nod, and then at Munn, who had a *Let's get some* look on his face.

God, it was good to be with his team and in the field, he thought. Ember was back. And he was starting to feel like maybe John Dempsey was too.

CHAPTER 25

Dempsey sat in the front passenger seat of the crappy cargo van, his knees jammed against the dashboard console. He would have greatly preferred to be in an up-armored truck, or have the spaciousness of a Chevy Suburban, but he'd learned long ago that you go to war with the assets available, not the ones you wish you had. He glanced over at Martin, who was in the driver's seat, tapping his thumb quietly but persistently against the steering wheel.

"We should be getting an update from the satellite feed any second, then we'll get going," Dempsey said. "I want to have a good handle on thermals inside and around the electronics store before we move."

"Yep, it's all good," Martin said, but Dempsey could feel the pent-up energy leaking from his teammate.

Dempsey got it. Martin was anxious to get out of the van and hit the target. No matter how experienced an operator was, the waiting was always the hardest part. Finding a way to contain and retain the adrenaline and energy during the pre-op pause—instead of letting it burn off like jet fuel in a plane holding at the end of the runway—was a goal for every operator.

And Dempsey was no exception. He'd spent decades trying to master "waiting," but even as a seasoned pro, impatience still sometimes got the better of him.

"Is the weapon okay, Ria?" Grimes said from the bench seat behind Dempsey. "You look . . . concerned."

The comment made Dempsey turn to see Ember's sniper in residence gesturing to the rifle in the NIA agent's lap. Ria, who was medium height and build, looked small beneath the kit they'd put together for her.

"Yes, I believe so," Ria said after a beat, but her voice betrayed her. "I've fired assault rifles, but this one seems different from the ones I trained on."

Dempsey noted that instead of gripping the weapon with positive control like the rest of the Ember operators, the short-barreled Wilson Combat SBR Tactical was resting on her lap, her hands limp at her sides.

"Don't worry; it will handle the same . . ." Grimes said.

The team had contracted with Wilson Combat to design an assault rifle that would be standardized for the SAD members, an initiative Munn had undertaken while Dempsey was in Russia. The result was one of the best tactical rifle platforms Dempsey had ever handled, so he had no complaints.

". . . it packs a little more punch than a standard M4 since it's chambered in 300 HAM'R instead of 5.5, but these are precision-made, custom-spec'd, high-end rifles, so you'll probably not notice any additional recoil."

"Okay," Ria said and shifted her right hand to the pistol grip. Dempsey suspected firing recoil wasn't what had the NIA agent worried, but he admired how Grimes smoothly distracted her with the information anyway.

"Yankee Actual, this is Dark Horse," came Baldwin's clipped voice in the tiny receiver/transmitter in Dempsey's left ear. The signals director had insisted on the call sign Dark Horse after some thriller novel he'd read and loved, and they'd indulged him since he rarely made such a request. Wang, who was running comms and signals from back at the NIA safe house eleven miles north of them, was Homeplate.

"Go for Yankee One," Dempsey said.

"Well, we made another pass and have an update for you," Baldwin said, not even trying to keep within comms protocol to be short, concise, and to the point. Dempsey resisted the urge to sigh. After all, having Baldwin and Wang in his ear was familiar and comfortable and felt like home. "The target building has no thermals suggesting sentries, but we have two heat signatures inside—"

"Only two?" Dempsey said.

"Only two *confirmed*. Understand, Yankee, structural interference prevents us from seeing into the basement. Intelligence suggests this is where the bombmaking activities take place. Unfortunately, we have no idea how many tangos may be in residence down there."

A pause ensued, as if Baldwin were waiting for comment. Thank God no one fired off a snide remark, as Dempsey would hate for someone to hurt the Professor's feelings.

"So, anyway," Baldwin went on, "the lot behind the electronics shop is empty, but it does have structures on both sides. One is listed as a butcher shop; the other appears to be the Nepalese version of a convenience store. As is typical, the business is located on the ground level with residence apartments above. It is possible that one of the neighboring units could be owned, or occupied, by al Ghadab and harbor a quick reaction force. We have four signatures in the unit to the east, and two on the west. Lastly, there is also a black sedan parked in front of the target shop on the street to the north, but the vehicle is unoccupied."

Another pause . . .

"Copy all, Dark Horse. Anything else?" Dempsey finally said.

"No, my report was comprehensive. Over and out for Dark Horse."

"One, Homeplate," came Wang's voice now. "All future comms will come from me, and I'm receiving all data from Dark Horse in real time."

"One," Dempsey said.

"Two," Munn acknowledged from where he was staged in the other vehicle, ready to lead the second stick of Prescott, Fender, and Lewis. "Thank God for Homeplate," Munn added, apparently unable to resist getting in a dig.

"Two, One—let's roll. Homeplate, Yankee is leaving Miami," Dempsey said, using the checkpoint code for the staging area south of the X.

The hardest part of this op was how tightly packed the buildings were throughout Kathmandu and the overwhelming volume of people and vehicles in Nepal's largest city. Even nearing midnight, the trip from the X back to the safe house—a mere eleven miles—was briefed to take over forty minutes.

Martin maneuvered the van east toward Shital Street, where the X was located. Munn's stick would wait at the intersection of Fulbari Purba Street and loiter around the main road of F23 and the rare empty lot just behind the target house. The existence of the empty lot decon-flicted the infil and breach tremendously.

Sometimes it's better to be lucky than good . . .

"I wish we had that drone the head shed promised for the op," Martin said, referring to the Predator UCAV Baldwin supposedly arranged to have in orbit from the Indian Air Force, but which had not arrived yet.

"Yeah, and I wish I had a pet dragon I could ride, but it is what it is," Wallace said from where she sat alone, fully kitted-up and looking badass, in the third-row seat at the rear.

Dempsey chuckled at the dig, then said, "We've got satellite coverage."

"Yeah, I know," Martin said. "I'm just sayin'."

Minutes later they arrived at the checkpoint by the target build-ing, and Dempsey was relieved to find no streetlight illuminating the empty lot. There was, however, a beat-up pickup truck parked close to the target building.

"No thermals in that truck, One," Wang said, anticipating Dempsey's every need for data. "And the engine is cold, so it's been there a while."

"Check," Dempsey said.

Lights out, Martin pulled them quietly into the lot, turning slowly to angle the truck back toward Fulbari Purba Street for the exfil. If all went well, they'd black-bag bombmaker Zafar Saeed and take him off the X and out the back, where he'd ride to the safe house with Dempsey's stick.

"Yankee One is Cleveland," Dempsey said.

"Two is Dallas," Munn said. "We'll move in on your call."

Dempsey turned to face his teammates. "Let's not forget our HVT is a bombmaker. You never know when or how those crazy bastards are going to decide to blow themselves up."

He got nods of acknowledgment from his team.

"Two," Munn acknowledged for his stick.

"All right, Grimes, you're up," he said.

Grimes jerked the door handle, pulled the slider door open on her side, and slipped into the night. Dempsey watched her dart across the empty lot, angling for a small two-story home to the east of the target, where she would set up as overwatch. She carried a highly customized sniper rifle—built using the Wilson Combat Tactical Recon platform— on her back while she scanned over her SBR. She disappeared into the shadows of an alley to begin her climb. Then, after what seemed like an impossibly short amount of time to get into position, she reported in.

"Yankee Eight is now Mother," she said, announcing she was ready and able to rain death from above for her team.

Dempsey could picture her stretched out, breathing slowly, scanning around them through her Leupold 5HD and the AN/PVS-30 she would have added for night vision. Knowing she was there was like having God looking over your shoulder.

"Roger, Mother," Dempsey said and opened his door quietly. "We're going, Two," he said.

A double click told him Munn had heard.

The plan was for Munn's vehicle, which had stopped a block away, to slowly creep toward the X. Bravo team—Munn, Prescott, Lewis, and Fender—would not exit their vehicle and begin the assault from the front until Dempsey called "Denver," signifying that his stick—Alpha squad—was in position and ready to breach from the rear. Bravo would breach seconds later, taking the defenders inside by surprise.

Dempsey led Alpha through the night and toward the bushes to the left side of the heavy industrial door at the rear of the so-called electronics shop. There, he raised a closed fist, pausing them in the shadows.

"Stay close," he whispered to Ria and pointed to a spot trailing him at his eight o'clock.

When she didn't respond, Dempsey looked over to see her nodding slowly, but her eyes didn't look confident. To her credit, though, they were not filled with the fear he'd expected to see. And her rifle was in a reasonable combat carry, her trigger finger tapping away nervous energy outside the trigger guard.

"We'll take care of the shooting," he said. "You just stay behind me."

"Okay," she said, and this seemed to relax her a bit.

Dempsey chopped a hand, and Martin and Wallace took up a position on the other side of the door. He watched Wallace press a preformed breacher strip onto the door at the handle and dead bolt, connect the det cord to the bottom of the strip, and then press against the wall with a compact detonator in her hand.

The former SWCC officer looked up and held Dempsey's eyes, signaling she was ready.

"One is Denver," he said, then turned his head and closed his eyes to preserve his night vision.

A three count later, she detonated the breacher with a thud and metallic reverberation that shook his chest. Dempsey whirled to the gap in the door as Martin rolled a flash-bang grenade through the crack just as shouts sounded inside.

A louder, percussive *whumpf* followed, accompanied by a flash of light, and the lead breachers—Martin and Wallace—went through the door.

Dempsey followed a heartbeat later, sensing Ria was in tow just to his left. He surged forward, knowing Martin would be clearing the right rear corner and Wallace the left. He scanned over his SBR Tactical through the Aimpoint Micro T-2, moving the red dot across the small back office.

Almost immediately a shooter popped into view, appearing from behind a metal bookshelf in the main room of the shop. Dempsey moved the red dot onto his forehead and squeezed. His rifle burped a round through the Whisper suppressor, and a puff of dark red erupted from the man's head as he pitched backward. At the same time, two rapid cracks of gunfire echoed, along with muzzle flashes, to his front left. Twin muffled return shots from Wallace suggested she had eyes on the tango.

A breacher detonation followed, signaling Munn and his team were entering from the front.

Time passed in a blink, and soon Alpha and Bravo teams met in the middle of the shop. Munn and Lewis took position at the bottom of the stairs leading up to the residence above the store while the rest of the team cleared behind shelves, display cases, and the desk with a cash register.

Dempsey heard footfalls from above.

He watched Munn squat low and fire twice up the stairs in rapid succession. Dempsey heard the racket of a man and rifle tumbling down the stairs and sprinted to join Munn, squeezing in beside Lewis.

"Secure here," he barked to Lewis and turned to give instructions to the rest of the team. With hand signals, he said, "I want two at the back door to cover our six; three here in the shop covering the front entrance and that door leading to the basement stairs. Two and I are clearing upstairs."

Without words, the seasoned Ember operators repositioned as ordered.

"What about me?" Ria asked.

"You stay here. I'll be back."

She nodded and shifted to stand next to Martin.

Based on thermal imagery from Baldwin, there was a single remaining tango upstairs. Dempsey's gut told him that heat sig was Zafar Saeed, their HVT. If not, they would be forced to clear the basement, a task he would prefer to avoid.

Dempsey moved rapidly up the stairs, side by side with Munn, their footfalls nearly silent.

"I still show one thermal upstairs," Wang said. "Top of the stairs, turn left, last room on the north side, which is your right . . ."

"One," Dempsey said softly.

On cresting the top of the stairs, he turned left and cleared the hallway.

"The figure is crouched in a corner, possibly kneeling," Wang continued, filling in the tactical picture. "He appears to be hiding inside a closet or bathroom. He's holding something, body position suggests it's a rifle. I can't make out all the details, but he's definitely there, not moving, in the northwest corner of the room."

Dempsey double-clicked his acknowledgment.

The last door on the right—leading to the target room—hung partially open. Dempsey stayed low in a deep crouch as he moved silently down the hall. On reaching the doorframe, he stopped, exhaled, and stuck his head out for a quick look through the narrow gap between the door and the jamb. As quick as he popped his head out, he snatched it back again while his mind processed the split-second imagery he'd collected. The bedroom appeared empty on first blush, but that was the beauty of thermal imaging. The shooter was hiding in the shadows of a closet on the far side of the room—invisible to Dempsey, but not to Wang.

Dempsey craned his neck to look back at Munn. In a barely audible whisper, he said, "Closet in the corner."

Munn nodded.

Dempsey exhaled, clicked on his gun light, and surged into the room through the gap between the door and the doorframe. As he did, his left shoulder hit the door and knocked it the rest of the way open, but his attention and focus were entirely on his target and the white beam of his gun light. The shooter was waiting in ambush, giving him the advantage, but Dempsey had kinetics and experience on his side.

Everything seemed to dissolved, save for the circle of light ahead of him. The focused beam illuminated the inside of the closet as his target materialized from shadow. Dempsey put his red dot center mass on the man deep inside the closet, cradling the rifle. Squinting hard against the light, the man tried to aim his weapon, but Dempsey immediately shot him, shifting his aim left so the 300 HAM'R tore through the fleshy part of the man's right shoulder.

Processing the man's facial features, Dempsey's brain flagged the tango as their HVT and mission objective—Zafar Saeed.

The bombmaker screamed and dropped his rifle. Dempsey kicked the closet door open and shot him again. This time his bullet tore through the man's right hand, blowing it apart and rendering it a useless, bleeding mass of flesh.

While Dempsey covered, Munn leapt into action, dragging the bleeding terrorist out of the closet and rolling the man onto his stomach. Dempsey watched with detachment as Munn pulled a tourniquet from his blowout kit and secured it to the terrorist's upper arm to stanch the bleeding. The arterial spray from the terrorist's blown off hand slowed and then stopped.

Munn looked up at Dempsey. "We need this guy alive, dude."

"He'll live," Dempsey said, finally lowering his rifle to a combat carry.

"Yeah, thanks to me."

"And thanks to me, this asshole won't be building any more bombs or killing any more Presidents," Dempsey said, his voice a throaty growl as he stared at the bloody stump below the man's wrist.

Munn held Dempsey's eyes a moment, then jerked the terrorist to his feet.

"I can't argue with that," he mumbled.

Dempsey led his teammate and their prisoner down the stairs, where Munn marched Saeed to a spot by the cash register and forced the bombmaker to sit. Dempsey glanced over at Ria and saw her eyes go wide, staring at the terrorist's wounds. When she didn't say anything, Dempsey turned his attention to the terrorist.

"We know you speak English and that you are Zafar Saeed," Dempsey said.

The man looked up at him, the shock in his eyes now ebbing. It had been replaced by seething hatred.

"How many men are downstairs?" Dempsey demanded.

The terrorist stared back, his eyes burning fires of malice.

"Are they your junior bombmakers?" Dempsey continued. "Bomb-makers in training?"

"Whoever or whatever is down there, the odds that the basement is booby-trapped are pretty high," Munn said.

"You've lost," Dempsey said, turning to tower over the bomb-maker. He held the terrorist's stare with a malevolent gaze of his own. "How much more you lose is up to you. Your life doesn't have to be over, but your bombmaking days are behind you. Now, you're going to open the basement door and show us everything."

"No," the man said in English, and his voice cracked.

"If you refuse, I will take your other hand . . ." He let a smile curl the corners of his mouth. "Then your right foot. Then your left . . ."

The man looked away, dropping his eyes to the floor.

"And I will take your eyes next, Saeed. But I won't let you die . . . I promise you that. You will spend the rest of your days in darkness, in a hole, unable to walk, feed, or clean yourself. Or you can disarm the bomb connected to that door and open it."

The terrorist cleared his throat. "I'll do it."

Dempsey nodded and turned to Martin. "Take him to the door."

Martin jerked the bombmaker to his feet and led him to the heavy metal door. Then, he quickly backed away, joining his teammates who were maintaining a standoff distance in a semicircle behind the display cases and register.

"Homeplate, Yankee is Jackpot," Dempsey said on the secure network. "Cleaning house, then out in ten."

"What if he trips a booby trap on purpose?" Ria whispered in his ear from beside him, her voice tight with worry.

"He won't," Dempsey said, the red dot of his Aimpoint on the back of Saeed's head nonetheless.

"How do you know?"

He turned and gave her a tight smile. "I've been hunting, killing, and interrogating men like him for two decades. I know."

They watched as Saeed opened a box beside the door and typed in a code. A red light turned green, and the door clicked. The terrorist opened it with his one good hand and turned to Dempsey, his eyes still burning with pain and hatred—but now also with something else.

Shame.

You should *be ashamed. You're a coward, sending kids to blow themselves up for your cause while you live safe and happy in your little apartment . . .*

His hand tightened on the grip of his SBR Tactical, but then he reminded himself that he still needed this asshole to find Umar.

"You first," Dempsey said as he approached Saeed, rifle still leveled at the terrorist.

They descended the dark stairs in a line behind the bombmaker, Dempsey's rifle in the man's back while Munn and Martin trailed tight, prepared to shoot over and past him at any threat waiting in the basement. But when they entered the cavernous cellar, they found it dark and deserted.

Dempsey scanned the room. Eight rectangular workbenches with metal stools were arranged in a tidy grid of two columns and four rows. Each station had a desk lamp, a toolbox, and stacks of clear plastic trays, but no bombs in various stages of fabrication.

"Where is everyone, huh?" Dempsey asked, prodding Saeed in the middle of the back with the muzzle of his SBR.

The bombmaker said nothing, but Dempsey could see his respiration rate was elevated as he clutched his stump.

"Yankee, you have local police inbound to your position; six mikes," Wang reported, urgency in his voice. "But Dark Horse has a cover op in place already."

The arrival of Nepalese police after Ember was gone was a necessary and critical element. To help preserve their NOC, they needed this raid to look like a local, organic operation, *not* like American or Indian spec ops.

"Dude, there's nothing here. We need to go," Munn said.

"But there was something here," Dempsey said, picking up a tray of little electrical components from a nearby workstation. "This is an assembly operation."

"Found a laptop," Martin announced as he made a sweep through the room.

"Yankee, exfil," Dempsey said, then to Munn and Martin added, "Quickly grab what you can; we'll destroy what's left behind."

Dempsey grabbed the terrorist by his collar and led him back up the stairs as Munn and Martin swept the basement for phones and other electronics of importance. As soon as they were up from the basement, Dempsey pulled two grenades from his kit, lobbed them into the cellar, and closed the heavy door behind him.

"Homeplate—sitrep on inbound police?"

"Yankee, this is Homeplate. Locals are three mikes out, will arrive from the east on Shital. They're northbound on Ganesh Street now. You need to boogie to avoid detection."

Dempsey signaled for Bravo to exit the front, then chopped a hand toward the back door of the shop for his team. "Alpha and Bravo vehicles both exfil west to F23 northbound. Mother, you're Yankee Eight—meet us at the van."

"Mother," came Grimes's cool reply, acknowledging she was leaving her sniper roost and giving up the overwatch call sign as she did.

"Grenades into the center of the building as we go," he ordered as the muffled explosions from the basement shook the floor beneath him. "Maybe it'll look like the guys blew themselves up."

"Roger that," Munn called on his way out.

"To the world, you no longer exist, Saeed," Dempsey said as he dragged the terrorist bombmaker out of the shop and into the empty lot at the rear where their vehicle was parked. "Blew yourself up by accident in the middle of the night, it seems. Too bad no one will mourn you."

Moments later they were pulling out of the empty lot behind the electronics store, fires burning already from their grenades, sirens wailing in the distance. Dempsey had taken one of the fold-down jump seats in the cargo hold to keep an eye on Saeed, who was sitting cross-legged on the floor. The bombmaker was clearly in significant pain, rocking and holding his wrist. To Dempsey, the man looked on the verge of going into shock, which wasn't surprising. They needed to get their HVT back to the safe house fast so Munn could do his thing, get fluids into the dude, and get him stabilized.

Dempsey verbalized as much to Martin, who was driving.

"Roger that, boss," came the reply from up front.

Dempsey glanced at Grimes, who was riding shotgun. She must have felt his eyes on her because she turned and fixed him with a weary smile. For a moment, she looked like she was about to say something but instead turned back to look out the windshield. He turned to Ria, who sat on the jump seat beside him, staring at her hands.

"Are you okay?" he asked.

She looked up at him, her dark eyes wet. He wondered if she'd ever been so up close and personal with violence before, or if she'd only experienced it secondhand in after-action reports.

She nodded, then said, "But you shot that man's hand off . . ."

"Yes, I did," he said and held her eyes, not sure if what he saw was disapproval, contempt, or just shock.

"Why? Why did you do that?" she asked after a long beat.

He could have lied and said it was self-defense or that he'd been protecting Munn. But the bombmaker had already dropped his rifle when Dempsey pulled the trigger on that second shot. No, he'd done it for another reason. For the same reason the American government had sent him on a hundred capture/kill missions as a SEAL. For the same reason Jarvis had sent him to Russia, where he'd collaborated with the enemy, Arkady Zhukov . . .

"To take a chess piece off the board."

When she said nothing in reply, he leaned into the backrest, pulled a tin of wintergreen snuff from a pocket on his kit, and packed himself a well-earned dip.

CHAPTER 26

PHIL H. BUCKLEW NAVAL SPECIAL WARFARE TRAINING CENTER

NAVAL AMPHIBIOUS BASE CORONADO

CORONADO, CALIFORNIA

1655 LOCAL TIME

The classroom, for all its academic pressure, was generally a place where the candidates at least got a short respite from the constant adrenaline surges from stress, fear, and physical challenge. This morning, though, Jake felt his pulse pounding in his temples, his breath coming in rapid gulps through his nose, and he felt his stomach turn at the images on the screen at the head of the room. In front of that screen, SEAL Master Chief Brewster paced, giving a short description of the time and place of each atrocity. With each image Jake felt revulsion but also an anger that simmered into rage.

"Iraq, 2004," Master Chief Brewster said as a new image came to the screen. Corpses of a man and a woman, tied to chairs in a walled-in porch. In front of them were three pools of blood. "This couple was executed behind their house in Ramadi. They were accused of talking to Americans who were searching for terrorists nearby. The pools of blood are from where their three children were murdered in front of them before the parents were shot in the head."

Click.

"Afghanistan, 2009," Brewster said. The image showed four headless bodies draped over a large wooden log. Behind them stood triumphant terrorists, each holding a bloody knife in one hand and a freshly decapitated head by its hair in the other.

Click.

"Syria, 2019 . . ."

Click.

"Cambodia . . ."

Click.

"Yemen . . ."

Click.

"Nigeria . . ."

Click.

"Mogadishu . . ."

Click.

"Israel, just north of Gaza, last year . . ."

With each image, Jake's revulsion lessened and his rage grew. He became aware that both of his hands were balled so tightly into fists that his nails dug into his palms. His mind filled with images of his own: pictures he'd seen of the attack on the Tier One SEALs in Yemen and the remains of the TOC from the simultaneous attack in Djibouti, the TOC where a boy with explosives in his rectum had blown himself up, killing everyone, including Jake's dad. He remembered the attack in the Georgia Aquarium where he'd personally taken on a terrorist hell-bent on killing as many innocent men, women, and children as possible. He remembered the look on the man's face. The bloodlust. The determination. The compulsion to martyr himself no matter—

"Did you hear what I asked, Kemper?"

Jake looked up to find the master chief staring at him.

"I'm sorry, Master Chief," he said, his jaw clenched.

"Don't be," the SEAL said. "This shit should bother the hell out of you. I asked what you felt when you saw these images."

"Rage," he said without hesitation, but regretted it after. This was a briefing on morality and ethics of warfare. That was probably *not* the right answer.

"Good," the SEAL master chief said, pacing back up to the front. "If you don't feel revulsion, you might be a sociopath. If you don't feel anger, you are probably in the wrong business. These are the same type of animals that killed our President, the Prime Minister of India, and tried to take out the Israeli Prime Minister. You can hate them. You can feel rage. You can thirst for the chance to mete out justice."

The SEAL arrived at the front of the classroom and crossed his thick, powerful arms across his chest.

"However," he said, scanning around the room, "if we operate based on that rage, then we risk becoming no better than the enemies we are charged to fight."

He clicked his remote again and the horrible images disappeared, replaced by the SEAL creed in a fancy font, overlaid on the image of an American flag.

"Who wants to read this aloud?"

Every hand in the room went up. The master chief pointed to Jay Maxwell, one of two officers in their SQT class. Maxwell stood and began to recite the creed. He turned to the class as he did, not needing to read from the screen.

"In times of war or uncertainty there is a special breed of warrior ready to answer our Nation's call . . ."

Jake felt something stir inside as he heard the words he, too, already knew by heart, words describing the life he'd chosen. He knew that his life would be forged by adversity just as the creed described. An elite warrior's life of sacrifice, loyalty, patriotism, service, honor, and integrity. He was shocked to feel tears rim his eyes as he heard those words, unable to not think of all the heroes who had gone before, heroes, including his own father, who had fought and died to build the proud tradition and feared reputation he was committing to uphold.

". . . I will not fail," Maxwell ended. Then he took his seat.

"Hooyah," breathed every SEAL candidate in the room, including Master Chief Brewster and the Senior Chief standing by the door.

"Ketron, stand up."

"Yes, Master Chief," Randy said, snapping to his feet behind the long common desk where he sat beside Jake.

"What part of the SEAL creed do you believe most applies to the warrior ethics we've been discussing, before I showed you all those fucked-up pictures?

"I serve with honor on and off the battlefield," Ketron said. "The ability to control my emotions and actions, regardless of circumstance, sets me apart from others. Uncompromising integrity is my standard. My character and honor are steadfast . . ."

"Correct," the master chief said. "That is what sets us apart, gentlemen. There have been a few who have fallen from that standard over the previous decades. Only a few, but they soil the Trident and reputations of all who go before us. That is unacceptable. Who agrees?"

"Hooyah," the room replied.

"The execution of my duties will be swift and violent when required," Jake said, rising to his feet without being called on, "yet guided by the very principles that I serve to defend."

The master chief stared at him hard but smiled.

"And what do you think that means, son?"

Jake let out a long breath.

"It means that when I am confronted with these pure evil assholes, I have to fight them with the honor and integrity and principles that make us better than them. Otherwise, Master Chief," he said, feeling the eyes of his teammates on him, "whether we kill them or not, they win."

"Take a seat, Kemper," the master chief said, and Jake did.

"That is the absolute truth. If we become no better than the evil bastards we fight, then they do indeed win. Just as your teammate said. We put our team and mission first, and we fight with honor and integrity at all times. Can you do that?"

"Hooyah."

Jake felt a swell of pride at the journey he was still just beginning. But there was a comfort in it too. He liked the black-and-white world he was entering. He liked the mandate to destroy those who would do harm to his country and its people, and he liked knowing that violence of action was just.

This is a world where I can be a warrior, and maybe still keep my soul . . .

Jake felt energized, despite the horrible images that still stained his mind—both from the presentation and his own memories. But he believed he was ready to face that kind of evil. The Navy was providing him the tools. He would bring his own moral clarity to the table.

"You'll be heading out to your East or West Coast sites for small-unit tactics tomorrow morning," the Senior Chief barked from the door. "While you are there, I want you to think and meditate on what the master chief taught you in the lecture today. Not once. Not a few times. Every fucking day. This is the difference between good and evil. This is the difference between us and the enemy. And, in the end, it is the difference between victory and defeat."

CHAPTER 27

NIA SAFE HOUSE

JUST OFF GOLFUTAR ROAD

NORTHERN EDGE OF KATHMANDU AT SHIVAPURI NAGARJUN

NATIONAL PARK

KATHMANDU, NEPAL

0215 LOCAL TIME

Elizabeth Grimes glanced over at the sofa where Tess Wallace was bullshit-ting with Prescott and Fender about SEALs and fast boats and SF diver qualifications. Ember's newest female SAD operator seemed upbeat and completely at ease. She didn't wear her heart on her sleeve or carry a chip on her shoulder. She wasn't a firebrand or a flirt. She didn't appear to have a hidden agenda, an ego to service, or a vendetta to satisfy. She was just Tess, a badass chick ready and willing to kick doors and drive fast boats.

She's the exact opposite of how I was when I joined Ember, she thought. *And on top of that, she bakes . . .*

Grimes's journey to acceptance and operational proficiency had taken nearly two years, whereas for Wallace it seemed to have happened overnight. She couldn't help but feel crazy respect for the woman, and annoying jealousy at the same time.

"What is going on down there?" NIA Agent Ravi Chauhan said, addressing no one in particular, but his voice oozing with accusation. By *down there*, Chauhan was referring to the basement where Dempsey was interrogating the captured terrorist bombmaker, Zafar Saeed.

Alone.

Dempsey had insisted on being alone, which concerned Grimes despite her not saying so or challenging Dempsey on the decision. She'd wanted to, had felt compelled to, but when Buz didn't say anything, she hadn't either.

The old Lizzie Grimes would have. *Why didn't I today?*

"Okay, so nobody is going to answer me?" Chauhan said, his gaze for some reason settling on her.

"What's going on *down there*, Ravi, is an interrogation of a bomb-maker suspected of blowing up your Prime Minister, our President, and thirty-five other innocent people," she said, a little more combatively than she intended. "What did you think was going on?"

"Clearly, I am concerned about the nature of that interrogation, which is why I'm asking the question," Chauhan clapped back.

"I think what my colleague is saying, Elizabeth, is that we have heard plenty of stories about the CIA's *enhanced* interrogation techniques," Ria said, stepping in. "I hope you understand that we, the NIA, cannot take part in or condone anything that violates international law."

"Or human decency," Dak added softly from beside Ria. "That is not our way. The ends don't justify the means. This is what separates us from the terrorists . . ."

Grimes felt her temper flare. The compulsion to defend her friend and teammate fueled a response that—she realized while she was speaking—she would later regret.

"You're absolutely right. The bombmaker is our guest, and we should treat him accordingly. We should give him the nicest bedroom in the safe house. Wallace can bake him cookies. I'll make him a latte. And Ravi, maybe you can massage his feet while we're at it."

"We are serious, and you mock us," Dak said, shaking his head.

"He's right, Elizabeth," Ria said, her expression hardening. "We are trying to have an important conversation with you."

"I know," Grimes said, realizing she'd taken it too far and trying to dial down the temperature, mostly her own. "But by implying that my teammate is violating international law, you've insulted our organization and our morals. You've questioned the professionalism of my teammate, and you've implied that lines have been crossed without any discussion about what those lines are."

"Lines like shooting off people's hands?" Ravi countered boldly.

That's when Grimes realized that her teammates on the sofa had stopped talking, and that the room had gone dead quiet. All eyes were on her.

"What're we arguing about?" a cheerful-sounding Munn said from somewhere behind her.

She turned to see Munn running his hands through shaggy wet hair after having emerged from the back hallway wearing blue jeans and a worn and tattered "Bars of Virginia Beach" long-sleeve tee.

"I need to talk to you," she said.

"Okay," he said with an easy smile.

"Alone."

His smile faded. "Roger that," he said.

He turned around and headed back to the bunk rooms. She followed him and shut the door behind her.

"What's up?" he said.

She was grateful for the fact he didn't try to make a joke or push her buttons.

"What happened in the electronics shop when you guys bagged Saeed?" she asked, resisting the urge to put her hands on her hips. "How did he lose his hand?"

Munn let out a long, weary exhale. "JD just blew it off."

"To disarm him?"

"No, Saeed was already disarmed."

"Was he reaching for a weapon?"

"No. We'd already shot him in the shoulder. Saeed had his hands up and JD just, uh, shifted his sight and squeezed."

She let out a long, exasperated sigh. "What did you do then?"

"I put a tourniquet on the sonuvabitch so he wouldn't bleed out."

"And what did you say to JD?"

"I asked him why the hell he did it."

"And what did he say?"

Munn chuckled. "He said something like, so that asshole wouldn't be able to make any more bombs to kill any more presidents, or something to that effect."

A wave of exhaustion suddenly crashed over her. She took a seat on the edge of the bottom bunk's mattress. Munn, following her lead, did the same on the bunk opposite her so they could still talk face-to-face.

"Dan, do you think the *old* Dempsey would have done that?" she asked, looking at a spot on the floor halfway between them.

"By the *old* Dempsey, do you mean the man he was before he came back from Russia?"

She nodded.

Munn thought for a moment. "I think my answer might surprise you, but yes, I do. The difference, however, is *that* Dempsey would have tried to justify it. Probably would have even lied about why he did it. And after he cooled down . . . he would have regretted it. But the guy downstairs in the basement, he just owned it."

A snippet of a conversation between Ria and Dempsey in the van on the exfil came back to her.

"You shot that man's hand off . . . Why did you do that?"

"To take a chess piece off the board."

"I'm worried about him," Grimes said.

He nodded. "I know you are . . ."

When he didn't finish the sentence, she said, "Aren't you?"

Munn fixed her with a closed-lip smile and shook his head. "He went through some shit over there, that's for sure, but he's back with us now. We're his family, and he just needs a little time to reconnect with us and purge the cold, zero-sum Russian mentality they live and die by over there. I think that Arkady Zhukov got into JD's headspace, and maybe it's our job to help get him out."

She nodded and felt a little better. Munn wasn't a bullshitter. He knew Dempsey better than anyone, so his words had weight.

"Ria and her team think he's torturing Saeed in the basement right now," she said. "I defended him, but what if they're right? I mean, what do you think he's doing down there?"

"You mean because of the whole *I'll take your hands and feet and eyeballs, but leave your ears* bit he said at the electronics shop?" Munn said with a chuckle.

She screwed up her face at him. "What the hell are you talking about, Dan? The Indians are pretty upset."

"It's from a movie, Lizzie. JD was just fucking with Saeed, trying to get in the guy's head so he'd open the basement door."

"What are you talking about?" she said, even more confused.

"'Your ears you will keep, and I will tell you why,'" Munn said with a grin and a deeply flawed British accent. "'So that every shriek of every child at seeing your hideousness will be yours to cherish. Every woman who cries out "Dear God, what is that thing?" will echo in your perfect ears.'"

She stared at him, perplexed.

"Oh, come on! Seriously? Lizzie, please don't tell me you never saw *The Princess Bride*?"

"Oh my God," she said, shaking her head. "You're both children."

"We're man-children," he said. "There's a difference."

"I think that's actually worse," she said, unable to help herself from laughing. Which got him laughing too. Damn if Dan didn't always find a way to make her feel better, no matter how dark and dire the circumstances.

"So you don't think he's down there chopping off Saeed's other hand right now?" she asked, getting back on topic.

"No," he said with a chuckle, "but if you want to put your mind at ease, I'll walk down there with you, and we'll see what we see."

"Really?"

"Yeah, let's go," he said.

He stood at the same time the door to the room pushed open, and Dempsey walked in.

"Go where?" Dempsey said, looking back and forth between them.

"To find you," Munn said. "Lizzie to wanted make sure you weren't chopping off the bombmaker's other hand."

All the goodwill she'd had for Munn instantly evaporated, and she shot him a look that could melt paint off a wall. To her relief, Dempsey nodded, unfazed by the comment as if it were an entirely legitimate concern.

"No, I let him keep that. I was able to keep things on the psychological end of the abuse spectrum."

"Oh, that's good," she heard herself say. The crushing weight of worry and anxiety she'd been carrying suddenly lifted. "Did you learn anything significant?"

"Oh yeah. You know how these guys get when they realize they're screwed. He sang like a songbird for me," Dempsey said. "I confirmed that Abu Musad Umar is the leader of al Ghadab. Also, Ria's working theory was right—Umar moved the command and control of the operation out of Pakistan and into Nepal nine months ago. The main base of operations for al Ghadab is here, on the outskirts of Kathmandu."

"Did he give up the location?" Munn asked. "Or are you still working on that?"

Dempsey grinned. "He did indeed. There's a compound in the mountains just outside the city. He gave me the name of the street and a hotel supposedly located next door."

"What about the bombs?" Grimes asked. "You said that basement looked like a friggin' bombmaking assembly line, but we didn't recover jack."

"He confirmed that he'd just completed a large order, and that the reason the basement was empty is because Umar had recently picked them up. There was nobody working because he has no additional tasking."

"How recently were they picked up?"

"Earlier that day."

"Damn it," Munn said. "Just missed it."

"Did he say where they were taken or what the next target is?" she pressed.

Dempsey shook his head. "He insisted that information is compartmentalized, and that Umar never shares plans with him."

"And you believe him?"

"Yes. I pressed hard and threatened to remove additional body parts if he lied."

She pursed her lips, not loving the idea that al Ghadab was likely gearing up for another attack. "I wonder if Umar is still in country," she said, thinking aloud, her mind already racing to the next logical step. "Maybe Umar moved the bombs to the mountain compound. Hell, maybe he's holed up there right now. Did you ask Saeed that?"

"I did, and he claimed not to know," Dempsey said, with remarkable patience as she grilled him. Then, smiling, he shifted his gaze from her to Munn. "But there is a way to find out."

Munn nodded, and she could see the fire in his eyes.

"Please don't tell me you guys want to run another op *tonight?*" she said.

Dempsey cocked an eyebrow at Munn. "What do you say, old man—you up for it?"

Munn popped to his feet. "Hoo-fucking-yah, frogman."

"But we haven't planned it. And even if the NIA folks are on board with it—which I doubt they will be without a little damage control first—there aren't enough hours of darkness left to mobilize, surveil, and execute the op," she said, not willing to indulge this idiocy a minute longer. "It's a hard no for me."

Munn came over and put his arm around her shoulders. "Come on, Mom, please. I promise we'll behave."

"Absolutely not," she said and glared at Dempsey, who made her wait for a ten count before finally replying.

"Well, we tried, Dan, but looks like we've been overruled," Dempsey said with theatrical headshake that told her they'd both been messing with her the entire time. He then walked over and put his arm around her from the other side so that she was sandwiched in between them. Unlike Munn, who was clean and smelled nice, JD kind of stank.

She ducked, stepped out of their teasing twin embrace, and turned to face them.

"How about you guys talk to Buz and Ria, fill them in on what you know, and get the green light for tomorrow? That will give us time to get properly prepped, surveil the location, and, if we're lucky, get the damn IAF drone on station this time."

"Okay, but what are you going to do?" Dempsey said, shifting his arm so it was around Munn's shoulder.

"I'm going to hit the shower," she said and turned to leave. At the threshold she stopped and turned to face her man-child teammates. "Oh, and JD, one more thing?"

"Yeah?"

"I suggest you do the same. Because 'Slider,'" she said, quoting the only movie she actually did have memorized, "'you stink.'"

CHAPTER 28

Abu Musad Umar sat at the modest desk in the rear office of the complex he secretly used as the headquarters for his Kathmandu operation, letting his long, sallow fingers gently caress the thick manila envelope stuffed full of cash. He'd been in the compound since long before the Chinaman had come offering him money, technology, and, most importantly, intelligence support—and it felt like home.

Only now it felt different. *More*, maybe.

The young man across from him stared at the envelope, eyes wide with awe—not because of the money inside, Umar knew, but because of what it represented.

Umar smiled and leaned back in his chair.

"You will personally deliver this envelope to the family of Yusuf, our brother martyred for jihad in Delhi," Umar said. Yusuf had given the ultimate sacrifice for Allah in the war against the infidels, and his sacrifice had made a true difference, killing the American President, who truly was the Great Satan. "You know what this payment represents, Azban?"

"Of course," Azban said, his voice a reverent whisper. "This is the Shahada payment for Yusuf."

"It is," Umar said, trying to match the reverence in the boy's voice. There would be a time when he might call on Azban to martyr himself for the cause as well, and moments such as these were of pivotal importance. There had been times where he, too, had prayed that Allah would allow him to die a martyr's death—to arrive in Paradise a hero of jihad—but no longer. No, it was now apparent to Umar that Allah had called him to a much higher purpose.

He slid the envelope across the desk where Azban picked it up, cradling it in his hands for a moment.

"You can imagine the wrath of Allah that would follow should someone take from this Shahada payment."

Azban's face went pale, and his mouth dropped open.

"I would sooner cut out my own heart . . ."

Umar raised a hand and smiled, satisfied with the reaction.

"Of course, my son, I trust you completely. I did not mean to imply you would be so tempted. You are one of my most dedicated and purest believers. No, I meant only to remind you how important it is that you protect this payment as you travel to deliver it to the family."

"With my life," Azban said as he slipped the envelope inside his thin coat with trembling hands. "I swear it."

"I know," Umar said. "I trust you, as I did with the Shahada payments to the families of Ahmed and Khaled. When you are done, stay a while in Faisalabad and visit your family, Azban. You have earned their pride and deserve time with them. I will summon you soon, as I know Allah has much more for you to do."

"Thank you, sir," Azban said, rising and bowing before hurrying out of the room.

Umar watched the boy go with a wave of nostalgia. Not long ago, he would have teared up at the enormity of what Yusuf had done. Life had been simple: Allah had called Umar to battle, and he had fought with passion and skill. He had given his all and sacrificed much, losing friends and even his brother in the war against the infidels.

But Allah had not rewarded him with a martyr's death, despite all the death that had surrounded him. And now he knew why.

Umar let out a long but satisfied sigh. Since the death of the American President, his life and the future of al Ghadab had changed in ways he could not have imagined. The Chinaman had promised there would be a new future for al Ghadab in the wake of the killings, but nothing had prepared him for the last week. He'd taken calls of congratulations from the regional leaders within ISIL as well as al-Qaeda. His own regional leaders reported a massive influx of volunteers, to the point where they were running out of places to house them. Suitcases full of cash had been left at doorsteps inside his compound in Lahore.

This, he decided, was what Allah had wanted for him all along. This was his reward—not in Paradise, but here on earth where he now believed it would be him, the son of a shoemaker from Kasur, who would lead the caliphate. The Chinaman had been but an instrument of Allah's will; he saw that now clearly. Soon enough, he would no longer need the help of the nonbeliever whose motives were impure.

He thinks he's fooled me, but I know better.

The Chinese operative didn't *really* support the cause. In Shazi's mind, al Ghadab was simply a chess piece in a high-stakes geopolitical game China was playing against the West.

But I am no pawn. I will not be so easily sacrificed.

Umar smiled. He looked forward to his upcoming meeting with Shazi. They had much to discuss. He rose and stared at himself in the dirty mirror attached to the file cabinet behind the desk, turning his head left and right. He needed to trim his beard. He needed a proper haircut. And, desperately, he needed new clothes. He was now the face of the new jihad and needed to look the part. This new jihad was to be led by a new generation, not goat herders from the mountains but men of education and sophistication. He would not be a living in squalor in a cave somewhere, dressed in rags.

That is clearly not Allah's will for me.

And, after too many years of poverty, it was most certainly not his will for himself. There was no one left from his family, all victims of either poverty or the war against the devils of the West. He was done living like an animal. He would need—no, it was okay to admit to himself that he *desired*—new clothes worthy of his new station.

The satellite phone on his desk chirped.

"Yes?" he said, seeing the number 1 on the screen. He hoped Shazi was not calling to say he would be late.

"Your bombmaker is dead," the Chinaman said with little emotion. Always, the man's voice was even and calm, something Umar had to admit he admired greatly. "I imagine your own people will be notifying you soon enough."

Typical Shazi—needing to remind Umar that he was always a step ahead.

No matter. This would all change soon.

"It won't matter," he said. "We have the weapons secured already. We can still proceed when we are ready."

"Not if the Americans and the Indians hit your compound next, Umar," Shazi said softly, a hint of condescension in his voice. "We must leave immediately. It is time to get you back into India for the next operation anyway. We must assume that they may have determined your location. It is dangerous to stay."

"The weapons are not here," Umar said simply, glancing again at himself in the dirty mirror and now imagining what he might look like in a Western-style suit.

"What? Where are they?" Shazi sounded impatient now.

"It would never have been safe to keep them at the compound. I have already arranged for their transit. If you are concerned about my safety, then I agree to go with you now."

"How generous," Shazi said, and Umar decided to ignore his sarcasm.

For now. I may have money and people beyond what I had prayed for, but I do still need the intelligence only he can provide.

"I will send a message shortly detailing where we can meet, and we will travel together to Delhi. But first, I suggest you leave a little surprise for the Indian and American operators who will no doubt come for you."

"What kind of surprise?" Umar asked, but he already knew and liked what Shazi was thinking. His mind was already generating the list of who he would leave behind, to earn their own place in Paradise and their own Shahada payments for their families . . .

CHAPTER 29

UNNAMED ROAD

SEVEN MILES NORTHWEST OF CITY CENTER

KATHMANDU, NEPAL

0150 LOCAL TIME

The nudge woke Dempsey from a deep sleep on the floor in the back of the unmarked cargo van. He'd told Munn to wake him up when something interesting happened or when they were ready to go. Apparently, that time was now.

He cleared his throat and opened his eyes to find Grimes, not Munn, staring down at him. She sat on a flip-down jump seat against the right wall of the van, wearing a coy little smile.

"Did you just kick me with your boot, Kate?" he said.

A ripple of confusion washed across Grimes's face. "Dude, you just called me Kate."

He hoisted himself up into a sitting position with his back against the opposite wall. "What? No, I didn't," he said.

"*Yes*, you did."

"Oh, sorry, I was . . . never mind."

At this, her smile returned. But it was accompanied by her

unmistakable *I'm worried about you* look, one he'd come to know well since he'd returned from Russia.

"You were dug in like a tick down there—totally comatose," she said, then raised her index finger to the corner of her mouth. "Looks like you got a little drool . . ."

He wiped his beard at the corner of his mouth. Finding it dry, he scowled at her.

"Gotcha," she said and chuckled, delighted with herself.

His brain, still half caught in the undertow of sleep, wanted to dive back into the ocean of REM. Unlike most of his dreams of late, this one had been nice. More than nice, come to think of it: friggin' wonderful. It had felt so real, as if he'd been transported back through space and time to relive the moment exactly as it had happened:

Jake had been six at the time, and Dempsey's marriage to Kate had been at its best. There'd been so much love between them, so much mutual adoration for each other and for their son. It was a Saturday, and they'd all gone to Longboat Key, just off the coast of Sarasota, for the weekend. In an unusual turn for the normally placid Gulf, there had been decent surf that day, waves just big enough to teach a six-year-old how to bodysurf. Jake's initial enthusiasm to learn had quickly turned to defeatism after a half dozen failed attempts and an ill-timed breath that had resulted in a lungful of salt water for his boy. But Dempsey had been patient with his son.

No, not Dempsey. Kemper—Jack Kemper had been patient.

His son's tears and little tantrum hadn't fazed Kemper a bit. No judgment. No lecturing the boy to "be a man" or to "toughen up." Just patience. And love. Lots of love.

And Kate smiling.

God, that smile could melt icebergs.

"What are you grinning about?" Grimes said.

"Just thinking about old times," he said, meeting her eyes.

"We've sure had some laughs along the way, haven't we?"

"Yeah, we have," he said, not having the heart to correct her assumption.

He exhaled, breathing away the disappointment of no longer being Jack Kemper as the nostalgic reunion with his family faded. Like beach sand through his fingers, the connection to his past dissolved from his mind as he became fully alert and attuned to his environment.

So strange . . .

John Dempsey was supposed to be a character. An NOC. A legend that he used at work, then shed like a uniform at the end of the workday. But these days, he never took John Dempsey off. In fact, it had taken this dream for him to remember what it even felt like to be Jack Kemper. The Dempsey NOC had somehow absorbed him. Consumed him. Become him.

A strange ache now settled in the pit of his stomach, and with it came a disturbing thought:

If Jack Kemper could meet John Dempsey, he probably wouldn't like him. Wouldn't like him one bit.

"He's awake," Grimes said to Munn.

The lumberjack/doctor/SEAL stood in a hunch, looking over Wang's shoulder at the mobile workstation at the front of the cargo compartment. "Must be nice," he said, glancing over his shoulder at Dempsey.

"What must be nice?" Dempsey asked, lobbing a slow pitch right over the plate for his best friend.

"To take a nap while the rest of us work," Munn said with a shit-eating grin.

Dempsey shrugged. "I'm old, and old people need their sleep."

This comment earned a chuckle from Ria, who sat in the jump seat opposite Grimes. Dempsey had said it to be self-deprecating and get a laugh, but at some level, he couldn't help but wonder if there was a measure of truth in what he'd said. He'd always prided himself at being able to sleep on demand, but this was different. They were in the field surveilling the target compound, and he didn't care. His body told him it desperately needed sleep, and his ego happily obliged.

No guilt. No shame.

Some might call it the ultimate demonstration of trust in his teammates, and a form of operational self-actualization. But on the other hand, it might be a sign he was losing his edge.

"Gimme a sitrep, dude," Dempsey said, pulling down a jump seat and hoisting his stiff body onto it. He was now at eye level with the rest of them.

"Believe it or not, tonight Baldwin actually got a drone on loan from IAF, and it's up and turning donuts with good thermals, which is what I wanted you to see," Munn said.

Dempsey leaned to get up and squeeze his way forward, but Wang stopped him.

"Don't get up; I'll throw the feed to your tablet," the Ember cyber lead said.

Dempsey grunted something halfway between a thanks and an acknowledgment as he pulled a small tablet from his kit. Onscreen, he saw the three-building al Ghadab compound, as well as a fourth building that sat on an adjacent plot of land. *The* probable *al Ghadab compound,* he reminded himself, assuming the intel he'd extracted from Saeed had been accurate. The pre-op surveillance was meant to not only collect tactical intel but confirm this compound was indeed the target.

Dempsey counted eight thermals in the centermost building of the compound—six were horizontal, presenting as sleeping; one sitting, probably watching TV; and one patrolling and holding a rifle. The other two smaller buildings appeared to be empty. A fourth building, on the lot next door, had nine thermals distributed in ones and twos in individual, equal-sized rooms on the west side of the building—most presenting as sleeping—and a single thermal on the east side of the building, sitting at a desk.

"What is this building over here on the west, with ten thermals?" Dempsey said, turning the tablet screen toward Wang and pointing to the building next to the compound.

"It's listed as the Happy Stay Hotel and Hostel Kathmandu. It has a website and legitimate web presence and history," Wang said.

"How long is legitimate?" Dempsey asked.

"Three years, seven months."

"We have been watching it for over three hours," Ria said. "It looks and behaves like a hotel."

"Mm-hmm," Dempsey said, looking from Wang to Ria, then back down at the tablet. "Have we had any activity in these two outbuildings that appear vacant?"

"No. They've been empty since we set up shop," Wang said.

"What's on your mind, JD?" Munn asked. "Does something have your antennae up?"

Dempsey cleared his throat again. "The readiness posture inside the compound seems a little lax given that we just hit the electronics store and snatched Saeed last night. You'd think they'd have a higher level of readiness."

"Yes, but you're assuming they know about our hit on Saeed. It is entirely possible that they don't. It is also possible that Umar compartmentalized the bombmaker's activities and location from these guys. Otherwise, why maintain and operate two different sites?" Ria said.

Dempsey looked from Ria to Munn. "What do you think, Dan?"

"I think . . ." Munn began, before pausing to blow air through pursed lips, "that I don't know. Both scenarios sound reasonable to me. It's also possible that Saeed fed us a line of bullshit, and this is just some random house next door to a shitty little hotel west of Kathmandu."

Dempsey didn't say anything for a long moment. Then, he turned to Grimes. "How does a single-night vacation at the Happy Stay Hotel and Hostel Kathmandu sound to you? All expenses paid."

Grimes grimaced. "I mean, the roof of that hotel has great sight lines. But, JD, do you really want me plinking targets above the hotel room of some kids who are backpacking around the world? What if the tangos in the target house return fire at the hotel and it's really a legit hotel? We're risking innocents. The north slope would be safer from a collateral standpoint."

He shook his head. "Take Luka as your spotter and set up on the roof. If we do our jobs properly, there shouldn't be any return fire."

She nodded, but he could tell she didn't love being micromanaged on her overwatch selection. Too bad, because his gut told him the Happy Stay Hotel and Hostel was not the innocent, coincidentally located lodge that it seemed from outward appearances.

Dempsey turned to Ria. "Do you want to come along on this one?"

She shook her head. "Not this time. After seeing how you guys work, and the complexity of this breach, I am certain I would be a liability more than an asset."

Dempsey silently breathed a sigh of relief. "Understood. Besides, why willingly walk into a gun battle when you can stay here in the van, sip cold coffee, and fly drones with Dick Wang's joystick? I mean talk about a wild night out on the town."

This comment garnered laughs from everyone except for Wang, who threw up his hands.

"You know I love you, Richard," Dempsey said, "but I had the shot and couldn't resist taking it."

Wang smiled despite himself.

"You ready to rock and roll?" Munn asked, looking at Dempsey.

Dempsey let his hands, which were already checking the loadout on his kit, answer the question for him.

CHAPTER 30

SUSPECTED TERRORIST COMPOUND NEXT TO

THE HAPPY STAY HOTEL AND HOSTEL

SEVEN MILES NORTHWEST OF CITY CENTER

KATHMANDU, NEPAL

0234 LOCAL TIME

Lying prone in the weeds, sixty meters out from the presumed terrorist compound, Dempsey scanned the three-story main building through an advanced night-vision monocle. The scope was equipped with an X27 camera module that rendered full-color, photorealistic imagery and made this dead-of-night operation feel like it was happening during the middle of the afternoon. It also had optical and digital magnification, which allowed him to zoom in to ridiculous levels. According to Munn, Chunk's team over at the Tier One had field-tested and approved the tech, which Ember had since adopted. Their helmet-mounted NVGs were also X27 enhanced, and Dempsey was blown away by the upgrade.

"This tech is a game changer," he murmured as he scanned every balcony and window of the three-story building, feeling less than zero regret at saying goodbye to the grainy green-gray monochrome rigs he'd used his entire career.

"Is this your first time using it?" Prescott asked from where he lay next to Dempsey.

"Yeah," he said. "I thought the gel body armor was cool, but this is something else. I wonder what they're going to dream up next."

Dempsey had split the team into two sticks, with him leading Prescott and Wallace while Munn was paired with Fender and Lewis. He'd teamed Martin with Grimes, not just as a spotter, but also as an insurance policy in case Dempsey's hunch that not every guest in the Happy Stay Hotel was an innocent civilian proved prescient.

"Maverick One, Eight—the roof deck is clear. Overwatch is set. Eight is now Charlie," Grimes said in his ear.

"Roger, Charlie," he said, then pinged Wang for a status report. "Jester, sitrep?"

For this op, Dempsey had let Lizzie pick the call signs, and she'd chosen character names from *Top Gun*, which he'd learned last night was her favorite movie of all time. As overwatch, she'd traded her usual Mother for Charlie, the code name of the civilian contractor Charlotte Blackwood in the movie. Using Maverick for the team call sign was a no-brainer. Wang had insisted that *he* be Iceman, but he'd been unanimously overruled by the team and dubbed Jester. Remaining film call signs had been assigned to the rest of the op's checkpoints and milestones. Presently, they were holding at Goose, conducting surveillance while Grimes and Martin moved into position.

"Maverick, Jester—no significant change to thermals. Everything looks good. You have a green light," Wang reported.

"Copy," he said, then checked in with Munn, who was set up on the north side. "Two?"

"Looks quiet, but I'm not loving the entry and egress options. There's no cover in a fifty-foot radius around the building. The bottom-level windows all have iron bars, and there are balconies that wrap three-hundred-and-sixty degrees around on the second and third levels. I hold no doors on the north side on the ground level, which means we'll have to breach through the wall or climb up to the second story. If they have cameras or we trip an alarm on the infil, their shooters will have the high ground, and we'll be stuck in no-man's-land with no cover," Munn said. "Also, the infil is uphill on three sides."

Dempsey, who had made similar observations, didn't say anything for a moment.

"But if you're ready to go, Two is all in," Munn said, possibly reading Dempsey's silence as a rebuke.

"Two, hold," Dempsey said, while he contemplated an adjustment available to him, one that his gut didn't like.

As if reading his mind, Wang spoke in his ear. "There's a door on the east side of the main building. Since breaching front and back is a nonstarter, you could breach south and east at a ninety-degree offset. Not ideal, I know, but something to consider."

"Two concurs. We'll still approach from the north, but on arrival shift around to the east side to breach."

"Charlie?" Dempsey asked, hoping that Grimes had good lines on the interior through the windows of the target building's east façade.

"I have good viz of the exterior, but nothing inside. I can't tell for sure, but if I had to guess, it looks like the windowpanes have been blacked out with paint," Grimes came back. "But I have great lines on the roof and second- and third-level balconies."

"What are you thinking, boss?" Wallace asked Dempsey, her voice tentative.

He got it. After the training op on the Farm and the hand incident with Saeed, Tess probably assumed that beast mode was his *only* mode, and that he was going to lead them charging into a dangerous, unpredictable situation. But he had no intention of doing that.

"I'm thinking that, on closer inspection, this nut might be tougher to crack than we initially expected," he announced. "I'm considering punting the op to tomorrow night and conducting another twenty-four hours of ISR."

"Maverick, this is . . . Jester Two," Ria said, speaking on the comms circuit for the first time. "I wasn't going to say anything until after the op, but since you are considering postponing, I will tell you that my team and I have been recalled to Delhi. We are leaving in the morning.

The Nepalese have voiced concerns to my government about our joint operations here, and I would not be surprised if similar talks are happening with your government . . ."

Well, that didn't take long, he thought with a grimace. *Maybe blowing up the electronics store was overkill.*

"Ain't that a peach," Prescott said, his voice thick with sarcasm. "We come here to exterminate the cockroaches in their kitchen, and they thank us by kicking us out of the house."

Dempsey, having played this game longer than anyone else in Ember—except for Buz, of course—wasn't surprised by this development.

"I hesitate to tell you this because I didn't want it to affect your tactical decision-making," Ria continued.

"Copy all," he said. He was annoyed—not at her, but at the situation.

Ria didn't want to force Dempsey's hand, but the practicalities of what she'd told them did just that. Buz was a pragmatist and not a man who shied away from risk, but by default he erred conservative. Having cut his teeth during the Cold War, Buz had learned the hard way what happens when you antagonize an ally. If their operational presence in Nepal was creating enough friction that NIA was pulling out, Ria's assumption that they would be pulled as well seemed valid.

If we were officially sanctioned outside of the White House, and maybe the ODNI . . .

Still, what was *President* Jarvis's risk threshold likely to be? Or Mike Casey's, who he didn't know as well? If Umar was inside the compound, and by inaction Dempsey let the terrorist bastard disappear into the night, he'd never forgive himself.

Damned if we do, damned if we don't. The Ember motto.

Dempsey ran his tongue between his lower lip and teeth, wishing for a dip. He was trying to quit, again, and he'd already cheated once tonight. Feeling agitated, he raised the monocle to his eye and scanned the building, this time looking for dome-style security cameras under the roof eaves and on the corners of the balcony decking. From his vantage point he didn't see any, but that didn't mean they weren't there.

What to do, what to do, what to do?

"Listen up, Maverick," he said, the high-tech microtransmitter in his left ear canal doing dual duty as both earbud and microphone. "I don't want to lose this opportunity, so we're going to hit the house. I'm not comfortable with Two breaching the east door. I don't want your backs to the Happy Stay Hotel until we're sure these guys don't have an overwatch of their own set up. So, you're going to infil from the north, but on reaching the compound, move south along the west wall to join up with our squad. We'll breach as three pairs through the front door."

"Two," Munn said, acknowledging all with his call sign.

"Charlie copies," Grimes added.

"Jester concurs," Wang said from the mobile TOC in the lead van.

Dempsey pressed up from his prone position into a low crouch. He stowed his monocle, lowered his new color NVGs into position, and unslung his Wilson SBR. "Maverick is a go. Call Hollywood."

On hearing a double click from Munn, he chopped his hand forward, leading Wallace and Prescott in an inverted V formation through the tall grass and up the hill toward the south side of the target house. The hour nap he'd taken in the van was paying dividends now because he felt every bit as alert and refreshed as he did twenty years ago when he had youth backstopping his performance. The unspoken reality, though, was that the time he'd spent in IK-2 *had* aged his body. It wasn't something he wanted to think about, but he felt it every day.

If only Baldwin had a biological upgrade for me equivalent to what the X27 did for night vision, he thought with a wry grin as he advanced, scanning for targets.

"Richard, I think we have a problem," Ria's voice said over the comms circuit.

Irritation immediately bloomed in Dempsey's chest at the undisciplined interruption.

She must have left her radio on vox . . .

He was about to scold her, but the tone in her voice caused him to hold his tongue and listen. He couldn't hear Wang's response to her because Wang's radio was not keyed.

Then, a beat later Ria said: "I know, I saw it before. This guy . . .

sleeping here just rolled over, and his leg went off the side of the mattress. Ten minutes ago, I swear I saw it happen, the same exact thing . . ."

"Maverick, hold," Dempsey said, raising a closed fist as he took a knee. "Jester, what's going on? And FYI, Jester Two's mike is on vox."

"Roger . . . we're looking into an anomaly with the drone feed," Wang came back.

"What kind of *anomaly*?"

"Jester Two thinks . . ."

"Jester Two thinks what? Come on, guys. I'm holding the team in no-man's-land," Dempsey said.

"I think we're watching a recorded loop on the drone feed," Ria said, answering for herself.

Dempsey glanced at Prescott, who he remembered had some experience with drones. "Is that even possible?"

"Dude, don't look at me," Prescott whispered.

"I thought you were a drone guy?"

"No, that's Martin."

"If the drone was hacked, it's possible," Wang came back. "It was turning counterclockwise donuts at ten thousand feet. Hold on, I'm on with the pilot—"

Wang's voice cut off midsentence.

"Jester, do you copy?" Dempsey said, scanning the target with fresh scrutiny. When he didn't get a reply from Wang, he tried Munn. "Two, One—sound check."

"Two," Munn's voice said in his ear.

"Charlie," Grimes said, proactively.

Dempsey breathed a sigh of relief.

Thank God we didn't lose all comms.

Then, gunfire erupted all around him.

CHAPTER 31

OPEN FIELD OUTSIDE THE TERRORIST COMPOUND

SEVEN MILES NORTHWEST OF CITY CENTER

KATHMANDU, NEPAL

0253 LOCAL TIME

Dempsey got low, swiveled, and sighted as muzzle flashes and rifle reports from the second-story balcony shattered the silence like a thunderstorm. Their stealth approach had just been blown, and the timing couldn't be any worse. They were crossing the wide-open grassy lawn between where they'd been surveilling in cover and the ground floor of the three-story target house.

"Heavy contact east," Munn's strained voice said in Dempsey's ear as he returned a volley of suppressing fire.

Thanks to the new X27 night vision, he could easily see the two shooters on the upper of the two balconies that completely wrapped the first and second stories of the target building. The blocky design of the tall, residential home reminded Dempsey of a square watchtower, built into the slope of the mountain. He sighted and dropped one of the tangos with a single shot, then flipped the selector on the SBR with his thumb to three-round burst, juking right then quickstepping forward.

Shoot and move . . .

In an ambush firefight like this, if you hesitated, you died, and Dempsey moved with the instinct born from decades of combat experience. In his peripheral vision, he saw both Wallace and Prescott vectoring through the tall grass while firing on the compound, opening the range between each other as their stick closed on the target.

Dempsey slid his targeting reticle onto center mass of the second balcony shooter as his boots pounded the dirt, but before Dempsey could pull the trigger, the man's body shuddered and the muzzle went dark as simultaneous volleys from Wallace and Prescott shredded the fighter's torso and exploded his head.

In that moment, the immediate mortal threat vanquished, his brain found time to catch up and parse Munn's report.

Heavy contact *east*, Munn had said.

The Happy Stay Hotel and Hostel was east, and Grimes was on the roof of that building with Martin.

And I ordered her there.

"One, Two," Munn said, his voice nearly drowned out by gunfire. "We have shooters inside the Happy Stay Hotel. No cover—so repositioning to the west wall . . . Shit, we've got contact south from the target house. We're caught in a cross fire."

Dempsey's brain was in overload as he tried to manage three tactical problems simultaneously. Their drone and Wang's comms were compromised, Munn's squad was being targeted from shooters in the Happy Stay Hotel to the east and from shooters on the target building simultaneously, and Grimes and Martin were trapped on the roof of a building occupied by enemy fighters—a roof that very well could have been booby-trapped.

I need our fucking eyes in the sky back.

The Predator B UAV they had in orbit was an older export model from the United States on loan from the Indian Air Force to NIA.

"Charlie, sitrep?" he barked, hoping to get a bird's-eye picture of the tactical situation from Grimes on the roof.

His legs churned as he climbed the grassy hill toward the south side of the target house, *toward* the shooters, but once his stick was beneath the balconies, they'd have a line on the west-facing windows of the Happy Stay Hotel and be difficult to spot and shoot at from the house itself.

Instead of Grimes, the next voice he heard was Wallace's.

"Incoming from above!"

Ears tuning to the threat, Dempsey heard the incoming whine of the Predator's turboprop engine—the pitch increasing with Doppler effect—as it screamed straight toward them. He glanced up and over his left shoulder, and his mind automatically calculated the kamikaze drone's impact vector. Harnessing every stored unit of ATP in his body, Dempsey whirled left, sprinted five strides, and threw his body into Prescott's.

Wrapping his teammate in a full-body tackle, Dempsey drove the other man to the ground just as the twelve-thousand-pound, thirty-six-foot-long drone slammed into the side of the hill with a deafening crash. The ground shook with the impact, and chunks of earth and debris rained down on his back as Dempsey shielded Prescott with his body. Eyes squeezed shut, he readied himself for the agony and the impending fireball that would engulf him and burn the flesh from his bones . . .

But the heat never came.

"Dude, you can get off me now," Prescott said.

Dempsey rolled off his teammate and whipped his head around to the impact site. The Predator hadn't exploded on impact, but its blended carbon-and-quartz fiber fuselage was annihilated. Fractured chunks of metal were scattered in an arc of destruction fanning out away from them. The long grass shined wet with 95 octane aircraft engine fuel, and Dempsey felt wetness on the back of his pant legs.

Thank God it didn't catch fire or I'd be burning . . .

He did a quick self-assessment to make sure that the flying shrapnel had not gifted him any new and unwelcome bodily orifices. Finding none, he scanned for Wallace and spied her in a prone firing position thirty feet away, scanning the target compound.

"Five, you good?" he called.

"Five is intact," she called back, then laid down a prolonged volley of automatic covering fire, strafing the upper and lower balconies, corner to corner, to deter any shooters inside the house from coming outside to play sniper.

"What the fuck just happened?" Prescott asked, taking a knee next to Dempsey and bringing his rifle up.

"Pretty obvious, I think. Somebody hacked our Predator and tried to murder us with it," Dempsey said, working hard to tamp down the flare of anger in his chest.

An orange spark from the wreckage at the impact site ignited the grass, which had been doused in five hundred pounds of fuel. Like a demon serpent emerging from hell, a curtain of flame rippled across the lawn, slithering straight toward Dempsey's squad.

"Don't know about you guys, but I got hosed down with gas," Dempsey said. He chopped a hand northeast. "Let's get the hell out of here."

Heavy gunfire reverberated from the other side of the compound, where Munn's squad still bore the brunt of the counteroffensive from the hostel and target compound itself. Dozens of rifle reports echoed off the mountains, creating a bizarre stuttering, repeating pattern. But with the structure of the target house between him and Munn's squad, Dempsey couldn't see anything.

"Two, sitrep?" Dempsey called as he squeezed off a preemptive volley at one of two barred windows on the lower level. The pair of corner windows were ideally positioned to rebuff Alpha squad's assault from this vector.

"We're pinned down. Six is hit but in the fight," Munn's voice barked in Dempsey's ear, all fury and gravel. "We're not going to last another five minutes at this rate."

"Copy, Two. Charlie—talk to me?" he said, praying Grimes and Martin were intact in the fight.

"One, Charlie—trying to thin the herd, but I've got no easy targets. Dropped one on the third-story balcony, but I have eyes on nothing else. They're all inside now, shooting from behind the barred windows," she said.

"What about the hotel? What's the situation over there?"

"I see tracers and hear fire below. I estimate there are multiple shooters in bedrooms here, but I can't see to confirm," she said.

"Two confirms," Munn shouted. "I count three shooters in building four. One on each level of the hotel."

Dempsey strafed the other barred windows on the ground level as he and his two squad members closed within ten meters of the covered basement-level entrance. Muzzle flashes from the first window flared in his vision, momentarily washing out a section of his NVGs. The bullets whistled past, splitting the gap between him and Prescott with, what felt like, no more than a foot clearance from his left ear. Wallace, who was trailing a stride off Dempsey's right shoulder, fired two three-round bursts at the hot window, giving the defender something to think about.

Legs on fire, Dempsey pushed hard into the homestretch. The grass gave way to a gravel driveway and parking area, empty of vehicles. Gravel flying from his boots, he sprinted the final twenty feet to the target house unscathed. He spun, slammed his back flat against the cinder block wall between the window and the basement door. Prescott arrived a heartbeat later, falling in on Dempsey's right, followed by Wallace on his left. She took a knee and sighted on the door while Prescott covered the barred window. As long as the enemy didn't have a fifty cal, they were probably safe from being cut down through the walls from inside.

"What's the plan?" Wallace called over her shoulder.

"We breach and clear the rat's nest."

"It's three stories, and there's only three of us," Prescott said. "And if the drone was hacked and the video on a loop, we have no clue how many shooters are inside."

A flashbulb memory of the bathroom brawl in IK-2 filled his mind's eye—where he fought alone against a squad of Russian guards with batons. In that moment, he'd unleashed the wolverine and fought savagely as they clubbed him to near death. They'd hurt him, but he'd hurt them worse.

All of them.

Gooseflesh stood up on his forearms. A bolus of adrenaline flooded his veins. And a carnal thirst to shred, and crush, and destroy energized every cell in his body.

"Ya znayu," he growled in Russian. *"I my zastavim ikh zaplatit'."*

I know. And we're going to make them pay.

CHAPTER 32

ROOFTOP OF THE HAPPY STAY HOTEL AND HOSTEL
SEVEN MILES NORTHWEST OF CITY CENTER
KATHMANDU, NEPAL

With her Wilson Recon Tactical sniper rifle propped on the knee wall atop the Happy Stay Hotel and Hostel, Grimes scanned the terrorist house four hundred meters away for targets. Beside her, Martin was doing the same, using a high-powered spotter scope. The Happy Stay Hotel was ideally suited for overwatch, with the entirety of its west-facing façade giving her unobstructed sight lines on the target building as well as the downward-sloping northern approach.

Gunfire rang from the bedroom windows below in asynchronous bursts as multiple terrorists fired on Munn's squad. The terrorists—presumably posing as regular peace-loving civilians—must have rented rooms and deployed here in advance. Dempsey's instincts to send Martin with her had proven prescient. The joint NIA–Ember snatch-and-grab mission to black-bag the al Ghadab bombmaker had telegraphed a fresh counterterror operation . . . something that the terror cell had not previously faced in Kathmandu. Umar, the seasoned, paranoid terrorist commander and the high-value target they were here to bag, had taken steps to maximize al Ghadab's readiness.

Whether or not Umar knew who was hunting him was a question yet to be answered.

"I have no targets," she said, her voice ripe with agitation. "What about you?"

"I got nothing," Martin said, then after a beat added, "Fuck this. I'm going to clear rooms."

"Not alone you're not."

"Come on, Grimes. I'm less than useless to you right now. I can't just sit up here and let our teammates get cut to ribbons."

"I didn't say it wasn't the right call. All I said was you're not doing it alone."

Gripping her sniper rifle, Grimes spun one hundred and eighty degrees and dropped down below the edge of the wall. Holding the rifle across her lap, she pressed her back into the cinder block and looked at her teammate.

She set her sniper rifle on the roof deck and picked up her SBR. "Dempsey's not gonna like this," she said, meeting Martin's gaze.

"Yeah, but at the same time, it's precisely what he would do."

She nodded and keyed her mike. "One, this is Charlie. Securing overwatch to prosecute enemy shooters in the hotel. Charlie is now Eight."

To her and Martin's mutual surprise, Dempsey appeared unfazed. "Check. Maverick is breaching. Happy hunting, Eight."

"Hooyah, that's what I'm talking about," Munn's voice said in her ear. "You've got two shitheads on level three and one on two. Counting from the north, we've got muzzle flashes from the second and sixth windows on level three . . . and the fourth window on level two."

"Did you catch that?" she said to Martin before responding, wanting to double-check for her own memory.

"Second and sixth windows on three. Window four on two," Martin said.

She nodded and keyed her mike. "Copy, Two, hang in there. We're bringing the pain."

"Music to my ears, baby," Munn came back.

She felt a twinge in her chest at hearing that, and suddenly she felt a powerful undertow of urgency to save him. During Dempsey's absence, she and Munn had formed a stronger, closer friendship. Strange that her own awareness of this fact hadn't happened until right now, at the worst and most distracting time.

If Dan dies because I was too slow, I'll never forgive myself.

She popped into a low crouch and chopped a hand forward. "Let's go."

As the Ember sniper, she rarely cleared rooms. It wasn't that she *couldn't* clear rooms; it was more a matter of proficiency. Excluding kill house training runs, the last time she'd cleared rooms in the field for real had been in Odessa, and, oddly enough, she'd been paired with Martin.

Is that why Dempsey made Martin my spotter? she thought with an epiphany. *Did he anticipate this scenario?*

"You want to lead or trail?" she said as they sprinted across the roof to the stairwell access.

"Wallace and Fender have all the breacher charges, which means busting doors the old-fashioned way," he said. "I'll lead. If the slab is left hinged, I'll go left. If it's right hinged, I'll go right."

"Roger that."

She stopped at the closed door of the little rooftop shed that housed access to the stairwell. She grabbed the doorknob and, in a quiet voice, said, "Three, two, one . . ."

On the zero beat, she pulled the door open, and Martin slipped past her, sighting over his rifle.

"Clear," he said and charged down the narrow staircase with her right behind him.

Their booted feet reverberated with every impact on the wooden treads as they descended from the roof to the third floor. At the first landing, Martin moved into position next to the doorframe, ready to clear. Grimes grabbed the door handle, counted down, and yanked. Martin slipped through the gap in a combat crouch, clearing left. She followed a second behind, turning right to find the corridor terminated five feet away in a dead end.

"Clear," she whispered, knowing her voice would be amplified for Martin by their sound system. She whirled to face the closed door of the room at the end of the hall and directly across from her.

"Clear," Martin said. In her peripheral vision, she could see him sighting down the length of the hall.

"North is this way," she said with a head nod to her right. "Question is . . . how many windows per room?"

"One or two is my guess," he said.

"Agreed. So, the second window could be this room or the one next door," she said, gesturing with her muzzle at the closed door three feet away.

"I don't hear any screaming. Nobody running for their lives. Either the real guests already left or they're sheltering in place."

"Or they don't have any *real* guests."

A pop of rifle fire sounded from the other side of the facing wall. She gestured with her barrel to the door beside her. Martin quick-stepped into position to breach. He cautiously tried the door handle, and she could see it was locked. Then, he turned to look at her.

"This one's a freebie, but after this the other shooters will likely be ready for us. We have to watch our six," Martin said. Then, reading her mind, he added, "Shoot to kill. We need Umar alive, but in the unlikely case he didn't skip town, he sure as shit ain't in this hotel providing cover fire."

She nodded, shifted into a ready combat crouch, and brought her holographic sight in line with her right eye.

Fresh rifle fire sounded from inside the room, and a surge of adrenaline—or maybe it was nerves—kicked her heart and respiration rate up a few notches. She shifted her finger off the guard and onto the trigger.

"On your count," she said.

"Three . . . two . . . one . . ."

On zero, Martin slammed his left shoulder into the door, which gave way with an impressive crack and splintering of wood. He cleared left and fired. She followed him and cleared center because there was nothing to the right but wall. She put two rounds in the chest of the same surprised jihadi shooter that Martin had shot a heartbeat before her. The bearded fighter didn't look a day over nineteen and was dressed in blue jeans and a T-shirt. He crumpled into a bloody heap while she did a quick sweep of the tiny hotel room, which had nothing more than a bed, dresser, and nightstand.

She surveyed the west wall and noted it had only a single window, which answered that question. Unlike American hotels, this room had no bathroom. Her brain, which was processing and drawing conclusions on autopilot, decided that the Happy Stay Hotel and Hostel must be set up dormitory-style, which meant there was a shared bathroom somewhere on the hall.

"Two, Eight—one tango down," she said, keying her mike to notify Munn of their progress.

"Got his radio," Martin said, kneeling by the dying shooter.

She whirled and quickstepped back toward the hall as Martin's warning about minding their six replayed in her brain. She took a knee at the doorframe and popped her head around the corner for a quick look. The corridor was empty. She counted doors and, at door number six, hovered her targeting dot at chest height above the door handle. She felt Martin's hand on her left shoulder as he swept behind and around her to take the lead. She quickstepped after him down the hall, her torso perfectly level and her quads complaining from the effort.

At door six, they split and took positions on either side. Martin held the captured radio to his ear to listen to the enemy chatter, hoping to learn if the hotel shooters were aware of their presence. After a few seconds, he mouthed, "Clear channel."

She nodded, and Martin moved into position.

A part of her wanted to hold until she heard rifle fire from inside the room, when the shooter would be engaged and distracted. But every volley at Munn's team was a roll of the dice that one of her teammates could end up wounded or killed.

"Two, Eight—breaching window six, level three," she said.

"Check," Munn came back.

She glanced at Martin, giving him the go-ahead, and he counted with a nod of his head.

Three . . . two . . . one . . .

Using his body as a battering ram, the former MARSOC Raider slammed into the door, splintering the doorjamb and cracking the slab as he did. Gunfire erupted, and Martin returned fire. Grimes shifted right, opening a line on the target—in this case, *targets.* She fired a three-round burst center mass into the figure on the right and indexed left to fire a volley at the other shooter.

In her peripheral vision, she saw Martin take a knee.

She swiveled back to the right, where the first terrorist she'd shot was still upright. With sniper precision, she put a round into the dude's head, dropping him. She indexed back left, to the second tango who'd been shot by both her and Martin. The crumpled body wasn't moving, and the man's rifle lay dropped on the carpet beside a limp hand. She turned to her teammate.

"I'm hit," he said, inspecting his chest and abdomen.

She swiveled to check their six, sighting on the hotel room door, before sidestepping to take a knee next to him. For tonight's op, they were wearing the new sheer, antiballistic, gel body armor. It was supposedly rated to stop 5.56 and 7.62 rounds, but to her knowledge the only person who'd been shot wearing it so far was Dempsey. And if memory served, he'd been shot with a 9mm. At least for now, though, Grimes didn't see any blood leaking out the bottom of Martin's kit, so that was a good sign.

"You think it punched through?" she asked, eyes flicking to the doorway.

"Pretty sure," he said, shoving a hand under the bottom left side of his shirt and kit. He pulled out bloody fingers. "Might have clipped me just below the skirt of the vest. I took a volley center mass . . . but I'm breathing okay."

She glanced back at the door, then said, "Unzip your vest; I need to know what we're dealing with here."

The new kits had an overlapping Velcro flap that ran from armpit to waist on the left side. Martin yanked the flap and peeled the bottom left corner of his vest up and away. Letting her rifle hang, Grimes leaned in and pulled Martin's Under Armour shirt up to expose his muscular abdomen and chest. Her gaze went first to the bleeder, a small crimson hole to the left of the operator's belly button, two inches from his side and above the hip. Hopefully the slug came out shallow and didn't punch through his intestines or other vital organs, but it was hard to predict the path of a bullet once it entered a human body and began rattling around. She gave his chest a quick once-over, where she saw three welts already forming hematomas, but no other holes. The ballistic gel apparently worked as advertised.

"Roll," she said, pulling on his arm. "I want to see the exit wound."

Whereas entry wounds were tiny and tidy, exits were typically horror shows. Slugs were designed to deform and spin when passing through tissue. A gory, nasty chunk of flesh was missing from Martin's flank. There was a lot of blood pouring from the wound, and Grimes felt uncharacteristically queasy. She wasn't squeamish when it came to blood in general but seeing it from one of her friends and teammates was different.

"That bad, huh?"

She didn't answer. In her mind, she calculated the trajectory between entrance and exit. It was possible the bullet had not entered his abdominal cavity at all.

Possible . . . not likely.

She gave him a tight smile without answering and then checked their six, raising her rifle and sighting on the hallway door long enough to collect herself. With a heavy exhale, she lowered her rifle again and let it hang while she pulled a blowout kit from her thigh pocket.

Working quickly and methodically, she heavily packed both wounds with gauze infused with a blood-clotting agent, placed trauma pad dressings over both and taped them tightly in place, and then wrapped his midsection with a four-inch self-adhering bandage. They had drilled trauma care constantly since she'd been at Ember, every time they spent a day at the Farm, and the whole thing took under a minute.

While she worked, she listened to comms. Having dispatched two of the three enemy snipers who had been ravaging Munn's position, she imagined his team was now concentrating their covering fire on the lone remaining shooter in the hotel and had repositioned to safety on the west side of the target house. Dempsey's stick had breached the target house, but she wasn't hearing anything from them either, and Wang had yet to come back online.

"Thanks, I got it from here," Martin said, pushing her hands clear as she tried to pull down his shirt.

"Are you sure you're—"

"I'm in the fight," he said in an uncharacteristically stern voice.

She slapped him on the shoulder and rose, her rifle up and ready. She understood all too well. Martin wasn't upset with her, nor was he upset with the inconvenience of being shot. The *never out of the fight* ethos was woven into the DNA of everyone at Ember. The only two conditions that would prevent Martin from finishing the op were unconsciousness or death.

She advanced on the door, stopping at the threshold to listen. Hearing nothing, she quickly peeked around the corner, then jerked her head back.

"Clear," she said as Martin joined her. The look on his face—all piss and vinegar—told her everything she needed to know.

"One more to go on level two," she said.

Just then, the radio Martin had taken from the first shooter squawked to life. Grimes, who'd developed only a rudimentary knowledge of Arabic, couldn't understand a thing.

"Is that Arabic?"

"No," Martin said. "I think it's Urdu. Most of these guys are from Pakistan."

"Do you speak it?"

"No, but this is the second call he's made. I bet it's the dude on two checking in with his teammates, asking why they stopped shooting."

It made sense, but it was just an assumption. The speaker could just as easily be someone radioing from the main house. "Are you going to be able to breach the door with your injury?"

"Yeah," he said, but she could see he was wondering the same thing himself.

"All right. We take the north stairwell down to two and finish the job. I'll lead."

"Check."

She was first out into the hall and cleared left while advancing on the stairwell at the north end of the corridor. Martin cleared right and took position on her right shoulder, and together they quick-stepped down the length of the hall. The operator hunched slightly, bracing against the pain he must have been feeling, and twice Grimes saw his left foot drag a bit. On reaching the door to the stairwell, she paused for him to take position, count her down, and open the door. She surged into the stairwell and sighted down the descending flight. Martin entered behind her and cleared the other direction.

"Clear," she said.

"Clear," he echoed.

She was already heading down the stairs when the door at the bottom of the landing below swung open and a figure charged into the stairwell. On hearing their footsteps, he whirled left and sighted on her. She placed her targeting dot center mass and squeezed the trigger. Her round found its mark, but before he collapsed, the terrorist returned fired.

Grimes felt a stripe of fire light up the left side of her jaw.

She froze, gripped by panic that she'd just had the bottom of her face blown off.

Suppressed rifle fire rang beside her left ear as Martin finished the shooter with a double tap to the head.

Hesitantly, she released the forward grip of her rifle. With her index and middle fingers, she touched the side of her face to make sure it was all still there.

Cheek, jaw, lips . . . Oh, thank God.

She turned to face Luka.

"That was a close one, Lizzie," he said, eyes fixed on the side of her face while he pressed his left palm against his lower back. "Centimeter to the inside and you would've lost half your jaw."

"How bad is it?" she asked, looking from his eyes to her bloody fingertips and back again.

"Just a deep cut. You're vain enough to want a plastic surgeon to close it," he said with a wink, "but it's not bad. Come on, that was probably our guy from level two, but we need to clear it and get back to the roof."

"Are you good?" she asked.

He nodded, his jaw clenched. He was clearly in pain but showed no signs of shock.

She nodded and resisted the urge to probe the wound on her own face as she felt blood run down the side of her neck. At the bottom of the stairs, she put another bullet into the head of the very dead terrorist sprawled on the landing.

"Asshole," she said with a growl.

Then, feeling both grateful that God had saved her face and furious that she'd been a half-second too slow in the engagement, she followed Martin into the second-level hallway. They needed to clear the last room to make sure that the dead terrorist in the stairwell was the last shooter, and then they needed to get back to the roof to finish what they'd started.

CHAPTER 33

Dempsey watched Wallace strip a length of breacher tape from the roll, place it on the door, and connect the leads. The process was faster, simpler, and more precise than using the old stuff, but the wolverine inside Dempsey didn't care. The Wolverine just wanted to get inside the target house and unleash hell.

But beneath the fury, a quiet, pragmatic voice reminded him that he'd only become the *Rosomakha* to survive IK-2. To survive Russia.

But I'm not in IK-2 anymore . . .

He was back with Ember, and the Wolverine was not what the mission needed him to be. More importantly, it was not who his teammates needed him to be either. He forced himself to take a deep, controlled breath and tamp down the fury. For Ember to evolve, he needed to occasionally take a step back and let others lead, so every member of the team could become an interchangeable part of their lethal machine.

He turned to Prescott. "You want to lead this one?"

The operator looked shocked by the question. "Um, hell yeah. You sure, boss?"

Dempsey nodded and took a step back to change places.

"Cool," Prescott said, and Dempsey could see a change in the man's posture as he leaned into his swagger.

"One, this is Charlie. Securing overwatch to prosecute enemy shooters in the hotel. Charlie is now Eight," Grimes said in his ear.

A year ago, Dempsey might have questioned the call. Two years ago, he would have bristled at the audacity of her securing herself instead of requesting authorization. But the Lizzie Grimes up there on the roof today had proven herself to be a cool, calculated tactician under pressure. He trusted her completely.

"Check," he replied. "Alpha is breaching. Happy hunting, Eight."

"Hooyah, that's what I'm talking 'bout!" Munn cheered. "You've got two shitheads on level three . . ."

"Ready," Wallace said, looking first at Dempsey then Prescott.

Dempsey tuned out Munn's report to Grimes, nodded, and pulled a flash-bang from his kit. Prescott did the same and gave the count.

"Three . . . two . . . one . . . go."

Wallace detonated the breaching charge, which blew out the door handle and lock mechanism and a nice chunk of the doorframe. The door slab, however, rattled in place and remained shut, so Prescott gave it a kick and tossed a nonlethal flash-bang into the void. Dempsey hurled his own grenade with power, sending it deep into the room. Like twin lightning strikes, the basement flashed and roared with double thunderclaps.

Prescott charged into the haze, followed by Wallace, with Dempsey taking the rear. Both his teammates had already engaged targets by the time Dempsey crossed the threshold. They were in a common room—a sofa and club chairs on the left, dining table in the middle, and a kitchenette built into the back right corner. Prescott cleared left, Wallace right, and Dempsey surged up the middle.

While his teammates dispatched the two shooters who had been harassing them from the windows, Dempsey glided forward, his body and mind linked and hyperattuned to the rhythm of combat. Ahead, he had no immediate targets, so he vectored left and toward a short hallway leading to a staircase to the upper levels and what he anticipated to be a bedroom, bathroom, or closet. Once in the hallway he counted three doors—all shut: one left, one right, one center at the end. He heard the shuffle of booted feet behind him and felt a thick hand on his right shoulder a moment later, letting him know his teammate—probably Prescott—was behind him. They hadn't had any building plans to study before the op but based on the dimensions of the house and placement of the hallway and doors, Dempsey could guess the layout: bathroom left, bedroom end of the hall, stairwell right.

At the first door on the left, he paused, grabbed the doorknob, and gently turned it. Once Prescott had drifted past him to the other side of the doorframe, he pushed it open and sighted inside.

Empty bathroom, clear.

He glanced over his shoulder and hand-signaled for Tess to cover the right-hand door and hallway behind while he and Prescott cleared the room at the end of the corridor. She nodded, and he and Prescott advanced silently on the closed door six paces ahead. On reaching the door, Prescott silently counted down with fingers: *Three . . . two . . . one.*

Dempsey opened the door, and the former Green Beret surged into the room, clearing left. Dempsey trailed a stride behind, clearing right.

"Clear," Prescott said, swiveling toward Dempsey.

"Clear," Dempsey said, seeing nothing but a couple of dirty old mattresses with rumpled sheets on the floor, along with piles of trash and empty water bottles.

"Two, Eight—one tango down," Grimes said over comms, and Dempsey mentally logged her progress.

He trailed Prescott into the hall where Tess still covered the closed door, which Dempsey figured by process of elimination led to a staircase. Breaching and ascending the staircase would be the most dangerous part of the infiltration. They'd be trapped in a kill box, and by now they'd lost the element of surprise. The upstairs shooters knew they were coming, and there was only one way up and in.

Normally, he'd have Grimes start putting high-velocity rounds through windows to give the bad guys something to think about, but she'd secured as overwatch. As Dempsey weighed their options, Wallace pulled a frag grenade from her kit and raised an eyebrow at him. Dempsey thought a moment. They needed Umar alive, but this entire op felt more like an enemy lying in ambush than defending an HVT. The odds the terrorist mastermind was here seemed incredibly low, and Dempsey had no intention of risking any more teammates' lives. They would figure things out from whatever intelligence they could pull off the X.

"You wouldn't happened to have been a softball player as a kid, would ya?" Dempsey said. "Cuz if that thing doesn't make it to the top and rolls back down the stairs . . ."

Pride flashed in her eyes. "We were 5A high school state champs two years in a row, and I was the starting pitcher."

"Dude, please don't tell me you're going to throw it underhand," Prescott said, with no-bullshit concern in his voice.

She flashed him a crooked grin. "Hell yes I am, and it's going to be a rocket."

"Do it." Dempsey said. He turned to Prescott. "Tony, let's not take any chances. Give 'em something to think about just in case."

Tess Wallace slung her rifle and snugged it tight while Dempsey moved into position with his hand on the doorknob. Prescott took a kneeling firing stance, sighting on the door to blast any potential tango covering on the other side.

"If there's a door at the top of the steps, don't throw it," Dempsey said.

"Obviously," she said with snark.

He grinned at her. "On your mark, Five."

Wallace took a deep breath, rolled her shoulders once, and said, "Now."

As Dempsey yanked the door, she pulled the pin. Prescott fired a quick volley up the stairs and leapt clear. Then, Dempsey watched Wallace whip her arm around in an underhand softball pitch that sent the fragmentation grenade up the steps with a velocity that had to be sixty miles an hour. With the payload airborne, he slammed the door, and they all ducked and covered.

The grenade exploded with a resounding roar at the top of the stairs. A heartbeat later, Prescott led the charge up the steps with Wallace following close behind and Dempsey once again bringing up the rear.

The staircase was enclosed on both sides by plaster walls. The left wall went all the way to the ceiling, but the right side terminated as a hip wall, which served as a railing separating the stairwell from the room above. Prescott stopped at the top of the steps and crouched below the hip wall. Not willing to be outdone by Wallace, the former Green Beret pulled a frag grenade from his own kit, yanked the pin, and lobbed it using a twisting sky hook over his shoulder, a move that would have made Kareem Abdul-Jabbar proud. The grenade exploded on the far side of the room, and Dempsey heard a shriek of pain.

On this cue, Prescott ascended the final few steps and skirted around the hip wall, firing from a low crouch. Wallace followed, disappearing from Dempsey's view, her suppressed SBR burping volley after volley. By the time Dempsey rounded the corner, the firefight was over, and his two teammates were standing over three very dead terrorists.

He mentally inventoried the dead: *Shot two on the balcony during approach, two downstairs, three here, plus the one who Grimes capped makes eight. Which should account for all the thermals we noted pre-op. But still no Umar. These were all low-level shooters.*

He clenched his jaw in frustration.

"One, Two—Bravo squad is in cover behind the west wall outside, ground level of the target house."

While Munn talked, Dempsey spied a metal spiral staircase in the corner that led to what looked like a loft. This unexpected fourth level had not been cleared yet, and Dempsey brought his rifle up, sighting at the top where the staircase entered the ceiling.

Ain't no way in hell I'm fitting up that skinny staircase. He hand-signaled for Wallace and Prescott.

"Copy Two," he said. "Level one and two are secure. Eight KIA. Getting ready to clear a loft we found. I don't think any of these shitheads are Umar."

"Do you need backup?"

"Negative. How is Six?" he asked, referring to Fender, who'd taken a round.

"Pissed off and bleeding, but nonurgent."

"Roger that."

Dempsey watched Wallace as she scampered up the spiraling rungs with no trouble. At the top, she tossed a flash-bang into the loft. After the flash and the *whump*, she disappeared through the hole in the ceiling. Prescott followed, but she called it clear before he'd even gotten his torso through the gap.

"What's up there?" he hollered. "Weapons cache, bunch of bombs? Cyber cave?"

"Negative," Wallace called down. "Just a bunk room."

Annoyed, Dempsey turned back to look at the dead terrorists, double-checking that none of them had resurrected and wondering if any of them were Umar, perhaps intentionally trying to blend in with his fighters. His gut told him no, that their HVT was in the wind and had ordered these guys to set a trap and martyr themselves, but you never could tell. After all, nobody knew what Umar looked like, so it was possible the dude was among the dead. Sometimes the terrorist bigwigs picked up a rifle and joined the fight, though not often. They'd need to get pictures and DNA from everyone and take whatever materials they could find off the X. He switched his radio to vox before kneeling to reposition the first of three bodies so the face was visible for photographing. If all they did was bag some low-level fighters, then this op was a fail. Finding and taking Umar was the priority because they needed, desperately, to know what he had planned next.

While he worked, he radioed Grimes. "Eight, One—target house is secure. How are you doing over there?"

Her reply took a long second. "Three tangos KIA. Sweeping the property for more. Be advised, Three is intact but took a hit. Urgent surgical."

"Copy," he said, not liking that news that Martin had been shot. Two wounded on this op was unacceptable, especially since they had not bagged Umar. The assault was complicated, but impossible with the loss of comms and eyes in the sky. That the terrorist network had the ability to hack the Predator drone was terrifying. "We need to get the hell out of here. Wrap it up over there ASAP."

"Roger that."

He turned to Prescott and Wallace, who had just returned from the loft. "Photograph and swab these assholes. One of them might still be Umar." If they had inadvertently killed the terrorist leader, that might be better than the alternative—that he was in the wind with an assload of explosives. "And remember, there are three dead dudes on the balconies. Search the bodies for IDs and bag all mobile phones while I look for laptops. Somebody here hacked our drone and comms. We need to find out how."

"You got it, boss," Wallace said and pulled a sample collection kit from a thigh pocket.

"Maverick, this is Jester," Wang's voice announced on the party line. "Comms reestablished. Sitrep?"

Dempsey breathed a sigh of relief at hearing Wang's voice. He'd been starting to worry that their mobile TOC had been physically targeted, not just hacked. "Compound is secure; we're taking pics and bagging electronics. We have two wounded, so we'll need to expedite to the jet. What about you? Are both vans intact?"

"Jester One and Two are intact, but we repositioned after the drone was commandeered just in case."

"Yeah, about that, Jester," Dempsey said, his voice ripe with fresh irritation after being reminded that he'd almost been killed by their own friggin' drone. "Please explain to me how the hell someone turned our Predator into a kamikaze and used it against us."

"Technically it wasn't *our* Predator; it belongs to the Indian Air Force . . ."

"Mm-hmm," Dempsey said while he rifled through an old wooden desk along the wall, looking for a laptop computer.

". . . but that said, we do need to figure out what happened. Predators are piloted from trailer-mounted ground control units," Wang continued. "Whoever did this didn't just hack our comms, they hacked into the GCU at Bareilly Air Force Base."

Dempsey didn't say anything while he contemplated Wang's report. Then, his temper getting the better of him, he slammed the desk drawer and kicked the desk so hard one of the legs broke and it tipped over.

They hadn't hit a completely dry hole tonight, but they'd also not found a room full of bombs or anything to suggest cyber operations. He was 99 percent certain that Umar was not among the dead. Everybody important in the operation had already bugged out. These guys had been bait.

Then, he noticed it, sliding into the corner of the now tilted desk. An external hard drive, the light still flashing blue with power, had been left behind. A cable still snaked out from the device where a computer had been plugged in. One of the minions, in their haste to get out before the attack and ambush, had disconnected a computer or laptop but left the drive behind.

The corner of Dempsey's lips curled up as he picked it up, inspected it, and slipped it into a bag he pulled from a cargo pocket.

Gotcha, you sloppy sons of bitches . . .

Prescott came back into the room from their quick inspection of the rest of the house. He shook his head and frowned.

"Nothing, boss," he said. "They bugged out and took all their electronics with them. The whole thing was meant to be an ambush on us, it would appear."

"Da, no eshche ne vse poteryano," Dempsey said, holding up the bag.

Prescott gave him a confused look.

Dempsey realized he'd slipped into Russian again. "It's not a total bust—I just found this external hard drive for Wang to hack."

"Oh, good," Prescott said. He was still giving Dempsey a strange look.

A beat later, Wallace was back from the balcony. "Swabbed everyone on this level and the balcony. I'm heading downstairs to get the rest."

Dempsey nodded. "Exfil in three minutes. Jester, pick up on the road out front. Jester Two, I need the rest of your team to break down all gear at the safe house and haul ass to the airfield so we can all fly out together."

"I'll expedite access to the airfield, Maverick One," came Ria's curt reply.

"Maverick, this is Viper," said Buz's calm voice unexpectedly in his ear. It suddenly occurred to Dempsey that Wilson could be a dead ringer for the actor who played "Viper" in the film, with his '80s 'stache. "We're already packed up and are loading to leave. We must assume the safe house is compromised. If they could hack a drone, they likely triangulated our comms. On the road in minutes and meet you at the jet."

"Viper, we have two wounded, one urgent surgical, so let Homeplate know to prep the med suite on the Boeing," Dempsey said, relieved that the experienced CIA spook was not just on the team but with them in Nepal. "Looks like Doc Dan is going to be busy when we get back."

PART III

The master sees beyond what is obvious.

He sees the unseen, feels the unfelt, and hears the unheard.

—I Ching, The Book of Changes

CHAPTER 34

EMBER'S EXECUTIVE BOEING 787-9

TAIL NUMBER N103XL

RAMP IN FRONT OF THE NEPALESE MILITARY HANGAR

TRIBHUVAN INTERNATIONAL AIRPORT

KATHMANDU, NEPAL

0407 LOCAL TIME

Dempsey watched while Munn worked on Martin in the back of the cargo van. The former Navy surgeon had flipped a switch and transformed from badass operator to combat medic in the blink of an eye, a transition that always amazed Dempsey. The doc already had an IV drip going and was now probing the former Marine's abdomen with two fingers.

"Dude, for the last time, I'm not going out with you no matter how you touch me," Martin joked, but his eyes showed he was in real pain.

Fender's wound had been superficial, apparently: a big chunk torn out of his left shoulder all the way through muscle, but no nerve, artery, or bone injuries. He sat on the bench seat beside Prescott, a dressing wrapped around his upper arm and shoulder, blood staining through the gauze and his eyes still in combat mode.

Their van pulled up right beside the Boeing, and Dempsey saw a black SUV was already there, indicating Buz was back from the safe house with the NIA agents. The bombmaker Saeed was probably aboard the jet as well. As the rest of Ember piled out of the van and began hauling gear into the jet, Munn checked pulses in Martin's neck, groin, and his wrists, then pulled a small bottle from his kit that had a spray attachment.

"Ketorolac?" Grimes asked from the rear door.

Munn nodded affirmation. "Won't lower his blood pressure, but it treats pain as well as narcotics without side effects, BP issues, or addiction concerns . . ."

Ketorolac nasal spray—yet another thing that had changed while he was in Russia.

"Let's get you aboard and into the medical suite," Munn said, helping Martin out the back of the van. Dempsey came around to the other side, slinging Martin's left arm over his shoulder while grabbing a loop of the operator's rigger's belt.

"Guys, I'm fine. I can walk," Martin complained.

"Good," Dempsey said. "In that case, shut up and walk."

The trio maneuvered up the airstair, and, to his credit, Martin still had much of his strength, stumbling only at the top over Munn's size-eleven boot. They moved past Prescott and Wallace, who were heading back to the tarmac to get another load of gear, and made their way to the plane's onboard medical suite.

"You're next, bro," Munn said, as they passed Fender en route aft. "You might want to reinforce that shoulder dressing once we're airborne—looks like you're bleeding through."

"Aye, aye," Fender said, giving a little two-finger salute.

The med suite was located near the rear of the plane and spanned three-quarters the width of the fuselage. It had surgical lights on the ceiling, an operating table in the center, and racks of supplies bolted to the walls. At the back, two narrow recovery beds were set up, bunk-bed style, to accommodate a prolonged transport of multiple wounded. Lying in the bottom bunk, his remaining good arm secured to the frame, was Saeed the bombmaker. He watched Martin, glassy-eyed, as they brought him in.

"What are you looking at, fuckstick?" Martin said, seeing the terrorist's eyes on him.

Saeed grinned.

"Ignore him," Munn said. "You need to focus on you."

"Look at the wall," Dempsey said to the bombmaker, "or a black bag is going over your head."

Saeed frowned but did as he was told.

"Am . . . am I going to need an operation?" Martin said, his voice suddenly taking on a tentative timbre.

"It's gonna be okay, bro," Munn said as he stripped his kit and midlayer off, leaving only a black Craig Morgan *God, Family, Country Tour* T-shirt and his cargo pants. "I'm going to do an ultrasound of your belly, and then I'll know more. But you're still hemodynamically stable, so I'm feeling good."

"Okaaaay," Martin said, his skepticism prominent.

"It's possible that the bullet didn't even go into your abdominal cavity, Luka," Munn said. "But if there is an occult injury—something we're not aware of—it could become life-threatening if we don't address it. I'm not hoping to operate on you. Let's see what I see with the ultrasound, okay?"

"Okay," Luka said as Munn helped him pull his kit off.

The jet began to move, taxiing away from the hangar, already in preparation for takeoff.

"If I can't ensure that everything's good, then we can always just do a quick laparoscopy—you know, make a tiny hole and put a camera inside to have a look and be sure."

"A tiny hole?" Martin said, laughing nervously. "Isn't the problem I got too many holes in me already?"

Munn squeezed the man's shoulder. "We'll let you sleep through it if we need to have a look. It's going to be okay."

Martin glanced up at Dempsey, trying to look stoic. Dempsey helped him get his base layer off, then assisted him onto the narrow OR table in the center of the small room.

"You want the dressing off?" Dempsey asked, noting that the front dressing was completely dry, but the rear dressing was already soaked with blood.

"No, leave it on for now," Munn said as he maneuvered a small cart beside the table.

Dempsey could feel the jet taxiing as Munn pulled the quick-release lanyard connected to his rigger's belt and connected it to a handy D ring on the OR table. He glanced at Dempsey.

"We're going to be in takeoff in just a sec, so put a strap on Martin and then take a seat."

Dempsey did as he was told, securing Martin to the table with a wide Velcro strap across the man's waist just below his hips. Then he took a seat on the bench by the door.

"This is going to be cold," Munn announced and squeezed some clear jelly onto Martin's exposed abdomen, streaked with dirt and blood.

"Oooh, hell yeah it's cold," the operator responded.

As the aircraft turned, the pilot's voice came over the intercom system.

"We're cleared for takeoff, everyone, so keep your seats—or find one if you're not already seated. Should be smooth flying today, but maybe a few bumps on the climb out."

As the jet finished its left-hand turn, Dempsey heard the engines spool up, and the aircraft began to accelerate. Munn rolled a wide ultrasound probe around Martin's belly, staring at the little monitor. To Dempsey it looked like nothing but gray and white squiggles—maybe a black-and-white version of a fish-finder on a boat—but Munn stared at it intently as he moved the probe along the left side of Martin's belly. The former Marine winced as the probe got close to the bullet hole near his left flank.

Dempsey watched Munn expertly change the angle and direction of the probe, scanning next along Martin's flank, already black and blue all the way up to his chest, and low on both sides of his belly. Next, he scanned up high, where Dempsey knew the liver lived on the right side—no one wanted to get shot in the liver, which was a great way to die fast.

Dempsey's ears popped as the jet headed up in a steep climb, and Munn set the probe in a holder on the edge of the cart, which he'd had locked down into a little track with his boot. The surgeon turned the machine off.

"Am I good?" Martin asked.

"Yeah, you're going to live," Munn said with a smile. "But . . ."

"But what?"

"I don't see any obvious injuries to your liver or other major organs. I tried to look at the track of the bullet, but that's always a challenge. I can't see well enough to say it didn't penetrate your peritoneum—which is the lining that surrounds your abdomen . . ."

"But I feel fine, so we can just see what happens?" Martin asked hopefully.

"Nope," Munn said. "You've got fluid in your gutters—fluid down in the dependent spaces of the inside of your belly. That's not normal. So, it could be that you have a little bleeder or, potentially, that you nicked your bowel or colon."

"Wonderful," Martin said with a sigh.

"Exactly, which is why I need to take a look and make sure."

"With the little camera through a small hole?"

Munn nodded. "If I see something that needs fixing, I can probably do it through the scope, so no big whack. I'd only open you up if there's something I can't fix laparoscopically, okay?"

"Roger that," Martin said.

Munn turned to Dempsey. "Get Prescott back here to pass gas, okay?"

Dempsey raised a curious eyebrow. "Say what?"

"'Passing gas' is what Dr. Dipshit here calls giving anesthesia," Martin said with a nervous laugh. "Thinks he's funny. When you were in Russia, he ran us all through an advanced medical training so we could assist him if he ever had to do some bullshit like this."

"Normally, I'd tell you to get Fender, but our new pararescue medic happens to be the other guy who got shot, so we'll have to settle for someone else."

"I'll get Prescott." Dempsey rose from the canvas bench seat, feeling the outsider and hating it. "We'll get a briefing together with Casey while you work, and I'll turn Wang loose on the recovered hard drive. Then we'll get data to Baldwin and the boys and see if we can figure out what these assholes are planning next."

"Still in the fight, JD," Martin declared.

"We'll see, Luka. You might need a day or two, depending on what we find," Munn said, managing expectations, then turned to Dempsey. "He's going to be fine no matter what. Nothing going on here I can't fix. And send Fender back too. I want to take a quick look at his shoulder while we get Martin sedated."

Dempsey gave his teammate a thumbs-up, then headed through the mini-OR doors and maneuvered through the center hall, a hand on the wall to stabilize himself as the jet continued to climb.

He turned into the conference room TOC. He again felt out of place, as this was yet another once comforting and familiar area on the Whale that had been changed by Casey in his absence. The conference room now truly had a TOC-like feel, with workstations along the starboard-side wall, where Wang already sat in front of multiple computers. Buz sat beside Wang, also typing away.

"Hey, Tony," Dempsey said. Prescott looked up from where he sat with Lewis, Wallace, and the NIA folks at the central conference table.

"Yeah, boss?"

"Munn needs your help back in medical."

"Is Martin okay?" Grimes asked, concern furrowing her brow.

"Yeah," he said. "Munn says he's going to be fine, but he has to take a look inside with a scope. Promised a full recovery, but still sorting it out. Grab Fender, will you, Tony?" he called after Prescott, who was already heading out the door. "Munn wants to take a look at his shoulder while you get Martin prepped."

"On it."

"Where are we?" Dempsey asked. He grabbed a bottled water from the fridge in the corner, took a long pull, and then took a seat at the table across from Wallace and the NIA investigators. The moment he hit the chair, a weariness descended on him, all his adrenaline now burned off. He felt a few aches and pains that had been hiding behind his combat focus and drive, especially the familiar cries of his lower back and the stinger that shot down his left leg from his old injury.

No, that was Jack Kemper's injury.

"Well," Wang called out from his workstation, "I'm sure it comes as a surprise to no one that I've already breached the password protection and encryption on the external hard drive. I'm just getting ready to look at the files—and there are a ton of them here."

"Yes, you're a genius," Grimes said. "An insecure baby of a genius who needs his little ego stroked at every opportunity."

A few laughs sounded around the table, but the mood, despite Grimes's attempt at levity, remained dark and heavy.

Two wounded teammates, and with Umar and the bombs in the wind, it can only mean another attack on the horizon . . .

"Put what you're seeing up on the big screen, Richard," Wilson said, leaving his station and moving to a seat beside Dempsey. "We'll get all our eyes on it together. And get it sent to Ian's team right away so they can also dig in."

Data started filling a window on the main screen, and Baldwin's face appeared in a pop-up window. "There we are," the man said, through the room's speakers. "Well done, Richard. That certainly didn't take you long."

"I do what I can," Wang said, feigning humility. "But it is nice when *someone* appreciates my brilliance."

"Yes, yes," Baldwin said, already pouring through something on his own computer. All Dempsey could see were tiles of data flickering onto the screen too rapidly to make sense of—strings in another language, some pictures, some schematics, lots of messaging boards . . .

"Stop," Ria called out from where she was sitting. "Can you go back?"

The tiles of data stopped populating, and Wang began to scroll backward through the already downloaded files.

"How far?" Wang asked.

"I don't know," Ria said. "Just keep going until . . . There!"

Dempsey stared at the image of a familiar government building.

"What is that?" Prescott asked.

"Oh dear God," Dak said from across the table.

"That's our building. That's NIA headquarters in New Delhi," Ria said. "Keep advancing . . ."

The images continued to scroll by.

"And *that* is a detailed architectural schematic of the building," Amir said.

"Complete with all security locations, cameras, everything," Ravi added. "How in the hell could they have gotten this? This is highly classified data. You can't find this on the internet."

Dempsey frowned at this disturbing new piece of evidence.

"Ian, I want a rapid analysis of these files. See if you can find any documents that might support the case that NIA headquarters could be al Ghadab's next target," Buz said from beside Dempsey.

"I don't get it," Dempsey said, his voice louder and harder than he'd intended.

"What's wrong, John?" Buz said. "You don't think NIA headquarters is a possible target?"

Dempsey sighed with aggravation. "Maybe it is, maybe it isn't, but that's not what's bothering me."

"Speak your mind, John."

"I think we've been asking the wrong questions. The question we should be asking ourselves now is this: How is it possible that Abu Musad Umar has been consistently one step ahead of us? And not just us," he said, looking at Ria. "Ria and her team have been trying to locate Umar since he went off the radar nearly a year ago. Will somebody please tell me how a poor kid orphaned at a young age, who grew up in the slums of Pakistan, learned the cyber skills to not only acquire confidential building plans for NIA headquarters but also to hack into our encrypted comms and take control of an IAF Predator drone midflight and turn it into a kamikaze? How did he obtain the intelligence necessary to plan the attack on President Warner and Prime Minister Chopra? How did he know how to penetrate the multiple layers of close protection provided by US Secret Service and the PM's security detail?"

When nobody said anything, he continued:

"Here me out on this . . . If al Ghadab was running a massive cyber operation out of that mountain compound, why didn't we find any empirical evidence to support it? I didn't see any remnants to suggest that facility was a hacker haven—no routers, no server racks, no flat-screen monitors, no satellite dish on the roof."

"Well, I hear what you're saying," Wang said, "but they could have packed up all their gear as soon as they learned about our hit on Saeed. They had a couple-hour window before we had eyes on the house."

"Yes, they could have. But if that was truly their version of a TOC, shouldn't we have seen some other evidence of that? Cables and wires and wall-mounted monitor brackets?" He paused, ran his fingers through his hair, and turned to look at Baldwin. "Ian, I have a question."

"Fire away, John," the Professor said.

"After I interrogated Saeed and passed the location of the target we just hit to you guys, did you monitor it and try to collect SIGINT?"

"Yes, John, we most certainly did," Baldwin said.

"And what did you collect?"

"Precious little. In fact, we observed virtually no cellular or internet traffic from the target house. All the traffic was out of the hotel."

"What about the dead fighters we swabbed and photographed? Have we managed to ID any of them yet?"

"Yes, we confirmed the identities of two: Raheem al Gazi and Ahmed Matri," Baldwin said. "I should note that both of these men were already flagged as possible al Ghadab members in the NCTC and SSEUR databases."

"Okay, so that's valuable confirmation," Ria said. "We know we hit the right place, at least."

"There is also another hit from the photos you sent, but it doesn't make sense. One of the dead terrorists is identified as Abu Musad Umar. But we had scoured all of this before and there were no photos of the al Ghadab leader anywhere."

"Well, what does that mean?" Dempsey asked.

"It would appear that the photo was *planted* in the intelligence files, and quite recently," Baldwin said. "We do not believe this man is Umar. A deeper dive flagged him as Mohamad Amit, who was part of a small ISIS terror cell in southern Pakistan and recently joined the al Ghadab network."

"So now al Ghadab is planting fake data files?" Dempsey folded his arms over his chest. "I'm telling you, guys, we're missing the forest for the trees. Either Abu Musad Umar is not who we think his is, or we've missed something."

"Ockham's razor," Wang said, his voice just above a murmur.

"What was that?" Ria asked as all eyes went to Wang.

"Ockham's razor says that the simplest explanation is usually the correct one. If the capabilities we're seeing from al Ghadab don't seem plausible, or even *possible*, for a terror group with their history and footprint, then maybe we should accept that as the answer."

"I don't understand," Ravi said.

"He's saying that if all the evidence suggests al Ghadab doesn't have a cyber operation capable of doing the things we're seeing, then they most likely don't," Grimes said.

"Then how are they pulling all of this off?" Ravi asked. "The attack in Delhi? The drone hack? How did they get these plans? And how could they possibly plant a picture in existing intelligence files?"

Wang shrugged. "Maybe they didn't. Maybe they've outsourced their cyber operation. Or, better yet, maybe some outside group is helping them."

Dempsey nodded, pleased to see the conversation evolving. *This* was what made Ember so formidable.

"What about Iran?" Tess proposed. "They're the biggest sponsor of terrorism in the region, and they aren't shy about spending money."

"It takes more than money to do this," Grimes said. "Even if VEVAK dedicated all their cyber resources to helping Umar, I'm not sure they could accomplish what al Ghadab has seemingly achieved."

In the corner of his eye, Dempsey saw Baldwin nodding on the screen. "We agree completely. I don't want to speak prematurely on the matter, but we have a couple of leads we're pursuing. Once we have evidence to back up the theory, we'll share it."

"Well, you need to hurry, Ian," Dempsey said, "because we have a hard drive with the confidential building plans for NIA headquarters, and if Saeed made an assload of bombs like we believe—and we have no friggin' idea where they are now—then there is another attack coming. And we are running out of time if we're going to stop it."

CHAPTER 35

Jarvis watched Petra smooth the wrinkles from the gray pencil skirt of her suit while she looked at herself in the mirror. It boggled his mind that God could make anything so beautiful and strong and shrewd as this woman . . .

"Serious and professional," he said gently from the doorway as she turned to him.

"What?" she said, smiling but confused.

"You were wondering how you looked—how you would be received. You look serious and professional," he said, crossing the short distance and wrapping his arms around Petra's waist. "And beautiful."

"Thank you," she said. Her body language suggested she wasn't asking for compliments. "In my role as your chief of staff—at both ODNI and as Vice President—I was a behind-the-curtain consultant. Your *confidant*, you called it once."

He laughed, remembering that moment on the porch at the Naval

Observatory—the Vice President's residence—though it felt like another lifetime ago.

"You said it made you sound like a concubine," he said and kissed her neck.

"I don't think I used the word *concubine*, but I remember saying something like that." Petra touched his cheek. "When I first met you at the Tier One, I only had two wardrobe choices—Navy khakis or cammies—so looking good was not something I had to worry about. A part of me misses the simplicity of a uniform."

"Me too," he said, tugging on his starched white collar, "but you could show up wearing a paper bag, and they'd still have to listen to you. Casey knows you were part of my inner circle all along. And they know your pedigree at both ODNI and the Tier One. You will be taken seriously."

Now she chuckled. "I wasn't worried about being taken seriously— at least not until you said that."

"What, then?" he asked, crossing his arms over his charcoal-gray suit, hating already how often he found himself wearing a tie since becoming President.

"Kelso, I was also an analyst. I'm very good at seeing patterns, at interpreting data, and at drawing conclusions. I'm pretty good at turn- ing that into potential tactical options."

"I would say *very* good at that," he said.

"Thanks," she said, but she seemed more annoyed than comforted. "But that's where my experience ends. I was excellent at being your sounding board—your *confidant*—but, to do this effectively and provide cover, not for you, but for the office of the President, I need to be the one making the decisions regarding Ember now."

"And you will be," he said. "But you don't have to do it alone. You can lean heavily on Mike and Buz. They're both experienced and insightful in a broad range of disciplines. Partner with them and ask their opinion. But don't be afraid to consult with me whenever you need. I don't need cover, Petra."

She nodded, her smile tight again, and looked him in the eyes.

"It's a lot of responsibility, Kelso," she said.

"And no one could shoulder it better."

She smiled for real now and then walked back to give him a hug.

"I have a plane to catch to Tampa," she said after a moment in his embrace.

"I know," he said. "The OC is all in place?"

"Yeah," she said, breaking from the hug. "The First Lady is meeting with kids from a private school, talking to teachers, reading to children . . . First Lady stuff."

"You'll be great at that too," he said. Then he became serious. "I need you to do something else for me, while you're there."

"Of course," she said. "What?"

"You need to brief Mike that I'll be flying to Delhi soon to complete the deal that Warner negotiated with Chopra before the assassination."

"What? When? Kelso, that's a terrible idea with all that's going on right now."

A sly grin curled his lips.

"It's not as simple as that. The trip is going to satisfy dual agendas—one overt, one covert. I sent official correspondence through the SIPRNet system to Andy and others, briefing them on the overt component. But I need you and Casey for the covert element, which will involve Ember."

She looked at him and raised an eyebrow. "Okay, you definitely have my attention. How about reading me in, Mr. President?"

Jarvis took her hand and shared his plan with her.

She listened without interruption. When he finished, she did something that took him by surprise. She said, "Okay."

"Okay, what?" he said, now his turn to raise a suspicious eyebrow.

"Okay, I agree. I think the overt piece is necessary and the covert piece might just work. I'll brief Casey, and we'll get the ball rolling on all the logistics."

"Great," he said, surprised how easy that had been.

"Secret Service could be a problem . . ." she said, her mind searching for trip wires.

He smiled. "Yes, but they work for me. And besides, I've got Tony to bulldog them into submission."

"That you do."

He extended his arm to her. She tucked her hand inside the crook of his elbow. Feeling like the luckiest guy on earth, he escorted her downstairs to where her Secret Service detail was waiting to take her to the limousine for her flight to Tampa to meet with Ember's head shed in person for the first time.

On the landing at the bottom of the steps, she leaned in and gave him a peck. "Wish me luck."

"Good luck," he said and kissed her back. "Oh, and if you happen to see Lieutenant Commander Redman when you're on the compound, tell him the President says *Hooyah*."

She chuckled. "Roger that."

In her parting glance, he saw both hope and worry in her eyes—hope in the audacity of his plan and worry about what could happen to him if it didn't pan out.

CHAPTER 36

Shazi sat at the polished black dining room table inside the luxury apartment and checked his watch, then groaned in irritation.

Umar was thirty-five minutes late for their meeting. Given the global manhunt that he knew was now underway for all al Ghadab members, Shazi should have been worried that the world's most infamous terrorist had been captured or killed. But he suspected he knew the real reason his apprentice was overdue. When Umar finally did arrive—dressed in a black tailored suit and wearing new stylish eyeglasses and expensive shoes—Shazi's suspicions were confirmed.

Celebritydom had gone to Umar's head.

In the short time since the assassination bombing, dark money had flowed into al Ghadab's coffers like a flash flood. Umar's organization had gone from broke and bootstrapping to brash and bursting with cash and volunteers overnight. With this change of fortune had come a change in focus for Umar. The quiet, driven, methodical man Shazi had partnered with and helped develop for over a year had now morphed suddenly into someone he scarcely recognized. Umar looked every bit a Dubai playboy prince—a caricature of the of very Muslim apostates he used to denounce.

"You're late," Shazi said in English, turning from the dining table to look at Umar, who, to Shazi's gut-wrenching dismay, was accompanied by an attractive woman carrying several shopping bags from fancy stores.

Umar ignored the comment.

"This is the businessman from Hong Kong I was telling you about," Umar said to the woman, in English. "See, I told you he'd be upset."

She grinned and even giggled a little. "I apologize," she said in Indian-accented English. "It's my fault that Zayn is late. He told me he had business meeting, but we were having so much fun."

Zayn. So that is what he told you to call him.

Shazi eyed the woman, who still wore her oversized designer sunglasses despite having come inside. She was one of the most strikingly beautiful women he'd ever seen, but her features and fair skin tone looked more Persian than Indian. Then again, during his time in India, Shazi had witnessed the full spectrum of skin colors from deep brown to creamy white. Similar to China and Korea, in India fair-skinned women were often deemed more desirable. Colorism was a hot topic across all of Asia but not something that Shazi had either the time or the inclination to worry about. What he did find interesting, however, was that Umar had clearly pursued a woman who, by Delhi standards, was elite.

Shazi forced a smile. "I appreciate the apology. I'm leaving for Hong Kong in a few hours, so if you could excuse us, I'm sure Zayn will contact you when he's free."

"Oh, too bad," the woman said with a pout. "I thought you said you were going to give me a tour."

"It is a rental apartment," Shazi said quickly before Umar could answer. "Nothing special. It was very nice to meet you."

"We haven't actually met, now have we?" she said, setting the shopping bags on the floor and walking over to Shazi with her right hand extended. "I'm Sunita."

"Li Mucheng," Shazi said, shaking her hand.

"Charmed," she said. "Zayn says you're an investment banker?"

Shazi forced a patient smile on his face. "That's right."

"And you're interested in investing in his company to help it grow internationally . . ."

Shazi nodded. "My firm sees a lot of potential in both his vision and products."

She smiled at Umar and held his gaze for a moment before saying, "I'm sure you have many important business matters to discuss. I'm very thirsty, but after I get myself a water, I'll leave you men to do your negotiations."

She made her way into the kitchenette as if she owned the place. Shazi watched her go to the refrigerator and retrieve a bottled water. Something about the woman felt familiar to him, but he couldn't quite put his finger on it.

"Mr. Li," Umar said, his tone quite forceful.

Shazi turned to the terrorist. "Yes?"

"I'd like to postpone our meeting for an hour."

"Impossible," Shazi said, the word a line in the sand. "We meet now, or I depart and the fund caps our investment at where it stands today."

"Have your meeting, Zayn," the woman said, leaning against the counter and standing in a pose that seemed to accentuate her perfectly proportioned breasts, hips, and legs. "I wouldn't want to be the thing responsible for you losing an important investment. Besides, without more money, how can you buy me things?"

She laughed at her own joke, walked over and kissed Umar on the cheek, then picked up two of the three shopping bags and headed for the door without another word or even a parting glance.

"How are you going to get home?" Umar called after her.

"I'll call my driver," she said with a laugh. She disappeared out the apartment's front door, letting it slam behind her as she did.

"What the hell was that all about? And who is that woman?"

"That was Sunita. And if everything goes according to plan, I'm going to sleep with her tonight," Umar said, turning from looking at the door back to Shazi. "Can you imagine sex with *that*?"

"Where did you meet her?"

"Chanakya," Umar said, shrugging off his suit coat and hanging it on the back of one of the chairs at the table where Shazi sat. He then walked to the kitchen, picked up the half-empty bottle of water Sunita had left on the counter, and began to drink from it.

"And when did you meet her?"

"Today."

"You met her today and brought her here? Are you an idiot?" Shazi barked, scowling at the younger man who now, upon closer inspection, looked like he'd also visited a fancy barbershop or salon. Umar's hair was styled with gel, and his beard now looked expertly manicured, with precise shave lines along the jaw and upper cheeks. "First of all, Chanakya is place with many cameras and high visibility. Your face was certainly recorded by multiple cameras. But even worse, you brought a total stranger to this safe house, knowing that I would be here!"

"Why are you so upset, Shazi? No one knows my face. You assured me of this personally. You said your comrades in PLA Unit 61398 have made sure of it—that the enemy databases have been scrubbed, and they have nothing on me. The Americans don't even know my real name," Umar said and took a sip of water. "And as far as your identity is concerned, I used your NOC with Sunita. That's what NOCs are for. Besides, you think a woman who looks like that is going to commit your name to memory? Five minutes from now, when she's driving away in her Range Rover, she won't even remember your face."

"It's not me I'm concerned about," Shazi said, which was only a half truth. "Two superpowers are hunting you and your men. A counterterrorism hit squad ambushed the Kathmandu compound last night, and it appears there are no survivors."

Umar leaned casually against the wall and laughed. "That was the point, Shazi. Your people were supposed to put Amit's face on my file. This is good news. They will think I'm dead. The plan is working."

"I don't think you understand how dangerous the situation has become, and how capable and tenacious our adversary is. The Americans have the most robust intelligence community and counterterrorism operation on the planet. They will not be fooled so easily. All I've done is buy you time."

Umar chuckled. "I appreciate your concern, friend, but I think you are overreacting."

"We have a major operation planned for tomorrow. You will not leave this apartment or see that woman again until after the mission is complete. Do you understand?"

Defiant anger flickered in Umar's eyes. "Last time I checked, Abu Musad Umar was the leader of al Ghadab, not Liu Shazi."

"Maybe you have forgotten, *friend*, but we are partners in this venture. We have been from the beginning. If not for me, you'd still be living in squalor in Kasur. Without my country's money, support, and technology, al Ghadab would be nothing."

"Maybe, maybe not, but you are not one of us," Umar said with superiority and a hint of something new, something Shazi took to be disdain. "You're not Pakistani and you're not Muslim. You're *Chinese*."

This comment stoked immediate ire in Shazi. He considered walking out, but he managed to center himself and find guidance from his readings of the *I Ching*:

The superior man controls his anger and restrains his instincts.

Maybe it had been a mistake to come back to India. Maybe Director Dongxing had been right. An unexpected and tremendous victory had been won; the prudent move was to savor the moment and cut all ties so that the trail from al Ghadab to Shanghai would decay to nothing. The MSS had planted intelligence linking the attack to al Ghadab, just as he'd planned—focusing the Americans' attention on destroying the terrorist organization he had used for his purposes. Instead of taking the win and waiting for Umar and his organization to be wiped off the map by JSOC operators from the West, though, Shazi had returned to the lion's den at the worst possible time. He was now in a trap of his own making.

But how could he walk away when his deep cyber hack into the

American intelligence network indicated that the newly sworn in American President was brazenly returning to Delhi to meet with the new acting Prime Minister? In failing to eliminate Jarvis in Tel Aviv, he'd created an adversary far more capable and dangerous in the Oval Office than Rand Warner had ever been. Thanks to Umar's assassin's failure, a Tier One Navy SEAL now sat behind the Resolute desk, a Navy SEAL whose ethos and mentality had been forged in combat and a profession that solved every problem with direct action. This was what concerned Shazi the most.

The truth was, his failure to kill Jarvis was the real reason he'd returned. To undo the mistake. To set things right.

It's convenient to blame Umar, but Jarvis becoming President is my fault . . . and only I can fix it.

"The reason I'm upset, Abu, is because I have new and important intelligence to share with you that will change our operation tomorrow," Shazi said, realizing he needed to swallow his pride and do whatever it took to get the old Umar back and focused on the mission.

Curiosity piqued, Umar said, "What new intelligence?"

"You'll not believe it, but President Jarvis is coming to Delhi."

"When?"

"Tomorrow."

Umar jerked back at the news, as if he'd been physically smacked. Then he walked to the table and sat down opposite Shazi, his eyes burning with intent. "Are you certain?"

Shazi nodded.

"Why would an American President take such a risk?" But the terrorist's eyes burned now with excitement and maybe a hunger.

"Simple: hubris," Shazi said. "He's a former Navy SEAL. Think about his reaction to the assassination attempt in Tel Aviv. This is a man who, instead of running away from danger, runs toward it. He wants to show the world that he is not afraid. That America will not be intimidated by al Ghadab—or anyone else, for that matter."

Umar rubbed his chin and smiled. "You were right to be angry with me. We have much work to do and very little time to do it. The girl can wait. *This* is the priority."

CHAPTER 37

89TH AW, 1ST AIRLIFT SQUADRON C-32A

CALL SIGN EXECUTIVE-ONE-FOXTROT

ON THE RAMP IN FRONT OF BUILDING 48

MACDILL AIR FORCE BASE

TAMPA, FLORIDA

0911 LOCAL TIME

Petra Jarvis, First Lady of the United States, sat patiently on a semicircular sofa in the middle of the enormous jet sitting on the tarmac at MacDill, waiting.

She glanced at the clock on the bulkhead.

9:11 . . .

The irony of those numbers was not lost on her, and she had an awful memory of how she'd felt that day, when she'd been a very young Navy Intelligence officer. That today she had traveled aboard a Boeing 757 essentially by herself, save for her new FLOTUS chief of staff and her contingent of Secret Service agents, seemed the most atrocious waste of taxpayer money imaginable. She understood the security issues and the optics, but the 89th Air Wing also operated a Gulfstream 550 corporate jet as the C-37. That would have still been decadent beyond words, but one helluva lot more cost-effective than a 757.

But this was not a choice she had the authority to make, it turned out. In fact, FLOTUS was a position that came with far less authority over anything than her last job as chief of staff to the Vice President. And even that position had bordered on superfluous, compared to her role at ODNI when Kelso had been director.

I'm going backward . . .

She sighed. This was her life now, she supposed.

At least it was for the next few months, something Kelso seemed to genuinely believe. A part of her prayed it was true, that they might be able to find that ranch he had talked about and lead a simple life. But when she tried to picture her husband—former Tier One Navy SEAL CSO-turned-chief spook, now the President of the United States—relaxing with a drink and watching the sunset, she couldn't. For a few nights? Definitely. A couple weeks? Probably. A few months? Doubtful.

And forever . . . ?

She smiled.

"Just a few more moments, ma'am," Anita Sanchez, her chief of staff, said. The simple gray suit the woman wore didn't make her look any less military, with her hair pulled back tight in a regulation bun, her shoulders squared, and her hands clasped behind her back. "Secret Service has a vehicle ready; they're just posting along the route."

Petra tilted her head at the woman, who she knew better as Captain Sanchez: Marine officer and the intelligence liaison for MARSOC when Petra had been assigned to the Tier One. Their paths had crossed numerous times, and though she'd never gotten to know the brilliant analyst well, she always imagined they had much in common.

"Tell you what, Anita," she said. "If you promise to call me anything other than *ma'am* when we're alone, I'll promise to call you Lieutenant Colonel Sanchez, or Colonel, or Marine—whatever you like."

Sanchez's shoulders dropped. She laughed, the ice broken.

"Deal," she said, unclasping her hands and stepping closer. "And Anita works fine."

"And I'd prefer Petra—like the old days," Petra said. "If you can swing it."

"I'll try, ma'am—I mean, Petra."

Now they both laughed.

"Maybe it helps that this FLOTUS billet is more of a TAD thing," Petra offered. "There's an election in a couple of months, and then two months later, it'll all be over."

"Well, we'll see," Sanchez said.

"What's that mean?"

"Seriously?" Sanchez stared at her, confused. "The whole country is rallying behind the President like some Jason Bourne action hero. There are polls saying he would win in a landslide that would make the Reagan election look like a razor-thin margin. He'd have the whole party, nearly all of the independents, and one poll even says he'd get close to half the voters from across the aisle. Hell, even Margaret Whalen said in an interview yesterday that she'd support him, but of course she promised to carry on his leadership if not. There's never been anything like it."

Petra considered this a moment. She'd seen the footage—again and again, in fact, as it was now a favorite clip on all the networks, as well as among the White House staffers. There were a few media talking heads on the fringes who were calling Kelso's actions reckless or worse, but she was not unaware of the impact his heroism was having on the country. At a time of war and uncertainty, their President was an action hero. That he was a reluctant President made him only more attractive.

"Well, I can tell you that's not likely to happen," she said with a wry shake of her head. "He never wanted to be President. Hell, he never wanted to be Vice President. He answered the call but hated every minute of it."

Her chief of staff glanced around to be sure they were still alone.

"But it must have made the . . . other thing"—her voice had fallen to a whisper—"a lot easier."

Petra shook her head. She'd read Sanchez in on her own current role with Ember—well, *partially*. She'd realized immediately when Kelso had tasked her that she'd need help, logistically if nothing else.

She'd done that for Kelso, after all, when he'd secretly provided tasking to Ember on behalf of Warner. She needed to have someone just to juggle schedules, meeting, connections with Casey . . .

She had not told Kelso about reading Anita partway in. She felt awful about it. She wanted to tell Jarvis everything and valued his opinion above anyone's—but like the details of her management of Ember, this discretion was required. He was the President. There absolutely had to be a degree of separation between him and Ember, but she simply couldn't do the job alone.

She saw that her chief of staff still waited patiently and quietly for a reply.

"Not as much as you might think," she said. "Yeah, he had access, but the VP is largely a ceremonial position. Or maybe more like a QRF, you know? Ready to go, but mostly on standby. There was also far more scrutiny on the VP than when Kelso was the DNI. It made it hard to stay under the radar."

The former Marine spook nodded her understanding. Sanchez was proving herself every bit as insightful and quick as Petra remembered her being more than a decade ago. With some guilt, Petra reminded herself that she'd pilfered Sanchez from a great assignment as deputy assistant to the Commandant of the Marine Corps for Intelligence. The Marine officer had been in a dream job with a pipeline to colonel, and likely general, until Petra had called her and put up a significant roadblock to that once-in-a-lifetime opportunity.

"I can't imagine it's going to be much easier for you," Sanchez said.

"Nah, I have you," Petra said, giving the Marine officer a solemn look. Sanchez, whether she knew it or not, was going to be the key to the whole thing. "You have no idea how grateful I am that you came on, Anita. I really needed you."

The Marine officer shrugged.

"Call of duty, Madam First Lady—I mean, Petra," she replied.

"Madam First Lady?" a new voice asked.

She looked back to see the head of her detail, Secret Service Agent Troy Stallone, peering in. The other agents called him Rocky.

"Hey, Troy," she said. "Ready?"

"Yes, ma'am," he replied.

Sanchez raised an eyebrow.

Petra noticed. "It's different when he says it, Anita. I don't know why."

"Did I say something wrong, ma'am?"

"No, not at all," she said, and rose from the sofa. "No press, right?"

"As requested, ma'am. There will be press at the school event, however."

"Of course," she said. "But not on base."

"Correct," he said. "We had CENTCOM issue a security elevation to keep civilians away."

"Okay, then," she said.

They'd released that the new First Lady was shy and terribly private to keep press off the flight. She imagined the press pool had sighed with relief, actually. No one wanted to cover the new First Lady visiting Cambridge Christian School in Tampa to congratulate them on being a blue-ribbon private school, talk on the importance of school choice with the faculty, and then read to preschoolers—at least not with world tensions in the wake of the assassination of President Warner and another foreign leader. There was little room in the news cycle for her school visit.

Which makes it the perfect cover for my real visit.

She descended the airstair where the base commander, Colonel Adam Szczepanik, gave her a salute—which she'd been instructed, as First Lady, not to return. The officer shook her hand.

"Welcome to MacDill, Madam First Lady," he said. "But then I understand you've spent plenty of time here, ma'am."

"You did your research, Colonel," she said. She had indeed spent enormous amounts of time at the Florida base, which was home to both CENTCOM and SOCOM, while she was working with JSOC and later with the ONI. "This is Anita Sanchez, my chief of staff. She's in fact *Colonel* Sanchez, on loan to me from the Marine Corps. I'm blessed to have her with me."

"Good to meet you," the colonel said, shaking Anita's hand.

The colonel escorted them to two waiting SUVs, where Secret Service Agent Bellamy Williams opened the door for her.

"Ma'am," Williams said as Petra stepped into the large, up-armored, deeply tinted Suburban.

"Thanks, Bell," she said. She liked to know everyone's name. It usually came easy to her, but between the Office of the First Lady staff and the Secret Service details for both her and Kelso, remembering them all was becoming more of a challenge than usual.

The caravan pulled away. As they left the flight line, the rear SUV turned right, toward where she remembered the Morale, Welfare, and Recreation department had a beach, boat rentals, and a large campground set up on Hillsborough Bay. There was a restaurant there as well—a pretty good one, if she remembered correctly. The second blacked-out SUV was meant to be a distraction, providing uncertainty as to where FLOTUS was going, and the contingent of Secret Service agents would be fools if they didn't roll the feint into a good meal.

Petra's SUV turned left, paralleling the flight line along Hangar Loop Drive before turning left onto Zemke Avenue. She stared out the window, thinking about all she had to accomplish today, as they circled around the enormous building that housed United States Central Command, weaved past the base exchange complex, and finally crossed just north of the main runway, eventually leaving the paved four-lane for a small access road that seemed to go off into nowhere.

"Where exactly are we going, ma'am?" Sanchez asked from the captain's chair beside her.

"You'll see," she said, smiling at her chief of staff. "They'll be expecting us at the gate, but we might still have to prove who we are, First Lady or not."

The guard shack looked unimpressive. She'd never been to this secret part of the base but imagined there was more to it than met the eye. They were waved through quickly, but not until their credentials were checked by the guard, who, though he was dressed in the gray uniform of a government contractor security guard, had the thick arms, sleeve tattoos, and hardened face of a soldier with a more lethal pedigree.

Their SUV pulled into a lot full of cars, and she saw two prefabbed buildings that looked more like construction trailers. The one to the left, she knew, was the home of the new JSOC Tier One SEAL Team, the team her husband had once led and that she had once served in. The other building housed something else entirely, and something almost no one on earth was read in on—including most of the members of the JSOC team working in the building right next door. The official cover was that the building housed an experimental intelligence analysis unit.

"Like to make one more pitch that you let us accompany you, Madam First Lady," Agent Troy Stallone said from the front seat once they had parked. His eyes suggested he knew his plea would be pointless.

"At least one of us, ma'am," Bell Williams said from the rear seat behind her.

"I wish I could, but I'm afraid that would be impossible, Rocky," she said, expecting the long, tense sigh he let out as soon as she said it. "I assure you, I'll be as safe as anywhere in the world."

Resigned, the agent got out of the driver's seat and opened the door behind him, allowing Anita Sanchez to exit. Somehow Petra managed to slip out her door before the agent in the passenger's seat, whose name she couldn't recall, could open it. She gave the Secret Service agent a sheepish shrug.

"We'll be out shortly—within the hour, I hope. I can always call you when we're done, if you want to go grab something to eat or whatever," Petra said.

She and Sanchez mounted the four wooden steps to enter the low trailer. As she knew he would, Agent Stallone shook his head.

"We'll be right out here, ma'am," he said. "Just in case. Please inform any security that we are out here and responsible for your safety."

A fully kitted-up man, who looked like a special operator, waited for them inside, standing beside an elevator door.

"Welcome, Madam First Lady," the man said, eyeing Sanchez with unmasked suspicion.

"Colonel Sanchez is with me. She's my chief of staff and will be accompanying me today."

"Let me just . . ."

The elevator doors slid open before he could call his supervisor, and a man she recognized emerged with a tight smile on his face. Mike Casey wore simple khaki pants, comfortable shoes, and an unmarked black sports shirt. His close-cropped hair was flecked lightly with gray, but the former submariner had barely a wrinkle. *Must be the lack of sun damage*, she thought, *from all the time he spent underwater.* Casey's engineering and submarine warfare pedigree, while atypical for leading a Spec Ops task force, brought a unique and analytical perspective to the job, which was the main reason Jarvis had handpicked him as Shane Smith's replacement.

"It's great to have you with us, Madam First Lady," Casey said, extending a hand.

"Good to be here," she said, finding his handshake strong and dry.

"Colonel Sanchez, I heard you might be joining us," Casey said. The two shook hands. "Well, let's get to it, then. We have a pretty busy day again."

They entered the elevator. Inside, Casey swiped his CAC, which instead of closing the elevator doors simply illuminated a black glass panel with a red light. When he pressed his hand onto the glass, the red halo of light around the scanner turned green and the doors closed. The elevator began to descend.

Only one destination, apparently . . .

"So, Mike," Petra began with a patient smile, "I know this is all a little awkward, but if it's going to work, I need you to dispense with all the *Madam First Lady* BS. Can you do that?"

The former submarine skipper chuckled. "I expected as much, because I had the same conversation with your husband when he became Vice President."

Now it was her turn to laugh. "I have no doubt."

"May I ask how deeply read in the colonel is?" Casey asked pointedly, giving a polite smile to Anita. The woman clenched her jaw but managed to smile back somehow. No one liked to be out of the loop.

"She is aware that my husband has tasked me to liaise between his office and Ember for the next few months. She knows you are tasked with finding those responsible for the assassination of President Warner and the failed effort in Tel Aviv. She is my chief of staff, but also a trusted adviser. Of all my staff, I'll be working most closely with her, and I need her to be able to coordinate our interactions and meetings, as well as manage cover stories for all in-person events such as this."

Casey nodded. His eyes told her that he got it—Sanchez was read in on what she was doing, but not on the full details of the most secret direct-action team in the world. She knew Casey would make sure it stayed that way, unless instructed otherwise.

The elevator slowed to a stop and the doors opened.

"Welcome, Colonel," Casey said.

"Call me Anita. If we're both calling the First Lady of the United States 'Petra,' I imagine I can dispense with the title as well."

Petra could tell that Casey warmed to Sanchez immediately with that. He led them down a short hall and then opened a heavy door, gesturing with his head toward a wall of cubbies, each with a plastic bin inside.

"Regular SCIF rules," he said.

Petra and Sanchez placed their cell phones and, in Sanchez's case, an Apple watch into the bins. Then they followed Casey through another heavy door into a lobby of sorts, but without any reception desk.

"I heard you did some remodeling," she said. "Of course, I've never been here, so . . ."

"Yeah, well, I just made it a little more efficient and streamlined," he said, then opened a door. "This is us."

The room held a long conference table with a standard large-screen monitor across from the door. There was a podium, but it was shoved in a corner and, Petra guessed, rarely used. Seated at the table was the bespectacled Ian Baldwin, flanked by two analysts she knew only as Chip and Dale. At the head of the table to her right was Amanda Allen, the former CIA officer Dempsey had rescued from terrorist abductors in Syria, now an integral part of Ember's intelligence team.

"Good morning, Madam First Lady," Allen said.

Petra sighed. "For Ember meetings I want you to call me Petra, okay, everyone?"

There were nods all around. Allen seemed to relax a little.

"And this is Anita," she added, gesturing to her chief of staff.

"Hello, Anita," Baldwin said and rose politely, giving a little wave. "Delighted to have you with us. You've done great work in your position as Deputy Assistant for Intelligence. Your reports are flawless." He gave her a goofy grin.

"How does he . . . ?" Sanchez began.

Petra shook her head to cut her off, and they all took their seats.

"Let's get started," Casey said and updated her and Sanchez on all the events of the past seventy-two hours since Ember SAD deployed to Delhi.

"So where are Umar and the bombs now?" Petra asked when he finished.

"We don't know," Baldwin said simply, as if talking about losing his favorite coffee cup.

"The open border between Nepal and India makes the movement of people and contraband difficult to monitor," Allen said, leaning in, elbows on the table. "Our concern is that Umar has fled Nepal for India. He may have the bombs with him. And we believe the target may be the NIA headquarters in New Delhi."

"Well, that's a problem, Mike," Petra said, turning to Casey.

He held her eyes but said nothing.

It was time to continue the conversation she and Jarvis had begun, but this time with the people most able to cybersleuth the answer. "Do we really believe that al Ghadab is capable of hacking a Predator UAV in flight and hacking NIA to steal the building plans? It seems a stretch for a bootstrap jihadist organization from Pakistan."

"We do not," Baldwin said, answering for Casey. He took a sip of tea from a cup beside him, then set it back down on a little saucer.

"We put the mathematical probability that they could have designed and executed these attacks unaided at less than four percent," Dale said from his wheelchair, his sinewy arms crossed in front of him.

"Three-point-two-four," Chip said.

"Which is less than four," Dale said, glancing over at his teammate.

"Unaided?" Sanchez asked, not missing a beat.

"There is a growing consensus that al Ghadab—operating in a vacuum—lacks the network, funding, and frankly the sophistication to have pulled off the attacks in Tel Aviv or New Delhi," Casey said. "Much less the technology to hack an operational drone or gain access to the intelligence needed to time the attacks in Tel Aviv and New Delhi."

"They could have conducted the attack in Patan Durbar Square in Nepal, though," Baldwin said and took another sip of tea, crossing his legs at the knee as he did. "In fact, I'm of the opinion that it was a dry run for the assassination bombing in Delhi. I think they were validating the shape charge explosive vest design to make sure it had the directional yield needed. Regarding the rest of the cyber activities, we are exploring possibilities, partnering heavily with our colleagues at NSA and the other various acronym agencies and looking for digital fingerprints. But we still have not uncovered any concrete evidence linking al Ghadab or Umar to any specific external organization."

Petra knew that Baldwin and Ember as a whole would be focusing on capabilities, the nuts and bolts of executing the attacks. But Petra had been thinking about something else: motive. Maybe it was time to say the quiet part out loud.

"I think we have to ask ourselves this: Outside of al Ghadab's paradigm of jihad, who has the most to gain from these attacks? Who has the most to gain from a disruption of that region of the world?" She paused to let the words sink in. "Who has the most to gain from a change in leadership of the US and India?

"The deal President Warner had outlined with India was multifaceted: a US arms supply component to the Indian military, a tariff reduction and trade incentive component, and US direct foreign investment in India. Had it gone through, China would have taken an enormous economic hit. It also would have destabilized the balance of power and influence in the region. Equally important, it diminishes Beijing's favorite weapon: exerting economic pressure on its neighbors to influence policy. Beijing has been waging an economic war against the West while benefiting from a most-favored-nation status and tremendous US foreign direct investment over the past two decades. Warner threatened to end all of that with this deal."

"Okay, let's say you're right. Let's say, as crazy as that sounds to say out loud, that the Chinese Communist Party is aiding the jihadist organization al Ghadab. Why try to kill Prime Minister Shamone? What does Israel have to do with US-India-China relations?" Allen asked.

"I've been thinking about that a lot too," Petra said, picturing her husband's face. She remembered the footage of him pulling the Israeli Prime Minister to the ground just in time, his SEAL instincts perfect as always. "I think that we have to consider the possibility that Shamone wasn't the target. I think the shooter was going after the VP and missed."

Petra felt all eyes on her as the Ember team ran that scenario through the machinery of their collective minds.

Sanchez broke the silence. "In my last job at the Pentagon, I was focused primarily on the growing China threat. We know that they have both the HUMINT and cyber penetration abilities to gather the intelligence needed to help plan these attacks. And it is not outside the MSS playbook to take a moonshot approach like this."

"What do you mean, *moonshot approach*?" Allen asked.

"I mean that we've seen a shift over the past few years. Beijing is getting bolder. They're not afraid to take chances and try audacious penetrations. I think we're seeing a new approach from them: *Let's throw a bunch of shit at the wall and see what sticks*. Is recruiting a jihadist as an asset that much different from recruiting a disgruntled US serviceman to trade military secrets? They already have a sophisticated global network of blinds and deep-cover agents, so it's possible al Ghadab's leadership might not even suspect there's any link to China, depending on how the approach was executed."

Petra felt a wave of satisfaction at her instinct to bring Anita on as her chief of staff. She resolved now to get Sanchez fully read in on Ember. She picked the thread.

"The chaos created by the loss of President Warner and PM Chopra would disrupt, delay, and possibly derail the Warner deal with India, especially if Vice President Jarvis had also been killed. In the aftermath, the replacement leadership in both countries would be laser-focused on finding who was responsible. It would give Beijing time to act. Time to get their fingers in the pie and provide alternative options and incentives to both countries to replace the plan Warner and Chopra had worked out . . ."

"I like that you're both looking at motive," Casey said, "and your theory is compelling. But without proof we're limited in what we can do, aside from continuing to look for Chinese fingerprints on the materials and data we've collected so far. But if you wanted to give us the authorization to take our investigation to the next level, I could direct Ian and his team to shift from playing defense to offense . . ."

"What exactly would that shift entail, Mike?" Petra asked, despite having a pretty good idea what he was going to say.

"It would involve active penetration of Chinese networks and agencies to identify the actor or actors involved," Baldwin said, jumping in. "Assuming China is involved at all."

"Is there a downside to trying?" she asked.

"I should let the submarine captain answer that one," Baldwin said and smiled at Casey.

"Remember in the movie *The Hunt for Red October*, when Captain Ramius orders one ping and one ping only?" Casey asked. "All submarines have active sonar, but despite it being incredibly useful at determining a target's range, we never use it. Do you know why?"

"Because if you ping a target with active sonar, you give away *your* position."

Casey nodded. "Not only your position, but also your stealth. The instant a submarine transmits, the enemy becomes aware of its existence and proximity. The same corollary holds true in cyberwarfare. Any aggressive cyber campaign by Ember against PRC targets would risk counterdetection by the enemy. Right now, I am confident that the Chinese are not aware of Task Force Ember's existence. What I'm proposing would potentially put that anonymity at risk."

"I see . . ." she said, dragging out the word. "In that case, this is a decision I need to think about."

And a decision I don't want to make unilaterally. Because it could put my husband at great risk . . .

"Roger that," Casey said.

Petra leaned forward in her chair. "There's something else we need to discuss—a plan the President and I need your thoughts on, as well as your help to execute."

"This secret plan wouldn't have anything to do with the President heading back into the lion's den, I hope?" Casey said, a flicker of discomfort skirting across his face.

"Yes, unfortunately it does. As you well know, my husband is not easily intimidated. And backing down from a fight is not in his vocabulary."

Casey chuckled. "We've seen the video footage."

"Chip and I wanted to have it playing on a loop on the big screen for your arrival, but Director Casey ixnayed that," Dale offered cheerfully.

"Thanks for sharing that, Dale," Casey said impatiently, though Petra could see the slightest hint of a smile. "We're ready to support however the President needs us to."

"President Jarvis has a plan to draw out the real mastermind behind Warner's assassination," she said. "But, for it to succeed, I need your help with the planning. And for the execution, we'll need Ember's SAD with Dempsey at the helm . . ."

CHAPTER 38

Jake looked across at Randy Ketron, who was grinning from ear to ear as the Seahawk helicopter from one of Carrier Air Wing 8's squadrons banked to port, screaming in over the trees of the Virginia countryside.

Still early in their land warfare block, the assigned exercise was pretty simple—infil by helicopter into the landing zone and then move rapidly to the tree line for cover. From there, they would reassess their situation and move to the target building only a quarter mile into the thick woods and assault the building from two sides.

They'd already conducted this assault once, debriefed what they'd done right and wrong, and now they were expected to do better. Simple enough, but Jake still found he had to think through every step of each component of the evolution. He imagined that, with the "two minutes out" call they'd just received, he would one day reflexively check his kit and weapons while double-checking his battle buddy—in this case, Ketron. But today, he still had to concentrate.

Checking his SOPMOD M4 was reflexive and easy enough—they'd trained on the rifle for what seemed like a million hours already. But checking his kit still took time. Extra magazines, radio, pistol, knife, grenades, fragmentation grenades, flash-bangs, medical blowout kit, and on and on and on—remembering *what* to check for was hard enough. But he also had to remember where the hell he'd put each item in his kit. They'd had a class on how to configure their individual kits but were told to set them up in a way that was most efficient for them. Like everyone else on his eight-man assault team, though, he had no idea what was most efficient for him. For now, most of them had just set things up the way they'd been shown in class.

He felt the Seahawk begin to slow. The crewman in the door held up one finger, signaling they were one minute out. Later, that would be communicated by either the jump master or rope master since most of the time they would exit a helicopter by parachute or by sliding down a fast rope. But since the air training block was still a few weeks off for their group, they had not been fully trained on either. Jake understood the efficiency of splitting things up for different groups within the training class—small groups meant the enormous advantage of a lot of individual attention, but it still made the training feel fragmented.

He imagined it all pulled together before the end, no matter how one navigated through the various blocks. And in any case, once they earned their Trident, they'd be back in training at SEAL Team Eight. In fact, training would be a daily part of his life for the next twenty years . . .

He watched the trees streak by, gave a thumbs-up to his eager friend, and tried to focus on the task at hand.

Instead of all the damn questions rattling around in my brain . . .

He'd been unable to let go of what Randy had told him: DNA collected from those killed in Operation Crusader did not include his dad's DNA. It seemed strange that Commander Redman and his dad could have crossed paths in a meaningful way that allowed them to become close if the SEAL officer arrived at the Tier One *after* his dad had died. Add to that incongruity the time on the grinder at BUD/S when Master Chief White said he thought he'd seen Jack Kemper alive.

Ketron had reopened Jake's own personal Pandora's box into which Jake had shoved all his unanswered questions. Each of the questions individually had reasonable explanations. But Randy was right about one thing—together they added up to *something*.

Jake physically shook the thought away, his ill-fitting combat helmet shifting on his head as he did so. Ketron gave him a curious look. He gave his friend another thumbs-up, just as the helicopter pitched up, flaring, and then settled gently onto the asphalt.

He was second out the port side of the bird, right behind Lieutenant Junior Grade Donny Maxwell, a man just a few years his senior, enough time to bang out four years at the United States Naval Academy and earn his commission—someone Jake had come to like and respect. The other two officers in their class were okay. He liked Lieutenant Capella, who was an ROTC guy who made it to BUD/S after a tour as a Surface Warfare officer, but the other Academy guy was a total tool.

Jake moved right in a low combat crouch like they'd been taught, heading aft toward the tail of the Seahawk and dropping onto his belly, searching through his old EOTECH holographic sight at the tree line, looking for threats. They were not supposed to encounter resistance until they made it to the X, a low building alone in the woods where they would take a high-value target in a capture/kill mission. That was the brief, but this was SEAL training. It would be no surprise at all if the instructors totally messed with the script the second time through.

In fact, I'm assuming that'll happen . . .

Jake saw no movement or other signs of enemy forces in the trees. The wind buffeted him as the helicopter rose, nosed over, and screamed away, signaling that the other five SEAL candidates had exited and completed the remainder of the circle around the helicopter, covering a three-hundred-and-sixty-degree arc, looking for threats. Jake rose to a knee as the bird departed, still scanning his sector for enemy targets—*tangos*, they now called them.

After a few moments, Maxwell rose and signaled for the team of SEAL candidates to move forward to the tree line.

They moved as two groups of four—one group heading straight

ahead, and Jake's four-man, with Maxwell in the lead, moving in a loose diamond formation toward the tree line farther west. Jake felt the adrenaline surging through his body, his heart rate quickening and his mind sharpening. No more pointless flutter kicks in the sand, cold water splashing in your face or running the beach with a friggin' telephone pole on your head. They were training for the real thing now.

They were *operating* . . .

Once inside the tree line, Maxwell led Jake's four-man diamond forward, then took a knee, raising a closed fist over his head. Jake shifted right and Ketron shifted left, fanning out their formation, while Dillinger moved up next to Maxwell, searching back toward where they'd entered the tree line, covering their six.

"Viking Two, One—sitrep?" Maxwell said into the boom mike by his mouth, his voice amplified inside Jake's green Peltor headset.

"Clear," came the voice of James Dewey, a second-class petty officer who'd served as an IT tech with the Teams before selecting for BUD/S. He was leading the other three candidates—Hanes, Comacho, and Christensen.

"Homeplate, Viking is Naples," Maxwell announced to their controller.

"Copy, Viking," came a firm male voice. "Proceed to Kingsville."

"Viking."

Maxwell circled a hand over his head, and Jake rose, falling into the diamond as they moved through the woods. He focused intently on scanning his sector—the two to four o'clock positions of their diamond—while also figuring out how to place his feet to stay quiet, simultaneously *also* reminding himself to stay in a low combat crouch. *And* to keep his hips in a level plane to minimize the movement of his trunk, stabilizing his shooting platform. *And* listening for radio calls while glancing frequently at Maxwell for hand signals. *And* trying to remember where the hell everything was in his kit . . .

One day—God willing, one day soon—this will all become reflex . . . right?

Gunfire off to his right—*simulated gunfire*, he reminded himself—made him jump, and he rose high up in his stance, nearly missing the shadowy figure moving toward him through the dense trees.

"Tango right—three o'clock in the diamond," he shouted, dropping into the dirt to make himself small just as another, panicked voice filled his earpiece.

"Viking Two . . ." There was a pause and then a burst of gunfire again. "Shit, this is Viking Two, we have, there's . . ."

"Enemy contact, left," came another voice from Dewey's stick—Jayden Hanes, Jake thought. "Multiple shooters."

More gunfire, then Jake saw a second figure moving through the woods behind the first. Both figures were maneuvering to attack his squad from the right rear quarter. Immediately, he was on his feet, pushing right and forward in a combat crouch, just like they'd drilled.

"Viking Three, contact right. Engaging two tangos . . ." Jake called in a tight but controlled voice.

Jake's movement opened a lane of fire on both shooters. He took a knee, a sudden paradoxical calm spreading over him as he dropped his sight on the closer target who was just now turning toward him in surprise.

Jake squeezed his trigger.

The crack of his rifle was muffled by the selective noise cancelation of his Peltors. The recoil felt nearly the same as if the rounds were not blanks, and the enemy shooter hesitated only a second, caught off guard, before dutifully collapsing to the ground—once the warble in his headset, set off by the sensors on his body armor, told him he'd been "killed."

"Red Seven KIA," a voice said, but Jake had already engaged and fired on the second tango, who dropped immediately as well.

"Red Five KIA."

"On me," Jake called and surged right, toward where the other half of their strike team engaged the enemy. "Shift left," he added.

"Viking Five, left with me . . . Seven, stay with Three," Maxwell ordered.

Maxwell and Dillinger pushed left, circling around to where the enemy force must have set up to engage Dewey and his stick. Jake sensed more than saw Ketron keeping pace just off his right, surging through the thick woods as they searched for targets.

Just like in the kill house . . . we got this.

Thighs screaming in protest, Jake continued east, away from the drop zone and toward where the other stick had entered the woods, searching over his rifle through the dense trees for the source of the gunfire and ready to drop his gunsight onto a target.

"Tangos left," Ketron said, his voice controlled but still tense.

He's loving this shit . . .

Jake took a knee and searched left, aware of Ketron spreading out to his right and still moving.

He saw a tango deep in the trees and set up a shot but must have missed. The shooter, one of the Red Team instructors from Group Two—maybe even SEAL Team Eight, for all he knew—shifted right behind a large tree, so Jake moved left, finding his own cover behind the massive root ball of a fallen tree.

Fire and move . . . fire and move.

More gunfire.

"Viking Eight KIA," came the calm voice of the instructor running the exercise from a dark room far away. ". . . Viking Six . . . wounded, but in the fight. Left leg injury."

Jake moved left around the cover of the tree and saw his target aiming toward Ketron. Jake dropped his sight on him and squeezed.

"Red Three wounded, right hip."

He squeezed again, and the man flailed and fell, to his credit adding some cinematic drama to his simulated death.

"Red Three, KIA."

Several bursts of gunfire to his right indicated Maxwell and Dillinger were in the fight, flanking the opposing force that had killed Christensen and wounded Comacho.

"Red Two and Six, KIA."

"All right," came a new voice. "Knock it off. Secure from the operation. Rally at the LZ."

He recognized the voice as the lead instructor, SEAL Master Chief Kevin Hacker from the NSW Advanced Training Center at Little Creek.

The gunfire stopped, and Jake felt suddenly spent. A microsecond ago, he could have climbed Everest; now he felt his legs and hands shake, and he took a knee, catching his breath.

Ketron, it seemed, was not nearly as affected. Jake felt a squeeze on his neck and turned to see his friend standing next to him, smiling broadly, rifle slung on his chest in a combat carry. Randy looked like he'd done this a thousand times.

"Dude," Ketron said. "That was totally friggin' badass. Oh my God, that was amazing."

Jake shook his head but smiled and stood up. "Dude, great work picking up those tangos."

Ketron shrugged. "Like spotting a buck on the first day of hunting season," he said. "No big thing."

They trudged back south to the edge of the woods, Maxwell and Dillinger joining them first, then Dewey leading Comacho, Christensen, and Hanes from their left.

"That was friggin' awesome," Allen Christensen said, sweat pouring from his face.

"Yeah, except where you got fuckin' killed, bro," Dillinger said, laughing.

"I don't even care," Christensen said. "That was incredible."

Hanes wiped sweat from his eyes and then his flushed, ruddy cheeks with the back of a gloved hand. "Better than sex," he said.

"How would you know?" Comacho asked, punching his teammate in the shoulder.

They hustled to where Master Chief Hacker already stood, in the circle at the end of the short, paved landing strip. His hands were on his hips and a scowl was on his face, his SPECWAR cap low over his eyes.

"Hustle on up, ladies," the SEAL barked. "Helos are here in a moment."

They formed a loose circle around the master chief, half the team of eight taking a knee. Jake took a long, satisfying pull of water from the mouthpiece at his shoulder. His throat suddenly felt so dry it ached, and his energy now returned after the adrenaline burn from a few minutes ago.

"Lieutenant Maxwell," Hacker barked.

"Master Chief?"

"We'll save the debrief for our return to the schoolhouse," the SEAL master chief said, crossing his arms on his chest. "But while we're still in the heat of the moment—how do you feel about the operation?"

"Well, Master Chief," Maxwell said, pulling at his chin. "The op was a failure. We did not make the objective before you called it off. We had one KIA and one wounded, though I don't know how urgent he was."

"What difference would that make?" Hacker asked.

"Well, Master Chief, if he was not urgent surgical, there would still have been an opportunity to make the objective, had we not stopped the simulation."

Hacker nodded, and Jake thought there might even be the hint of a smile. "Maybe," he said.

"With the Red Team KIA, based on the intelligence from the brief, the target might have been easy to secure—assuming there was no QRF and the eight Red Team we engaged meant only two shooters left at the X," Dewey added.

Maxwell gave him a nod.

"Maybe," Hacker said again. "We'll dig deep into all of that in the classroom when we get back. You should damn well have anticipated the ambush and reacted more quickly, Dewey."

"Yes, Master Chief," Dewey agreed, looking down.

"Nothing will ever, ever be what you brief. Always be ready."

Jake heard the distant sound of rotor blades beating the air into submission. He glanced east and saw the growing dots of two helicopters. His eye caught the group of Red Team shooters—experienced SEALs from the training cell—together off by themselves, laughing and talking. Two passed a plastic bottle back and forth, dribbling tobacco spit into it.

That'll be us.

"How do you feel about what Kemper did, Maxwell?"

That brought him back, and he felt his chest tighten.

Had it been a mistake to take off to the east? Should he have waited for the team lead to initiate? Shit, Maxwell was more than team leader;

he was a friggin' officer. Jake had the sudden sense he was in big trouble. He glanced over at Ketron, who gave a subtle shrug.

"He engaged the enemy when he saw them, Master Chief," Maxwell said, giving a nod to Jake, who felt only a touch of relief. Lieutenant Junior Grade Maxwell had no real authority here whatsoever. Jake turned to Hacker.

"And when he headed off to the east?"

Maxwell hesitated.

"I mean, I guess he could have checked with me. But if he saw a threat . . ."

"Maybe," Hacker said again. "But remember: this is the Teams, gentlemen. You are not aboard some ship. We are all—every one of us, from E-2 all the way to O-8—SEALs. That means we are all prepared, at all times, to both lead and to follow. Team before self."

"Hooyah, Master Chief," Maxwell said.

"Hooyah," the rest of them, Jake included, replied. The helicopters were flaring to land.

"After the debrief, gather your personal items. We'll be overnight at Little Creek. You'll get liberty tonight, but don't get shit-faced because you'll be touring your assigned Team spaces tomorrow."

There was a collective whoop. They loaded up, the SEALs from the Red Team piling into the second bird.

Moments later both helicopters were banking southeast, back toward Virginia Beach seventy-five miles away. Jake settled into his seat on the floor of the helicopter, where he clipped in and let his feet dangle out the port-side door, his rifle cradled in his lap and the wind whipping at his pant legs above his boots. He didn't know why he gravitated to this position in the helicopter. Or maybe he did. He'd seen several pictures of his dad, the legendary Jack Kemper, in Blackhawk helicopters, and in every one of them he'd been in the port-side door all the way aft.

He sighed, leaning his helmeted head against the doorframe as the rest of his teammates chattered around him. Something Master Chief Hacker said had his mind once more on questions best left alone.

Personal effects . . .

Jake lifted his head and turned to look at Ketron, who was lean-ing in and talking smack to Dillinger on the aft nylon bench seat. Jake looked outside at the ocean of orange and red—the trees giving up their last breath in brilliant, colorful celebration of autumn—and let his mind drift.

He could hear his mom in the other room of their house in Virginia Beach during that horrible time after the deaths of his dad and his entire team just a few years ago, talking to the ombudsman from the unit—the secret unit his dad had served in when he died. Even the legendary Tier One needed an ombudsman.

His mom had sounded urgent, talking in hushed tones.

"I really appreciate your help, and I'm not trying to be difficult, but I know it has to be there somewhere . . . No, it wasn't with his personal effects that they sent me . . . Yes, of course I checked again. I'm telling you it isn't there . . . I just really need someone to check wherever they were staying in Djibouti because I know—I know for certain—that he never, ever deployed without it. When he was on an op, he left it with his things because it had a picture of his son, but once he was back in his FOB or camp or wherever, he always had it on his person . . ."

Something missing from his personal effects. Jake had heard her talking to Captain Jarvis about it too. After the memorial service where Jarvis had given her his card, she'd called him about whatever it was that was missing—that it had to be there because everything else had been returned.

Even his damn shaving kit and toothbrush came back, but not this, she'd said.

He glanced again at Ketron, who must have felt his gaze because he looked over and gave Jake a thumbs-up. Jake smiled and nodded, then turned to look out at the Virginia countryside again.

No DNA evidence of Jack Kemper dying in the TOC in Djibouti . . .

No way he could have served at the Tier One with whoever the hell Lieutenant Commander Redman was . . .

Master Chief White from WARCOM—a measured, levelheaded,

blooded warrior who knew Dad better than most people, better than
Jake had—was sure he'd seen Jack Kemper long after his death, on an
op somewhere . . .

And something important and meaningful missing—impossibly,
according to Mom—from his personal effects . . .

*Ketron is right. Each alone is nothing. But all of it together adds up
to something . . .*

He leaned his head against the doorframe again, enjoying the cool
wind on his legs. He would call his mom tonight. He was due to talk
to her again anyway, and maybe he could figure out a way to ask her
what had been missing from Jack Kemper's effects. He hated bringing
things up from the past—picking at that damn scab—especially with
her seeming so happy these days. In fact, while his teammates were out
on the town tonight, maybe he could meet her for dinner. She lived
nearby, and she would love the surprise, he suspected.

He let out a long sigh and clenched his jaw. The more he mulled it
over, the more certain he was that his gut was right.

Navy SEAL Senior Chief Jack Kemper was alive. He was alive and
still operating somewhere.

And if he was, Jake would find him.

Because that son of a bitch had a lot of explaining to do.

CHAPTER 39

EMBER'S EXECUTIVE BOEING 787-9

TAIL NUMBER N103XL

RAMP IN FRONT OF BAY THREE

INDIRA GANDHI INTERNATIONAL AIRPORT

DELHI, INDIA

1928 LOCAL TIME

Dempsey took a seat at the conference table in the TOC and leaned back in the leather task chair. While he rubbed the sleep from his eyes, somebody—probably Munn—put a mug of black coffee in front of him.

"Thanks, dude," he said with a nod as the doc dropped into the chair beside him.

Munn raised his mug in reply.

They'd all been operating on minimal sleep over the past forty-eight hours, and when Dempsey had finally gotten a chance to go horizontal, his brain had gone totally comatose. For the first time in as long as he could remember, he hadn't dreamed. It was a blessing. A quick scan of the weary faces of the assembled—Grimes, Munn, Prescott, Fender, Wallace, Wang, and Wilson—told him he wasn't the only one who was dragging ass.

Ria and the rest of the NIA folks had left in the early morning hours after learning that NIA HQ could be al Ghadab's next target. They'd insisted on taking custody of Saeed, which neither Dempsey nor Buz had fought them on. They weren't equipped to keep the dude on the Boeing, nor did they want to have to provide ongoing medical care for the wounded terrorist. Dempsey, for one, was happy to let someone else take out the trash.

Before departing the airport, Ria had pulled Dempsey aside for a one-on-one talk. He'd expected her to lecture him about crossing lines when he'd interrogated Saeed and warn him about what would happen if he did it again, but that's not how it went down. Quite the opposite, in fact. She'd thanked him and wanted to shake his hand. She'd said she'd learned a lot during their brief but whirlwind operation in Kathmandu. He thanked her for her support and told her that coming on the raids like she had was a very brave thing. After that, they'd traded mobile numbers and agreed to keep the other informed of any developments.

While they'd only spent a short time working together, his gut told him that he'd not seen the last of Ria Keltker. Friction with new international partners was both expected and inevitable, but despite it all Ember and the NIA's crackerjack CT investigation team had worked through the problem and gotten results. Plus, he'd made a friend and found someone he could trust in Delhi, and that was what mattered most in his line of work: building a network of allies around the world he could call on in times of trouble.

He drained half the mug as Wang established the secure connection for their video conference with Casey and Ember HQ.

"First order of business," Casey said the moment his face filled the screen. "I wanted to update you on Martin. He's stable, in good hands, and on his way to Germany. He'll spend a day or two at the hospital in Landstuhl, then fly back to Tampa to recover. He's not showing signs of infection following the colon injury Dr. Munn repaired. In fact, I was told he's still complaining that we wouldn't let him return to immediate operational status."

Dempsey smiled. Even though Martin came as a replacement early on, he still felt like *original* Ember. He knew the former Marine would be back in short order.

"It's the right call," Munn said. "He needs to recover from the internal injury, but that giant chunk of missing flesh on his flank at the exit wound is going to take time to heal before he can operate at anything close to one hundred percent. We don't want to rush it."

"Agreed," Casey said, all business. "Next, I want to update you on a meeting we had with Petra Jarvis . . ."

Dempsey listened with disbelief as the Ember director informed them that President Jarvis and a contingent of staffers—including the Deputy Assistant Secretary of Defense for Irregular Warfare and Counterterrorism—would be arriving in New Delhi tomorrow at 1600 local time.

"What?" Wallace said, her eyes going wide. "Whose incredibly stupid idea was that? We can't have the President here with Umar in the wind and planning more attacks. Hell, we should be evacuating our diplomats and FSOs from Delhi, not bringing people in. I'd like to talk to the dumbass who thought that was a good idea."

Casey grimaced. "Unfortunately, that dumbass is President Jarvis."

"But that's crazy," Munn said. "He of all people should know better. I understand the optics of showing strength and not perpetuating a narrative that al Ghadab has power over the United States, but coming here now is reckless."

"He feels that the initiative with India—what he is now calling the Warner Initiative—is too important to let evaporate from both a national security and an economic security point of view. He feels that cementing the agreement is important enough to risk the trip. That said, those of you who know Jarvis well know that he always has a plan," Casey said, and a sly smile curled his lips. "This trip will serve two agendas—one diplomatic and one tactical. The latter is where Ember comes into the picture. What the President and First Lady have cooked up is brilliant, complicated, and very dangerous. Participation in the decoy convoy will be entirely voluntary. We have less than twenty-four hours to plan and prepare, so I will not begrudge or judge any member of SAD who opts to sit this one out."

Wearing a crooked grin, Dempsey turned to look at Munn.

Munn flashed Dempsey a toothy smile back and said, "Dude, he had me at *decoy convoy . . .*"

CHAPTER 40

From the front passenger seat of the up-armored black Suburban SUV, Dempsey watched Air Force One taxi from the main runway toward the secure tarmac. Per protocol, the President's plane would be parked alongside the Air Force C-17 from Joint Base Andrews, which had arrived eight hours ago in the middle of the night carrying the President's advanced Secret Service detail, the three vehicles that would comprise the presidential motorcade, and a special contingent of CIA Ground Branch shooters who would augment Ember SAD for the decoy mission—code name *Operation Fury.*

Unbeknownst to the world at large, however, the C-17 had also transported a VIP not listed on any passenger manifest or security memorandum: the President of the United States.

Jarvis, wearing a green bag flight suit, had boarded the heavy-haul military transport with the flight crew at Andrews and departed half a day before Air Force One left CONUS. Only a handful of people on the planet were read in to the highly compartmentalized operation, and no electronic records or documentation of the plan had been created. This particular C-17 had been selected for the mission because it had already been previously modified with a fully enclosed, soundproof communications suite and SCIF inside the cargo hold. This room was where Jarvis would remain for the duration of his visit to Delhi, and it was where he and India's acting Prime Minister would meet in less than one hour to sign the Warner-Chopra Trade Pact. Hindon AFS, India's largest air base, had been chosen over Indira Gandhi International for the President's arrival because it offered much tighter security and access control. Ember SAD had arrived before sunrise, under cover of darkness, and worked with the advance team to ready the vehicles and brief the mission.

But the highlight of the predawn craziness was the fifteen-minute window when Dempsey, Munn, and Grimes had been able to shake hands with the new President of the United States and catch up over coffee.

Jarvis looked good, fit, and lean, but he'd definitely aged since Dempsey had last seen him. During the brief chat, Dempsey had watched their old CSO closely for tremors, but he'd not seen any. He'd asked Munn later if Parkinson's was a disease that could go into remission, and Munn had said he'd heard of one or two documented cases but that generally the answer was no. Dempsey hadn't asked Jarvis about his health—that would have been inappropriate and awkward as hell—but Dempsey hadn't been able to prevent himself from thinking about it. The lion's share of the conversation had been Jarvis asking about the new team members and reminiscing about old times. The visit had been all too short, but the President was a busy man. Despite being stuck in that SCIF, away from prying eyes, every spare minute of his day had been scheduled.

"So, I guess we're supposed to put in this curlicue earpiece doohickey now?" Munn asked from the driver's seat next to him, referring to the infamous and overtly visible throat mikes that close protection agents wore.

"I guess," Dempsey said. He stuck the ridiculous thing in his right ear and turned to look at his best friend. "By the way, have I told you that you look, like, eight years old without your beard?"

"Yeah, well, you look just as old and just as ugly without yours."

No surprise, Munn had complained the longest and the loudest about having to go clean-shaven for the op. None of the agents on the presidential protection detail wore beards, so to look the part, Ember couldn't either. Dempsey didn't really care. His beard grew so fast he'd look back to normal by the end of next week. In addition to shaving, they had to clean up their haircuts and dress as Secret Service agents, which meant dark gray suits.

"Looks like it's showtime," Munn said as the airstair was driven over from the hangar.

Dempsey jerked the door lever, pushed the heavy passenger-side door open with his foot, and climbed out of the nice, air-conditioned interior of the Suburban onto the tarmac and the hot, humid Delhi air. The Ember "Secret Service" contingent—Dempsey, Munn, Prescott, Fender, and Wallace—were joined by seven Ground Branch operators who were augmenting their team. With Martin out of commission and Grimes reserved for overwatch, they needed extra firepower. Dempsey didn't know or recognize any of the dudes, but they all walked the walk and talked the talk. To a man they'd been handpicked by Casey, so Dempsey knew they were pros, which was enough for him.

Dempsey resisted the urge to tug on the collar of his starched white dress shirt as they crossed the tarmac to the airstair. He could not remember the last time he'd worn a suit, let alone a necktie.

I'd rather be waterboarded than have to spend all day every day in this monkey suit . . .

A pair of armed Marines stood guard at the bottom of the stairs. Dempsey had never been aboard Air Force One, and for some reason he felt a spark of excitement to step aboard the world's most famous airplane. Maybe *excitement* was too strong a word—he didn't get excited about much these days. *Curiosity*, maybe. He followed Munn, who'd taken the lead, up the stairs.

On reaching the top, Dempsey made eye contact with a real Secret

Service agent standing just inside the aircraft. Munn executed the code word challenge–response protocol with the armed agent, who stepped aside to let them enter. A second agent stepped up to greet them.

"I'm Alex," the man said and stuck out his hand to Munn. "Are you John?"

"Nope," Munn said, shaking the man's hand and gesturing with a chin turn, "he is."

"Whoa," Alex said, turning to Dempsey, "I see why they picked you. Same height, same jawline, same build. Throw on a pair of shades and a ball cap to cover your darker hair and from a distance you'll be a dead ringer for POTUS."

"I've known Kelso Jarvis for twenty years," Dempsey said, doing his best Jarvis voice. "I can talk like him; I can walk like him; hell, son, I can even chase down assassins who miss their kill shots through the streets of Tel Aviv like him."

"That's pretty damn impressive," the agent said with a chuckle. "You and I are going to head forward into the President's office; the rest of you guys turn right and wait in the hall outside the medical office and main galley."

Dempsey followed the agent into the President Air Force One office—with its cream-colored walls, rich mahogany wood tones, and blue carpet. The President's desk faced aft, but the desktop was angled at forty-five degrees so that the President could swivel in his chair to face a leather sofa, also angled and wedged into a little corner. A tall, expensive-looking leather chair sat empty behind the desk, and behind it the presidential seal decorated the bulkhead.

So, this is the Oval Office of the stratosphere, occupied for the first time by a Navy SEAL.

"Since you know him so well, it should come as no surprise that the President hates neckties, so you'll need to take yours off," Agent Alex said. "And I'm going to trade you this bomber jacket for that suit coat you're wearing."

With a satisfied exhale, Dempsey shed his tie, undid the top button of his dress shirt, and shrugged off his suit coat. Next, he donned Jarvis's presidential bomber jacket and a navy-blue ball cap and put on a pair of aviator-style sunglasses.

"How do I look?" he said to the agent.

"You look every bit the part. My work is done here," Alex said, then gestured for Dempsey to head back to join his team.

"Dude, I'm impressed," Munn said as Dempsey walked up, channeling the mannerisms and posture of his current and former boss. "You don't look like his twin, but you could definitely pass as brothers."

"I'll take that as a compliment, Dan," Dempsey said, approximating Jarvis's voice. This earned him a laugh from the assembled team of operators. Then, strangely, he noticed that they were all looking at him expectantly, as if waiting for a speech or pep talk.

Guys, I'm not really the President, he wanted to say. Instead, he decided to lean into the moment.

"All right, guys," he said, switching back to his real voice, "the op is pretty straightforward—we're bait, so anyone that hits the trap, we kill. We've briefed it already, but it is worth repeating that we have no idea if the enemy knows we're here. No idea if the enemy plans to target the President's convoy. And if they are targeting it, no idea what they are going to throw at us. We're heading out there with a target on our backs. If and when the shit hits the fan, there will be no backup. Whatever happens, we will adapt and overcome."

"Hooyah, frogman," Munn barked.

Dempsey fell in behind Munn, Prescott, and two Ground Branch shooters who were also dressed as Secret Service offices. Together they exfilled the President's door on Air Force One.

Dempsey moved with purpose, imagining himself as Jarvis in this situation. He maintained close separation from his bodyguards in front and hunched in an ever-so-slight combat crouch. The objective was to be seen but not seen. Nobody was supposed to know the President was here. Nobody was supposed to be watching, but at this point, Casey and Baldwin were convinced that al Ghadab was not working alone. Until the compromise in White House security was identified, they had to operate as if this performance was being monitored.

Parked ten feet from the bottom of the airstair, the presidential limousine—the Beast—was waiting for him. A pair of real Secret Service agents were standing by the vehicle with the rear door open and ready. Dempsey quickstepped across the tarmac, ducked his head, and clambered into the most advanced and secure Cadillac on the planet. Prescott got behind him, and the heavy armored door slammed shut.

Noise from the outside world instantly disappeared, and Dempsey felt entombed, or maybe enwombed, in a pod of luxury and antiballistic isolation. They'd been briefed on the two-million-dollars-a-pop Fort Knox on wheels that was the centerpiece of the presidential motorcade. With military-grade armor plating, run-flat Kevlar tires, internal fire suppression system, and self-contained atmosphere to withstand CBRN attacks, the Beast was truly a marvel of modern engineering. A black hard case sat on the floor of the rear passenger compartment, but instead of containing champagne and shrimp cocktail, it held their kits and weapons. Dempsey took five seconds to recline into the supple leather seat and enjoy the experience of being "the President."

Just as quickly, the moment was over. He took off the sunglasses, ball cap, and bomber jacket. Looking at Prescott, he laughed.

"Man, I'm not going to lie, I'd hate being President."

"Amen to that, brother. The day I can't operate is the day I want you to put me down, like a stallion with a broken leg."

Dempsey knew Prescott was kidding, but as Munn was fond of saying, *There's a little bit of truth in every joke.* The sad truth of the matter was that Prescott's joke pretty much summed up Dempsey's deepest and darkest fear.

He smiled at his teammate. "C'mon, it's time to kit up."

CHAPTER 41

Elinor Jordan felt 99.9 percent sure she'd found and identified Abu Musad Umar. That she'd done it before IB, NIA, CIA, NSA, and even Task Force Ember, proved once again that she could make a difference—especially when unshackled from the oversight of nation-state bosses.

Of course, she couldn't take all the credit—it had been a group effort. Her team had found Umar; she'd simply been the one who made the approach, won his trust, and placed the bug. Her little organization, Athena AG, had only five members. They were lean, agile, adaptive, and, most importantly, highly motivated. Jordan's vetting process was meticulous and comprehensive. Besides being technically and tactically elite in their field, each potential hire had to possess a moral compass, set of guiding principles, and similar geopolitical worldview to Elinor.

For Athena to succeed, every member of the organization had to function as an extension of Elinor herself. By design, Athena was everything the nation-state intelligence agencies were not. And, by God, she meant to keep it that way.

She'd worked late last night, and the night before she'd gotten no sleep, so she'd decided to sleep in this morning. Assuming nothing happened to change her mind, today was going to be the big day—she would contact Ember and provide all the intelligence and imagery Athena had collected on Umar and his organization in Delhi.

To find Umar, she and her team had *followed the money*—a time-tested technique taught to her by the Israeli spymaster Levi Harel. Before the assassination, this had been impossible: either no money was flowing into al Ghadab or it had been through channels unknown to Athena. But afterward, the network of financiers who facilitate and orchestrate the global jihad economy had bustled with activity. Inside this network of illicit bankers, crypto traders, and couriers, Athena had paid informants and cyber exploits. It was only a matter of time before she got a hit, and when she did, her team had made quick work tracing the funds and identifying Umar's account. From there, she'd found his credit card; then, following his digital footprints, she'd found him.

When to inform Ember had been a major source of consternation for her over the past twenty-four hours. As the Americans would say, in handing over this intelligence she was delivering them her golden goose, her magnum opus. In this one act, she would make good on her promise to Jarvis; pay forward the kindness and allegiance Levi had shown her, even after her unmasking as a double agent; and prove to Dempsey that she could be trusted as a partner.

She didn't want to screw this up by being wrong. But wait too long to deliver the goods, and the opportunity would be lost. She needed to save the day before Ember found Umar themselves.

And before Umar had a chance to strike again.

Balancing a drink holder in one hand, she keyed the passcode into the apartment lock touch pad with the other. An LED flashed green, the dead bolt rolled open, and she opened the door.

"Good morning, boss," said Gaëlle, a former member of French DGSE, France's foreign intelligence agency.

"Good morning," Elinor said. She set a latte in front of the young woman, who sat at the dining table working on a notebook computer. "Any developments? Where is Umar?"

"He is at a McDonald's . . ."

"At a McDonald's? Where?"

"*Ici*," Gaëlle said, pointing to a red dot on a bird's-eye view map of Delhi on the screen, "across from the, eh, Red Fort in Old Delhi."

A pulse of nervous angst flared in Elinor's chest. "That's an odd place to go. What is he doing there?"

"He's working on his computer."

"Do we have eyes on?"

"Yes, Zara is surveilling."

"Did he go alone?"

"*Oui*," Gaëlle said, looking up at Elinor through a pair of chunky, blue-framed eyeglasses. "Are you worried?"

Elinor ignored the question. "What about the supposed investment banker, Li Mucheng? Where is he?"

"We do not have eyes on him. The last observation was by Christian, entering the ITC Maurya hotel late last night. But you were here for that, *mais non?*"

"I was not . . ." she murmured, annoyed. Elinor flipped open an idle notebook computer and used it to find the location of the hotel on Google Maps. Her breath caught in her chest. "Oh shit . . ."

"What?" Gaëlle said.

"This hotel is located in the diplomatic enclave."

"So?"

"It's directly across the street from IB headquarters."

"You don't think . . ." Gaëlle said, her voice trailing off.

An adrenaline dump sent Elinor's heart rate into the roof. She ran to the gun locker and grabbed a vest and a pistol.

"Where are you going?" Gaëlle asked.

"To bag Umar," she said. "Zara can't do it. She's not an operator."

"Take Christian's motorcycle," Gaëlle said, tossing Elinor a set of keys. "The traffic is terrible. If you're right, and something is about to happen, you'll never make it in time by car."

"Gaëlle, you're running the TOC. I assume Jacob relieved Christian, and Christian is in bed?"

"*Oui.*"

"Wake up Christian and warn Indian Intelligence that IB headquarters may be the target of an impending attack," she said as she ran out the door.

CHAPTER 42

Shazi sat alone in a chair, looking out the window of his sixth-floor deluxe hotel suite. He'd reserved a room facing northeast, overlooking the Intelligence Bureau headquarters and training campus, which was one of the targets for today's operation. He'd provided Umar with an external hard drive containing dozens of files related to the NIA headquarters' building and instructed the terrorist to leave it behind for the Americans to find in the event they raided the mountain compound . . . which they had.

Over the past twenty-four hours, he'd validated that this misdirection had worked. Chinese intelligence had confirmed a flurry of activity and chatter around NIA being al Ghadab's next target. Staffing reductions, protocol changes, and ramped-up security on the campus had been observed.

The plan had worked.

The actual target was IB headquarters, but this too was misdirection.

The attack on IB headquarters was designed to create chaos and distraction from the *real* objective: to attack President Jarvis's motorcade. The American Navy SEAL President had, as Shazi had hoped, lived up to his cowboy reputation and was flying into Delhi today. This visit had not been publicized or announced and was being executed with the utmost secrecy by the Americans. But Shazi's cyber team had penetrated the Office of the National Cyber Director, responsible for securing communications within the White House. Thanks to this breach, he knew the confidential details about the President's schedule and had passed this information to Umar. Shazi had volunteered to conduct the attack on IB headquarters using only drones, thereby saving all al Ghadab's manpower for the attack on the presidential convoy.

A new generation of heavy-payload multirotor drones was set to revolutionize terrorism. Using a fictitious front company, al Ghadab had procured a dozen JOUAV PH-20 high-endurance drones three months ago from the Chinese manufacturer. Each hexacopter was rated to carry a payload of up to ten kilograms, had an endurance of thirty minutes when fully loaded, and a five-thousand-meter altitude ceiling. Taken together, this meant the attack armada could be launched at a significant standoff distance. They'd positioned PH-20 launch boxes on eight different rooftops around Delhi. The launch boxes and drones inside were remote operable via the command-and-control program Shazi was running on his computer. Every drone was equipped with an advanced CPU, GPS, and cellular modem. The targets and flight plan were programmed and downloaded into the drones' onboard computers in advance.

He looked at the countdown timer in the upper left-hand corner of his screen, which read *87 seconds*. When the countdown reached zero, the launch box lids would open, the rotors would whir to life, and the drones would zip across the rooftops of Delhi armed with six kilos of C-4 encased in six kilos of ball bearings. Half of the drones would target the IB campus. The other half were reserved for the convoy.

His encrypted satellite phone received an SMS from Umar, who would be coordinating the attack from a café.

Convoy is delayed by five minutes.

Delay drone launch accordingly

Shazi added five minutes to the countdown time and messaged back.

5 minutes added

While he waited, Shazi's thoughts drifted to Sunita, the fashionable woman who Umar had foolishly brought back to the rental apartment. After the woman had left, Shazi demanded Umar have her followed by one of his men. The underling, who was driving a motor scooter, had observed her getting picked up several blocks away by a Range Rover, but the fighter had eventually lost her in Delhi traffic. This report had not surprised Shazi—jihadists were not clandestine agents trained in tradecraft—but it had angered him nonetheless.

Something about the woman's sudden appearance in Umar's life felt off.

The master sees beyond what is obvious, he reminded himself. *He sees the unseen, feels the unfelt, and hears the unheard . . .*

Maybe it was simply that Shazi had been blindsided by her arrival. He'd pressed Umar for details about how he'd met the girl, and Umar insisted that he had pursued her and not the other way around, but that assurance didn't set Shazi's mind at ease. Every intelligence agency used honeypots to penetrate closed networks. This woman could easily be an American asset or agent of the National Intelligence Agency working undercover.

And she saw my face, he thought with irritation.

Out of an abundance of caution, Shazi considered the apartment compromised and had ordered Umar to vacate. They'd argued for ten minutes over this, but Shazi had come out on top. After sunset, Umar had relocated to a secondary, nonluxury property in a lower-income neighborhood—the type of neighborhood where Umar had always set up shop before coming into cash. Shazi had spent the night in a hotel on the opposite side of the city, but he'd left before dawn and not revealed the location from which he intended to coordinate the drone strike on IB headquarters. He'd checked into the hotel using an alias that Umar was unfamiliar with in the event that Umar was captured and tortured for information.

It was time to sever the connection. After today, he would never see Abu Musad Umar again.

The computer chimed with the one-minute warning on the countdown timer, breaking his rumination and drawing his attention to the screen. He checked his phone for any new messages from Umar. Finding none, he texted:

> Convoy status? Sending drones in less
> than one minute.

The reply from Umar came an instant later.

Convoy underway. Send drones

Shazi watched the countdown timer reach zero, then clicked the LAUNCH button with the computer's touch pad. The graphical user interface, which depicted the twelve launch boxes, lit up with color as all the red boxes changed to green in near perfect synchronicity. He watched the individual drone icons also change color as the hexacopters went through their start-up sequences and took flight.

One of the twelve drones, number nine, slated for the convoy attack, generated an error signal and failed to launch. Shazi tried rebooting the drone and launching it again, but the same error occurred. Annoyed, he shifted from the command screen to the navigation pane, which showed the position of the airborne drones overlaid atop a map of Delhi. Eleven drones were on the move, buzzing their way over the world's second most populated city.

The routes had been planned using AI, so that drones one through six would arrive at the IB campus simultaneously regardless of their launch points. Only the drone with the most distant launch box would travel a direct route. All other drones would fly random, indirect patterns. The closer the launch box to the target, the more circuitous the flight path. This had been Shazi's idea: to generate target confusion just in case the Indians were somehow able to track them. He seriously doubted this would be possible thanks to the hexacopters' small size and low-altitude flight paths, but why not use the best strategy available? The same tactic was employed for Salvo 2, the drones targeting the convoy.

He messaged Umar:

Drones airborne and en route to targets.

Salvo 1 ETA is 7 mins, 22 secs.

Salvo 2 ETA 11 minutes, 22 secs.

Drone #9 failed to launch

Umar acknowledged the message without comment.

Shazi set his computer down on the foot of the bed and went to the bathroom to empty his bladder while he still had time. When he returned, the Salvo 1 drones were four minutes and fifteen seconds from the Intelligence Bureau campus. The next several minutes passed slowly, and he felt his anxiety and worry ratcheting up.

He'd intentionally ceded all responsibility for managing the convoy attack to Umar. His instincts told him that this attack would be al Ghadab's last. The Americans would pursue Umar with ruthless, unyielding commitment. If they didn't catch him today, they would run him down like a pack of wild dogs until he was exhausted and out of options. As much as Shazi would have liked to have coordinated the attack and watched the death of President Jarvis himself, the prudent move was to take a step back and observe the bloodiest part of the battle from afar.

Regardless of the outcome, tonight he would fly back to China.

His computer chimed, notifying him the drones were on final

approach. He watched the icons accelerating toward IB HQ on his computer screen—six triangles speeding toward the target from six different directions. In addition to closing range, each drone was changing altitude. Three would attack at near horizontal vectors, and three were climbing to drop straight down from an altitude of five hundred meters. This pop-up and attack-from-above strategy was a tactic used by the American Javelin missile, and Shazi had decided to try it. If the IB campus had antidrone countermeasures in place, this would be a good experiment to see which attack profile worked best.

A message flashed on his screen:

TERMINAL HOMING IN FIVE SECONDS.

This warning meant he had five seconds to abort. After that, the drones could not be stopped. On this cue, he looked away from his computer screen and out the window, counting down in his mind:

Three . . . two . . . one . . .

Six explosions rocked the Intelligence Bureau campus, detonating like daisy-chained firecrackers. Cars crashed, people screamed, and sirens began to wail. Purple-gray plumes of smoke rose in the distance, and he saw pandemonium on the streets below.

Mission accomplished. Umar's jihadists will attack the breached building now, but they will all die rather quickly. But the feint is now done . . .

Shazi closed the drone management application on his notebook computer and initiated a total SSD operating system reformat. He packed the computer in his luggage and set it by the door. Next, he texted Umar one final message—that the first drone strike was complete—before removing the SIM card and mechanically destroying his mobile phone. With a controlled breath, he surveyed the hotel room one final time and walked out.

The rest, as Umar often said, was in God's hands.

CHAPTER 43

SRI DIGAMBAR JAIN LAL MANDIR (JAIN TEMPLE)

CHANDNI CHOWK AREA

DELHI, INDIA

1051 LOCAL TIME

Grimes stretched her back and rolled her neck. She barely fit in the uncomfortable roost inside a tiny room atop the northern spire of the temple complex. One thing was for sure—if things did go sideways, her contribution would come exclusively from here in the sniper hide she'd set up. A lot of guesswork had gone into picking this location as the most likely place the convoy might be hit on the route. If she and Dempsey had guessed wrong, and the convoy was attacked somewhere else along the decoy track, then her contribution would be zero.

The oblong, domed, red-tile twin roofs of the temple stretched more than a hundred feet in the air, and getting all the way up here—with clear lines on the northern approach to the Lahori Gate entrance into the historic Red Fort—had taken her nearly twenty-five terrifying minutes. She didn't envy the maintenance workers who routinely navigated the rickety ladders and walkways inside the domes. She'd feared for her life more than once on the climb. Without a parachute or some sort of rappelling gear, getting back down would take her every bit of another twenty minutes. If they needed her for a running gun battle, it would be long over by the time she got to the fight.

She took a long, slow breath and pressed back into the Leupold 5HD sight mounted on her custom Wilson rifle. She scanned the crowds on both sides of the street along the entire stretch from the gate north along Netaji Subhash Road. The police presence—both overt and covert—was quite easy to spot. The Indian counterterrorism agents were harder to pick out, perhaps, but she could see them as well, mingling among the crowd at the popular Lahori Gate.

Grimes frowned.

They're in the wrong position. If I was planning the hit, I'd attack on the approach from the north, before the entrance into the expansive park around the gate.

But their presence was better than nothing, she decided. They didn't know the convoy was carrying a decoy POTUS; they thought this was the real thing. As far as this crew was concerned, the new American President was en route to meet the new Indian PM to sign a historic trade agreement. They weren't acting.

She scanned the businesses on the east side of Netaji Subhash: a couple of clothing stores, a floral shop, a travel agency, and a large, bustling coffee shop at the northern corner of the complex housing the Red Fort. On the west side of the road sat the Lal Qila metro station and an electronics store. Grimes scanned the few higher sites beyond the north corner, where a road circled counterclockwise around a block dense with businesses and restaurants—places that an enemy sniper could be in play. She swept her reticle over rooftop hides and windows, looking for places *she* might set up if she were playing for the other side.

Nothing.

She frowned again.

She also didn't see any suspicious marks in the crowd, young men who fit the profile of al Ghadab jihadi shooters or suicide bombers. And this surprised her because spotting terrorists trying to blend in was literally her superpower.

To counter the building stress she was feeling, she ran through a series of four-count tactical breaths. She didn't stop until that tension began to ebb.

What if we were wrong? What if Operation Fury had given al Ghadab too much credit for their cybersleuthing ability, and they didn't learn about the "surprise" Air Force One visit in time to plan a hit? President Jarvis had leaked the information through the same internal channels used for scheduling Warner's trip to meet with Chopra, but had the enemy just gotten lucky that time? What if instead of targeting the convoy, Umar decided to target a shopping mall or major tourist site like the Taj Mahal instead? The lives of innocent civilians would be on her conscience if that happened.

"Mother, Eagle lead. Radio check?"

"Loud and clear, Eagle," Grimes replied, aware her voice had taken on the singsong cadence she knew came with being in position on the long gun.

"Mother, Fury One is in position," Dempsey said next in her ear.

"Fury Two, set," came Munn on his heels.

"Copy, Fury," she breathed. "No joy on targets."

She scanned slowly along the route again.

"They're there," Dempsey said. "Or they will be."

She said nothing but mumbled a little prayer that he was right. Because if he was wrong . . .

The route from Hindon Airport, just barely outside Delhi proper, would take the President's convoy along Wazirabad Road, lined now with Delhi police and American Secret Service. From there it was a turn south onto Outer Ring Road, which would become Nataji Subhash just a half mile north of her position. That road would bring the convoy here. The Red Fort was the perfect place for the American President to secretly meet with the new Indian Prime Minister. As far as the public was concerned, the site was closed to tourists today for "maintenance." The final approach would funnel the presidential convoy into an irresistible kill box, Dempsey had said. And looking at it from her bird's-eye position, she agreed.

She glanced at the Suunto watch on her wrist.

They would be here soon.

Another round of four-count tactical breathing kept her calm and focused as a variety of scenarios unfolded in her mind—none of them very good. And it was in that moment that she realized she wasn't sure whether she should be praying for Dempsey to be right or wrong with his kill box prediction.

This was a common theme in her relationship with him.

The seconds ticked by, then minutes. She scanned incessantly, but nothing got her radar up.

"Eagle is turning south," came the Secret Service call. "Ten minutes out."

Sudden movement made her question whether, for some incredibly stupid reason, the bad guys had a false start. Then she realized the people she saw running were New Delhi police, as well as the three agents from 22 SG near the Lahori Gate. They were all sprinting to vehicles. Police lights suddenly began to flash from unmarked cars, which tore onto the street heading south.

"Mother, Fury One, this is Homeplate—be advised IB headquarters has just come under attack. We're about to lose most of our local support," Wang announced from his post in the TOC aboard the Boeing.

"Don't you mean NIA headquarters?" she said, assuming he'd misspoke.

"No, I mean the Intelligence Bureau headquarters," he said.

Well, there's one thing we were wrong about . . . I wonder what's next.

"Fury, be advised that the attack on the IB headquarters appears to be an airborne assault," Baldwin said from where he and Director Casey were watching in real time on the other side of the world. "We are showing an attack by multiple suicide drones with massive damage to the south wall of the IB building. Wait, there now appears to be multiple gunmen firing at the building and more drones inbound. This is Outfield, by the way."

Grimes felt her chest tighten and her pulse quicken. She pulled her eye from her scope to scan the sky, but she saw nothing but smog-stained air to the horizon. Normally, she felt safe and secure up in her perch, but not when kamikaze drones were in the mix. Against an incoming fast mover at altitude, she was a sitting duck.

"Outfield, Mother—promise me you're keeping an eye on the sky at my pos, because I don't have anybody watching my six," she said as she leaned back into the cheek pad on her rifle to resume her scan. "And being blown up by a drone would really ruin my day."

CHAPTER 44

MCDONALD'S

ALMOST TWO BLOCKS WEST OF THE LAHORI GATE TO THE RED FORT

CHANDNI CHOWK ROAD

DELHI, INDIA

Abu Musad Umar sat in a corner booth by himself, wishing his butter chicken "burger" was made of beef, but enjoying his cheese fries nonetheless. He ate only to keep his nerves—no, his *excitement*—at bay, so it didn't matter that much. But once he received the message from Shazi, his benefactor who had now helped finance not one but *two* of the greatest terror attacks of all time, his thoughts about fake McDonald's fast food disappeared and he was filled with anticipation.

Sure, Osama bin Laden's body count had been higher, but Umar had not only pulled off the assassination of the Prime Minister of India—a secular ruler and enemy of Allah's plan for the Muslim people of Kashmir—but also had assassinated the President of the United States, the Great Satan. Those attacks, despite the missed opportunity in Tel Aviv, had made him perhaps the most famous jihadi in the world. Though the intelligence machine had kept his name out of the press, the name al Ghadab, which to him was a literal synonym, was on every media feed and social media stream around the globe. Money had poured in from other jihadists and nation-states alike. Volunteers had been so numerous, he had a whole team now assigned to vet them, and many had to be turned away. After this attack, he had decided he would post a video claiming leadership of the most powerful terrorist organization in the world and outlining their plans for the new caliphate.

Al Ghadab needed a face—and that face was his.

Already, his life had been completely altered by the success that Shazi claimed for himself. Umar knew better. This was *his* destiny, and it would come to pass with or without the Chinese spook he had now outgrown. His organization would now and forever be well funded and well staffed without the help of the Chinese infidel.

And there had been other perks—more personal and enjoyable perks. He was sitting in Delhi in a suit worth more than what a few years ago had been a month's wages, and he'd paid more for his haircut than he used to live on for a week. Allah's rewards for his faithfulness, the devout part of him rationalized.

And I deserve it either way, the pragmatic doubter he'd become reassured him.

With this attack, and a second presidential assassination only minutes away, he would be known as the greatest jihadist of all time. The splintered factions of ISIL and al-Qaeda, the shadowy al Qadar, and even his own Jaish-e-Mohammed in Pakistan, having waxed and waned over and over since the Kargil War nearly a quarter of a century ago now, would coalesce around him. No, *under* him. Long after bin Laden was forgotten, Abu Musad Umar would be a name on the tongue of every believer and every infidel on earth. After so many failed attempts, the first true, successful caliphate would be led by him.

And with it both the power and the wealth I have very much enjoyed becoming accustomed to . . .

He glanced around the McDonald's, then maneuvered the touch pad on the laptop in front of him, tapping to open the collapsed screen at the bottom. He was annoyed that he still depended so heavily on Shazi. That would change soon enough. With contributions at an all-time high, he would surround himself with tech experts who could do what Shazi did for him.

Except, maybe, the incredible intelligence he is somehow able to deliver. That I have no idea how to replace.

Perhaps he would need the unholy alliance a little longer. But it would now fall on him to manage Shazi, in the same way perhaps that the spy had always tried to manage him. With more power would come an increasing codependence.

The screen of the MacBook Pro filled with a split-screen image, and his worries about what came next faded away. The left side of the screen showed streaming, real-time images from the four cameras he'd set up on buildings at the corners of his kill zone. The convoy was not yet in any of the four images but should be picked up by the two north-facing cameras at the south end of the square very soon. The right side of his screen, meanwhile, showed the six—no, the *five*— green triangles converging on the Lahori Gate to the Red Fort from both the south and northwest.

He picked up his burner phone, glanced around again, then pressed the contact labeled "B."

"Yes?"

"Time?" he said softly, his latest-generation earbuds easily picking up his voice and making the single word crystal clear.

"Perhaps two and a half minutes," the voice of his fighter Ahmed said, no fear in his voice despite the rather low probability of his surviving this attack. *Although,* Umar thought, *if the drones cause enough destruction to the convoy vehicles and enough of the security presence has redeployed to IB headquarters, who knows? Ahmed may yet be again at my side.*

Not that it mattered. He would have the pick of the crop.

"Very well. You may command initiate the vehicles to the south."

"Of course."

The phone went dead. The fighter leading his attack was brave and passionate, and if their religion was true, his reward would be great if he did not survive. Umar wondered if he still had that passion, that warrior drive, somewhere inside him. Fighting and leading Allah's warriors and their incursions into India for half a decade, he'd felt that rage and that drive. But perhaps Allah had created him for more than that, and that was why he was in the position he'd earned. And why not have a reward both here and in the afterlife, if it existed?

"Inshallah," he muttered.

Three green triangles moved across the map over Qutab Road while two others converged from the south of Humayun's Tomb. The timing would be close to perfect. He wondered for a moment whether this impending success was truly Allah's will or just a demonstration of the skills of the Chinaman. He'd once believed so passionately that he was an instrument of that will. He was less sure now.

Umar felt suddenly overwhelmed with the need to see the culmination of his work for himself. He had time to make it to the corner of Chandni Chowk and Netaji Subhash Marg. He deserved to see his victory with his own eyes—and despite the paranoid worries of his benefactor, he'd succeeded in staying in the shadows. No one knew who he was, much less what he looked like. That would change soon enough, but for now it gave him the safety to observe his victory firsthand.

As far as they're concerned, I will be one more terrified tourist . . .

He pushed away the fake burger, slipped his laptop into his leather satchel, and hurried from the fast-food restaurant, jogging east along Chandni Chowk and smiling.

CHAPTER 45

Seated in the back of the presidential limousine with his Wilson SBR Tactical in his lap, Dempsey craned his neck to look out the starboard-side window for incoming drones. They were the middle vehicle in the three-vehicle convoy. A typical presidential convoy would have two or three times as many vehicles, including a second identical presidential limousine to confuse any would-be attackers about which Beast actually carried the President, but Jarvis was only willing to put the minimum number of lives at risk for this ploy. Two up-armored Suburbans bookended the limo, taking the lead and tail positions.

"You see anything?" Prescott asked from beside him, where he was looking out the other side window.

"No," Dempsey grumbled. Then, through gritted teeth, he added, "At least not yet . . ."

"Fury, this is Homeplate," Wang said, his voice a bass string of tension. "We hold five airborne targets converging on your position.

These appear to be the same hexacopter drones used in the attack at IB moments ago. ETA is less than a minute."

"Fury One, roger. Mother, can you—"

Dempsey was interrupted by a squeal of rubber as Wallace—who was driving—slammed on the brakes. The instant deceleration catapulted both Dempsey and Prescott forward and into the backward-facing bench seat across the cabin. If not for the padding on the backrest, Dempsey probably would have gotten a concussion from the impact.

He scrambled to look through the ballistic glass divider separating the passenger cabin from the driver compartment, which allowed him to see out the windshield. Three gray SUVs stopped nose to tail had pulled in front of the convoy to block the entrance to the Lahori Gate complex.

"Fury Two," he called out to Munn, who was in the rear escort vehicle. "Back up!"

"Negative, Fury One," came Munn's tight voice. "We've got three Mahindras blocking us from the rear."

"Fury element, stay in your vehicles," Dempsey barked. Yes, they were sitting ducks in the halted convoy, but at least they had antiballistic protection. He knew the Beast was rated to withstand an RPG attack, but he wasn't sure about the Suburbans—and he had no idea what sort of explosive payload the incoming drones were carrying.

He stared again out the windshield at the three SUVs blocking the road. Dempsey couldn't see inside the aggressor vehicles because of blackout tint, but he assumed the Indian-made Mahindras were packed with jihadi shooters. The same was undoubtedly true of the blocking SUVs in the back. Any second the shooters would come pouring out to assault the convoy.

Damn, I hate when we're right . . .

"Fury, Mother has a line on all target vehicles," Grimes reported from her spire hide, high above and behind him. The moment the jihadists emerged, she'd start smashing pumpkins.

But, he realized, *they're not going to emerge. They're here to pin us in place until the drones arrive.*

"Drones in fifteen seconds," Wang announced as if confirming the thought.

"Fury, Outfield," Baldwin said, proving he could be concise if he wanted to. "We believe inbound bogeys are JOUAV model PH-20 hexacopter drones and fitted with explosive payloads—"

"How much payload can they carry?" Wang asked, talking over Baldwin and asking the exact question on Dempsey's mind.

"Fury," Baldwin said, urgency in his voice, "the drones can carry a payload of ten kilograms."

"Please tell me the armor can withstand—" he heard Allen say in the background.

"Ten kilos!" Munn shouted over her. "If they're carrying bricks of C-4, we're fucked!"

"Mother, we need you to shoot down the incoming," Dempsey ordered, his brain working the problem. "Repeat, shoot down incoming bogeys."

"Copy . . . scanning . . . I have no visuals," she came back, her voice strained. "Homeplate, you gotta help me."

"Drones are approaching from the north at high speed," Wang said, "bearing 340 from your pos."

"Roger, I see them," Grimes said. "Shit, they're fast for quadcopters."

"Hexacopters," Baldwin corrected.

Through her mike, Dempsey heard the dull *whump* of her Wilson Recon burping out 6.5mm Creedmoor rounds through the QUELL Titanium suppressor.

Two rounds . . . three . . . four . . .

"I've disabled one drone, which just dropped onto the roof of the floral shop," Grimes said, her voice frantic. "I can't stop the rest; it's impossible to track them in my scope while they're moving with such a high bearing rate . . ."

"Whoever is driving presidential limousine, listen very carefully to me," Baldwin said, his voice uncharacteristically direct and focused.

"Driver is Fury Nine," Wallace said. "Ready for instructions."

"Open the center armrest console. Inside you should see plexiglass cover over a box labeled TED. Lift the clear cover and press the black button labeled ARM . . ."

"Standby . . . I found it . . . Arming . . ." Wallace said. Dempsey heard, and felt, a thrum that seemed to be coming from inside the Beast. "System armed."

"Now, on my mark, Fury Nine, I want you to press the red button labeled DISCHARGE."

"Anything else?" she asked.

"A prayer wouldn't hurt," Dempsey heard someone say.

"Standby, Fury," Baldwin said, "in . . . three . . . two . . ."

CHAPTER 46

Umar heard the squeal of tires just as he reached the corner. A smile spread across his face as he approached the sawhorse barriers blocking Chandni Chowk from the crossroad at Netaji Subhash Marg. He was about to witness firsthand the execution of the newly sworn in President of the United States—an execution, and a victory for jihad, that he had planned and led. From this moment forward, entire nations would fear him. The power he would wield would be greater than most countries. He would have a nation-sized army of followers and soldiers. India would be the first to fall, but others would follow as his power and numbers grew.

I have done it. And it all starts right here.

People were screaming and running from the unfolding chaos in the streets. It had become clear what was about to happen as soon as the terrorist SUVs surrounded the presidential convoy. In mere seconds, the street had cleared of all but convoy vehicles and the six Mahindra SUVs containing his own army of Allah's warriors. Civilian vehicles were abandoned in the road, doors left open. A half block south, Umar noticed a woman or a small man sitting on a motorcycle, staring upward in shock.

He reminded himself that the drones carried ball bearings as well as explosives. Those would leave the detonation at the speed of bullets, so before impact he would need to hide around the corner—perhaps even move farther west.

His pulse quickened on hearing the whining buzz of the drones. Looking north, he saw the triangle formation of three PH-20s headed toward their target. Five of these demons would still be enough. Anyone who survived would be finished off by his hidden shooters waiting in the coffee shop, floral shop, and clothing store nearby.

His men had been instructed to grab what was left of the American President and drag him through the street while filming the entire victory, taking his bloody body back to the vehicles waiting for them in the lot behind the Jain temple. If they got away—which seemed likely, thanks to Shazi's plan to distract Delhi's police presence by forcing them to respond to the attack on IB headquarters—then the shock value of what they would do with that body on social media was worth millions in contributions and volunteers to the cause.

Suddenly he heard a repeated, dull *whump* from above him. He looked up but didn't see the source. Then he noticed one of his drones suddenly spiral out of control and disappear, likely crashing onto a roof somewhere in the densely packed city.

The Secret Service has a sniper up there. Well, my four remaining drones will be enough.

The rising scream of the next wave of approaching drones became an abrupt silence, and for a moment Umar was confused. His head jerked left and right, searching for the drones—which should be in terminal acceleration toward their target. Instead, the air had become eerily still. Umar's mouth dropped open as the silent drones fell from the sky, arcing like thrown toys toward the ground, before crashing onto the street with little fanfare and no explosion. Umar turned left in time to see the other two drones fall as well, one of them bouncing off the roof of the center Mahindra SUV behind the presidential convoy.

"No," he breathed. "It's not possible . . ."

He pulled out his phone to order the attack on the convoy to commence without the drones. The SUVs carried RPGs. Their mission could still succeed.

But the screen of his phone was black.

He looked around, noticing for the first time that every light in every building, every billboard, every traffic light—even the headlights of the trucks and cars on the road—were dark. The only sound was the idling of the small old motorcycle just south of him, whose rider now seemed to stare directly at him.

Should he run into the street and lead the charge himself, pull his warriors from their SUVs, and spur them into battle? He'd led many a charge such as this in his life.

But is that my mission now? Have I not a greater purpose?

Just then, the doors of the presidential convoy vehicles and the Mahindra SUVs of his brother jihadists opened in unison.

And the battle began.

CHAPTER 47

Dempsey didn't feel the EMP go off, but the device definitely worked because as soon as Wallace pressed the button, the incoming hexacopter drones dropped from the sky like bricks. Secret Service had not briefed them on the electromagnetic pulse system built into the trunk of the Beast, but somehow Baldwin had known about it, and Dempsey couldn't help but wonder how. He also couldn't help but wonder how many times the man's attention to detail and brilliant mind had saved his ass that he didn't know about.

"Comms are down," Prescott said.

"Noticed that," he said, checking his compact radio for lights and finding none.

Unfortunately, in addition to bricking the drones, the pulse had also shut down their comms. There was no fresh tactical information from Wang or Baldwin coming to him any time soon. He also couldn't communicate with Grimes in her overwatch position or the other members of his team in their convoy vehicles. His mind performed a quick cost-benefit calculation about whether to shelter in place in their armored vehicles or to exploit the moment of confusion and assault the enemy SUVs.

The decision didn't take long.

He'd never be a shelter-in-place kind of guy.

He turned to Prescott. "We could probably survive whatever those guys try to throw at us in the Beast, but our escort vehicles aren't built to the same specs. I say we assault the enemy before they get organized."

"Check," Prescott said and moved into position on the driver's side rear door.

Dempsey knocked on the divider glass between the driver and passenger compartments. Wallace and the Ground Branch shooter in the passenger seat both turned to look at him. He signaled no comms. They both nodded, then Dempsey signaled for Wallace to stay put in the driver's seat but for the Ground Branch soldier to exit and engage.

They both nodded again. It was on.

Dempsey burst out of the SUV, rifle up and ready, scanning forward at the three Mahindra SUVs that blocked their path ahead. They'd gotten a two-second jump on their jihadi adversaries. Dempsey placed the red dot of his gunsight on the man who was just now exiting the rear driver's side of the Mahindra and squeezed, shifting right as he did. The shooter's head puffed red gore, just as a bullet from another shooter crouching by the Mahindra pinged off the Beast to Dempsey's left. Dempsey backpedaled, moving his sight to the new threat—but a 6.5 Creedmoor round from Grimes's sniper rifle, fired a quarter mile away, exploded the man's head like a melon.

The remaining al Ghadab shooters had taken cover behind their vehicles on the far side. But Dempsey knew that Grimes still had a line on them from her high perch, and the steady *whump, whump* from her Recon sniper rifle was met with screams as she dropped the jihadists one by one. Dempsey fell back to the rear bumper of the Beast, where he crouched beside Prescott.

"Looks like they bought it hook, line, and sinker," Prescott said with a tight grin. "Jarvis's instincts were right. The decoy convoy worked."

"Yeah," Dempsey said as Munn and his squad engaged the shooters in the SUVs behind them. "But maybe too well. Those drones almost did us in, and now we're stuck in the middle in a cross fire."

"We've been in worse."

At that comment, a chilling thought occurred to Dempsey. Umar had proven himself to be both clever and cunning. He would have anticipated that the shooters in the SUVs would be killed or incapacitated by the kamikaze drone attack. He doubted those Mahindras were armored, and anybody outside of the vehicles at the time the payloads detonated would have been blown to bits.

So if Umar planned for those guys to be martyred, he'd need a mop-up crew—a reserve contingent to assault the wreckage of the convoy after the bombs went off.

Dempsey scanned the sidewalks and storefronts to the west, looking for new threats that could engage them from a third direction. Presently, they were only exchanging fire front and back, but their left and right sides were also vulnerable.

A burst of gunfire erupted, followed by a shout from Munn, confirming his fear.

"Contact left . . . Contact left!"

Dempsey spun left and brought his rifle up in a kneeling firing stance, just as four enemy shooters appeared seemingly out of nowhere. The assaulters coalesced into a modified diamond formation, firing on full auto and strafing the convoy along the passenger sides of the vehicles. Dempsey placed his sight center mass on the lead man and squeezed off a three-round burst. As his tango dropped, the head of the shooter marching behind exploded in a burst of gore.

Way to go, Lizzie, he thought. *But damn it, we need comms . . .*

Then he remembered something Baldwin had said once in a training session about how EMP discharges didn't actually "fry" electronics like people thought. More often than not, the pulse would overload the circuit and trip it off, but rebooting was often possible—just like cycling power to a bogged down Wi-Fi router would reset the circuit and get it working again. Dempsey cycled power to his radio and the light came on. His earpiece crackled to life and Wang's voice filled his ear.

"I say again, Fury, this is Homeplate . . . how do you copy? We have eyes on. You have shooters on both sides of the street now engaged . . ."

"Cycle your radios," Dempsey shouted. "I have comms up."

Munn, who'd heard the call, repeated the instruction up and down the line. Within seconds, Fury element had their radios back.

"RPG right!" Prescott shouted.

Dempsey spun right to see a jihadi terrorist taking a knee and bringing up a shoulder-mounted weapon—a Russian RPG-7 or a Chinese variant. He sighted and squeezed the trigger. A three-round burst found the target, just as the jihadist's body began to jerk from Prescott's rounds pummeling the assaulter's torso simultaneously. The RPG streaked out of the weapon in a plume of smoke and fire, passing over the lead Suburban and striking the façade of the ornamental gate into the courtyard at the Lahori Gate, where it exploded.

A muzzle flash in Dempsey's peripheral vision caught his eye, and he shifted left too late. The incoming round smashed into the upper receiver of his rifle, missing his hand but driving the weapon into his chest and knocking him backward into the Beast. He felt the pain flower in his chest, and only then did he realize that the round had punched a hole through his rifle and slammed into his body armor.

He unsnapped the quick release on his sling to abandon the weapon, as someone on his team returned fired and dropped the shooter with a double tap to the face. Relieved of his damaged rifle, Dempsey's hand found the butt of his custom full-size SFX9 pistol in a holster on his kit. He pulled the weapon and scanned the right side of the street for shooters as fresh gunfire sounded all around him.

His gaze settled on the corner of a nearby cross street, closed behind sawhorse barriers that blocked all vehicle traffic south. Whereas the rest of the pedestrian crowd had fled from the gunfire, one man stood at the intersection, conspicuously alone. He looked like a wealthy Afghan or Pakistani, and his black hair was coifed like a male model's. He was dressed in a suit, wearing eyeglasses, and had a leather satchel slung over his shoulder. Like a field marshal, the young man was surveying the running gun battle raging up and down the convoy line.

And he was smiling.

As the man swept his gaze across the battlefield, his stare settled on Dempsey. They locked eyes.

That's Umar, Dempsey realized. *Gotcha.*

Dempsey's face must have betrayed him because the young terrorist turned on a heel and sprinted west on Chandni Chowk Road and disappeared around a corner. Without a thought about the surrounding gunfire, Dempsey took off after him.

"Where the hell are you going?" Prescott shouted.

"I saw Umar," he shouted, letting him and anyone who had comms back up know that he'd found the terrorist mastermind. "And I'm going to bring him in."

CHAPTER 48

Dempsey hurdled the line of sawhorse barriers that separated Netaji Subhash Marg from the road down which Umar had fled. Dempsey had run only a quarter mile, and his knees were already aching. Not a good omen for how this chase might play out.

Equally irritating, Baldwin had begun to babble in his ear.

"For reference, John, you're running west on Chandni Chowk Road, a two-lane divided promenade that extends one point three five kilometers between the seventeenth-century Mughal fortress and the Fatehpuri Masjid. Normally, this would be a very busy area, but it appears on our satellite feed that most of the crowd at your end of the block has fled . . ."

I can't imagine why, Ian.

". . . so you should be able to maintain excellent visual contact. But in case you lose him, we are tracking the target."

"Check," Dempsey said between breaths.

Abandoned bicycles, pedal rickshaws, and ubiquitous green-and-yellow motorized tuk-tuks lined both sides of the street. The gun battle at the convoy had sent the crowd of locals and tourists fleeing from the violence, and Dempsey could see the tail end of the human stampede as it flowed mostly west, in the same direction his quarry was running. Merchant stands and wheeled carts lined the south side of the street, and the north side was crowded with tightly packed storefronts. Brightly colored, disorderly signage created a visual hodgepodge that extended as far as the eye could see, advertising electronics, computers, and mobile phones of every brand imaginable.

The terrorist leapt over the road's center island, which was filled with low shrubbery, and angled away from Dempsey. To Dempsey's surprise, the dude was pretty fast.

We'll see how long he lasts at this pace.

Dempsey, who was no stranger to foot chases since joining Ember, had both speed and endurance—or, at least, he had them before IK-2. With the way his knees were complaining, maybe he'd wear out before his quarry, which would be a first.

Not going to happen, growled the SEAL inside.

Ahead, he saw the jihadist vectoring toward a tipped-over motor scooter.

No, no, no . . . Dempsey silently screamed, then cursed when he saw that the lucky bastard had somehow found a scooter that was unlocked and operable. Umar looked over his shoulder and locked eyes with Dempsey. In the man's eyes, Dempsey saw fear, but also something else.

Swagger?

Dempsey sighted with his pistol as the terrorist revved the motor scooter to life. He fired a three-round volley, but given the vehicle's range and acceleration, none of his bullets found their target. Jaw clenched in aggravation, he scanned the immediate vicinity for any transportation. He saw plenty of bicycles and tuk-tuks, but nothing he could commandeer which might actually catch the fleeing terrorist.

Suddenly, the whine of a motorcycle engine behind him caused Dempsey to whirl. A leather-clad rider on a bright-red motorcycle was screaming toward him. Finger on the trigger, he held fire while assessing the threat. An instant later, though, his brain de-escalated based on two key details: one, the bike was slowing; and two, the driver was not holding a weapon.

The motorcycle braked to a hard stop beside Dempsey. The rider turned to look at him, flipping the helmet visor up to reveal a striking and familiar face.

"Elinor? What the hell are you doing here?" he said, a flurry of questions flooding his mind.

How did she know I'd be here? Did Jarvis tell her about the decoy convoy? Does she know that man is Umar? Was she tracking him already, and if so, how did she find him?

"Helping you catch Abu Musad Umar . . ."

I was right—that slippery sonuvabitch is Umar.

"Get on," she said, eyes burning with urgent intensity.

An unpleasant memory of the last time he rode bitch on a motorcycle popped into his head. He'd been chasing the Russian Zeta Anzor Malik, a.k.a. Valerian Kobach, through the crowded streets of Istanbul when he and Munn had commandeered a BMW motorcycle. Munn's insane driving had almost gotten them both killed, and Dempsey had vowed *Never again.*

"What are you waiting for? He's getting away!" she snapped.

With an annoyed growl, he holstered his weapon and grabbed the open-faced half helmet bungeed to a rack behind the pillion. He jammed it on his head and threw his leg over the back of the bike. As he settled onto the seat, he wrapped both his arms around Elinor's lower torso.

I suppose it ain't all bad, he thought with a smile, scooting his pelvis tight against her backside. *At least this time I'm not hugging Munn.*

"Please don't kill us," he shouted.

Her reply was to twist the throttle and accelerate so hard he had to clench his jaw to keep his mouth from flapping open.

"Fury One, please advise—who is that, and what are you doing?" Baldwin's voice said in his ear.

Dempsey ignored him and said, "Homeplate, can you put Elinor on our comms channel?"

"Hold on, did you say Elinor? As in *Elinor Jordan?*" Wang came back, disbelief in his voice.

"Yeah, that's the one."

"Even if I could, I don't know if that's a good idea, One."

"I'm not asking, Homeplate," he snapped. "I'm telling."

"Well, I can't do it while she's driving a motorcycle," Wang said. "There's encryption shit I need to do with her transceiver. And the kind of unit she's using makes a difference."

"Never mind." Then, shouting to Elinor, he said, "Do you see Umar?"

"He turned," she called back. "Hang on tight."

Dempsey gritted his teeth as Elinor braked hard and leaned the bike over at the last second to make a right-hand turn into an alley. Instead of trying to help control the maneuver, Dempsey forced his body to meld into Elinor's, and he let her muscle movements guide his own.

The red rocket they were riding handled like a roller coaster on rails, not skidding or losing an ounce of traction as they pulled out of the turn and returned upright. Squinting into the wind, Dempsey spied Umar's scooter entering a triangular courtyard formed by the junction of three streets. A massive tree—which was doing double duty as an electrical pole and structure for hanging shade tarps—grew in the center. Shanty shacks and pop-up vendor stands had been built all around it, creating a fork in the road.

The terrorist, who was sounding the scooter's horn and aggressively trying to navigate a path through a throng of panicked pedestrians, went left.

They were now several blocks away from the convoy, and the density of people to contend with was increasing. Elinor revved the motorcycle's engine and barreled ahead, anyone in her way be damned. People yelled and swore, leaping out of the way. A motorbike coming the opposite direction swerved violently to avoid a head-on collision in a game of chicken that Elinor won. Dempsey heard the man and his bike crash into a cart behind them.

A ludicrous mental image—Baldwin sitting with Chip and Dale, eating Dippin' Dots with plastic spoons in leather recliners while watching him via satellite feed on the big screen in the Ember TOC— popped into Dempsey's head.

"Uh-oh, watch out for the baby," Baldwin said in Dempsey's ear.

"Look out!" Dempsey shouted and squeezed Elinor's waist.

Damn if the eagle-eyed Baldwin wasn't right. A toddler was crawling in the dirt, crossing the road ahead.

Elinor executed a seemingly impossible half loop maneuver to avoid running over the child. A metal pole sticking out of the side of a shanty shack caught Dempsey's left shoulder and almost ripped him off the back of the bike, but his death grip on Elinor's jacket held.

"Shit, that was close," she yelled. She gunned the throttle, accelerating once again into the chaos that was the backstreets of Delhi.

"Talk to me, Homeplate," Dempsey said. "Any idea where this guy is going?"

"Dude, I don't think he has a plan. He's just running," Wang said.

"Check." Then, knowing he'd regret asking: "Outfield, give me a summary of what's ahead?"

"I'm glad you asked, Fury One," Baldwin came back. "And I'm happy to report that your target has chosen an untenable escape route. The alley roads only get narrower and more crowded in the direction he's chosen. I do not think he will be able to continue fleeing via motorbike for more than another block or two."

"Going to get real narrow and real crowded ahead," Dempsey shouted, giving Elinor a heads-up.

She didn't answer. It was what it was.

What happened next, at first, seemed like a good thing. The crowd between them and Umar parted like Moses and the Red Sea, and Elinor poured on the speed, rocketing them into the expanding funnel of human bodies. But Dempsey quickly recognized what was really happening. At the end of the funnel sat Umar on his motor scooter, stopped perpendicular to the alley, his torso rotated to face them. Worst of all, he was holding a machine pistol trained in their direction.

Elinor reacted instantly. She laid the bike out and sent it skidding along the ground at Umar like a missile. A stream of bullets raked the air above them. The maneuver dumped both of them, but Dempsey reflexively rolled out of the fall, his helmeted head smacking against something hard and unmoving as he came to an abrupt halt at the edge of the road. The machine pistol reports stopped, and Dempsey heard a loud crash as Elinor's motorcycle slammed into a street cart behind where Umar had been standing.

Dempsey shook off the stars, pulled his pistol, and reoriented into a prone firing position, intent on dropping Umar with a headshot. But the terrorist now had shoved a woman into Dempsey's line of fire before he could align his sights. Umar fired his machine pistol into the air, causing fresh panic in the crowd and generating moving cover for his escape.

Unable to risk a shot, Dempsey watched the terrorist disappear into the hysterical, jostling crowd. Cursing, he turned and scanned the ground and found Elinor lying against the side of a pushcart ten feet away, slowly getting to her hands and knees. He popped to his feet, ran to her side, and conducted a quick head-to-toe scan for major injuries or bleeders. Seeing nothing of immediate concern, he looked down the alley to make sure Umar hadn't circled back to take aim and reengage.

"Fury One, the target is on the move," Baldwin said, as if reading Dempsey's mind, "but we're tracking him. Recommend immediate pursuit on foot."

"Are you okay?" Dempsey asked, ignoring Baldwin and turning back to Elinor. He grabbed her under her right arm to help her up.

"I think so," she said, but as she tried to put weight on her right foot, she yelped and collapsed. "My foot's broken. I felt it snap when we dumped. I'm out, but you go. Hurry, he's getting away."

"No. I left you in Tehran. I'm not doing that again," he said, meeting her beseeching gaze.

On hearing this, she grabbed his forearm and squeezed it tight. "This time I'm giving you permission. I've got backup in the area. I promise I'll be fine, John."

"Are you sure?"

"Yes, just go get that fucker."

An operator's grin curled his lips, and he turned to leave. But he only managed two steps before turning back to her.

"What?" she shouted, exasperated.

"How will I find you?"

She winced in pain but still managed to flash him a coy smile. "You won't. I'll find you."

CHAPTER 49

Dempsey sprinted into the crowd, shouting for people to move out of his way as he did.

"The target is forty meters ahead of you, heading north," Baldwin said, "Hold on, scratch that, he just turned west. There's a dogleg ahead, John—I mean, Fury One. Now he's heading north again. You're going to turn left in ten meters . . ."

Dempsey rolled his eyes. *He's never going to change*, he thought, *but same goes for me. Just like family, we're stuck with each other to the end.*

He spotted the intersecting alley, exactly where Baldwin said it would be, and rounded the corner at full tilt. He began shouting, "Clear a path," hoping to make his forward progress a little easier through the densely packed alley.

"You should see a sign for USHA Cable on your right side. Turn north at this landmark . . ."

Dempsey noted the neon-pink sign in his peripheral vision and completed the dogleg to head north once again. As he turned, his mind's eye thought of Elinor hobbled on the ground and how Baldwin and the boys hadn't warned him that Umar had stopped to ambush them in that alley.

"Outfield, if the target stops and tries to set up another ambush like he did last time, you better fucking tell me," Dempsey barked.

"Roger, Fury. That one was on me. That section of alley was extremely narrow and shade tarps obstructed our view. We were waiting for the target to come out the other side," Baldwin said, his voice contrite.

"I don't need excuses," he said between breaths. "I need backup."

"Understood, Fury One."

Dempsey hurdled a wooden crate of bananas without breaking stride. Now that he was moving and warmed up, his knees were feeling pretty good. Or maybe it was just the adrenaline masking the pain. Either way, he'd take it.

As he dodged left to avoid a woman dragging a wagon, Dempsey collided with a man who stepped out of a doorway carrying several stacked boxes in front of him. Dempsey's two hundred pounds of muscle prevailed and sent the man and his junk flying. The impact caused Dempsey to stumble for a few strides, but he didn't go down.

"Target has turned west and is still on the move," Baldwin said. "Stand by to turn at an alley in twenty-five meters. You're closing the gap, Fury; keep it up."

Hearing that, Dempsey pushed himself a little further toward his personal redline, ignoring the burn from lactic acid buildup in his muscles. He was breathing hard and heavy now, but situations like this were what he trained for. Unless Umar trained regularly as a distance runner, he had no chance at outlasting Dempsey.

"Turn left in five meters . . ."

Dempsey rounded the bend, and as he did caught his first glimpse of Umar since he'd turned to fire on Elinor's motorcycle. The terrorist mastermind was struggling to push through a dense pocket of crowd, and Dempsey could see why. Five meters past Umar, a delivery truck was blocking half the available walking space in the alley. Dempsey's mind identified this as a natural spot for Umar to try another ambush.

He said as much to Baldwin as Umar disappeared from view.

"We concur, Fury One. Seems likely . . . Watching . . . Target paused briefly but now is back on the move, still heading west," Baldwin reported.

"What's to the west? Is it possible he's got an exfil vehicle waiting?"

"In fifty meters, the target will intersect— Yes, Chip, I realize that . . . Of course, I'll tell him— As I was saying, Fury, in forty meters the target will intersect HC Sen Marg, which is a two-lane road with heavy vehicle traffic. At this juncture, he will be only a quarter of a mile from the DLI train and metro station. It could be his plan to flee by metro or rail. Or your instincts could prove prescient, and he may have an exfil vehicle waiting."

"Copy all. Tell me if you see him use his phone."

"Oh yes, we've been waiting for that."

Dempsey rolled his eyes.

"Move, move, move! Outta my way," Dempsey shouted, driving forward with his shoulder as he did. Like a predator closing in on flagging prey, Dempsey could practically taste the kill. All thoughts of taking Umar alive had long since vanished. He had a narrow opportunity to take the shot now before Umar exited the alley onto the busy street ahead.

I can make the shot, Dempsey thought. He stopped dead in his tracks and took aim at the back of the terrorist's head.

He put tension on the trigger and . . .

"Shit," he growled, desperately wanting to squeeze but unable to because there was just so much collateral: vendors manning street carts, a mother shepherding a gaggle of children, a tuk-tuk driver leaning against his cab trying to flag down fares, a skinny young man handing out flyers . . .

Damn civilians fucking up my op.

"The target has reached Sen Marg," Baldwin said in his ear. "He's hesitating, may be scanning for a ride . . . Target is on the move, cutting across traffic and heading west."

Dempsey shoved his way through the agitated crowd—shouting at people to move—until he finally burst onto the more open but traffic-filled Sen Marg. Compact cars, minibuses, tuk-tuks, and three-wheeled bicycle-powered rickshaws jockeyed for position in a traffic jam that extended as far as the eye could see in each direction.

Thirty feet away Umar dodged and weaved his way across the busy thoroughfare.

A man on a bicycle swerved to avoid a toppled bag of groceries and fell directly in front of Dempsey, who hurdled the man without breaking stride and surged toward the crowded four-lane street Umar was already crossing. Horns blared and voices shouted as the terrorist dodged cars. Dempsey juked around a yellow-and-green tuk-tuk and then slid feetfirst on his left hip across a car's hood and landed on his feet on the other side. He held up a hand to stop a minibus going the opposite direction. The driver sounded his horn, but the bus stopped, and Dempsey skirted the gap so close he could have reached out and touched the windshield. He surged through one final gap between a line of tuk-tuks and emerged on the other side, panting and scanning for Umar.

"It appears the target is entering a construction project," Baldwin said with the tone he always used when he found something curious or perplexing. "According to what limited information we have, the structure you're looking at is a future shopping mall and luxury galleria."

Dempsey spotted Umar ducking into a gap between vertical corrugated metal panels that formed a perimeter around the massive construction site. The bones of the main structure—the concrete foundation, support columns, and second and third floors—were completed, but access to the interior of the mall was wide open because no exterior walls, doors, or windows had been installed. A massive ten-story crane stood unmoving behind the building like a sentinel watching over the project.

"Fury One, be advised we've lost visual contact on the target. Proceed with caution," Baldwin said.

"Check," he said and paused at the gap in the perimeter fence, alone now without eyes guiding him from above.

He took a knee and sighted through the narrow opening, scanning as best he could before slipping between the corrugated panels. A metal burr on the right-hand panel caught the fabric of his shirt as he did, and when it snapped free, the panel shook and vibrated loudly.

Cringing, Dempsey sprinted to cover behind a cement mixer.

Clutching his pistol, he looped around the back side of the cement mixer and advanced deeper into the construction site. Metal scaffolding had been erected in dozens of places, and ladders connected each level of the scaffold—the only apparent way to move between the ground floor and higher levels.

Pounding footsteps sounded from inside the galleria, and Dempsey ran toward the noise, silent in a high combat crouch. He swiveled right and then left and back to clear but saw nothing. Pulse still pounding from his run, he forced himself to take measured, controlled breaths and tried not to think about how much he wished he had a rifle instead of a pistol.

A loud, metallic clang sounded to the left, and he dropped to a kneeling firing stance, sighting on the base of a tall column of scaffolding where he'd heard the noise. Seeing nothing at ground level, he scanned upward, then fired twice at a flicker of movement on level three.

The rounds clanged sharply off the scaffolding, echoing in the otherwise still construction site.

Then silence.

He held, waiting and scanning for something to shoot, but no target presented itself.

Where are you planning to go, dumbass?

Dempsey shook his head at the terrorist's stupidity—but at the same time, pursuing Umar vertically was an equally stupid and dangerous proposition for Dempsey. The terrorist had the high ground, and Dempsey would be completely vulnerable during the ladder climb. After a moment's consideration, he decided to hold and wait for Umar to screw up.

A heartbeat later, running footfalls on metal echoed from above. Then something happened he did not expect to see: Umar flying through the air and making a very long jump between the scaffold platform and the third-story floor, which encircled the central atrium. Dempsey eyed the distance between the scaffold and the ledge, then looked at the vertical drop, which had to be close to forty feet.

Hell no, I'm not doing that.

A backlit form appeared on the third level, and the stillness was again broken, this time by a burp of submachine-gun fire.

Dempsey dove left for cover behind a tool cage as the volley of rounds ricocheted off the concrete floor where he'd just been standing. The line of bullets dragged right and pummeled the other side of the tool cage, shaking the metal and raining sparks. Then, as abruptly as it started, the maelstrom stopped.

"It's over, Umar," Dempsey shouted. "You're trapped. There's nowhere left to run."

"If it's over, then why are you cowering down there? Come up here, and we will settle this battle like men, face-to-face," Umar called back.

Dempsey assumed Umar's magazine was spent. The dude fired without discipline, but the terrorist had also proven himself to be wily. Dempsey had no intention of underestimating the terrorist who had pulled off the assassination of an American President. No matter how much help Umar may have had, the operation took balls. Down to a half a magazine, Dempsey swapped mags now while he had a pause.

"The President wasn't in the convoy. You know that, right? It was a charade—a trick to lure you out of hiding," Dempsey called.

As he talked, he estimated the firing angle on Umar in his head, then visualized himself making the impossible shot: *steep up angle, at a backlit target, with only the top 15 percent of the torso visible, at an eleva-tion of thirty-six feet and a range double that.*

". . . and it worked, because here you are."

"Congratulations . . . but I still killed President Warner and Prime Minister Chopra. I showed everyone how weak, unprepared, and vulnerable you are. America is a paper tiger, and now the entire world knows it. Even if I die, al Ghadab will carry on. And if al Ghadab crumbles in my absence, other warriors will rise to carry on the battle and deliver the caliphate."

Dempsey pressed up into a ready squat, gripping his pistol with both hands. "There's something I don't understand, Umar. How did you hack that Predator drone in Nepal, huh? That's way beyond your capability."

As soon as Umar began to answer, Dempsey made his move:
"You Americans always underestimate—"
Dempsey rotated left around the edge of the cage, sighted, and fired. Trigger squeeze, squeeze, squeeze . . . squeeze.

The first round hit Umar in the right shoulder, the second one in the side of the neck, the third in the face, and the fourth missed as Dempsey's volley walked a tight, upward sloping line to the left. He watched the terrorist waiver momentarily, then collapse forward and tumble over the concrete lip of the third floor. The body turned a revolution and a half as it fell—heels over head—before landing with a nauseating splat on the concrete floor, close enough that spatter from the impact of the body sprayed across Dempsey's right pant leg and boot.

Dempsey stared at the mess for a moment. "Homeplate, Fury—mission complete."

"One, Two—where the hell are you?" Munn's voice asked in Dempsey's ear.

"I'm with Umar, or what's left of him," Dempsey said. "Sorry I ran off and left you guys . . . I assume the gun fight is over and we won."

"Yeah, we won," Munn said, but Dempsey could hear the thinly veiled irritation in his friend's voice. Knowing Munn, that irritation was rooted in the fact that Dempsey had taken matters into his own hands and abandoned his team in the middle of a firefight.

But if I hadn't, Umar would have gotten away.

"Great, then come pick me up," Dempsey said, turning his back for the last time on Abu Musad Umar and walking back toward the road. "I'm ready to go home."

CHAPTER 50

BOMBARDIER CHALLENGER REGISTERED TO CHINA TELECOM

ELEVATION: 41,000 FEET—EASTBOUND OVER BHUTAN

EN ROUTE TO SHANGHAI, CHINA

1522 LOCAL TIME

Liu Shazi opened his eyes slowly to the gentle tap on his shoulder.

"I am so very sorry, sir," the corporate flight attendant said in Mandarin as he looked up at her. "I do not wish to disturb you. But may I get you something to eat? We have a wonderful selection of appetizers, or I can prepare you a meal from our menu. A glass of champagne, perhaps?"

"Green tea," he said patiently, smiling at the woman who had pulled him from his meditation.

"Of course," she said, returning the smile with bright-red lips. "Anything to eat?"

"No, thank you," he said. "And we have a long flight, and I will be spending much time in meditation and in thought. Would it trouble you to leave me undisturbed? I promise to let you know if there is anything at all I need."

"Of course, sir," she said with a respectful bow. "I so apologize. And I will not disturb you again."

"There is no apology needed, I promise. And you have not disturbed me. You are doing your job wonderfully, and I will report just that to Mr. Chen on my return. I hope you will take my pensiveness as an opportunity to relax and enjoy the flight as well. Prepare yourself a meal, perhaps?"

"Oh, I am not permitted to do that, sir. But your kind words are a blessing."

"Even if I insist? If I demand it?" He gave her his very best smile.

"Well," she said, her smile genuine for the first time. She looked up at the ceiling. "I suppose if you were to *demand* it, I would have no choice."

"Then I demand it," he said, smiling still.

She gave another short bow.

"I will prepare your tea," she said and headed to the front of the jet where the galley was located.

Shazi sighed. Disturbed from his breathing the Original Breath, his mind no longer a clear lake reflecting the sky, he opened his laptop again. His finger tapping the side of the mahogany table of the oversized club seat, he watched the four separate videos on the split screen again. His breathing quickened, and he felt his right eyelid quiver.

That Umar had been killed was of little consequence to him. A satellite pass sent to Shazi from his mentor, Zhao Feng, showed the terrorist's inglorious death, and he felt nothing at the sight. Even if Director Dongxing at SSAB didn't order it, Shazi would have executed the man nonetheless, to severe the last tie between al Ghadab and China.

But the operation was not a success. Was it?

Again, the American President had won. Shazi zoomed in the screen at the top left, trying to see the eyes of the operator at the rear of the lead vehicle, but the magnified image was too grainy. The American President and this man in the video. These were the men who had bested him. Jarvis had sprung a trap of his own, as if he knew—somehow actually *knew*—what Shazi had planned. That was impossible, of course. There could be no leak because there was no one to leak anything. Only Shazi had known the plan. And Umar, of course, but he had waited until the last possible minute to share anything with the al Ghadab terrorists for that very reason.

No. The American President was prescient.

He zoomed in tighter on the operator in the picture, which only made the face blurrier.

Or perhaps you are the prescient one, my friend. Perhaps this American operator is the real reason I failed.

Already he had run facial recognition—another favor generously offered by Zhao Feng—and it had come up with nothing. This man, it seemed, was a ghost. At least a ghost within the American intelligence community, whose databases he perused at will, like shopping for clothes on Amazon. Neither the American nor the MSS databases had any matches.

Perhaps somewhere else in the world a match existed, though. If so, Shazi would find it.

You will not remain a ghost for long, my friend . . .

He closed his laptop. With a smile at the attendant, he accepted the green tea, including the sterling pot to freshen his porcelain cup when needed, then turned and looked out at the deck of clouds beneath the jet. Something occurred to him that he should have thought of before. It seemed very unlikely that the woman Umar had brought to the apartment in Delhi was an operative who had somehow penetrated the al Ghadab organization, especially on such short notice—but she had, nonetheless, seen Shazi's face in the same room with the Pakistani terrorist.

Obviously, that simply wouldn't do.

Shazi picked up the smaller of the two satellite phones on the table. Only one ring was necessary.

"Yes?"

"The girl from the apartment that I told you about . . ."

"I remember. We pulled photos from the building cameras. She seems never to look at them—always her head is turned—so facial recognition is not possible."

That was strange, wasn't it?

"We have her name from our man who owns the apartment."

Or at least the name she used . . .

"You wish me to find her and make sure she is who she says?"

Shazi thought a moment. It seemed reckless to take a chance.

"No," he said softly and then took a sip of his tea. The temperature was perfect. "Find her and kill her. It no longer matters who she is."

"It will be done."

He set the phone back down.

Yes, he'd been beaten. All he was doing now was minimizing the damage. President Jarvis might already be sitting down with the new Prime Minister of India. Even now he might be pitching the security and economic agreement Warner had negotiated with Prime Minister Chopra to this temporary PM ahead of an election in India. In the wake of the two terror attacks, the Indian government would be even more eager for the agreement—an alliance that would cause great economic hardship for China, Shazi predicted—than before the first attack.

My mission has not just failed—it has made things worse . . .

He would try, if at all possible, to meet again with Zhao Feng before returning to Shanghai. He needed his mentor's advice now more than ever.

The other phone chirped.

Shazi sighed, performed a series of Original Breaths to center his Qi and bring peace to his troubled mind, then answered.

"Yes?"

"Where are you?"

"I am returning from vacation," he said. "I apologize. I know you asked me to stay away longer; however . . ."

"No, it is for the best," Director Gua Dongxing of SSAB said. "There has been a development."

"What has happened?" Shazi asked, sipping his tea.

"That terrorist has attempted another attack—an attack against the Americans in Delhi, of all things. He was killed, but it is a mess. This will likely galvanize the relationship between the new heads of state, just as you feared. We need you back immediately. We may need to put you back in play."

"Of course," Shazi said. "It is my honor to serve. I can be in Shanghai in a few hours."

"Call me when you land, Liu Shazi. We have much to discuss."

The line went dead, and Shazi set the phone down. He stared out the window where the tops of the clouds reflected orange light from the sun. It was strange how the universe brought people and things together again and again until everything was set in balance. It seemed that he and the American President might yet find another opportunity to dance.

He opened the laptop and stared at the blurry image on the screen. *The American President and his shadow warrior . . .*

CHAPTER 51

EMBER'S EXECUTIVE BOEING 787-9

TAIL NUMBER N103XL

ELEVATION: 43,000 FEET—WESTBOUND OVER THE CASPIAN SEA

EN ROUTE TO RAMSTEIN, GERMANY

1844 LOCAL TIME

Dempsey collapsed into one of the oversized recliner chairs in the lounge outside the bunk rooms aboard Ember's jet. He was exhausted, not just from the last sixty hours of nearly constant sustained warfare activity—between the hit on Saeed, followed by the hit on Umar's compound, followed by the ambush of Umar's al Ghadab fighters—but also all the hours of tedious intelligence analysis, mission planning, and briefs in between.

No, he was exhausted from what he now thought of as his "apology tour" he'd made over the last hour.

He pressed the buttons in the armrest of his favorite chair and let it recline halfway, the footrest coming up to meet his calves, then leaned his head back and closed his eyes. He'd decided to skip the meal that waited in the galley and enjoy a moment of solitude in this chair—the one he'd relaxed in after so many missions with Ember. It was one of the few things that was still familiar on the revamped Ember jet, and he felt grateful that Casey had the insight to leave it for him.

Dempsey unconsciously probed at the deep-black bruise in the middle of his chest where the enemy slug had punched into his body armor after trashing his rifle. It had stung at the time, but then he'd forgotten about it until they were back aboard the Boeing. Munn had insisted on an X-ray in the medical suite, but the doc hadn't found a fracture of the sternum. He'd done an EKG also, but Dempsey didn't fully understand—nor did he really care about—the explanation of how an EKG could detect a bruised heart.

Living with a bruised heart is my default state anyway . . .

Munn had cleared him for duty with no follow-on tests, but his best friend had been strangely quiet during the exam, throwing out only one sarcastic comment about Rambo, which Dempsey had blown off. But later, when Buz had assembled the team for the after-action debrief, the look on Munn's face revealed exactly what he thought of Dempsey running off on his own to chase Umar. Whatever Munn's concern—whether it be the risk Dempsey took pursuing the HVT on his own, consternation over the reemergence of Elinor, or the fact Dempsey had left the team one man short in the convoy firefight— Munn had kept his thoughts and criticisms to himself.

Of course he did, because Petra Felsk—no, Petra Jarvis—had tuned in remotely for that debrief.

Munn was a team-before-self guy to the core and would have never thrown Dempsey under the bus in such a forum. Later, Dempsey had found Munn and apologized, but the lumberjack had simply shrugged.

"All good, bro," he'd said, barely managing a smile. "That's just who you are now."

Those words still rattled in his mind as he lay on the recliner with his eyes closed. What the hell did that even mean?

Am I so different after Russia?

After three-plus years at Ember, thinking of himself as a SEAL had a foreign and unfamiliar feel to it. The man he was before Ember felt like a distant and faded dream, but that was understandable. He'd lost his SEAL family and forsaken his real one. And in the aftermath, Ember had taken their place.

For the Russia mission, he'd been forced to walk away from his family yet again—this time, his Ember family. He'd not wanted to do it, but he'd not had a choice either. When he said yes to Jarvis on that beach, he'd had to accept the fact that he probably wasn't coming home. He had to resign himself to the fact that assassinating Vladimir Petrov was a suicide mission—a suicide mission he couldn't have completed without severing ties first.

But I didn't die . . . I completed the mission, and I came home.

But no sooner had he thought it when Munn's words echoed in his head.

That's just who you are now . . .

Yes, Russia had changed him, but only for the better. The man and operator who'd come home was stronger, harder, tougher. Like a blade tempered in fire, his time in Russia had only made him more lethal.

He shook the thought off and took a long, soothing breath.

No one else at the brief had batted an eye—not Prescott or Lewis, and of course none of the newbies. And Buz, who was never shy about doling out criticism when criticism was warranted, hadn't said a thing. Neither had Casey. The debrief had ended with a "Great job, everyone" from Casey and an impassioned thank-you from the new FLOTUS, and no one in leadership had made any specific mention of what Dempsey should or should not have done on the decoy op.

So what was Munn's problem?

He'd thought maybe Grimes could shed some light on the matter, but he'd not found time alone with her yet. Everyone was getting cleaned up and rested before they arrived in Ramstein. There, they'd pick up Martin and refuel for the last leg home. Casey told them that Baldwin and the team in Tampa were still interrogating data and hoped to have more information on whether the Chinese had or had not been assisting al Ghadab. In the meantime, they had successfully cut off the head of another terrorist snake, and that was something to celebrate.

Unless Jarvis needs me to assassinate another foreign head of state . . .

The thought came so suddenly and was so unwelcome that he sat bolt upright, only to see Wallace, the former SWCC warrant officer, in the doorway, freshly showered and wearing jeans and a black long-sleeve tee.

"Sorry, did I wake you?" she said.

"Uh-uh. Not at all. Just relaxing before I hit the showers myself."

She nodded and smiled. "So . . . um, is this how it always is at Ember?"

He studied her, looking for some subtext of accusation or dissatisfaction behind the question, but her expression appeared earnest.

"What do you mean?" he asked, pushing the armrest button to raise the recliner.

"I mean, is it always this badass?" she asked through a laugh. "I did some cool shit with the Teams, but this—this is next level. We destroyed a terror cell single-handedly. That's insane!"

Now it was Dempsey's turn to smile. He liked Wallace. She was a skilled operator, a great breacher—and dude, her chocolate chip cookies were ridiculous.

"This unit is very good at what we do and backstopped by great leadership. From what I've seen so far, you're a great fit here. We're lucky to have you."

He thought about what she'd just said. Was Ember that much better than everyone else or just better positioned to do the work?

"Honestly, Tess," he continued, "with the right people and support, Ember is simply proof positive of what highly skilled operators can do when the big boss lets you take the gloves off. Most of the operators I've served with in my career could do what we do, given the chance and the resources we have."

"I like hearing that," she said, then after a moment added, "There's a rumor that you were once with the Tier One, so you may have an elevated expectation of what can be accomplished by a unit with such a small footprint. But I like the sentiment anyway."

She didn't seem to be looking for confirmation about who and what he was before Ember, so he didn't give her any.

The lounge door opened just as Wallace reached for it to leave.

"Oh, hey, Elizabeth," Wallace said and stepped aside to make room for Grimes to get by.

"Hey, Tess," Grimes said.

"I'm heading to the galley to see what kind of oven setup they have and what the dry-goods situation is in stores. I was thinking about baking cinnamon rolls," Wallace said.

"Oh, hell yes," Dempsey said. He glanced at Grimes, expecting to see an eye roll, but the redhead death-dealer just smiled politely.

"See you guys," Wallace said and turned to leave.

Grimes gave a little wave and then shut the door.

"How are you doing, JD?" she asked, staying by the door and crossing her arms.

"Great," he said, rising from the recliner and feeling a twinge of pain in his chest as he did. "Dan says no fractures and no heart bruise or whatever, so I'm five by. How about you?"

"I'm good, but you know that's not what I meant."

He sighed but flashed her his best innocent look.

"In that case, I'm doing great. It's good to be operating with the team again. I missed you guys," he said, thinking that a bit of emotion might appease her. He wanted to cross his arms and remind her he had been cleared by a team of shrinks at Bethesda, and then by the private therapist Director Casey had made him see. He was fine. Why the hell couldn't everyone just act normal around him?

"We missed you too," she said, softening. Then, unexpectedly, she crossed the carpet and wrapped her arms around his chest in a big bear hug and squeezed.

He hugged her back. Lizzie was like his kid sister, and they'd hugged all the time. Why did it feel so uncomfortable this time?

After releasing him, Grimes stepped back and looked at him. "Why didn't you tell us about Elinor?"

She butters me up with a hug, then hits me with that.

Dempsey let out a long sigh. "We were on mission. I reported the initial contact up the chain to Casey and then put it out of my head.

Honestly, I felt like that was my only option. Otherwise, she would have been stuck in my headspace, mucking around with my emotions the entire time. I fully planned to tell you and Dan as soon as the mission was over and the time was right."

"I get being in mission mode, John," she said, but seemed unconvinced. "But this was different. I mean, she betrayed us. Shit, she betrayed more than just us—she was a double agent for VEVAK. Her showing up could have impacted our mission. Hell, it *did* impact it— just, you know, not in the way any of us would have expected."

He nodded, trying to retain his calm. He really didn't owe her an explanation.

"I guess I didn't see it that way, and it seems Casey didn't either or he would have read you in. Like I said, I passed the contact on and got back to work. I was as surprised to see her at the Red Fort as you guys."

"Well, not quite as surprised," Grimes pointed out, "since we all still thought she was dead."

"Okay, that's fair I guess."

Grimes shook her head, as if still battling disbelief. "That you just took off with her of all people, without questioning anything . . ." She let out a long, exasperated exhale. "Whatever; it's over now. Casey says they're briefing the whole incident up the chain, and I'm sure Petra will let the Israelis know about her."

"Right," he said.

Dempsey suspected the Israelis already knew. Harel had been a man who was always one step ahead of the rest of the world. Elinor had attended his funeral, which meant Levi and Elinor must have reconciled. The Israeli spymaster had let her live for a reason . . .

Probably the same reason I opened my hotel room door and let her back into my life.

"So, anyway, Buz wants us back in the conference room for a quick hooyah over dinner," she said.

He nodded and was about to let her go, but then said, "Do you think China was pulling the strings behind the assassination?"

Normally, he would have left the matter for the head shed and policy wonks to worry about, but for some reason he cared and couldn't get it out of his mind. He was curious to hear what Grimes thought too. Yes, she was a demon on the long gun, but before she came to Ember, Grimes had been a brainiac at the Brookings Institute. Besides being a damn fine operator, she also happened to be one of the smartest and most insightful people he knew.

"Hmm," she said and paused a moment. "I think Petra makes a good case that because of the Warner-Chopra Pact, Beijing had reason to feel threatened and motive to act. We'll see what Ian has for us, but this seems excessive even for the Chinese. Then again, the rules of the game are always changing."

He wondered if there was *Russia mission* subtext in that last comment, and if so whether it was a jab at him. Instead of getting annoyed, he shook it off. "My gut tells me it was China."

She fixed him with a tight smile. "If so, are you prepared to go up against them? That's a whole different kind of thing."

"Yeah, but so was Russia."

"But you'll have a helluva time blending in on the streets of Beijing compared to Moscow."

"I go where the fight takes me, Lizzie. And if there is some group in China—sanctioned or unsanctioned—that played a role in killing Warner . . ." He felt his jaw twitch. "Well, let's just say that's an op I look forward to running."

An awkward pause followed, but Grimes ended it by hugging him a second time. This time, however, it felt warm and right and nice.

"It really is good to have you back," she said.

"Team before self," Dempsey said.

Then, feeling more like himself than he had in a while, he followed her out to join up with the rest of the team.

He might never feel like Navy SEAL Jack Kemper again, but Ember was his family—and John Dempsey had finally made it home.

EPILOGUE

SQT BARRACKS, ROOM #314

PHIL H. BUCKLEW NAVAL SPECIAL WARFARE TRAINING CENTER

NAVAL AMPHIBIOUS BASE CORONADO

CORONADO, CALIFORNIA

1943 LOCAL TIME

Jake knew it was time to make the call.

He and Ketron had a long way yet to go, but with each passing phase, his confidence grew, as did his realization that his best friend was going to be one badass operator. SEAL Team Eight was going to be very lucky to have both of them, he was slowly able to admit to himself, though he imagined he would never be able to say it out loud.

The two men had been consistently the top team in most evolutions, and in the top three scorers in every phase. They'd set the class record in both speed and accuracy in the kill house before small-unit tactics. They mastered Land Nav. They'd finished number one and two in the small-unit tactics course. They still had a grueling medical course to complete, which Randy was sweating for its academics, and they'd heard horror stories about SERE school. But next they headed to Air Phase, where they would master HALO and HAHO jumping and ropes training—which would be fun.

They had work to do, sure. But it was fun, exciting work.

Jake was nervous about what he might find out, but it was becoming more distracting to worry about making the call, and he didn't have time for distractions now. He'd had dinner with Mom in Virginia Beach, but it had been simply too perfect for him to bring up the pain of Jack Kemper. She'd seemed so happy. She'd seemed so proud of him, despite the fears he knew she kept to herself. In the end, he'd wanted too much to savor the evening.

So he didn't ask about the missing personal effect from her dead ex-husband.

Would it even have mattered what she'd told him in that moment, though? He'd already known he had to dig deeper.

And so he had. Jake looked at the screen of his laptop and the several dozen names he had, in random order, typed on the Word document. Many of these people were dead, killed in Yemen or Djibouti during Operation Crusader, and Jake had highlighted these names in yellow. Several others had died during the twenty years of wars in the Middle East, dating all the way back to 2003. The sheer number of dead Special Operators in Iraq, Afghanistan, Syria, and other places was sobering for a man at the very beginning of what he hoped to be a long career as a United States Navy SEAL.

But he still had a good dozen names of people who, like Master Chief White, had served with his dad but never gone to the Tier One. Those were the names he needed to dig deeper on.

There was a path forward to connect with those people and learn more. And with Randy's help, he had an avenue to connect with the mysterious Commander Redman who now served at the Tier One.

But those next steps had a cost. A cost for him and Randy professionally, perhaps, but also for those he reached out to. Sometimes, maybe, it was best to leave the dead buried. Digging them up had repercussions that could ripple out beyond his own growing need to know and could affect others with unintended consequences.

But he just couldn't do it anymore—leave the murky past behind with no real answers.

Could his mom tell him something that might sway his decision one way or the other? Would a conversation with her make his path clearer?

Maybe.

He picked up his phone and tapped *Mom* in the favorites in his contact list. The phone rang twice, and she picked up.

"Hi, sweetheart! Is everything okay?"

He heard the strain in her voice, the strain that she tried to mask, just as she had when he'd been a kid with a father who was in harm's way. It tugged at his heartstrings.

"Yeah, I'm fine. Everything is great. Just checking in. What's new for you?"

He heard her let out a sigh of relief, and then he let her ramble on about her day and a trip she and her husband, Barry, were planning, a trip to go lobstering in the Keys.

"Wish you could go with us. I miss you. But we'll be there for your graduation, and then you'll be so close that we'll see you tons, right?"

"Right," he assured her, wondering what the training and deployment schedule would be like for him at SEAL Team Eight, and if he was just lying to her like Dad used to. No—she knew the deal. She knew what was ahead, maybe better than he did.

"Oh, Mom, I was thinking about something the other day," he said, trying to sound as casual as possible. "It's kind of silly, but I can't get it out of my head."

"What is it, Jake?" she asked.

"Well, not to bring up painful stuff, you know, but do you remember when we were at the memorial service for Dad and his team, and we were talking to Captain Jarvis?"

"Yes, of course," she said, and she didn't sound like his question had been the gut punch he worried it would be. She'd come a long way. She had a good life now. "I still can't believe that I, like, *know* the President of the United States," she laughed, and he relaxed a little. "Or knew him once, I guess. Your dad always looked up to him so much. He was a real mentor to him."

"I know," he said, closed his eyes, and dove in. "So, I keep remembering you talking to him about something—about some personal item that you never got with Dad's things. I know it's a silly thing, but I keep thinking about it. I think because I never knew what it was and never wanted to ask because you were upset about it at the time."

"Yeah," she said, and her voice did go far away, at least a little bit. "A lot of years have passed since all of that. It was a big deal at the time, though. There was something he carried with him all the time. He never took it on missions because he didn't want it to get damaged, but when he wasn't out doing his thing, it was always in his pocket—or at least he said so. Silly, I know, but I had hoped to get it back, because I wanted to give it to you."

"What was it?" he asked, swallowing hard, but trying to sound normal.

"It was a pocket watch—an old-style pocket watch. You could press a button and it opened up, you know? Like in the Old West. He bought it for himself years ago, which was weird because he never bought himself anything. But it wasn't special to him, I don't think, until I got a picture of him and you together and had it put inside the lid for his birthday. It was glazed right into the metal—hell, it probably cost more than the damn pocket watch. I guess I thought he would have wanted you to have it, you know?"

"So what happened to it?" Jake asked. Tears were rimming his eyes now at the thought of the man—the warrior—he thought he knew, carrying a picture of him everywhere he went.

"It was never found," she said. "I kept pushing and pushing but finally gave up. He was in the TOC, remember, so I thought he would have had it on him. At least it would have been with his things, and everything else made it back. I don't know . . ."

"Thanks for sharing that, Mom," he said. He looked at his watch. "Jeez, it's kind of late there . . ."

"Never too late to talk to my baby boy," she said with a laugh.

Jake looked up as the door to their room opened and Randy came in, carrying the pizza and six-pack of beer he'd gone out to get.

"I'll call you again before we head out Sunday night for Air Week," Jake said.

"Love you, Jake."

"Love you more."

He hung up and set his phone on the desk.

"Your mom?" Ketron asked, pulling a chair over from his desk and opening the box of steaming pizza.

"Yep," he said, reaching for a slice as Ketron opened them each a beer.

"And?"

Jake wasn't ready—maybe never would be—to tell his roommate about the pocket watch his dad had carried, with his own picture inside.

"You should reach out to the support guy at the Tier One," Jake said, taking a big bite of pepperoni-and-sausage pizza. "I want to figure out how to connect again with Redman when the time is right."

"We're doing this?" Ketron said, in full-on conspiracy theory mode, a big smile on his face, as he took a huge bite of his own slice.

"We're doing this," Jake answered, then took a long swig of cold beer. "It's time for me to know the truth about Jack Kemper . . ."

ACKNOWLEDGMENTS

Thank you, Andy and Kathryn, for helping us push this one across the finish line. We couldn't have done it without you!

GLOSSARY

ATS Anti-Terrorism Squad

BUD/S Basic Underwater Demolition/SEAL Training

CAC Common Access Card

CBRN Chemical, Biological, Radiological, and Nuclear

CENTCOM US Central Command

CI Counterintelligence

CNI Centro Nacional de Inteligencia (in Madrid)

Comms communications

CONUS Continental United States

CSO Combat Systems Officer

CT Counterterrorism

DGSE Directorate-General for External Security (France's foreign intelligence agency)

DNI Director of National Intelligence

EEOB Eisenhower Executive Office Building

EFP Explosively Formed Penetrator

EMP Electromagnetic Pulse

Exfil Exfiltrate

FOB: forward operating base

FOIA Freedom of Information Act

FSO Foreign Service Officer

GCU Ground Control Unit

GID General Intelligence Department

Guóanbù China's Ministry of State Security

HAHO High-Altitude High Opening

HALO High-Altitude Military Parachuting

HUMINT Human Intelligence

HVT High-Value Target

IAF Indian Air Force

IB Intelligence Bureau

IC Intelligence Community

IDF Israel Defense Forces

Infil Infiltrate

ISR Intelligence, Surveillance, and Reconnaissance

IT Information Systems Technology Technician

JDAM Joint Direct Attack Munition

JO Junior Officer

JSOC Joint Special Operations Command

MARCOS Marine Commandos

MARSOC Marine Forces Special Operations Command

MEDEVAC Medical Evacuation

MSS Ministry of State Security (China)

NCTC National Counterterrorism Center

NIA National Investigation Agency

NOC Nonofficial Cover

NSA National Security Agency

NVGs Night-Vision Goggles

OC Official Cover

ODNI Office of the Director of National Intelligence

OPORD Operation Order

OPSO Operations Officer (sometimes spelled as *Ops O*)

OSTP Office of Science and Technology Policy

Pogue Disparaging term for military members who do not engage in direct combat

PRC The People's Republic of China

QRF Quick Reaction Force

ROE Rules of Engagement

RPG Rocket-Propelled Grenade

SAD Special Activities Division (of Ember)

SBR Short-Barreled Rifle

SCIF Sensitive Compartmented Information Facility

SERE Survival, Evasion, Resistance, and Escape

SF Special Forces

SIB Subsidiary Intelligence Bureau

SIGINT Signals Intelligence

SiPRNet Secret Internet Protocol Router Network

Sitrep Situation Report

SOB: Small of Back

SOCOM US Special Operations Command

SPECWAR Special Warfare

SQT SEAL Qualification Training

SSAB Shanghai Secrecy Administration Bureau

SSD Solid-State Drive

SSEUR SIGINT Seniors Europe—a.k.a. the Fourteen Eyes

SWCC Special Warfare Combatant-craft Crewman

TAD Temporary Additional Duty

TOC Tactical Operations Center

UAV Unmanned Aerial Vehicle

UCAV Unmanned Combat Aerial Vehicle

UPS Uninterruptible Power Supply

VEVAK Ministry of Intelligence of the Islamic Republic of Iran

WARCOM US Naval Special Warfare Command

PARTNER PAGES

Andrews & Wilson actively promote and partner with veteran-owned small businesses that demonstrate a mission of giving. The organizations featured here donate to and support the health and well-being of US service members as well as their families. We encourage you to learn about and support our partners and to spread the word about the important and uplifting work that they do.

BONEFROG

Tim Cruickshank is the founder and CEO of Bonefrog Coffee Company, a veteran-owned and operated premium, small-batch coffee roastery located in the Pacific Northwest.

After serving twenty-five years in the US Navy, he created Bonefrog Coffee Company as a tribute to the "brotherhood" of US Navy SEALs, the Naval Special Warfare community, and all Americans who bravely served, or who are currently serving, in our United States Armed Forces. Each label the company creates tells a story to remind us of battles fought and great American heroes who answered the call.

www.bonefrogcoffee.com

DECLAN JAMES
WATCH CO.

As a former Navy SEAL, founder Brian Dougherty was instilled with a higher purpose, a purpose that guides his company today. It is not just about creating watches with fine craftsmanship, flawless design, or uncompromising standards. It's also about his desire to create a meaningful legacy and a company that his sons can be proud of for generations to come. This is why, to Brian, watchmaking is not just a business—it's a time-honored tradition.

Every Declan James piece pays tribute to the heritage of watchmaking. It honors not only those who came before us but also those who will come after. The company's history is rooted in service. It continues this lineage of humbly serving its customers with pride, integrity, and dedication.

www.declanjameswatchco.com

Founded by Army veteran and retired Delta Force Tier One operator Tom Satterly and award-winning filmmaker Jen Satterly, the All Secure Foundation provides resources, education, posttraumatic stress injury resiliency training for active-duty units, warrior-couples workshop retreats, and family counseling for special operations warriors and their warrior families. They believe that every family member deserves tools to heal from war trauma and that no one is left behind on the battlefield on the home front.

www.allsecurefoundation.org
Email: information@allsecurefoundation.org

Since 1977 Wilson Combat has been the leading innovator in high-performance, custom 1911 handguns, tactical long guns, and accessories. With over forty-five years of experience as champion competitors, gunsmiths, and component optimizers, Wilson is the world's expert in custom firearms manufacturing. Wilson Combat has deep ties to both the military and law enforcement communities, servicing and producing firearms for the Department of Homeland Security; US Border Patrol; HQ SOCOM; US Marshal's Service; US Army, Navy, Air Force, Marines, and Coast Guard; Diplomatic Security Service; Texas Rangers; and many more elite law enforcement and military units worldwide. They also proudly support the needs of thousands of law-abiding private citizens in the United States and in many other countries abroad.

Wilson Combat has been instrumental in helping Andrews & Wilson "get it right" in our novels and partnered with us to design the weapons that would be used by Task Force Ember as well as the Tier One operators in the Sons of Valor series. We consider the team at Wilson Combat not only partners but also good friends.

www.wilsoncombat.com